# METAL GEAR SOLID

## GUNS OF THE PATRIOTS

### PROJECT ITOH

# METAL GEAR SOLID

## GUNS OF THE PATRIOTS

### PROJECT ITOH

Translated by Nathan Collins

**HAIKA SORU**

San Francisco

**METAL GEAR SOLID: GUNS OF THE PATRIOTS**

© 2012 Konami Digital Entertainment
© Project ITOH 2008, 2010
First published in Japan in 2010 by KADOKAWA SHOTEN Co., Ltd., Tokyo.
English translation rights arranged with KADOKAWA SHOTEN Co., Ltd., Tokyo.

English translation © 2012 VIZ Media, LLC
Cover design by Kam Li

**HAIKASORU**
Published by VIZ Media, LLC
295 Bay Street
San Francisco, CA 94133

www.haikasoru.com

Library of Congress Cataloging-in-Publication Data

Itoh, Project, 1974-2009.
 [Metaru gia soriddo ganzu obu za patoriotto. English]
 Metal gear solid : guns of the patriots / by Project Itoh ;
translated by Nathan Collins.
     p. cm.
 ISBN 978-1-4215-4001-6
 I. Collins, Nathan.   II. Title.
 PL871.5.T64M4813 2012
 895.6'36—dc23
                    2012012918

 Printed in the U.S.A.
First printing, June 2012
Second printing, August 2023

# CONTENTS

## PROLOGUE

LET ME TELL you a story about a grave.

The lone man was placing a bouquet beside a gravestone. No name was inscribed upon the stone, only the words IN MEMORY OF A PATRIOT WHO SAVED THE WORLD.

This was, after all, a cemetery for the unknown. For those whose names could not be determined. For those whose identities were not permitted to be recorded.

White flowers carpeted the cemetery grounds. Their name, the star-of-Bethlehem, evoked the light of the kingdom of God. (Also, a moniker shared with the trinket placed atop Christmas trees.)

But the graves in this potter's field belonged to those cast out from the light of heaven.

Do you know why graveyards for the nameless are called potter's fields? The answer can be found within the book of Matthew. A repentant Judas brought back his thirty pieces of silver to the Jewish priests, but the priests turned him away. Said it was his own problem, not theirs.

Judas threw the silver coins to the temple floor, left, and hanged himself. The priests used the blood money to buy a field from a potter, which they turned into a graveyard for the travelers, for the exiled, and for the abandoned.

A graveyard funded by Judas's betrayal.

And so graveyards for the nameless are called potter's fields.

The True Patriot, exiled, her name stolen, her remains lost, left nothing behind but her gravestone. The stars-of-Bethlehem, virtuous and white, seemed to stand in memory of the grave's owner.

The Joy. That was her name.

She loved her country more than anyone, and her country was always in her thoughts. And yet, this proud, beautiful woman was exiled, buried here, and stripped of her name. By all rights, The Joy's remains should have been properly laid to rest at Arlington, not abandoned in distant Russia.

At the site of that same grave, fifty years earlier, another man's battle began.

Oddly enough, he too had placed a bouquet on her gravesite. It was a half a century ago—back when Russia was still called the Soviet Union, when the Soviets and the Americans threatened global destruction again and again, playing at their perilous staring contest with enough nuclear ordnance pointed at each other to destroy the world many times over and still have some to spare. The stars-of-Bethlehem had not yet taken root when the man stood there, motionless, his head tilted back to keep his tears from spilling. With that sorrow, that lonesome tableau, numerous battles were to begin.

No one knows the real name of The True Patriot.

The Joy had many names—"The Boss," "The Mother of Special Forces," and in Russia, "Voyevoda," meaning "Warlord." These were but a small sample, but the one name the man had never been able to learn was that given to her by her parents.

The man standing at her grave had once been known as "Snake."

To state it more accurately, he had been one of the Snakes.

The story I have to tell is about these Snakes.

One tried to change the world. One tried to destroy it. One tried to protect it. There were many Snakes, and there were many battles.

I want to tell you.

I want to tell you how our world came to be what it is.

I want to tell you the story of the Snakes who shaped the world.

## ACT 1: LIQUID SUN

LET ME TELL you a story about the Snake I know best.

The Snake who was my friend. The Snake who changed my life.

Seated on the back of a crowded military truck, his AK-47 propped up beside him, he was smoking—well, I wasn't there to witness it, not yet, but that man was never without his smokes.

If any of the other soldiers packed onto the flatbed minded the smoke, they didn't show it. They faced a far more imminent death than lung cancer some decades down the road. For them, to abstain from the simple pleasure of smoking would be absurd. Just minutes later, their brains might be spilling onto the ground through holes punched through their skulls. Bullets might be rolling around inside their guts as they writhed in agony.

Nothing would be as ridiculous as banning soldiers from smoking. The Nazis enacted the first nationwide tobacco ban as a measure of public health, but even Hitler couldn't keep it from the soldiers in the field. War and smoking come as a pair.

The man exhaled smoke and squinted up at the sun, too far inland for the cool sea air to reach.

The sun's harsh glare passed unimpeded through the crisp, dry air. Most of the soldiers had wrapped cloths around their heads to protect their vulnerable skin from the brazen sun and the sand storms carried by the arid wind.

The road was, almost without exception, unpaved—it was less a road than a tire trail. The single line of trucks—old and plain, but rugged—followed the path. From the gaps between the wooden boards running along the sides of the flatbed, the man glimpsed the occasional stone building, all of them abandoned.

They were approaching a city—or what had once been one.

Its inhabitants had long since left, for how could a family casually go about their daily routine with bullets flying everywhere?

A few men, known as operators, were mixed in with the soldiers jostling about on the backs of the trucks. Most of the soldiers were local militiamen of varied experience and training. The operators had been sent by PMCs, or Private Military Companies, to organize the rabble into a disciplined fighting unit.

My friend was there in the guise of one such operator. He registered with the local PMC and came to the battlefield as a mercenary.

PMCs were the enterprise of turning war into a living—the enterprise of providing the means to make war.

PMCs offered the tools of waging war to any who sought them. They turned people who had never fired a single bullet in their lives into capable soldiers. They worked with arms merchants to provide the necessary materiel. Training, equipment, command, transport, supply, medicine—all aspects of war were organized under the domain of business.

The actual act of the war itself was only one small fraction of the vast market.

Even the operators were commodities in the battlefield marketplace, simply workers selling their labor—only their work was combat and their workplace was the theater of war.

Half a century ago, mercenaries existed as independent contractors—even the largest groups of them were small squads—and they worked for whichever army would pay them. They didn't fight for the sake of any ideology, or for any nation's cause, or for a religious belief. They fought for the money, and nothing else. Without any reason to band together out of loyalty, there was no means for them to organize.

With the end of the Cold War, these outlaws began to form larger groups. The era of opposing superpowers capable of mutually assured destruction had passed, and small wars erupted around the globe. It was as though the hoops had fallen off a barrel. Some peoples hadn't been able to escape historical grudges, some zealously wanted to prove their god was absolute, and others, oppressed by hopeless poverty, gathered into armies.

If we at least have guns, we can kill each other.

With swords and axes and the like, people had to be close enough to watch their blade pierce helmet and skull. Unlike those primitive weapons, guns were tools for massacre and designed for ease of use. Just a squeeze of the trigger, and some distant foe would flop to the ground.

But to make war with them—that's a different matter. For that, a soldier needs to undergo the right training, to be given the right equipment, and to learn how to execute the right strategy.

The first company to begin filling those needs was a mercenary agency called Outer Heaven.

Considered to be the first PMC, Outer Heaven was headquartered in a fortress in South Africa, from whence it dispatched mercenaries to conflicts around the world.

Founded by a legendary mercenary who roamed the world's battlefields during the Cold War, the company was revolutionary, even when considering the history of conflicts that had followed World War II. In the chaos that came with the end of the Cold War, Outer Heaven announced to the world that war didn't have to be between the armies of nations.

The man who had destroyed that organization was sitting in the military truck, an old soldier exhaling cigarette smoke. He leaned against his propped-up AK, ready to throw himself once more into the flames of war, whipping every last ounce of life out of his relentlessly aging, improbable body.

His name was David.

He was the son of Big Boss—the legendary mercenary and founder of Outer Heaven.

David was also a legend. In the secret histories of war, he was known as Solid Snake.

~~~

Their enemies already knew they were coming.

Snake looked up and saw a Canard Rotor VTOL scouting craft, part helicopter, part jet plane, flying across the yellow sand and over the convoy. The governmental army would no doubt be waiting in the abandoned city ahead, taking up tactically advantageous positions based on the aircraft's reconnaissance.

The moment the trucks crossed into the ruins, the battle began.

The vehicles stopped, and waves of militiamen leapt from the flatbeds. If even half of them had been really prepared for the fight, things might have gone better. Worse still, the PMC troops hired by the governmental army had indeed known of the militia's coming and had set up snipers' nests in buildings a safe distance away.

Militia forces, armed only with AKs more suitable for relatively close-range combat, fell one by one, their heads shattered by the onslaught from two-man cells of snipers and spotters.

But there came a point when a soldier had to trust in his instinct and leap into the fray. One way or another, he'd have to throw his body into the maelstrom of bullets. But if he ventured into the chaos alongside everyone else, maybe the probability of the enemy targeting him would be lower.

Snake waited for his instinct to discern the right moment, then without further hesitation, he spurred his old, tired body and leapt to the ground.

Directly in front of him, a soldier whipped back. Red oozed out the back of the man's head, and a soft lump of fragmented brain tissue struck Snake's clothing.

Not that the seasoned warrior let it faze him. The instant Snake touched earth, he was already moving, headed straight for the nearest cover.

The area around the trucks was already piled with corpses.

The PMC snipers on the government's side expertly dispatched most of their targets with single shots to the head. Those targets unfortunate enough to have the bullets miss their heads or hearts and instead hit their lungs or stomachs lay on the sand twisting in agony. There was no luxury of a battlefield medic here.

Maybe the PMC unit was well aware of that reality. In previous wars, inflicting nonfatal injuries—legs, arms—was the more effective tactic. The downed soldiers' comrades would have to drag them to safety, tying up two or more combatants with one shot.

But the militia had no system to save the fallen and no techniques to administer aid. Moreover, they hadn't any medical supplies to use. Any casualties would be left behind. There simply wasn't any other choice. Without any benefit in simply injuring the militiamen, the PMC was better off shooting to kill.

Snake wound through the scattered bodies and dove into the shadow of a partially destroyed house.

Truck after truck passed through the city gate, spewing forth militiamen. Some soldiers, seeing the hellish battlefield, froze with terror. Others, who had taken the initiative and jumped from the flatbeds first, had their heads blown off before their feet hit the sand. The soldiers' fear was understandable—this wasn't a battle but a massacre.

Snake tested the action of his AK by firing three single shots. On the third, his trigger locked. The ejection port was jammed by a chunk of broken metal. Bad ammo. The casing had swollen inside the chamber.

Snake clucked his tongue in frustration and tossed down the useless weapon. The rifle clattered out from the shadows, where it was immediately hit by one of the snipers' shots. The impact of the shot kicked the jammed gun even farther out of reach.

Snake made a wry smile, appreciating the shooter's skillful aim despite the realization that the sniper had him cornered.

Just then, a low, angry, bestial bellow rumbled through the sky, the cry some cross between that of a cow and a pig.

The militia fighters looked at one another. The roar seemed a harbinger of a demon's descent to the battlefield. The cry was that of an animal, though doubtfully like any the militiamen had ever heard.

There. Snake saw them.

Off in the distance, large, unnatural shapes leapt through the spaces between the half-destroyed buildings. They hopped like frogs and quickly closed in on the battleground.

There was a thunderous crash. Snake turned to look at the source of the noise and saw that a military truck had slammed into the city gate. The overturned vehicle's driver slumped upside down, blood streaming from the bullet hole in his head. The anti-government forces were now cut off from their reinforcements. And in front of them waited only the ruthless PMC snipers and those approaching beastlike creatures.

Suddenly, silence fell over the battlefield. All the gunfire ceased like a conversation halted by an awkward silence.

"Death approaches," said one of the militiamen.

It was an oddly dreamlike moment. Several of the men nervously looked about.

Snake stood ready, knowing that the battle was only turning for the worse.

A giant object came down from above.

It was a kind of leg. What else could it be called? Some poor fighter was crushed beneath it, his body cleaved in two.

The creature's legs had the shape of a bird's, but bulged like two olive-drab sausage tubes stuffed full of meat. Perched atop the organic legs was a mechanical tank-shaped head. Indeed, the thing seemed to be a miniaturized version of the nuclear-equipped bipedal tank, Metal Gear REX.

Snake recognized the shape immediately. These things were Metal Gears too. Antipersonnel Metal Gears without nuclear warheads.

Unmanned weapons. The lives of soldiers in wealthy countries were worth far more than the lives of impoverished militia. To protect those valuable lives, economically advanced nations and the

PMCs hired by them had pursued new combat capabilities. Driven by artificial intelligence, these robots were capable of thinking for themselves and made decisions without the need for human input or control.

The robot was a superb combatant. It swung its legs, each as wide as a tree trunk, and sent militia fighters flying into the stone houses. As the men slammed against the walls, every bone in their bodies shattered. They were dead in an instant.

More Metal Gears were coming. They hopped through the help-less militia forces, scattering the fighters and kicking them into the air like soccer balls. The robots were produced by AT Corp under the code name IRVING, but were commonly known as "Gekko" or "Lizards." The machines quickly overwhelmed the militia with an adroitness befitting their moniker.

The militia forces dispersed into the ruined city. Perhaps that was the PMC's goal—to split up their opposition into smaller, weak-ened units and then pick them off one by one.

Snake realized it was time to go. He wasn't here to help the militia.

With the snipers' attention drawn to the scattered soldiers, he began moving away from the area in front of the gate.

Snake hadn't come to the battle to throw in with either side. History had seen its like in many lands and many times, and more would surely come.

But one point differentiated this war from those known to the past—this was a proxy war, fought by contracted mercenaries and manufactured unmanned weapons, not on behalf of any nation or ideology, and not for the purpose of obtaining resources or ad-vancing the cause of a people. ID-tagged soldiers carried ID-tagged weapons, used ID-tagged gear. Nanomachines inside their bodies enhanced and regulated their abilities.

Genetic control. Information control. Emotion control.

Battlefield control.

Everything was monitored and kept under control.

The PMCs were supervised and controlled. Battlefields, once the embodiment of chaos, were regulated, made routine.

Supervised battlefields. Supervised lives. Not the war to which Snake had become accustomed.

But even if the war had changed, Snake still had a role he must play in it.

His last role. His life's finale.

To stop his brother's plan to throw the world into chaos.

Three days earlier, I'd briefed Snake on his final mission.

The rotor blades of my helicopter hung over the cemetery, the downwash spurring the carpet of flowers into a mad dance. I climbed down from the helicopter and landed in the white field of the virtuous stars-of-Bethlehem and walked toward Snake, who stood fixed before one of the graves.

The graves belonged to warriors never spoken about—those convicted of war crimes, those whose records for some reason had all been stricken. Among them, some were regarded as heroes by more than a few soldiers.

Snake's back was to me, and he didn't speak loudly, but his low, powerful rumble carried clearly over the rotor's noise. "Otacon, even the dead have ears."

"Snake, we've got to go."

He turned to give me a dubious look. I responded, "You've got an old friend waiting for you in the helicopter."

He followed me through the rows of tombstones. Then, he said, "The test results..."

My reply caught in my mouth. Of course I'd known he'd ask. I'd thought and thought about how to tell him, but still I had no idea what I should say.

I started with the scientific facts. I tried to present them as objectively as possible.

"Proteome analysis was positive. But the mRNA analysis turned up negative. The wrinkled skin, the hardened arteries... Your early aging symptoms look like classic Werner syndrome. But none of the tests were able to pinpoint the cause."

"So?"

Snake wanted to cut to the heart of the matter—the painful end that awaited his body.

He wasn't afraid. He'd seen his body dying, and he'd accepted it. He'd accepted that he wasn't human, that he wasn't born from nature. From the very beginning, he'd seemingly accepted the fate that awaited his cloned body.

I was the one who couldn't accept it.

"Well...judging by how rapidly the aging has progressed, I'd say..."

My words trailed off. Snake was waiting for me to continue. I had to tell him. I had to give him the truth. He was ready to hear it; he'd long been ready.

But my throat was frozen with sorrow and fear. I opened my mouth, but no voice came. Instead, I felt tears well up.

"A year at best, right?"

My reply felt hollow. "Yeah..."

Snake paused to gaze at the bed of blooming flowers and the white petals kicked up into the air by the helicopter's wind. He watched them as if his life were floating away.

There was such sadness in his eyes, I found myself saying, "Snake...let's try another doctor."

"Some ordinary doctor won't make any difference. I'm not an ordinary man to begin with. Not to mention FOXDIE."

"You're right."

FOXDIE, a virus programmed to selectively kill specific people, had been injected into Snake's body as part of a plan nine years prior to annihilate the terrorist group FOXHOUND. It still lived on inside him.

I added, "But we don't know where Naomi is..."

Even if we found her, would she be able to do anything?

It was then I realized I was clinging to a narrow hope. No one in the world would better understand Snake's cloned body than Dr. Naomi Hunter. She had participated in the mission at Shadow Moses Island and helped create the FOXDIE virus.

But would she be able to stop his relentless aging?

I couldn't make myself think so. To a stranger, he'd likely seem to be in his seventies. In actuality, he was still in his forties. An ordinary man experiencing such rapid aging would be inconceivable. This was clearly a genetic disease stemming from his manipulated genome.

But old age was old age. No matter how extraordinary the circumstances of this one case, aging remained a mechanism within all life—a mechanism that mankind had not yet devised a method to halt. No one could escape death from old age. Neither I, nor Snake, could believe that Naomi would have any power to prevent it.

Snake turned at the sound of a familiar voice calling his name. An elderly man was seated in the back of the helicopter, leaning on a cane for support.

"Colonel!" Snake said, and I was relieved to hear a little brightness, no matter how brief, return to Snake's voice. Snake and I climbed into the helicopter, and he shook Colonel Roy Campbell's hand.

"I'm not a colonel anymore, Snake."

Campbell had long since retired from the military. But to Snake, he was both a superior officer and a friend, and he would always be Colonel.

Snake noticed Campbell's suit and grinned. This was the first time he'd encountered the man in anything but a uniform.

"I'd figured the only place I'd ever see you dressed like that would be at your daughter's wedding."

Campbell's face briefly darkened. Meryl. She was his daughter, though he still hadn't been able to tell her as much. Meryl was the result of an affair—with his sister-in-law. Campbell's brother later died in the Gulf War, and the colonel seemed too ashamed to tell her the truth. She knew Campbell only as her uncle.

We all are burdened by our sins. Even Campbell.

Even me.

Snake asked, "What are you doing these days?"

Campbell pulled himself back from thoughts of his daughter and replied, "I'm working for an organization under the UN Security Council—the analysis and assessment staff of the PMC Oversight and Inspection Committee."

"I remember the resolution being passed a few years ago."

"Snake, I came across some information in my work."

Snake narrowed his eyes.

Campbell continued. "We've found him…in the Middle East."

Him. Snake knew who that was in an instant.

"We've got to stop him," the colonel said. "Now. Before it's too late."

Snake looked at me.

I nodded. "Liquid's made his move."

The whir of the helicopter's rotor increased in pitch. The aircraft lifted off the ground, and the white stars-of-Bethlehem quickly faded into the distance.

"The Manhattan Incident triggered a serious public backlash," Campbell explained. "Now the US has to think twice before intervening militarily in other countries' affairs. This has fueled a push toward military privatization, with PMCs at the heart of that movement."

"Every age has its mercenaries," Snake said. "These PMCs are nothing new—we've been dealing with them since before the turn of the century."

"No, Snake. They're nothing like the mercenaries of the past. The Department of Defense's new battlefield control system has produced a decisive difference between the hired guns of the past and the PMCs of today."

I added, "The system was developed by ArmsTech Security."

A glimmer of recognition came to Snake's eyes. "ArmsTech? You mean AT Corp?"

Campbell nodded. "In recent years, AT Corp has shifted focus from weapons development to security tools. And since the establishment of AT Security, business has been booming. The system makes it possible to integrate not only micro-level information on individual soldiers and units, but also macro-level information about field conditions and order of battle."

Snake sighed. In an effort to recreate the prosperity of the Atomic Age in the post–Cold War world, ArmsTech and DARPA had worked together on the Metal Gear REX project. After the Shadow Moses incident and the death of ArmsTech's president as a result of FOXDIE, the company fell on hard times, but now it had undergone an unorthodox restructuring. If that president could now see the fruits of his labors, I wondered if he'd laugh.

"So," Snake said, "they've finally managed total real-time battlefield control?"

Campbell nodded again. "There's more. State governments and rebel groups can't match the maintenance price of standing forces. PMCs, by comparison, are reliable, easy to use. It wasn't long before everyone had them on the payroll. And as a result, regular armies began to decline worldwide."

I thought back to the graveyard of fallen warriors. The legendary mercenary, Big Boss, and the true patriot, The Boss—and all the other soldiers buried there—had fought for nations.

War has changed. Now there was no place for heroes or legends. They had been replaced with pure profit and efficiency.

"It's hard to believe, I know," Campbell said, "but PMCs are beginning to overtake conventional armies in terms of scale. Nowadays it's the PMCs that serve as standard battalions. They already make up sixty percent of all combat forces in conflict zones."

Snake was taken aback. "Sixty percent…"

"The fact is the world now depends largely on PMCs for waging its wars."

"I thought it was the UN that authorized the PMCs in the first place."

"The US abstained from voting on that resolution. In effect, Washington was endorsing PMCs without ever revealing its true intentions." Campbell drew in a deep breath. "Until they got wind of the uprising, that is."

I pulled a report out of my briefcase and handed it to Snake. The documents outlined the five major PMCs—Pieuvre Armement, Raven Sword, Werewolf, Otselotovaya Khvatka, and Praying Mantis.

"There are hundreds of PMCs in business worldwide," I explained, "and their numbers are growing. Currently, five of them are big enough to be labeled global powers—two in the US, and one each in the UK, France, and Russia."

Campbell nodded. "Reconnaissance has revealed that those five PMCs are run by dummy corporations that act as fronts for a single mother company. Its name—'Outer Heaven.'"

Snake's eyes popped open. "You mean..."

Outer Heaven. The place where soldiers could always find sanctuary. Big Boss had founded the mercenary agency, and Liquid Snake—his son and Solid Snake's brother—had attempted to reestablish it at Shadow Moses Island.

"That's right," Campbell said. "It's Liquid. He's taken command of this immense army and is now preparing to unleash an insurrection."

"I watched him die."

That was at Shadow Moses. Liquid was killed by Naomi's modified strain of FOXDIE.

"His will lives on," the colonel explained, "in the body of the man once known as Ocelot. He aims to fan the flames of war even higher—to create the perfect world once envisioned by Big Boss."

"The one world in which soldiers will always have a place."

A world where soldiers were needed. A world where a soldier could say, "This is where I belong." Many times had Big Boss and

Liquid Snake sought to bring about that world, and many times had Solid Snake stopped them.

The world envisioned by Big Boss was one in a constant state of war—a world where soldiers were needed in every nation; a world whose peoples killed each other endlessly.

It was time for Campbell to say what he had come to say. "He must be stopped—before it's too late."

Snake didn't say anything. Instead, he gazed out the window of the helicopter at the passing scenery below. I looked at his face, and in his eyes I saw such deep resolve and such strong will that I was nearly moved to tears.

Even now his body continued its slow, relentless deterioration. My friend was dying. His hypertrophic heart, enlarged like a piece of old, stretched-out rubber, hadn't the strength to send blood circulating through his body. His lungs, stiffened by pulmonary fibrosis, could no longer absorb enough oxygen.

But even with his body tortured by those and countless other afflictions, Snake continued to fight—to set right his curse, one not of his choice but rather placed upon him before he had been granted life in this world.

The helicopter tilted forward, and through the windows I saw *Nomad*, a large military transport plane with a capacity that put the USAF's Globemaster to shame, parked on an airport runway below. Its cargo bay could hold our helicopter with room to spare.

We landed on the tarmac, climbed out of the chopper, and ran to *Nomad*.

As we closed the distance, Campbell said, "Do you understand, Snake? Any means necessary. Just stop Liquid's insurrection. Even if it means—"

The colonel fell silent and stopped in place. We all did, and Snake stared right at Campbell, who looked away with a tortured expression.

"Killing him?" Snake spoke with no emotion in his voice. "You want Liquid dead. Isn't that right, Colonel?"

Campbell closed his eyes, cursing himself for asking the friend he'd been with through so many battles to perform what was essentially a murder.

"I'm sorry. I know...this isn't justice. It's a covert assignment—a hired hit. A wetworks op targeting the head of a major multinational corporation."

I shook my head. We'd been through a lot together, the three of us—the destruction of secret weaponry, the rescue of a kidnapped scientist, the prevention of a nuclear attack. And I'm not implying that we didn't have blood on our hands. But this would be the first time the mission was simply to kill.

Our last mission together would be to kill a man because we wanted him dead.

A cool, pleasant breeze blew across the open runway in open defiance of our solemn mood. The sky was clear and blue.

Snake looked up at the sun and then started to run toward *Nomad*. We followed.

"Why me?" Snake asked.

"Because of the military might of the PMCs and the effect they have on the economy. War is to the twenty-first century what oil was to the twentieth—the pillar that supports the global economy. The global community is concerned, but they're all too afraid of the war economy collapsing to do anything about it. The UN too."

"And any intervention through official channels would damage the economic system. America can't step in, and neither can the UN. So it falls to us outcasts to do something about it. Is that it, Colonel?"

"America has now turned war into a form of economic activity. Analysts are calling it the 'war economy,' in that it's picking up the slack for the downward-sloping oil market."

"Sounds pretty self-serving to me."

"Snake, this mission isn't an order from Washington—not like the old days. And it's not something the UN can officially sanction either. But we can't just look the other way while Liquid plots this insurrection. If we fail to act, he'll become the greatest threat the world has ever faced."

We'd reached *Nomad*. The hatch at the rear of the transport yawned open, revealing the massive, empty cargo bay. I lent Campbell my arm as we climbed up the ramp.

Once inside, Campbell stopped and looked into Snake's eyes. "Snake, you're the only man I can trust."

Snake returned the colonel's stare.

We'd arrived at our final destiny.

Kill Liquid. Sure, we could run. Sure, we could close our eyes. But in the end, we wouldn't be able to escape our fate.

"Fine," Snake said. "Let's hear it."

Snake pointed to a set of chairs in the temporary command center the colonel and I had established in the fore of the cargo bay. Even though the mission was urgent, the flight would be long, and *Nomad* was suitably equipped. There was a workstation complete with multiple LCD monitors connected to *Nomad*'s supercomputer, Gaudi. Equipment useful for military applications, including a medical bed, were readily available. A gangway led to upper-level living quarters complete with a bed, a shower, a kitchen, and a bathroom.

Campbell sat on a backless folding chair. "Our intelligence on Liquid's uprising originally comes via reports from US Special Forces, who were mobilized after we at the UN reported our findings. They're tracking Liquid's movements. About eighteen hours ago, he was spotted in the Middle East."

The colonel shifted his posture, unable to find a comfortable way to sit. "There's a rebel army there made up of ethnic minorities waging civil war against the regime in power. The core of that regime's army is provided by one of the PMCs under Liquid's control."

"What about the rebels?" Snake asked.

"The local militias have hired small numbers of operators as trainers and field commanders. And of course, they've got help from the local PMCs."

"Right," I added. "A proxy war between hired guns."

PMC versus PMC. A quagmire of war. All-too-typical victims of the new world economy.

Snake pulled out another cigarette. As he searched his pockets for a lighter, Sunny bounded down the gangway and snatched the unlit cigarette from his lips.

"S-Snake," the little girl said, "th-this is a non-smoking flight..."

Snake gave her a chagrined smile and scratched his head.

A dumbstruck Campbell watched the child go back upstairs and said, "She's...?"

"Olga's daughter," I said.

With a look of understanding, the colonel said, "The woman from the Manhattan Incident? The one with the daughter kidnapped by the Patriots to extort her cooperation?"

"Yes, that's her. Raiden rescued Sunny from the Patriots, and we took her in."

"Where's Raiden now?"

"I don't know. After he saved Sunny, we lost all trace of him."

Raiden.

When the president was kidnapped in a marine decontamination facility thirty kilometers from Manhattan, Raiden had been at first an unwitting pawn of the Patriots. But he joined us in that fight against Solidus Snake, the third "son" and clone of Big Boss—although the events ended in violence.

Truthfully, Solidus—and Liquid—were only struggling for freedom. They put their very existences on the line, resisting the secret organization, the Patriots, who attempted to control all reality. Looking back now, in the context of the Patriots, that shadow network that manipulated America and the world, I couldn't label Liquid and Solidus as simply evil.

"She seems to have some trouble speaking," Campbell said.

I nodded. "Sunny's stutter bothers her. After she was born, she lived under unusual conditions. She carries many burdens, and the stutter is their manifestation."

Snake added, "And I thought living with us was unusual enough."

He'd been getting at me to let her out of *Nomad*, to show her more of the world. But as long as the Patriots were watching, he couldn't convince me that letting her roam freely outside was the right thing to do.

"She's a child prodigy," I added. "She's different from other children. It's just how she is."

"She's a prodigy?" Campbell asked.

I pointed at the supercomputer rack against one of the cargo bay walls. "She's amazing at anything technological. She can comprehend the most complicated source code in an instant. She even has a substantial understanding of mechanical engineering. Take this, for example."

I stood and retrieved a robot from the rear of the cargo bay. The machine had an LCD screen, two legs, and a body just small enough to fit my arms around.

"Allow me to introduce Metal Gear Mk. II. It's a Metal Gear, just like REX. But this Gear's not a weapon. It's a remote mobile terminal designed to provide Snake with operational support."

"But what does that have to do with Sunny?" the colonel asked.

"She designed it with me. She had her hand in much of the code, from the auto-balance system to the image recognition routines."

I lowered the Mk. II to the floor and turned it on from my terminal. The robot booted up and deftly coasted across the cargo bay, rolling on two wheels on the ends of its feet.

"But she can't be older than seven or eight! That is impressive."

"She's a product of the next generation. I'm already obsolete."

"Obsolete or not," Snake said, "there's still much you have to do. We can't pass on our sins to Sunny's generation."

"I know," I said. "That's what we've been fighting for all this time."

Campbell nodded in agreement, then leaned forward, ready to return to the matter at hand.

"Snake, you'll be sneaking into the conflict zone via transport truck, disguised as one of the rebel army's hired operators. Your first objective is to make contact with our informants, Rat Patrol 01, shorthand RAT PT 01. They'll be expecting you."

"Rat Patrol, huh. They sound sneaky."

"They're a special forces team assigned to the army's PMC investigation unit, CID."

The Criminal Investigation Command (formerly the Criminal Investigation Division, and still referred to as "CID" for continuity) was a law enforcement agency within the army—basically, the army's police. They investigated all crimes within the army's jurisdiction, from crimes on the battlefield and occupied territory—such as mass murder of civilians or cruelty to prisoners—all the way down to simple misdemeanors on base.

Snake chuckled. "So they're the rats of the army."

Whether you deemed them necessary or not, those who sniffed around among your comrades weren't going to be popular.

Campbell shook his head. "No, I can vouch for them personally."

"Friends of yours?"

"You could say that."

Snake looked at Campbell with narrowed eyes, but the colonel ignored the look and went on.

"Transportation to the area will be provided under cover of a UN humanitarian aid mission with support from the US military. From there on, though, you'll get no protection—and no guarantees—from anyone." He paused for emphasis. "And you must not leave behind any evidence of your involvement in that area, let alone that of the UN. If word of this ever leaked out, it would spark a global firestorm."

"The same as always," Snake said. "Same as Zanzibar Land and Shadow Moses. It's like in Mission: Impossible—if you're caught or killed, we'll disavow any knowledge of your actions."

"Will you do this for me? Will you terminate Liquid?"

Now Campbell looked at me.

I nodded. We had to finish this.

Before Snake's life went up in smoke.

"Thank you," Campbell said, his words filling every corner of the cargo bay.

The words carried appreciation not only for the fight we now faced, but for all of Snake's battles and the painful weight with which they burdened him.

That is the man whose story I tell.

His code name was Solid Snake, but as well known as the moniker is now, it's hardly a code. Say the name Snake to anyone, and they'll say something like, "Oh, the legend." The hero of Shadow Moses. The mighty champion who crushed Outer Heaven and brought down Zanzibar Land. The man who made the impossible possible, the man who destroyed the devil's weapon, Metal Gear, again and again.

The legend.

Snake grew tired of being called that.

Truth be told, back when I first met him, I hadn't heard anything about him yet. I was just a science geek, and all I cared about was using the funds of a gigantic military corporation to build a robot like the ones I'd seen in Japanese anime.

Anime and technology—that was all that defined me. I devoted myself to my work, giving birth to a two-legged walking robot weapon, clueless in my childish naiveté to its actual purpose.

Yes, I created Metal Gear REX.

The American government requested—or should I say, ordered— Snake to a remote island off the coast of Alaska to destroy REX. The Next-Generation Special Forces unit FOXHOUND rebelled against the United States and took control of the Metal Gear, and with it, they could launch a nuclear strike anywhere in the world.

Shadow Moses Island was located in the Fox Archipelago, and there, in the deadly cold winds of the Bering Strait, training exercises with the Metal Gear were under way. FOXHOUND, which had been ordered on protective duty during the training exercises, seized the island and its stockpile of nuclear warheads. Using threat of nuclear attack, they made their demands of Washington. After the end of the Cold War, the island became home to an enormous stockpile of nuclear warheads no longer needed elsewhere.

The trouble with nuclear warheads, ICBMs and the like, is the expansive amount of money required to deploy them. And without a Cold War, there wasn't a need for that expense. Both Russia, whose government collapsed due to her failed economy, and her counterpart America were eager to restrain their spiraling military expenditures.

But not everyone saw it that way.

Some bureaucrats thought that order had been kept in the world because of the nuclear threat that could wipe out hundreds of thousands in an instant. Others saw the profitable industry fueled by the ceaseless development of new tanks and weaponry by the Soviets and the Americans as each stared down the threat of total annihilation.

Among the latter group were DARPA chief Donald Anderson and ArmsTech president Kenneth Baker. In hopes of restoring the prosperity each had found during the Cold War, they utilized black project funds secret from public accountability to start up development of a new Metal Gear.

The Metal Gear that FOXHOUND stole on Shadow Moses.

But no matter how many nuclear warheads the terrorist group got their hands on, the weapons wouldn't mean anything unless they could deliver the payloads across the sea and onto American soil. Why else had both sides of the Cold War pushed so hard to develop space rockets? But Metal Gear REX didn't need to rely on rockets to make its deadly delivery to any point on the globe.

A railgun was mounted on REX's right shoulder. Nuclear warheads placed on the rail could be shot at tremendous speed by a magnetic force created by an immense influx of electricity. Effectively,

REX was a cannon with no need for gunpowder. The basic mechanics were identical—only this cannon could fire projectiles into space.

And its ordnance was quite different from missiles or rockets, which relied on burning fuel for propulsion. A warhead fired by REX would have too high a velocity to be shot down and, with no smoke trail or heat signature, would be undetectable by satellite or radar.

The devil's weapon, Metal Gear REX, would usher in the twenty-first century.

FOXHOUND was led by one of the Snakes who changed the world. He was Solid Snake's clone brother and, in a sense, was Solid Snake himself. He tried to surpass Big Boss, and he failed. This was Liquid Snake.

Solid Snake had infiltrated Shadow Moses Island on orders to determine the extent of the threat posed by FOXHOUND and, once confirmed, put a stop to it. Solid Snake had once been a member of the next-generation US Army unit established by Big Boss on behalf of the Department of Defense to handle combat situations too politically sensitive to intervene in through public means. During this time, Big Boss also secretly founded the mercenary company Outer Heaven in South Africa, where he developed the first Metal Gear with the intent of global destruction.

The mission thrust upon the rookie soldier: You are to infiltrate the enemy fortress "Outer Heaven" and destroy their final weapon Metal Gear.

Big Boss chose the young and inexperienced Solid Snake for the role because he'd hoped the mission would fail. Publicly, Big Boss was the commander of FOXHOUND, but his second identity—the one that held his true allegiance—was as the commander of Outer Heaven.

Much to Big Boss's surprise, Snake proved himself a capable warrior. At the time, Snake didn't know he had inherited his innate prowess from Big Boss. But in the end, the young clone destroyed

Metal Gear and bested his original in combat. In effect, Big Boss was defeated by his own shadow.

Ironically, due to these events, FOXHOUND became known to the world, and the existence of Big Boss was covered up. Afterward, Big Boss fled to Zanzibar Land, a remote former Soviet satellite in the Middle East, where he fought as a mercenary, helping local freedom fighters secure independence for their nation. There, he built a second Metal Gear and once again sought to bring chaos to the world.

Big Boss believed that from this chaos would emerge a soldier's Utopia—a place where warriors would be able to discover their true selves. But Snake, called in by the US government, crushed Big Boss's plans once more. Then, when Snake faced his former commander, he learned the identity of his father—from his elder's dying words.

At Shadow Moses, Liquid made one demand of Washington—he wanted Big Boss's body.

Genes inform many traits—intelligence, personality, physique. One study suggested that some traits usually dismissed as entirely cultural or acquired post-birth—including political leanings—are decided to a certain extent by hereditary factors. Big Boss's genetic code contained the "right stuff" for soldiers, and his body was kept preserved in the Pentagon, a virtual library of soldier genes.

Through a method of gene therapy, Big Boss's genetic traits were given to select special forces soldiers. These soldiers would form the Next-Generation Special Forces, also known as the Genome Soldiers.

The Genome Soldiers were among Liquid's FOXHOUND forces at the insurrection on Shadow Moses Island. Once again, Snake, the man who made the impossible possible, was forced into duty.

But the Pentagon's true goal was only to send in Snake as a vector for a deadly virus—FOXDIE.

The virus, a biological weapon designed by Dr. Naomi Hunter

with ATGC Corp on behalf of the Pentagon, responded to individuals with specific strings of genetic code, inducing apoptosis in the heart and subsequent cardiac arrest.

Snake's orders—to rescue DARPA chief Donald Anderson and the president of ArmsTech, Kenneth Baker, and to prevent the launch of the nuclear warheads—were an outright lie. FOXDIE killed Baker and, finally, took Liquid's life as well.

I met Snake during the course of those events. As a scientist—or I guess I could say the chief engineer—I assisted Snake and threw myself into the battle to make the world a slightly less awful place.

After the events on Shadow Moses, Snake and I worked to combat the worldwide spread of Metal Gear derivatives. At the marine decontamination facility Big Shell, off the coast of Manhattan, we learned of the existence of the shadow network called "the Patriots" that controlled not only America, but the entire world. After that, we shifted focus from being "anti-Metal Gear" to being "anti-Patriots."

Snake and I have been together for a long time now. This is the story of the last battle of Solid Snake—my lifelong friend, the man who met that geeky robot-obsessed scientist Hal Emmerich on Shadow Moses and changed his life forever.

Snake grew tired of being called a hero, but I'm going to call him one anyway. Solid Snake was a real legend—to me, and to many others.

I want you to know his story.

## 2

A CHEERFUL VOICE rang through the sky above the ruins like a message from God.

"Acting under the contract of local authorities, the Praying Mantis PMC recently restored governmental control to this sector. Utilizing ArmsTech Irving unmanned vehicles, Praying Mantis conclusively delivered a swift and decisive outcome. We hope you'll consider the Praying Mantis solution for all your future combat needs."

A commercial. Not that Praying Mantis would find any new customers among the rebel assault force, seeing as they were all dead, their corpses awash in the blowing sandstorm.

Indeed, order had seemingly been restored to most of the city ruins. Snake took a drag of his cigarette. The rattle of gunfire had gone silent, and the low, unnerving roars of the Irvings were absent. Between the buildings, Snake could see a column of advancing PMC armored vehicles—made in the USA—and no signs of rebel resistance.

But the rebels hadn't lost this battle yet—they'd only gone underground to fight with guerrilla tactics. Here and there, Snake caught glimpses of rebel fighters scurrying through the streets.

He followed after them and soon found himself at what seemed to be an underground headquarters. Tailing the soldiers wasn't difficult—not for Snake at least. He hid in the shadows and sized up the gathering forces. The rebels had suffered heavy losses, but still had barely enough numbers to pull off one more attack.

Snake considered that the attack at the city gates might have been a diversionary ploy to sneak in this force. The labyrinthine corridors underneath the city were filled with the injured and the dead, but as Snake passed by the command room, he noticed commanders preparing to regroup their forces.

"Are you all right?"

Snake turned. Behind him was the Mk. II. Controlling the robot remotely, I'd been following Snake for some time. With its stealth camouflage engaged, the machine was practically invisible.

I spoke through the live video feed on the Mk. II's flip-out screen. "I'll be watching you with the Mk. II."

"Sounds like you're keeping cool," Snake said, "while I'm out here in the middle of a hot zone."

"Hey, I'll be with you in spirit. Anyway, because you had to

dress up as a militiaman, I had the Mk. II bring you some goodies."
I opened the Mk. II's storage port and withdrew the Solid Eye.
"Starting with this. Put it on your left eye."

"Looks like an eye patch."

Snake strapped the Solid Eye over his eye. The patch was black, angular, and loaded with sensors. With the Solid Eye on, I thought Snake looked just like Big Boss. Even Snake's father, the original, the legendary Big Boss, didn't complete all of his missions unscathed. He'd lost his right eye in a Cold War op and from then on wore an eye patch.

"It's an all-purpose goggle," I explained, "that displays radar images and other data in 3D. You can also switch it over to light-amplifying night vision or enhanced magnification."

Snake pressed a switch on the side of the Solid Eye, and a data overlay appeared across his vision. The Eye's software gathered pictures from hundreds of tracking points and extracted 3D locational data from the various viewpoints. Data could be transmitted from the Gaudi and displayed in 3D space. The image displayed in the Eye was not a virtual reality created from scratch, but rather an augmented reality.

The rebel forces continued to pour into the stronghold. Some of them were injured, but the majority were still at full strength.

"It looks like they've got the government's PMC troops beat," I said. "At least in numbers."

"And this is their home turf. Praying Mantis is playing psychological games, announcing their victory from the skies, but the real battle is yet to come."

"You miss your AK, don't you?"

"Jammed. I had to dump it. I tried appropriating some of the PMC's SCARs, but even with their safeties off, their triggers were locked."

"It's practically raining bullets out there, and you made it all the way here unarmed?" He really did make the impossible possible. "Snake, the PMC soldiers are using ID guns."

"ID guns?"

"The locks on ID guns are only disengaged when they recognize the nanomachine ID inside a soldier's body. Anyone not possessing nanomachines keyed to the System, or anyone who is keyed but not authorized to use that weapon, won't be able to pass the ID gun's verification process. And as long as the lock is engaged, you can't pull the trigger."

"So I can't use PMC guns."

"I'm afraid not. You're not registered with the System. And it's not just weapons. Vehicles, buildings—everything used for military purposes is secured with this ID control system. Without the proper IDs, it's impossible for PMCs or state armies to fight."

"So it's a way of identifying individual soldiers—like a dog tag, only at the nano level."

Everything on the battlefield was under the authority of tiny machines swimming through the soldiers' blood. Without the System's authorization, guns wouldn't shoot and armored vehicles wouldn't drive.

"Snake, I know this is a stealth mission, but you'll need to protect yourself."

I sent the Mk. II's manipulator arm back into its side storage port and withdrew an Operator M1911.

"It predates the implementation of the System," I explained. "By some miracle, it was never recycled. It's getting tough these days, finding decent guns that aren't ID-locked."

Snake took the gun into his hand and inspected the weapon's condition. He pulled back the slide, looked into the chamber, and checked the magazine's spring.

"You coming?"

"Of course," I said. "I'll follow you wherever you go. The CID informants who said they saw Liquid here should be a little farther up. Head for the rendezvous point."

"It's a battlefield out there."

"This Metal Gear has stealth camouflage. Like a wizard's cloak of invisibility. I won't attract any attention."

"I'm jealous."

"Jealous? Of what? The Metal Gear? Or me, back in *Nomad*?"

"Both."

~~~

As Snake emerged from the rebel's stronghold, a birdlike creature flew overhead. Snake quickly dove into the open doorway of a building, but his aged, weak lungs were already filled with sand from the desert storm. With some effort, he managed to force his mouth closed, stifling any cough that might have given away his position, but what he couldn't conceal was the cold sweat that rolled down his bandanna.

"Are you all right?" I asked. The Middle Eastern climate wasn't kind on his ailing body, and it pained me to watch Snake force himself through it.

But he didn't acknowledge my concern. He only asked, "What was that thing?"

"A Slider. A PMC aerial weapon. Look, here comes another."

One more flew directly overhead. The strange thing looked like a bird, only without a head or a tail, just wings. The Slider dove down and flew toward a distant building where the occasional burst of gunfire echoed. Then, as the creature shot back up into the sky, a giant explosion rocked the building, obliterating it.

"That," I said, "was a cluster bomb. A precision bombing UAV."

"And I thought I saw a rear-facing gun too. That's not something I'd like to go up against."

Snake swiftly scanned the room he'd ducked into. Through a shaft of light that cut through a skylight, motes of dust floated through the middle of the room. Aside from that, no other light cut through the dimness. But even in the darkness, this space was clearly unusual: parked directly in front of Snake was a Stryker armored personnel carrier.

Snake drew his Operator and cautiously approached the vehicle. An ice bucket packed with several cans of Narc Cola rested
on the floor. Narc had been a subject of controversy a few years
back because of its drug-related name.

But Snake was less interested in the bucket of sodas than what
was beside it—an M4 carbine rifle. Even if he had made it unarmed
into the center of the rebel stronghold, Snake felt insecure carrying
only a single pistol. His own gun still readied, he approached the
rifle and reached his other hand toward the larger gun.

Suddenly, Snake sensed a presence behind him. In one smooth,
swift motion, he put both hands on his semiautomatic and turned
to face the unknown presence.

A monkey.

Well, to be honest, neither Snake nor I was quite sure what the
creature was. Don't get me wrong, its body was technically that of
a monkey—a gibbon, to be precise—but this monkey hadn't a single
strand of ape hair. A monkey without hair is like a human without
clothes. I was struck by the (admittedly groundless) feeling that I
was being affronted by some terribly shameful sight.

The monkey opened its mouth.

Then the voice came: "Pretty sweet, huh?"

Snake blinked, worried that senility had joined the host of
other maladies old age had brought.

The hairless monkey grabbed an ice-cold can of Narc, pulled
the tab, and started gulping the soda down. The scene was so surreal, Snake could do nothing but watch it. Then the voice spoke
again.

"Whoa, hold it! I'd appreciate it if you didn't point that thing
at me."

This time, Snake could perceive that the speaker wasn't the
monkey, but someone beyond it, in the darkness. He held his
gun trained on the shadow of the APC, from which emerged an
African man with short hair dyed white and teeth dyed even whiter.
He wore a tailored suit coat and tan camouflage cargo pants, and

dangled a white handkerchief in one hand—perhaps as a white flag of truce.

The hairless monkey belched.

"I'm neither enemy," explained the man, smiling as he slowly walked toward Snake, "nor friend."

He waved the handkerchief, and like some magic trick, he pulled away the cloth to reveal a grenade in his other hand.

Snake looked down the barrel of his gun at the man and said, "You're not with the militia, and you're not PMC…"

The man nodded. "I'm a weapons wholesaler."

"ID guns won't do me any good."

Snake kept his pistol aimed at the stranger and his attention on the entire room.

The arms dealer wagged a finger at Snake. "No need to worry, 'cause all my shit's been laundered."

"Laundered?"

"You see, I take ID guns like the PMCs use and make some mods. Then you can use 'em without having to match IDs. In other words, I'm a gun launderer. You can call me Drebin."

"Drebin?"

"Yeah, you know, Drebin. *The Naked Gun*? Leslie Nielsen? The comedian? Don't tell me you've never seen it."

Drebin placed the grenade on the floor and laid the handkerchief over it. Then he plucked the cloth back up, and the grenade was gone.

"All of us in the profession, all over the world, share the nickname. Not that I ever met any of 'em personally. Me, I'm Drebin number 893."

Painted on Drebin's APC was a stylized revolver cylinder and the words EYE HAVE YOU!

Drebin put away his handkerchief. "You ain't a registered PMC employee, are ya? You need a guy like me." He picked up the M4 from the ground and handed it to Snake. "Consider it a welcome gift."

Snake didn't trust the man yet, but he took the M4 and ran

through a basic weapon check. With everything in working order, he slapped in a full magazine, aimed out a window, and squeezed the trigger.

"I can't pull the trigger."

"Really?"

Snake displayed the trigger, completely locked. It wouldn't budge.

"Wait," said Drebin, "I got it. I bet you're using an older generation of nanomachines. Sometimes they don't really jibe with the new System."

"Who are you?"

"My day job's working at ArmsTech Security. I'm in charge of production control—so I get my hands on the ID chips before they're even registered. It's a side of AT the public don't see." Drebin gave Snake and his muscle suit a once-over. "From the looks of it, you ain't with any state army. But you ain't exactly green, neither. You've got last-gen nanomachines. So I'm guessing...former US Army?"

Snake eyed the man suspiciously. Drebin said he was an arms dealer, but was that the real story? What if he worked for Liquid? Or the Patriots?

Drebin must have sensed Snake's doubts, and he stopped probing. "Let's talk business."

"Business?"

"I make my living off the war economy. I'm green collar—green like an army uniform, green like a tank. The only thing that separates me from bein' white collar or blue collar is that I earn my keep on the battlefield. The only thing I trust is money. So if you've got money, I can help you out. We'll keep it strictly business."

"What do you get out of it?"

"This," said Drebin with a theatrical gesture, "is a war zone. There's product coming in here by the truckload. Whatever guns you find and don't need, I'll take and buy 'em off ya. That'll earn you points you can cash in for services."

"Like what?"

"I'll launder your ID guns—no more locks. And I can also sell you the guns I've got in stock. Let me show you..."

Drebin waved Snake over to the rear of the APC. The hatch was open, revealing racks upon racks of weaponry stored on the interior walls of the vehicle. Drebin climbed inside and soon reappeared with a medical transport cooler.

"To ensure you can use non-ID guns, I'm gonna have to suppress the old nanomachines you've got in ya. Otherwise, they'll interfere with the System."

He took a plastic pouch from the cooler and tore off the top. Inside was a syringe.

"Here. Let me stick you with this. It's full of suppressor nanomachines."

Snake drew back. No matter how reasonable he sounded, this man was a stranger—worse, he was a stranger on a battlefield.

"Relax, it won't hurt."

"The pain isn't what I'm concerned about."

"What, you don't like shots?"

Snake laughed. As bad an idea as this sounded, he wouldn't be able to get very far with only the Operator. He acquiesced and held his neck out.

Drebin injected the needle into Snake's neck. The pain was intense, and the old soldier couldn't stifle his cry.

"See?" Drebin said. "No sweat. Now you can use non-ID guns, no problem."

Snake rubbed at the base of his neck, then took the M4 back into his hands. He aimed at the wall and squeezed the trigger. The muzzle flashed and the bullet lodged into the concrete.

"There, ya see? You name it, I can launder it. Well, I'd better be on my way."

Drebin started packing everything back into the APC. The monkey downed the last of his soda and let out a deep belch.

Drebin shook his head. "Man, he's gotta give that shit a rest."

"Looks like you're doing pretty well for yourself."

"And why do you think that is? System codes are the law now, and control's essentially absolute—paving the way for fat profits, if you're willing to bend the law. Demand keeps on growing thanks to the war economy. I sell ID guns to the PMCs and state armies, and naked guns to terrorist groups and paramilitaries. And these ID guns can't be sold on the black market. The System's practically a license for us arms dealers to print money."

He returned the ice bucket to his vehicle, saying, "Privatizing the military's made the PMCs big and bloated. And the fatter the PMCs get, the blurrier the line between civilian and soldier is gonna get. Sooner or later, the whole damn human race is gonna be green collar. More like, we're all gonna be fighting proxy wars. But hey, this war economy puts the food on my table."

Drebin closed the hatch from the inside, then stuck his head out the driver's side window. "You're green collar too, ain't ya?" He returned Snake's cold stare with a genial grin. "It's in your eyes. You've seen a lot of combat."

"What makes you think you know me?"

"Nothing to be ashamed of. I'm the same way. I grew up here too. I got no interest in the outside world."

The APC's engine started, and Drebin spoke over the noise. As he pointed first to his own eyes, then at Snake's, he said, "Eye. Have. You."

The vehicle sped out of the room and out of Snake's sight.

3

THE CID RENDEZVOUS point was located in a building on the outskirts of the city.

Removed from the area of the fiercest fighting, the location made a suitable meeting place. Not because the building wouldn't draw much attention—as the city fell into ruin, few structures stood out anymore, not even the ones in the city's center—but because the constant threat of cluster bombings within the city proper tended to put a damper on long conversations.

Drebin's M4 at the ready, Snake stepped inside.

Sunlight filtered through the cloth roof of the courtyard at the core of the five-story building. Any traces of life had long since gone.

I told Snake that the meeting point was on the top floor, and he started up a staircase decorated with colorful arabesque tilework.

Snake climbed one flight of steps. Then another.

He gritted his teeth, and I knew his ankles, his knees, his hips, all of his joints were crying out in agony. Snake was beset by old age and all its maladies—including osteoarthritis, arteriosclerosis, aortic stenosis, and a slowed healing process.

Normally, a person has decades to adjust to the gradual deterioration of the human body with age. Snake had to confront it over a period of years.

By the time he reached the last flight of stairs, he was breathing heavily. Muscle suit or no muscle suit, five flights of stairs were no easy feat for the body of a seventy-year-old.

I suggested he take a break, but he ignored me. With great effort, he made it to the top and exited to the roof. I bit my lip. Snake was fighting a battle between his body and the world, and there was nothing I could do to help him.

Once out in the open air, we saw that this was only half the roof—another partial floor occupied the remaining space. Taking care to walk silently on the balls of his feet, Snake stepped inside and into a room littered with empty bottles of liquor, formerly a bar. Snake passed through and saw his destination.

His rifle trained in front of him, Snake carefully pushed open the door to the room. Thankfully, the hinges were mostly free of rust, and no squeak broke the quiet. Through the crack in the doorway, Snake peered into the room. It seemed empty.

Just as he set foot inside, Snake sensed someone behind him and turned.

From behind the doorway stepped a soldier, armed and with his gun pointed at Snake's head.

"Drop your weapon!"

The soldier's voice sounded young.

Snake glimpsed the man's weapon out of the corner of his eye. It was trembling.

He was reminded of an incident on Shadow Moses. It was just like when Snake had first met Meryl. She resisted alone against the rebel FOXHOUND unit—maybe she was trying to live up to the memory of the man she believed to be her father, the Gulf War hero. When she saw Snake, she didn't know if he were friend or foe, and she'd held a trembling FAMAS at his head just like this man was doing now.

Snake dropped his Operator, raised his hands, and turned to face the soldier.

"Don't move!"

The man's voice was as shaky as his gun. Snake couldn't help but grin—this really was just like before.

"You haven't even taken the safety off, rookie."

"Careful, I'm no rookie! I'm a ten-year vet!"

Snake deliberately flicked his eyes to the safety on the soldier's XM8.

Lacking the confidence to see through Snake's bluff, the young man nervously glanced at the side of his rifle. The safety was off, but he didn't have time to bask in satisfaction. By then, the veteran Snake had already made the young man pay the price for letting his guard down.

Snake grabbed the XM8 and yanked the rifle forward. The young soldier lost balance, and Snake connected his elbow to the man's face. He hooked his leg around that of the soldier and, still gripping the rifle, sent him flying to the ground.

CQC—short for close quarters combat—was the hand-to-hand

fighting style developed during the Cold War by The Boss and her disciple, Naked Snake, aka Big Boss. Snake had mastered it.

Not one second after he had dropped his guard, the soldier was staring up the barrel of his own rifle.

This was a ten-year veteran? How the hell had he ever survived that long?

"Don't move!"

Now another gun was at Snake's head.

Snake's eyes moved up the ridiculously large barrel of the gun to find, with no great surprise, a Desert Eagle. The weapon was tremendously powerful for a handgun, but if a weaker female attempted to fire it one-handed, the recoil would probably snap the bones in her wrist.

But the voice that now spoke to him was definitely that of a woman.

"CQC...a real Big Boss, huh?"

Snake kept the XM8 pointed at the soldier on the ground as he eyed the woman with the Desert Eagle. She wore a balaclava, which hid all of her face except for her eyes.

"Lower your weapon!" she ordered. "Slowly now. I wouldn't try anything funny if I were you."

Snake noticed that there was more pointed at him than this woman's peculiar choice of a firearm. Two laser dots held steady on his chest.

Judging from the gear worn by the woman and the younger soldier, the two were likely with the CID special ops unit. No matter where the battlefield, Americans stood out. Then Snake noticed the emblem sewn onto the woman's combat chest harness.

A sharp-eyed fox holding a combat knife in its mouth.

"FOXHOUND?" Snake said.

The woman's eyes narrowed in suspicion, but soon a look of surprise washed over her.

"Snake?"

She lowered her weapon and pulled off her mask, revealing

a familiar face. She had grown up since Shadow Moses, and no youthfulness remained in her appearance. Only her chic hairstyle was unchanged.

Meryl Silverburgh.

Colonel Campbell's so-called niece who had fought alongside Snake on Shadow Moses Island.

"It's been four days," Meryl said, "since Liquid arrived in the area."

She handed Snake a photograph. He squinted and moved the glossy paper closer and farther from his eyes, trying to find the sweet spot where the photo wouldn't be blurry. Meryl looked away.

I wasn't surprised she hadn't recognized him at first—the aging had been so fast and severe, he looked like a different person than he had only years before.

When he told her about the disease, she couldn't hide her shock. Since she was little, she'd fondly listened to stories of the legendary man, and when she'd met him on Shadow Moses, her feelings toward him grew. Now, seeing the unthinkable transformation of the man she'd once fallen for, she seemed truly disturbed.

Though Snake could understand her feelings, he also knew there was nothing he could do about them. What surprised him most was that beyond the initial and short-lived shock, she was handling the news so well. She seemed unnaturally calm.

The picture was of a man once known as Revolver Ocelot.

An agent of the Patriots and a former FOXHOUND member, Ocelot had lost his right arm on Shadow Moses and had the limb replaced with one belonging to the fallen Liquid—some even thought that Liquid's personality had taken over through the transplanted arm.

Meryl gave Snake another photograph. The subject seemed to

be a woman, although her face wasn't clear—not only was she wearing a hood, the picture was out of focus.

"This woman's been with him the whole time. She doesn't look like a combatant. Probably some kind of advisor. Maybe a scientist."

Meryl leaned forward to get a closer look at the picture. Her face was near Snake's now, and close-up, the affects of his aging were undeniable. His skin was dry and mottled and blotchy, and innumerable wrinkles creased the corners of his eyes. She could even hear his wheezing breaths.

She began to tear up, and gently placed her hand on the shoulder of the man she'd once loved. But Snake shrugged her off. He would soon reach the end of his life, but he couldn't endure her pity. He'd hurt enough people already.

He tried to soften his rebuff, saying, "You've become a fine soldier."

But that wasn't what she wanted to hear—not some praise about her abilities as a soldier. "Maybe it's because someone taught me well. A certain legendary hero who suddenly disappeared?"

Snake never did know how to talk to women, despite how talkative he was over the wireless codec. (I even grew to think of him as a big mouth.)

"You quit the unit," she said. "Me...I never gave up on you—or on FOXHOUND."

She might have even been wearing the emblem of her own accord. I doubt the army had acknowledged its use, seeing the FOXHOUND Special Forces Unit was still kept secret.

"Snake...back then, I just wanted you to accept me. I wanted you to turn around and see who I was. But I've put the past behind me. I'm done playing at romance."

Meryl regained her composure. Snake looked pained, but just when I thought he might let his emotions come through, his face went blank. Every time his feelings began bubbling up, something seemed to crush them back down.

"C-Commander..."

It was the soldier who had surprised Snake from behind the door.

Without looking at him, Meryl sighed. "Akiba, what is it? The bathroom again?"

"Y-yes, ma'am. My stomach hurts again..."

"Is your stomach ever normal?"

"Y-yes, well, I think so...I'm sure it's been at some time, although I can't remember..."

Meryl had heard enough and waved Akiba off. Hands clutched to his stomach, he moved as stealthily as he could and still reach the toilet in time.

"He's a handful," Snake said.

Meryl put her head in her hands. "His name's Johnny Sasaki. But everybody just calls him Akiba. He handles traps, sensors, and cyber combat. He has a wearable computer on his right arm."

"I've come across a number of soldiers with bad stomachs," Snake said. "It must just be my luck. Maybe I had some taste for bizarre foods in a past life and now I'm doomed to encounter the scatological."

"Maybe it's been the same soldier all those times."

"Yeah, right."

They both laughed. Then Meryl asked, "So...what are you here for?"

"Threat assessment—the PMCs." That was partly true, at least, thought Snake. To discover Liquid's intentions, he would have to discover the threat posed by his PMCs.

"Really? Because I hear a rumor there's an assassin out there targeting their leader."

Snake feigned surprise. "Well, that's some rumor. I'm only here because the UN wants me to assess the impact and effects of PMCs on their refugee protection efforts."

"That's all?"

"More than enough for a retired vet like me."

Meryl sighed and, seeing she wasn't going to get anywhere,

returned to the subject at hand. "I know he's plotting an insurrection. But as long as AT Security's System is in place, there's no way he'll succeed."

"How can you be so sure?"

"They've implemented a system that monitors in real time every single soldier engaged in combat action—whether he's state army or PMC. Each soldier has been fully ID-tagged with nanomachines injected into their bodies for that purpose.

"The AI at the System's core not only collects data on the state of their bodies and the battlefield, it also monitors sensory organ data showing strong emotions such as pain and fear. This data is monitored at HQ to enable command to make quicker, more precise, and more rational decisions. It also enables crisis management for each individual soldier."

"Battlefield control..."

"It's being used by the US military, by state armies in allied countries, by PMCs. Even police agencies are starting to adopt it. Unless they agree to implement the System, PMCs aren't permitted to send troops anywhere."

Snake made a connection with something strange he'd sensed in Meryl's behavior.

"You've got these nanomachines in you too."

"Of course. Our unit plays by the rules, same as everybody else. It was creepy at first—knowing you're being watched twenty-four seven—but I've gotten used to it. It gives us a lot of advantages in the field too. We get a clearer picture of what's going on around us, so there's less confusion during missions. And our nanomachines communicate with each other, making teamwork a lot smoother."

Snake had sensed right.

Her unnatural calm—as if something inside her quelled her rising emotions.

Nanomachines. Nanomachines, and their link with the System, constantly scanned her mental state. They found an emotional instability and automatically stabilized her.

"And that's not all the System does for us," Meryl continued. "It's also a security guarantee against the PMCs."

"A security guarantee?"

"The PMCs don't fight out of nationalism or for a cause. They're just bodies, fighting on someone else's behalf. They're mercenaries. A commodity—it's easy to imagine them betraying their clients by joining the enemy or refusing to fight... or committing humanitarian atrocities. To keep these things in check, the System ensures that no one can use firearms or military vehicles without the proper System ID. It's true for every piece of equipment out there."

"So if the PMCs tried to mount a terrorist attack or coup d'état—"

Meryl cut in. "Right. They would automatically find themselves locked out of their weapons and equipment. They wouldn't be able to move, attack, or engage in combat of any kind."

Snake wasn't convinced. "What if someone tried to circumvent the System by getting the nanomachines out of their bodies?"

She chuckled. "They'd be losing their IDs in the process—so they wouldn't be able to use their weapons."

"We've progressed too far," said Snake. "We can do too much now."

The more impossible circumventing the System for Liquid seemed, the more uneasy Snake felt. The System appeared to be perfect, but there had to be something he wasn't seeing.

Snake was struck by a suspicion.

"And the Patriots are involved?"

"La li lu le lo? What's la li lu le lo?"

Word protection.

Her nanomachines were censoring him, interfering with her ability to hear what he said. Snake had seen this before—in the Manhattan Incident, he'd run into people under Patriot control who couldn't speak the group's name. When they tried, the word only came out in the gibberish phrase *la li lu le lo*.

Snake sighed. "Never mind. So this System is foolproof, huh?"

"Completely. They call it SOP."

"Standard Operating Procedure..."

"No. Short for 'Sons of the...' It's the network that monitors soldiers."

Sons of the Patriots.

Meryl continued. "The AI that controls it is a tightly guarded secret—both at ArmsTech Security, where it was developed, and at the Pentagon. There's no way a third party could get control of it."

"I just met a guy who said he could launder ID guns. The System does have holes..."

"There can't be more than a few hundred of those gun launderers. They're a grassroots organization. It's not like they can affect the entire PMC war machine."

"And Liquid won't be able to make use of his military forces?"

Meryl nodded. "His PMCs might even exceed the US military in terms of numbers. But as long as they're registered, their troops' activities are constantly being monitored. So long as the US responds immediately when Liquid makes his move, we can take them down by force."

Snake grinned wryly. *By force, huh? Typical thinking for someone in the US military*, Snake clearly thought—but didn't say. I knew that smile though. What he did say was this: "How did you get involved?"

"When Army Special Operations Command heard about Liquid's plans, they sent us to sniff around the PMCs. Took us three months to find him. When we reported that we'd found Liquid, our superiors ordered us to provide the UN investigators with intel. But I didn't know it'd be you."

"Didn't the colonel tell you he was sending me?"

"Colonel?" Waves of barely restrained hatred stirred her composed expression. "Don't tell me it's Campbell."

"You didn't know?"

"You've got to be kidding! You expect me to work with my uncle?" Meryl stood and paced around, kicking chairs, cursing—no longer attempting to hide her anger.

"Meryl, calm down."

"This is bullshit! He's not my father!"

Snake was at a loss for words. *She knows. She knows whose blood flows through her. Whose genes she inherited.*

Meryl considered her father a curse. Husbands and wives can choose their spouses, but children can't choose their parents. I guess that can be a kind of curse, even though most are lucky enough never to have to think of it that way.

But Snake and Meryl weren't lucky. Just as Snake hadn't chosen to be born as Big Boss's clone, she hadn't chosen to be born Campbell's daughter.

"So," said Snake, "you knew?"

"Yeah. Little violation of the need-to-know rule."

That unnatural calm had returned to her voice. Amid the nearby PMC and rebel gunfire, nothing was a bigger disturbance to a unit than its commander losing herself in a fit of anger. Still, Snake couldn't help but abhor those nanomachines for suppressing her real and valid anger.

"Then why are you still calling him uncle?"

"You're still calling him colonel."

"He's your father."

"As far as I'm concerned, we're still uncle and niece. I'll never forgive that womanizing piece of shit."

That was going too far. Snake shook his head. "Meryl, he's—"

"He remarried."

"The colonel remarried?" Snake reeled in shock, likely chastising himself that now, with life and death and the fate of the world on the line, was not the right time or place for all this small talk of cheating and remarriage.

Meryl's subordinates—Johnny, the burly African-American sniper Ed, and the giant mohawked Jonathan—were clearly uncomfortable, doing anything they could—inspecting their weapons and electronics, feigning sleep—not to look at the two.

"His new wife's about my age," Meryl said. "I hear she's even got a kid. It's as if he's given up on making up with his own daughter. Men. Selfish, egotistical pigs."

Snake's expression reflected guilt, as if she were accusing him. Which she probably was.

He changed the subject. "Where is Liquid now?"

Meryl suspiciously eyed the man who was working for the father she hated and said, "Liquid's camp is up ahead. I'll mark it on your map."

4

From the skies above the abandoned city, the giant birdlike Sliders—part tactical strike bombers, part mobile advertisements— tirelessly blasted out their promotional messages. *We hope you'll consider the Praying Mantis solution for all your future combat needs.* Staying out of the sight of PMC and militia ground forces was no longer enough for Snake—now he had to watch the skies. Carefully, he made his way toward the location Meryl gave him.

The closer he advanced, the thicker the PMC patrols became. Before long, the passing of armored vehicles became frequent. The PMC headquarters must have been larger and more fortified than we'd anticipated. Snake made a few adjustments on his muscle suit and enabled its camouflage. He'd need more than his own stealth to go any farther.

The OctoCamo system scanned Snake's surroundings and copied them across its surface.

The OctoCamo couldn't make Snake completely invisible like the Mk. II's stealth camouflage, but—much like an octopus's natural camouflage—the suit could read the surfaces around Snake and perfectly emulate them, providing Snake the edge he needed to stay out of sight.

The PMC stronghold was located in what used to be the city's administration complex. The building, a boxy structure surrounded by a sizable wall, looked like about what you'd expect from a government office—a healthy mix of authoritarianism and austerity. Easy to defend and hard to assault, the complex even contained a generously sized parking lot. All in all, the facility was well suited for military purposes.

Snake went prone upon the gravel, and his camouflage shifted to blend in. Slowly, he crawled through the open streets like an inchworm. The area outside the base provided no cover, but Snake, utilizing Native American tracking techniques, gave the soldiers nothing to see and nothing to hear.

Of course the OctoCamo was a major factor of his success, but Snake's sense of his connection with the world around him was even more crucial. He was a part of his surroundings, a part of the world. By closely matching himself in with that baseline, he could be more stealthy than what might seem possible.

With his senses attuned to the environment around him, Snake easily got inside the wall. Inside, neat rows of tents and transport vehicles provided better cover than outside the complex. This clearly was a command post—soldiers busily went about their duties, and compared to the patrols outside, they were far less alert.

It was always dark below the lighthouse, Snake knew.

The soldiers inside shouted at each other instead of using the wireless, providing a level of background noise sufficient that Snake didn't even have to worry about keeping quiet.

A Canard VTOL craft flew overhead with a thunderous roar. Snake's attention was drawn skyward, and then he saw the lone man standing on the roof.

A man with long gray hair. Even with sunglasses on, his face was unmistakable.

The man once known as Revolver Ocelot.

Now known as Liquid Snake.

But what should he be called, really?

At the Manhattan Incident, he'd called himself Liquid—the right arm, transplanted into another's body, awakened.

Was that even possible?

There had to be a better explanation.

When he confronted Ocelot in the sinking tanker off the coast of Manhattan, Snake had felt Liquid's presence in the man.

After the events at Shadow Moses and the spreading of Metal Gear technology throughout the world, Snake and I founded Philanthropy, an anti-Metal Gear organization. We monitored nuclear powers for any signs they were developing new Metal Gears. After receiving intel that the US Marine Corps was smuggling an anti-Metal Gear Metal Gear, RAY, inside a decoy oil tanker, Snake intercepted and infiltrated the ship in the Hudson Bay. He intended to get photographic evidence of the Metal Gear, which I would then leak to the Internet and reveal their secret to the world.

We were beaten to the weapon by Russian mercenaries intent on stealing it for themselves. The group was led by Colonel Sergei Gurlukovich, former head of the Spetznaz GRU and the father of Olga Gurlukovich—making him Sunny's grandfather.

Sergei successfully seized the tanker but lost his life when he was betrayed by a member of his forces. Betrayal might not be the right word, because Ocelot, who'd escaped Shadow Moses and left FOXHOUND, had only joined Sergei to spy on behalf of the Patriots.

That's how our paths crossed with him once more. There, as Ocelot's explosives doomed the ship, Snake saw Ocelot the man cease to exist. Though Ocelot struggled to resist the transplanted right arm, in the end, Liquid took complete control of his body. The man who stole Metal Gear RAY and successfully escaped the sinking vessel wasn't anyone if not Liquid Snake. Two years later, when the president was kidnapped and we faced Ocelot again, Liquid had taken full control.

The man was both Liquid Snake and Revolver Ocelot.

And now that man, unmistakably, stood atop the government building.

"I knew it."

Meryl's voice came over Snake's cochlear-implant radio. He dropped to one knee and quickly scanned the area for her squad, spotting them within cover in a concealed corner of the complex.

"Snake, you're here to kill Liquid, aren't you?"

"That's the mission. Are you going to stop me?"

"My mission," Meryl said, "is to inspect the PMCs. I'm not in a position to take action. All I can do is stand by and watch."

Whether by her own decision or orders from ARSOC, this was a tacit consent from the US Army.

"I can't help you," she said. "Understand? I'm a peacekeeper, here to keep order."

"Understood."

Snake cut the transmission and gave Meryl a small wave. She hesitated, dropping her eyes for a moment, then motioned her unit to move on.

Liquid seemed to be talking over his wireless. He was positioned where he could look down over the courtyard, where his employees, the PMC soldiers, were going about their various duties, transporting equipment and forming ranks.

Even Snake would likely not have been able to cut through their masses, but he could at least move a little closer to where he could better observe Liquid. Snake stood and carefully advanced.

Then the world fell apart.

~~~

His chest felt like it was being crushed. Blinking, breathing, every act of simply staying alive brought an avalanche of pain cascading upon him. He felt like his thoughts and awareness, and everything that made up his consciousness, were completely shut off from himself. He had only made it a single step forward, and from there, he could no longer move.

Snake's very steps told the story. *So, this is how it is. My end has come. Old age has brought an end to my tired life.*

*Is this as far as I go? Is this really it?*

Snake struggled to retain his consciousness. He fought against the crumbling world with everything he had. At the edges of his awareness, the other soldiers shared in the agony. They were all around him, some convulsing on the ground, others frothing at the mouth, a few shitting themselves uncontrollably, and on and on.

Snake looked for Meryl's squad. Ed, Jonathan, and Meryl had collapsed with their hands clutched at their heads. Only Akiba seemed unaffected, helplessly watching his comrades suffer.

Snake gritted his teeth. "It's not over. I can't fall here. Not yet," he told himself. "I cannot leave my fate, my curse, to Meryl and Sunny's generation. After I finish what I must, then I will happily die. But not now. I still must fight."

With a voiceless roar, he lifted his Operator and stumbled into the courtyard. He pushed his way through the throngs of writhing and flailing soldiers. He fought against waves of overwhelming nausea. With saliva streaming from his mouth, he closed in on Liquid.

Suddenly, Liquid pointed straight at him.

Snake froze as if pierced straight through.

Liquid gazed down upon the courtyard in chaos and boomed, "Brother! It's been too long!"

"Liquid!"

Liquid spread his arms in a theatrical motion. "Rejoice! We're not copies of our father after all!"

Snake could no longer focus his vision, and now Liquid appeared as two blurry forms. Snake's heart pounded, the palpitations threatening to burst his hardened arteries. With each beat, pain shot through his heart and his body.

Liquid pointed his right arm at the sun. "We are freed from the shackles of destiny!" He spoke as if he were pronouncing his victory over Big Boss, fate, and the world. "Snake! Brother! We are free!"

Something within Snake had been defeated. His legs refused to hold up his body. His knees hit the ground. His body submitted to the pain.

Liquid was still shouting. "I've surpassed my own creator!"

Snake collapsed to the earth. Even then he tried to lift his Operator and aim at Liquid, but he could no longer distinguish which blurry shape represented the man.

Then a pair of feminine legs walked into his vision.

The legs moved in steady footsteps—their owner apparently not afflicted by the chaos that struck Snake and the PMC soldiers. One step at a time, the legs approached Snake.

The world was silent, save for his own breathing. All seemed distant, dreamlike.

A familiar voice cut through the haze.

"Snake," the voice said.

Snake realized that he knew her. He had killed her brother, his old comrade. Snake had first crippled him in Zanzibar Land and stood by and watched him die on Shadow Moses. He was given the code name "Fox," FOXHOUND's highest honor. He was Big Boss's ally. Gray Fox.

Fox's sister took a syringe out of her coat pocket and slowly injected it into her neck.

She was Naomi Hunter, the creator of FOXDIE.

Snake muttered, "Naomi," but he couldn't tell if he had actually been able to voice the word or not. His consciousness was slowly fading.

Naomi discarded the empty syringe and turned her back.

"Snake, if you don't want to be a prisoner of your fate...then go. Fulfill your destiny."

Snake reached out for her, but pain shot through the straining muscles in his arm and chest, and he collapsed again. By the time he could look up, she was gone.

On the roof of the building, Liquid was boarding a transport helicopter, with Naomi already seated inside. Liquid removed his sunglasses and looked down at Snake with naked eyes. His face might have belonged to Revolver Ocelot, but the resentment festering within those eyes was all Liquid.

Liquid flashed a smile and got in the aircraft.

Snake found his life flashing before his eyes. "It's not just a saying," he told me later. "It really does happen."

In one instant he saw with complete clarity the events of his life. He began to slip beyond the plane of consciousness.

The Iraqi heat when he was a Green Beret disabling Scud missiles in the Gulf War. His infiltration of Outer Heaven, his first mission with FOXHOUND. When he'd grown tired of war and moved to Canada and was forced back into service to respond to the disturbance in Zanzibar Land. Shadow Moses, where he first met his brother Liquid. The tanker in the Hudson Bay he boarded on behalf of his anti-Metal Gear NGO. When he snuck aboard the Big Shell facility, home to the terrorist organization Dead Cell, led by his second brother, Solidus.

Somewhere inside Snake, a voice spoke.

*Hasn't this been enough for one life?*

*You've fulfilled your duty.*

*You've fought more than enough battles.*

*No one will fault you if you perish here.*

*It's time for you to fade into the shadows of history, Solid Snake.*

But Snake wouldn't be able to forgive himself.

If he died now, he'd die a captive of his own fate.

Snake let out a deep roar from the bottom of his gut. He raised his Operator to the sky and blindly fired until no bullets remained.

"I'll show you!" he shouted. "I'll make it to the source of my destiny!"

As the last vestiges of consciousness slipped away from Snake, the helicopter disappeared beyond the city.

## ACT 2: SOLID SUN

LET ME TELL you a story about another Snake I knew.

First, I'll have to be clear—this young man didn't carry the same genetic makings of Liquid or Solidus. He wasn't a clone or even a designer baby. His parents were a normal, loving married couple who did as normal, loving married couples do, and he was given life as a normal fetus inside a normal womb.

He was forced to relive Snake's battles—he was raised to become Snake. He was created in an attempt to produce another Snake, not through genes but through *memes*.

But he didn't become Snake.

He rejected the transformation. He found his footing and decided to walk his own path, not Snake's.

Because he met the real Solid Snake. Because he saw the other man's battles, the other man's life.

His name was Jack.

He was once known as Snake. And he was once known as Raiden.

We don't pay much attention to Africa. By "we," I mean most of the world. Even now, as I write this, the number of lives being lost there is staggering, and the widespread starvation is unimaginable.

More than half of the nations in Africa had an average life expectancy of under forty—a shocking difference when compared to our expectations of lasting into our seventies or eighties, with plenty of time for a comfortable life even after having raised children. But all everyone seemed to care about was global warming, endangered animals, or tomorrow's stock prices. No matter how high the bodies piled, those with food, clothing, and shelter continued about their days unperturbed.

Jack was from that Africa.

The Republic of Liberia was born with the return of slaves from America. The founders of the nation based their new homeland upon the structure of the country where they had been forced to labor—a constitution and code of laws, a bicameral parliament, and a president who would serve as the head of the government. One way of looking at Liberia was as a doppelgänger of America.

But in the second half of the twentieth century, Liberia was gripped by a succession of civil wars. A dark rift ran between the native Africans and the Americo-Liberians, and poverty and hunger fanned the flames of a seemingly endless struggle for power.

Jack was born to one of the few white Liberian families.

At that time, the insurgent forces of the National Patriotic Front of Liberia were clashing with the government army, which was backed by the Economic Community of West African States. Factions among them shifted, splinter groups formed, and old groups dissolved, and the war even spilled into neighboring Sierra Leone. The situation devolved into chaos.

Jack's parents were killed, and the young boy was kidnapped and conscripted into the rebel army.

He was forced to ritually chop off the arm of one of his friends as if it were a piece of kindling. He was indoctrinated to hate perfectly innocent villagers, given gunpowder to be snorted like cocaine, and made to watch *Rambo* again and again. In order for him to survive, his conscience rotted away. It didn't take long.

Jack's squad was called a "Small Boy Unit."

Too young to know fear or the value of their own lives, they were able conscripts. Adult soldiers were burdened by too many values to have any hope of easily reaching the children's grotesque, calm plateau.

Jack was haunted by the memories of this time—or, to be more honest, he ran from them.

He ran from the memories of the women, the little girls, and the fathers he killed with not a moment of hesitation, following orders.

He ran from the nickname—White Devil—that he earned through his fighting prowess.

With the end of the war, he was rescued by a human rights group and sent to America, where he joined the army and, eventually, the High-Tech Special Forces Unit FOXHOUND.

Jack focused all of his energy into his training and on a budding relationship with a woman named Rosemary. Through his pursuits, he ran from his past—from the casual slaughter prompted only by an order.

Some might say he had sought a petty and cowardly refuge in his new life, but for the first time Jack was able to find himself.

His first and only FOXHOUND mission was to rescue the kidnapped president from Big Shell—a marine decontamination facility and international symbol of environmental protection efforts that had been constructed to clean up the catastrophic oil spill left behind by the sunken tanker where Solid Snake was thought to have drowned.

When President James Johnson came for a personal inspection of the facility, a rogue counterterrorist unit, Dead Cell, seized control of the plant. The forces were aided by Russian mercenary forces and under the direct control of former US president George Sears.

Before given the code name Raiden for that mission, his FOXHOUND code name was Snake. The entire incident had been carefully planned to turn Jack into Snake.

From the terrorist stronghold in an isolated marine location to threats of kidnapping and nuclear attack, to countless smaller details, the Big Shell Incident was a purposeful recreation of the conditions Snake faced on Shadow Moses.

Believing that anyone faced with an identical story under identical circumstances would become Snake, the Patriots set the stage—they sank the tanker, spilled the oil, and built the cleanup facility.

Revolver Ocelot, along with Olga Gurlukovich, whose daughter had been kidnapped to coerce her support, worked as the engineers of this deception. Ocelot guided the former president—aka Solidus Snake, the "perfect" Snake—and his Dead Cell unit into an uprising against the Patriots, all in order for them to fill the role of FOXHOUND on Shadow Moses.

Behind the plot was GW, the command and control AI of Arsenal Gear, the Patriots' giant submersible missile carrier that was secretly docked beneath the Big Shell facility.

Between his budding career in FOXHOUND and life with his lover, Rose, Jack had stubbornly kept his eyes closed and his ears plugged. He convinced himself he was following a path he had chosen. But as he fought the battle the Patriots had chosen for him, he discovered the cruel truth.

Everything he thought he had chosen for himself had instead been chosen for him.

He had only been running from his past.

Because Snake and I went into Big Shell "off-script," we threw unforeseen wrinkles into the Patriots' scenario, and Jack was able to learn the truth. He might have wished we never had. The knowledge must have been difficult for him to face.

But Jack was man enough to take it.

Jack defeated Solidus and drew the curtain on the play—which had been the Patriots' plan all along. With their experiment successful, the Patriots announced the completion of a computer model.

The program had the ability to freely simulate stories—to recreate the Patriots' interpretation of the truth. It was known as the S3 Plan—the Selection for Social Sanity. With it, the Patriots could manipulate reality. The transformation of Jack during the reenactment of Shadow Moses was only an operations test to test the limits of the program's abilities.

But Jack hadn't become Solid Snake—even though the test had been executed perfectly.

The Patriots' AI told us that all of our sadness, our anger, our mourning were only byproducts—that our experiences off the coast of Manhattan had all been planned out by the Patriots.

But what was born within Jack wasn't the Patriots' story—it was Jack's. It was Raiden's.

But there's a tiny little story inside each of us, and Jack's refused to be a mere byproduct of the Patriots' plan. That story held Jack up as Jack and no one else, and prevented him from becoming a soldier like Solid Snake.

Jack was once known as Snake.

It had been decided that he would become Snake.

He filled Snake's role, and he fought like Snake.

But Jack kept fighting, even now, and he did it as himself.

Somewhere out there.

The smell of butter, oil, and sulphur.

Snake awoke. I was holding a plate of Sunny's fried eggs under his nose. The two yolks looked like they'd taken gunfire, and the whites had burned black. The smell was the best thing the eggs had going.

I admit I have no room to talk, but no woman I've ever personally met has been a good cook. I've heard that even Raiden's ex-wife Rose was bad at it. During our mission on Big Shell, Raiden let slip that he vastly preferred military rations to her cooking, so it must have been truly heinous.

And now Sunny too seemed to have fallen under my jinx. God must really be enjoying Himself torturing me with these women!

"Are those for you, Otacon?"

Snake put a hand to his head and sat up on the medical bed. *Nomad* wasn't exactly a smooth ride, and the turbulence was a source of annoyance and discomfort. But Snake had slept straight through it until now.

"Yeah," I said, taking in the broken yolks. "Sunny side up, only these suns collapsed." I sensed someone behind me and turned to find myself under Sunny's wrathful stare. "Oh, um, sorry. I'll dig in right away, Sunny. And would you make some for Snake too?"

Snake threw a glance at me that seemed to say, *Thanks, leave me out of this.* Then he said to Sunny, "Hey... none for me."

But she was already up the gangway, headed for the kitchen. Snake sighed and scratched his head.

"How long was I out?"

"The whole day."

Snake rubbed his eyelids. His voice was hoarse. "Someone saved my life."

"It could have been Meryl and her boys," I said, although I didn't know for sure. The PMC soldiers were wailing, puking, holding their heads in their hands, even trying to kill each other. It was hard to tell what was happening amid the chaos.

"Don't worry," I added. "They're doing fine."

But that didn't seem to reassure Snake much.

Groaning in pain and with a hand on his hip, Snake arose.

"Liquid got away," he said.

Suddenly, he began to cough violently. He put his hands on his knees and bent over, out of breath. I put my hand on his back, and after a short while, he recovered.

"Back there," Snake said, "my body... just seized up all of a sudden. It wasn't like normal. It wasn't my joints or muscles."

"It looked like the PMC soldiers all went haywire en masse. I thought it might be a form of an Active Denial System. But I didn't detect any electromagnetic aberrations. You were lucky—some of those guys' hearts simply stopped."

Then Snake remembered the woman. "She was there. Naomi was at Liquid's side. Otacon, did you see her?"

"No," I said. Noting Snake's disappointed expression, I quickly added, "But you're right. Naomi was there." I pointed to the syringe, a white autoinjector, on my desk. "I found traces of her DNA in that syringe you were holding."

"So it was Naomi. Why?"

"Here, let me show you something."

I sat at my computer and opened a file. Snake tottered over to look over my shoulder.

"Right after it all happened," I said, "I got a video mail from Naomi. It was sent to my old address. The data checks out—no viruses. The voiceprint matches Naomi's. And I'm fairly confident the picture hasn't been digitally synthesized either."

The video finished loading, and I clicked play.

Naomi's face filled the screen. The background was dark, but it looked like some kind of storeroom.

"Snake, I'll make this quick." Naomi's expression was urgent. She spoke in a whisper and kept looking over her shoulder. The picture was unsteady—she seemed to be recording herself with a handheld camera.

"I'm in South America. I've been captured and forced to do research. It's Liquid. His goal is to seize control of SOP—the Sons of the Patriots system that controls the soldiers. To do that, he needs to analyze the nanomachines' structure and find out how they communicate with one another."

"Was the madness I saw when I faced Liquid," Snake muttered to himself, "the result of that takeover? Did Liquid already control the System?"

"The nanomachines currently in use by the PMCs are third generation. But their design is derived from that of the first, and the technology is still the same."

"The first generation?" Snake said to the screen. Drebin had said something along those lines—that the nanomachines in Snake's body were "old nanomachines" and had caused the interference with the System and blocked him from using non-ID guns.

"I was the one who created the first generation," Naomi was saying. "A colony of nanomachines—part of which was FOXDIE. Nine years ago, at Shadow Moses, I injected it into your body, Snake. The technology used in FOXDIE was incorporated—inherited, really—by SOP. That's why Liquid is making me help him hijack the System. Because I know how FOXDIE works."

Viruses could be thought of as machines built from molecules of DNA or RNA—machines possessing the ability to utilize the cells of living organisms to reproduce. A man-made virus was, in essence, a nanomachine, and a virus found in nature might be said to be a natural nanomachine.

There was a loud noise on the recording, and Naomi turned. Sweat beaded down her forehead.

"Please rescue me." She was visibly distressed. "Liquid's found a loophole he can use to get into the System. Preparations for his insurrection are nearly complete. There's no time to waste. Snake, hurry!"

The video ended.

Snake covered his mouth in thought. Meryl had told him that Liquid's PMCs would be unable to stand up against the world governments—even if he was Liquid, the System couldn't be beaten by military force.

But if the SOP could be hacked, the PMCs would be freed from the System's control, and they could proceed to make war however they wished. The leaders of the war economy, now more powerful than the US military, could bare their fangs against the world that had used the war economy for its own benefit.

"This is bad," Snake said.

I nodded. "Naomi created the technology. Given enough time, I'm sure she could do anything."

The screen flashed CALL. I checked the encrypted ID tag and told Snake, "It's Campbell."

The line connected, and Campbell's office appeared on the screen. The colonel sat with his arms resting on his oak desk.

"Snake," he said, "as you'll recall, following the Shadow Moses Incident nine years ago, Naomi was detained by the authorities. But someone arranged for her escape."

Snake and I knew all about that. We had, after all, been official suspects. As fugitives, we kept a close eye on all of the charges against us—including the false ones. Snake and I have shared more than a few beers together while laughing at our names on the tops of the FBI website's wanted lists for crimes we certainly didn't remember having anything to do with.

Snake laughed sarcastically and said, "Yeah, I hear they added that to my rap sheet too."

"I suspect it was actually Liquid. He must have taken her prisoner and forced her to do research at his facility in South America."

I said, "Naomi sent her location data in a separate file. It was encrypted, but Sunny decoded it for us."

Campbell nodded, and then his expression turned even graver. "Chances are the location she gave us is the site of Liquid's main base."

As he searched his pockets for a smoke, Snake asked, "But is there any actual proof?"

"Yes," said Campbell. "There's an ongoing skirmish between a new regime put into power by PMCs and a rebel army formed by remnants of the old one. The rebels have hired a small-scale local PMC of their own to stir things up. It's the quintessential example of the war economy market. The new regime is still in shambles, so it's really Pieuvre Armement—one of the PMCs under Outer Heaven control—that's calling the shots. You might say it's a perfect place for Liquid to make his haven."

"Or it could be a trap."

"True. But even if it was, we'd have much to gain."

"I had Sunny trace the origin of Naomi's mail," I said. "The address was fake, but Sunny was able to track the message back through its proxies based on time stamps and data transfer volumes. Apparently, the message originated from a server in South

America. I wouldn't exactly call it one hundred percent credible though."

Out of gratitude for her help, I didn't tell Snake that she had hidden his cigarettes—just a modest trade to help ensure our continued stay on *Nomad* would remain a pleasant one.

Campbell said, "I've secured you landing clearance at El Dorado International Airport. You'll be acting as UN inspectors."

"South America…" I said. "That's about twenty hours from here. What happens when we get there?"

"I'll arrange for them to get you a four-by-four. The location Naomi gave us—the PMC's base—is in a mountainous region surrounded by forests. Use the four-by-four to get as close as possible to the PMC's security perimeter. From there on, Snake, it'll be a solo sneaking mission. The rebels are still pitched in battle against the PMCs. The commotion should help you slip into the facility unnoticed."

Snake changed the subject. "Colonel, how deeply are they involved in this?"

I looked at him and asked, "The Patriots, you mean?"

Even in the Middle East, we couldn't help but keep watchful for any sign of the Patriots' involvement. After the battle with Solidus over the Arsenal Gear in Manhattan, their AI had loudly proclaimed that they would regulate and control everything.

Snake nodded. "The data we got from Arsenal Gear was a load of crap. Twelve founders who've all been dead for a hundred years. Give me a break. We know they exist today. If the purpose of this battlefield control system is to control IDs, it fits in with their plans perfectly."

"Seizing control of the world's ID systems," Campbell said, "and then using them to manipulate the economy and the worldwide flow of information—for the Patriots, that's the ultimate prize. You might say that the Patriots are the embodiment of the war economy."

"Everything that Solidus feared five years ago," Snake said solemnly, "has come to pass."

The former president had turned to terrorism out of his desire to build a world free of the Patriots' control. Freedom. Human rights. Opportunity. These were the fundamental ideas that burned inside each and every American's heart in those glorious first days of their independence. But somewhere in the young nation's short history, those ideals were warped and twisted, and the Patriots' horrifying System was born.

It wasn't because any one person had been driven by a thirst for power, or that someone had desired control. America's commerce, economy, lifestyle—even the very essence of the nation itself—had given birth to the structure of the Patriots.

"Now with the media and global opinion under complete control," Campbell said, "not even the UN can stand up to them."

Snake asked, "Then Liquid's insurrection is against the Patriots?"

"Exactly. It would seem as though Liquid has taken up Big Boss's cause. An age of persistent, universal warfare for mercenaries freed from domination. In a sense, the 'Outer Heaven' Big Boss envisioned is already a living reality."

"You mean the PMCs and their war business."

"Right now," Campbell said, "Liquid is a slave to the Patriots, forced to fight their proxy wars for them."

"He must be dying to break free of their spell."

"Beneath the surface, a new cold war is brewing between Liquid and the Patriots over who will survive."

Snake turned away from the screen and looked up at the ceiling with a distant gaze. "And no matter who wins, the world will have no future. Until we stop Liquid and destroy the System, we'll never be free."

Isn't that what Solidus had wanted? He had been terrified of not leaving any legacy behind. Solid, Liquid, Solidus—the sons of Big Boss—had been born stripped of the ability to create offspring. They were just reproductions of Big Boss's genetic code.

But Solidus had wanted to achieve something. He wanted to prove he was more than a simple carbon copy of Big Boss's DNA. He wanted to prove he was free. He wanted the world to hear his silent cries—*I am free. I am me.*

I am free. And you are free.

"Snake," Campbell stated plainly, "what we call 'peace' is an equilibrium kept in check by the war economy. Destroying the System means wiping out the information society—the end of modern civilization. Like it or not, we may have no choice but to protect the System."

Solidus had tried to destroy the System, but it defeated him. As ironic as it might seem, Snake and I—and Raiden—believed our actions had saved the world. If we now took down the Patriots like Solidus had tried to do, only an endless chaos would await us.

But still, could you say that Solidus was entirely wrong? I didn't think I could.

"Got it," Snake said, rubbing at his shoulder, stiff from lying unconscious for an entire day. "We've got twenty hours until we land. I'll have a look at the documents. And I'd like to have a smoke while I have the chance. Otacon, have you seen where mine went?"

"Sorry Snake, I can't tell you."

I shrugged. He eyed me with suspicion but didn't press.

Since I didn't know where Sunny had hidden them, I wasn't exactly telling a lie.

2

AFTER FLIGHT CLEARANCE was granted by the local air force, *Nomad* touched down at El Dorado. Sunny pressed the button to lower the hatch. The thinness of the outside air startled her.

The air *was* thin. El Dorado International Airport was over eight thousand feet above sea level—an elevation high enough for air pressure to significantly affect the boiling point of water. I wondered if that would affect the taste of her eggs. Could it possibly be for the worse?

You might have inferred this already, because air traffic control was being performed by the military, but the El Dorado Airport was jointly a civilian and a military airport. The air force was in full presence, with old C-130s scattered everywhere. America had probably sold them off decades ago.

"I think those are PMC transport craft," Campbell said from the screen.

Emblazoned on the sides of the planes was Pieuvre Armement's ominous logo—eight tentacles poking out the eyes, nose, and mouth of a skull. *Pieuvre* being French for octopus. I've heard that people in southern France sometimes eat octopus, but whoever designed that fearsome image couldn't have been a fan of the dish.

As Snake performed one last inspection of his gear, Campbell decided to use the time to introduce Snake to his psychological counselor for the mission. He called her over next to his desk to get her in the video feed. She was young and attractive, with straight black hair.

"This is Rosemary," he said.

Snake and I looked at each other at the same time. But not just in reaction to her beauty. This young woman had been Jack's lover, and during the Big Shell Incident had carried his child. Rose would later tell me about how Jack returned from the Big Shell unable to put away his memories as a child soldier. He'd get drunk, and some nights he returned covered in injuries. Eventually, she had a miscarriage, and he disappeared.

When I first learned all of that, I had trouble accepting it. How could that have happened? For a brief moment, I even thought, *Why couldn't she have come to Snake or me?* But I know that neither of us could really have done anything for her.

But when her face appeared on the screen inside the cargo bay, I was suddenly reminded of something else I'd heard. I looked at Snake. He seemed to simultaneously come to the same realization, and it wasn't a pleasant one.

"Colonel," Snake said, "the woman you married, the one that Meryl was talking about..."

"Is Rosemary, yes. Didn't I tell you before?"

Snake and I sighed in unison.

"What were you thinking?" Snake asked. "She's young enough to be your daughter."

Campbell's response was only more depressing. "Yeah. Lucky me, huh?"

I nearly laughed at the absurdity. Snake, disgusted, said, "Now I see why Meryl won't have anything to do with you."

"Meryl said something about me?" The flippant tone had left the colonel's voice, replaced by deep pain. But neither Snake nor I were in the mood to feel sorry for him.

Snake flatly replied, "Yeah, I believe her words were, 'I'll never forgive that womanizing piece of shit.'"

"I see."

With none of us having any desire to linger on the aggravating and bizarre revelation, we instead sought refuge in our various battle preparations. I tested Snake's OctoCamo and calibrated the power assist on his Sneaking Suit. Then I ran the Mk. II's system tests and went through *Nomad*'s inspection checklist to prepare for our eventual departure.

When the time came for Snake to leave, Sunny stood at the edge of the cargo bay, waved goodbye, and called out, "S-see you, Snake!"

Snake returned a smile. He would be gone for at least several days—several days without having to endure her fried eggs. I looked at Sunny, watching Snake reach the edge of the tarmac, and I thought, *We're something like a family, aren't we.*

We weren't really a family, of course, but at that moment, I felt at peace.

If only everything could have stayed like that.

I shook my head. What was I thinking at a time like this? Snake was about to enter another battlefield.

Using an ID Campbell had provided, Snake passed through customs and immigration. He climbed in the four-by-four and headed up into the mountainous region on the other side of the border. Just a few years ago, the high altitude wouldn't have been a problem for Snake, but with his aged lungs Snake was having trouble adjusting to the low oxygen.

Fortunately, he'd have time to adjust—the mountains were quite far. But as the elevation increased, Snake only seemed to become worse off. He rarely spoke, and the occasional bead of sweat rolled down his cheek.

"Snake," I asked over the codec, "how are you holding up?"

Snake, as reluctant as ever to discuss his body, simply asked, "What's our current situation?"

I sighed. "Rebel guerrilla units are advancing on the base of the government PMC troops. The building appears to be Liquid's safe house. According to Naomi's data, she's being held prisoner inside the compound."

I sent a satellite image of the compound through the Solid Eye.

"That's where she is?" he asked.

"Assuming Naomi's data are correct. According to satellite imagery procured by Mei Ling, the facility where Naomi is being held is to the north, along a mountain road. I'm sending the location to your map."

Snake hadn't heard that name in a while. "Mei Ling?"

"Yeah."

Along with Colonel Campbell, Mei Ling was part of Snake's wireless support team during the Shadow Moses Incident. Back then, she was still a teenager, but now, nine years had passed, and she was a grown woman.

She'd become the captain of the USS *Missouri*, a battleship from the time when giant turrets were still the backbone of naval power. *Missouri* had a long and storied history (including serving as the setting for a Steven Seagal movie), but with the advent of carrier fleets, the expensive and inflexible battleship-class vessels became obsolete. Although cannon power attacks on coastal areas remained in sporadic use through the Gulf War, *Missouri* was retired as an aged soldier, no longer of use to the modern era, in the following year, '92. The rest of the battleships would meet the same fate by the mid-nineties.

Now the seas were dominated by frigate-class ships and cruisers powered by the mighty Aegis system.

After its decommissioning, *Missouri* was sent to Hawaii to live out the rest of its years as a tourist attraction, but after its museum contract expired the ship was recommissioned and used for virtual training. Rather than actual combat training, the goal seemed to be getting the sailors acclimated to seamanship aboard an analog vessel.

In short, everyone involved with the Shadow Moses incident had either become fugitives or had been sidelined into nonessential dead-end appointments. The same had happened to Meryl. She was wasting away in some desk job when Campbell pulled some connections in the army to place her within the PMC inspection unit—an assignment considered extremely dangerous even for the CID.

"Otacon," Snake said, "I just saw a PMC armored truck. I think I'm not far from Pieuvre Armement patrols. I even saw some giant billboard advertisements for them. 'Arms of the Octopus, Arms for Your War!'"

"That might sound appealing if you were desperate. But in the fog of war, even eight arms aren't enough."

Even some nonsense name like Octopus Armaments takes on an elegantly feminine quality when said in French. Pieuvre Armement. Personally, I found all this ebullience over the booming war economy distasteful.

I confirmed Snake's positional data on the GPS, then said, "You'd better ditch your car. That area's a veritable hornet's nest of PMC patrols."

Snake voiced his acknowledgment. He left the four-by-four hidden in a thicket of trees and lowered the Mk. II from the back. He adjusted the OctoCamo and took slow, even breaths to condition his breathing to the thin atmosphere. He studied his environment and attuned his senses and his intuition to the South American highlands.

The smell of the grass.

The smell of bugs.

The smell of the earth.

Crawling on the ground, the smells were unavoidable—and to Snake, they were an essential component of his senses.

When others were or had recently been nearby, they left ripples in what Snake liked to think of as a baseline. The forest and the earth were a delicate system within which Snake could pick out the traces of human disturbance. By attuning his senses to the ripples in the baseline, his situational awareness surpassed what most would consider possible.

Even with some of his attention dedicated to keeping track of PMC forces, Snake soon reached the path. Nestled in a dell at its mouth was a village with several houses, a barn, and a PMC armored truck.

The battlefront had arrived ahead of Snake.

Defeated rebel soldiers were gathered together on their knees. A number of battle-scarred corpses were scattered around the village, all of them antigovernment forces. The rebels had no uniforms and carried mismatched sets of whatever equipment they were able to scavenge or improvise. The PMC soldiers, of course, wore combat chest harnesses and Protec helmets, their equipment on par with that of the US Army.

Flames spewed from one of the houses. Likely, this village had been a rebel hideout. By blurring the line between the battlefield and civilian life, guerrillas could evade the attacks of conventional armies.

The guerrilla warfare tactics employed in the mountains of South America owed much to Mao Zedong. A mountainous expanse covered much of China's territory, and in farming villages in those highlands, Mao had made his stronghold. He knew that urbanized forces would not be suited to the steep ranges. South America, with a similar share of mountains and villages, had a lot in common with China.

At one with the forest, Snake observed the PMCs through his Solid Eye. A figure emerged from the flaming house. The man was noticeably taller than the PMC soldiers, and he wore a long black coat utterly out of place in a battlefield. Snake recognized him.

The man was one of the monsters of the rebel unit, Dead Cell, whom we thought had been shot to death by Raiden on the Big Shell. But death never seemed to take for him, as he could be stabbed in the chest or shot through the head and laugh it off.

The man's teeth had once been in Snake's throat, and Snake could still remember how his eyes had looked. Bottomless. Black. Lifeless. Like a vampire.

"It's Vamp," Snake said, and when I heard the words, time stood still.

Vamp. The heartbreak of seeing his knife stick into my sister's stomach had haunted me for years. How much better would it have been had the knife been pointed at me instead? How many times have Emma's last words echoed inside me just as I was about to fall asleep?

All I could do every night was grit my teeth and clutch at the bedsheets and endure the memory of her feeble lips forming the words *Call me Emma*. Reliving that moment reduced me to tears every time.

That man—that Nosferatu—killed Emma.

"Otacon!"

I snapped back to the mission. Snake must have been calling my name over the codec for some time. I put my hand to my chest and tried to calm my hastened pulse and breathing. No easy task with that man on the other side of the monitor—on the other side of Snake's Solid Eye.

"I'm sorry," I said. "He could be involved with Liquid's plans." Vamp had been working in concert with Ocelot on the Big Shell.

"It's possible. But I thought Jack took him out in Manhattan!"

I bit my lip. Was Vamp really immortal? Maybe I should have felt afraid, or incredulous, at the possibility of facing an enemy who couldn't die, but all I could feel was the rising anger for the man who killed my sister. I tried to fight it back, but my racing heart sent blood straight to my head. My temples started to ache from the intensity of my emotions.

"I swear, the next time I see him..."

"Otacon, get a grip!"

Snake's shouting broke me free from the magnetic draw of my hatred. For the moment, at least, I was thinking straight again.

The burning anger had subsided into an icy black river. I said to Snake, "Let's see what the PMC troops are up to."

Snake acknowledged and moved to where he could hear their voices, from which we gathered the Pieuvre Armement soldiers were searching for Snake's whereabouts.

The soldiers reported to Vamp that Snake hadn't been in the

village. Vamp's skin was whiter than it had been on the Big Shell, and veins stood out on his cheek like neural pathways.

"The guerrillas have scattered," Vamp said to the men, his voice low and smooth, straight out of a nightmare. "But they'll be coming to storm the safe house. He must be among their numbers. Sooner or later he will come. Don't let down your guard."

The PMC troops saluted, and Vamp climbed into the armored truck and left the smoldering village behind. Somehow, they knew Snake was coming.

"This could be a trap," I said.

"Yeah. We'll need to stay sharp."

## 3

THE PATH TWISTED, turned up the mountain, and wound in and out of the forest. But this wasn't a small, irregular trail created by the occasional passing of man and beast—it was a road of packed-down earth, complete with tire tracks laid down by military vehicles. From the look of the tracks, the trucks had been numerous and heavy, perhaps weighed down by armored plating and weaponry.

Or by materials brought in for research purposes.

Snake continued his crawl, hugging the earth like an inchworm. His OctoCamo constantly matched its patterns and colors with his immediate surroundings. He moved in a slow and steady rhythm, pausing whenever he sensed the slightest ripple in the baseline—perhaps some shift in the odor of the dirt—and once satisfied that no danger was present, he adjusted his senses to the change and pressed on.

This continued until a sudden call came from his codec and broke his rhythm.

The caller's ID tag was blank. Blended in with the background noise was the sound of odd, irregular breaths. No, odd wasn't quite the right word—the breathing seemed inhuman.

"Who is this?" Snake asked.

"Snake..."

Snake had heard that voice before. "Is this..."

"There is an APC parked up ahead. It looks junked, but a strange man is inside. It could be a PMC trap. Be careful."

"Is this Jack?"

The voice was unmistakably Jack's, although there was a mechanical tinge to it.

Jack.

Raiden.

The former FOXHOUND member who fought at our side on the Big Shell. Although, strictly speaking, he had only thought that he belonged to FOXHOUND—the group had been disbanded. After he'd rescued Sunny from the Patriots, he vanished without a trace, as if his role were over.

Where had he been?

"Jack is dead. Snake, I'm at your side."

The line disconnected.

"Otacon," Snake said, "is Rose there?"

I switched my feed to Campbell's office—his home office, to be exact. Rose was already at the screen, and I connected her with Snake.

"What's going on, Snake?" she asked.

"Rose, I just got a call from Raiden. It sounds like he's close by."

Rosemary took in a sharp breath. I couldn't tell if the confusion in her eyes was from joy or terror. With some effort, she assumed a calm expression.

"Did...did he seem okay?"

"Yeah, as far as I could tell from his voice."

Softly, she said, "That's great," but the words hadn't reached her expression. "Snake, I have a favor to ask."

"What?"

"Don't let him know I'm involved in this operation, okay? For now, I think it would be best for Jack if I let him be."

Did she really think that? From where I sat, it seemed like she was the one afraid of him. Filled with regret over abandoning him, over not being able to save him, she was clearly upset by his sudden reappearance.

Not many could ever escape their sins. The same way I hadn't been able to say something, to say anything, to Emma's final words before she slipped away.

Rosemary said, "After we lost our baby, all Jack did was avoid me—he blamed himself for the miscarriage—but Roy, his commanding officer, worried for me."

When he was a child, Jack was forced to kill many other children. But after the events on the Big Shell, he tried to face his past sins, but they only began to gnaw at him more and more.

The final blow had been brought by the death of his unborn child.

"Roy was so kind to me," Rosemary explained. "I know it sounds like I'm making excuses, but I needed to get over it, to move on with my life. I'm worried about Jack, of course, but...I'm also afraid of him."

If there were a man free enough of guilt to condemn her after that confession, he wasn't on the codec channel. I suppose Sunny would have been pure enough, had she been in the command center and not on the second floor immersed in her quest to make better fried eggs.

"All right," Snake said. "I'll keep my mouth shut."

"Thank you, Snake."

Snake soon came across the APC from Jack's warning.

Chipped paint revealed patches of rusted armor plating. I don't think many would look at the junker and see anything more than an abandoned vehicle.

But if what Jack said was true, someone—or some ones—waited inside.

Snake, keeping his presence concealed, inched toward the APC. But even right up next to it, he still couldn't sense anyone around.

Had the enemy not noticed us? Was there even anyone in there, waiting this still for Snake to come?

A preemptive strike on the occupants of the APC was out of the question. Any attempt to smoke the would-be ambushers out with a grenade or something of that kind would have alerted nearby PMC troops—an unacceptable risk considering that the APC might be deserted.

Snake slowly rose. He withdrew a cigarette from the pack he'd purchased at the airport and lit it as if to say, *If you're in there, go ahead, come at me.*

A small shadow whirred right past his nose.

Not a bullet.

An animal.

The creature climbed atop the APC with surprising speed, then started taking a leisurely drag from a cigarette. Only then did Snake notice the cigarette had disappeared from his mouth. He'd seen that animal before—the hairless gibbon in the Middle East.

The rear hatch of the APC opened, and from within came a cheerful voice.

"Yo! Over here."

At the same time, the rust and the damage on the exterior of the vehicle faded away. In its place was the smooth armored shell and a stencil that read EYE HAVE YOU!

OctoCamo. The whole body of the APC was coated with a layer of OctoCamo material.

From the rear hatch, Drebin was waving Snake over.

"Come on, hop in. It's getting rough out there."

The gibbon, cigarette in mouth, tried to climb inside, but Drebin shoved him away. The arms merchant pointed at the monkey's mouth and then the ground. Reluctantly, the animal rubbed Snake's smoke into the dirt. Snake dutifully picked up the snubbed-out butt and stuffed it in his portable ashtray.

Climbing into the rear hatch, Snake asked, "Have you been following me?"

Drebin closed the hatch and snapped his fingers—probably instructing the APC's computer system to re-engage the OctoCamo.

"You seemed like an interesting guy, so I decided to check you out. There's a lot of stories about you out there in the intel community—especially the CIA."

"How did you find me?"

"You know those nanomachines I injected you with back in the Middle East? They let me track your location."

Snake cursed his own carelessness. *Isn't that exactly how I got myself injected with FOXDIE before Shadow Moses?* Snake seemed to respond with the same inexplicable and baseless defiance whenever asked if he didn't like shots.

Drebin appeared genuinely pleased to see Snake again. "Figured it's only fair that I tell you. After you showed up in the Middle East, the five big PMCs all got orders to kill. 'Your number one priority is to eliminate Solid Snake on sight.' But from where I'm sitting, I'd say 'Old Snake' seems a little more appropriate."

"Old, huh?" Snake had thought he'd come to accept his accelerated aging, but hearing it from Drebin stung. After all, he was still in his forties.

To someone like me, having known him for about a decade, the whole business of Snake reacting to someone asking, "Do you not like shots?" was clearly him just putting up a strong front. He'd never admit it, but he dealt with the aging disease the same way. I guess that's one of the things we found endearing about the man.

"Drebin, I thought no one was supposed to be able to hack into the System. Are you with the Patriots?"

Drebin threw his head back and laughed. "No sir, I ain't no la li lu le lo."

There was that word protection again. Just like Naomi. That meant, whether he was aware of it or not, Drebin was within the System.

But then the man said with a laugh, "I mean...I'm no Patriot."

Snake sighed. Did this guy have to be so dramatic about everything?

"The nanomachines I got in me aren't military issue," Drebin said. "No speech restrictions for me."

*Still*, Snake and I both thought, *you know the Patriots exist.* Few people had heard of the Patriots, and most who did thought they were something dreamed up by paranoid nuts, like the Freemasons or the Jewish conspiracy. Almost none knew that the Patriots were not only real but continued to exist in the form of technology.

Thinking that Drebin must know something, Snake asked, "Who the hell are these Patriots? Are they human?"

"Not anymore, they ain't. They're the law of this world, created over the course of history. They're America, the world's greatest military power. They are the war economy. Which makes you and me just cogs in a much grander schematic. We're just the context."

The context. That was how the AI had explained it to Jack on the Big Shell.

"I mean," Drebin said, "someone obviously had to start the whole thing at the beginning. But now their law has taken on a life of its own."

"A life of its own?"

"Yup. The country, the war economy...It ain't run by people. It's run by the System. No need for high-level decision-making authority. It's all handled by a massive yet simple information processing system. An AI, you could say."

Snake wasn't entirely convinced.

The Patriots had built a marine decontamination facility to hide the construction of Arsenal Gear. In order to set the stage for that, they set a trap for Snake and sank a tanker with him in it. And after the Big Shell had served its purpose and the Arsenal Gear was made, they used the facility to reenact Shadow Moses as part of a test for a global information control system.

To do all that required the manipulation of a great number of people—their fates, their thoughts, their feelings. Jack, Rose, Solidus, the members of Dead Cell—even Ocelot, who thought himself to be one of the Patriots. Is a mere AI capable of such complexity?

Reading Snake's misgivings, Drebin spread his arms and said, "It works just like natural law. The world's a much simpler place than most folks realize."

"But what is the Patriots' AI, exactly?"

Drebin held up three fingers. "The Patriots' System is closely monitored by three peripheral AIs and a core AI that ties them all together. The SOP System, controlling the world's military power, is one part of that. It's all backed up by a foolproof control system. So not even yours truly can sneak inside the Patriots' AIs."

"What if, hypothetically, someone found a way?"

Drebin was startled by Snake's insistence, but he took a moment to think it over.

"If they could fool the Intrusion Detection System, I guess they could use it as a haven to lie low."

"A haven?"

"You know, like a tax haven. Online, we have net havens, data havens. An extraterritorial place where social conventions and the rules of the net don't apply. Last century, the superrich would open bank accounts in countries without income tax laws. Won't be long before people start using havens to escape from ID control."

"So, thinking along those lines, if someone got into the Patriots' AI…"

Drebin shrugged. "Either way, it's absolutely impossible to access the Patriots' AIs from the outside. No chance in hell. Like I said, there's no breaking into those AIs. Not from the outside."

But everything had a hidden side. Everything had a hole. Meryl had said that it was impossible to interfere with the SOP, and yet

Liquid proved it could be done. No matter how many times Drebin assured us the AIs couldn't be broken into, neither Snake nor I believed it for a second.

Snake pressed further. "But Liquid's got something in mind. You sure there's no way?"

Drebin let out a derisive laugh as if to say, *Give me a break already*, then said, "I'm just a gun launderer. Only reason I'm interested in you is 'cause you start a lot of fires."

"All right then, I guess I'd better take a few weapons that can cause some sparks."

Snake bought a DSR1, a German-made bolt action sniper rifle. After each shot, the shooter manually opened the breech to eject the spent shell and rack the next one into place. It was built more simply than automatics, making it more accurate and more reliable. Snake checked the weapon over and, satisfied with its condition, slung it over his back.

"Thanks, friend," Drebin said. "All right then. You need anything else, give me a ring. Eye. Have. You."

Snake dropped down from the rear hatch to see the APC's OctoCamo blur into the same markings as the PMC vehicles. And, just as it had in the Middle East, the vehicle sped away and out of sight.

An explosion sounded in the distance. The noise of battle, and of death.

Snake looked up the mountain path.

On the other side of the battle was the woman who knew the truth.

## 4

BRAVING THE BARRAGE of PMC gunfire, a lone bulldozer advanced.

Thick, welded-on steel plates protected its sides, and the front lifting blade repelled the PMC bullets at its front. The vehicle, a Caterpillar D9, came with enough horsepower to be unaffected by the added weight of the improvised armor plating. Not that its top speed really mattered much. For all the militia cared, it could crawl like a turtle as long as it smashed through the enemy barricades.

The D9s had been used to great effect by Israel in clean-up operations in Palestine. And once, an American citizen armored up a Japanese-made Komatsu bulldozer, went on a rampage, and destroyed much of a small town's main drag, completely impervious to SWAT team fire in his shell.

As Snake watched from a shaded cliffside, the militia's D9 smashed through a thick gate to the mansion safe house. The rebel forces poured through the opening, using the bulldozer as cover.

The militia was gaining momentum.

The rebel howitzers launched a barrage against the line of PMC forces at the perimeter of the villa's sizable garden. Snake steeled himself and moved onto the battlefield. As the relentless rain of shells tore chunks out of the earth, he advanced in a running crouch.

Snake's back gave out, and he lurched forward. Luckily, he regained his balance, avoiding a fall. As if the artillery fire and swarms of bullets weren't bad enough, now Snake had to worry about his back killing him first.

All he could do was grit his teeth and keep moving. He didn't have any other options.

Pushing aside the intense pain in his lower back, Snake resumed his advance. He was used to ignoring pain. Put in enough years on the battlefield and you developed the ability whether you wanted to or not. The trick was to separate the sensation of pain from your consciousness.

But the pain of old age wasn't like the sharp pain of a bullet or knife wound. It was dull, heavy. It reverberated. Compared to the many battle wounds Snake had endured, this was much harder to ignore.

Bullets whizzed past Snake's ears, but he was too preoccupied fighting back his pain to spare any room for fear.

Then there was the air. The air quality of the battlefield was, as one might expect, far from wonderful. Dirt flew, and clouds of powder smoke hung in the air, along with all the terrible smells of battle—burning houses, burning vehicles, burning people—and you didn't have to be there to know it wouldn't be easy on the lungs. Making things worse (and this he brought on himself), Snake was a heavy smoker.

Hacking and coughing, Snake somehow made it to the rear of the villa. Snake climbed into the house through a window on the terrace. Inside, PMC forces were rallying against the rebel army. The soldiers were exchanging shrill jeers with rebels outside—but their behavior was clearly different from the combat high combatants sometimes experienced. Each seemed unusually excited. Some leaned out front windows, wildly spraying bullets, with what any soldier would recognize as not the right timing.

"Otacon, something's strange about these guys."

"Yeah, the PMC troops have been operating at high altitudes for a while now, and we have reports that it's starting to upset the balance of the nanomachine control system. The change in concentration of oxygen in their blood seems to have an effect on the nanomachines—it's leading to heightened aggressive tendencies."

Perhaps that was another weakness in the System. At the very least, these soldiers were clearly not completely under its control.

Nature was causing interference in the SOP. Unlike ID guns or ID vehicles, the human body contained too many unknown elements.

"Get to the basement," I told Snake. "There should be an underground tunnel that leads to the research lab."

The mansion had a definite South American air to it, with touches of Spanish Colonial architecture all over. The quaint appearance of the villa formed an odd juxtaposition with the sight of the armed soldiers holed up within, where they fought their pitched battle.

Sneaking around inside confined quarters was Snake's strong suit.

He easily passed behind the line of soldiers and made it to the long underground tunnel. Snake was far more at ease with this sort of infiltration than he was with sneaking around in the middle of an open battlefield. He completed mission after mission via secrecy and stealth.

The tunnel was supported by wooden beams, and after some distance it ended in a vertical shaft with a ladder leading up. Snake climbed it and cautiously lifted the trapdoor at the top.

He was outside an isolated medical laboratory in the middle of a forest. Snake slowly clambered up to the surface, and alert for any disturbance in the baseline, he advanced toward the building. In stark contrast to the villa, the lab was a ramshackle wooden structure with exposed boards and peeling paint. But it wasn't unkempt. The grounds were clean and looked cared for—an impression certainly aided by the ring of blue flowers around the building.

Blue roses.

Snake pressed his back to one of the building's walls and looked in through an open window.

Most notable was the imposing GE-brand CAT scanner. Such a large and expensive piece of equipment was out of place inside the lonely clinic. In a country like this, that sort of machine might not be found in even the capital's university hospital or medical facilities for the very wealthiest. Everything else inside the shack, for that matter, was clearly state of the art, with high price tags and high precision.

This had to be Naomi's research center. Or, I should say, Liquid's research center.

Someone moved in front of the window. Snake ducked down. It was Naomi Hunter.

"Yes," she said into the cordless phone at her ear, "the next test. And things on your end?"

Letting the M4 hang from its sling, Snake drew his Operator and stepped in through an open doorway. Slowly, careful not to make noise on the floorboards, he moved to a room where he could better hear Naomi's conversation. She was in the connecting room, her back to him.

"I see. We're on schedule here as well. I know. Me too. Until then."

She hung up the phone. Suddenly, she gripped the edge of the desk and gasped as if struggling against something. Her shaking form revealed deep agony. Without stopping to think, Snake rushed forward to support her, but before he made it, she withdrew a syringe from her lab coat—the same type as the one she'd left in the Middle East—and jabbed it into her neck. Snake froze.

Finally, she took in a deep breath. For a time, at least, her pain had left.

"Naomi," Snake said.

Having only just caught her breath, she jumped back in surprise at her visitor's sudden appearance. When she saw it was Snake, relief flooded her face, but the coldness remained.

"Snake, I knew you'd come. You and I...neither of us can escape our fates."

Snake looked at her. Nine years since they'd last met, yet she still had that bewitching beauty behind which she kept her feelings deeply hidden. The sight of her conjured the words *femme fatale* in Snake's mind.

Was that sadness filling her shining eyes? Was there any truth behind her words?

Snake had been completely outfoxed by Naomi on Shadow Moses. He couldn't blame her for it, though. In Zanzibar Land, he had crippled her brother, Frank Jaeger, code name Gray Fox.

After the battle, Frank had become a test subject for an experimental exoskeleton. He had to be pumped full of painkillers to endure the searing pain as artificial muscles were grafted to his body. Armed with superhuman strength and speed, he escaped his confinement with one purpose—to find Solid Snake. His journey took him to far-off Shadow Moses Island.

Naomi used to hate Snake, the man who killed her brother. Perhaps she still hated him. Or perhaps, having learned that Frank gave his life to protect Snake, she'd forgiven him.

Snake asked, "Who were you just talking to?"

"Liquid. Although I suppose he's really Ocelot, from a medical standpoint."

"So he's not here then."

Naomi nodded.

Watching the video stream, I could only sigh dejectedly. Sunny stood behind me, worrying for me though unaware of what to say. I turned to her, saw the plate of fried eggs in her hand and sighed again.

"Don't worry, Sunny. It's nothing. I'm in the middle of a mission right now, so I'll eat later, okay?"

Sunny climbed back up the gangway, the concern still upon her face. I turned back to the monitor.

"Where are all the guards?" Snake asked.

"They know I won't escape."

"Tell me, Naomi. What happened in the Middle East?"

The chaos. The world falling apart.

It hadn't affected only him. All of the Praying Mantis soldiers had languished there, and some of them died. If Liquid were trying to seize control of the SOP, was that test a success, or was it a failure? Did Liquid already have the SOP within his grasp?

"What you saw was the soldiers' emotions run amok."

"Another product of the System?"

Naomi shook her head. "At first, Liquid thought—we thought—the SOP was an ID control system designed primarily to maintain order and control in battle. And we were right. But only partially. SOP has another function: to control people's senses."

Snake had seen Meryl's behavior—that sudden unnatural calm as the System automatically adjusted her emotions to their optimal state. With that amount of emotional control, the System would also be able to create artificial combat highs to increase combat effectiveness, as well as to dispel any bouts of panic during a battle.

"The skyrocketing demands of the war economy," Naomi explained, "have fueled the demand for more soldiers and more fighting. The System ensures a steady supply of battle-optimized soldiers at minimal cost. But you of all people surely understand..."

"That unlike combat technique, a soldier's senses can't be taught—only earned through experience. Does that have something to do with that test of yours?"

"At first, our goal was to release the soldiers' nanomachines from the System. But we didn't know about the mental control."

"And the nanomachines went berserk?"

Naomi shook her head. "No. Our test was a success. At least, it confirmed our hypothesis at the time."

"Confirmed it?"

"Just as we predicted, the nanomachines stopped functioning, and the PMC soldiers were freed from the grips of the System. But the moment the System stopped...all the pain, and fury, and sorrow, all the trauma and stress, all the hatred, regret, guilt...all the sensations that had been suppressed were unleashed within their hearts."

That chaos was the result of being freed from the System. With the spell of the nanomachines broken, the emotions simmering below the surface erupted all at once. The soldiers' memories, unlike their senses, weren't erased. Each enemy soldier they'd killed, each lost comrade, each threat of violence against the innocent. The emotional consequences of all of their actions had only been restrained, not eliminated, by the technology.

"In suppressing the user's mind," Naomi said, "the nanomachines exact a heavy burden on his heart. The user's body begins to reject the nanomachines; this reaction must then be suppressed with drugs. Before the user knows it, his mind is in complete shambles."

The instant they'd been freed from the SOP, the soldiers had been brought down by their own humanity. A chill ran down my spine.

Once Liquid's plans came to fruition, the hundreds of millions of green-collar workers around the world, wherever they might be, would all simultaneously be thrown into madness.

"Snake...remember Frank."

The sudden mention of his name took Snake by surprise.

Snake's superior, Snake's enemy, Snake's friend.

Naomi's brother.

"They twisted his body for their experiments and suppressed his broken heart with nanomachines. SOP has taken it even further and applied it to people with flesh and blood. The war-guilt these soldiers carried assaulted them in the form of unimaginable shell shock. The purpose and the methods of war may have changed, but the battlefield itself hasn't. Until the SOP was removed, those soldiers waged war as if it were a game. And then, suddenly, reality came crashing down upon them."

But what about Snake, then? No one could say that the legendary hero had made it through his battles unscathed. Even the "man who made the impossible possible" had suffered his share of setbacks. But Snake made it through his own doing, not thanks to nanomachines. Just like every other warrior of the previous century—no, every other warrior since man first made war.

Snake must have been having similar thoughts, because he asked Naomi, "But what about me? I've never been under the System's control."

Naomi nodded.

"That's why I want to examine your body. You need to know too. All right, Snake. Undress."

Old age comes to everyone.

There isn't a single human, mammal, or vertebrate who can escape old age. Not the rich, not the poor. Not the president, not the peasant. Death by old age is a protocol of life.

Aging primarily originates from what's essentially a self-executing program in the DNA. One's environment and lifestyle certainly have an effect, but improvements in those areas will never be able to entirely eliminate aging or death. The word *grow* is just another way of saying "age." To grow, to learn, to mature, is to age.

Granted, Snake's aging was far more rapid than that of other people. But as long as that aging was a process already etched inside his DNA, he wouldn't be able to escape it.

As Naomi ran Snake's body through her tests, she explained this to him.

Through the codec, I despondently listened to her talk. Had I been alone, I might have cried. I might have been unable to hold back the welling tears. I might have thrown my head on my desk and wailed. But Sunny was with me, and I didn't want to do anything to upset her. So I held my eyes on the monitor and silently listened.

Naomi's news didn't get any better.

At the end of chromosomes are segments called telomeres, and these determine how many times a cell can divide. The telomeres consist of repeated snippets of buffer code, and with each division of the parent cell, a little more of the buffer is lost. Once the telomere is completely gone and the chromosome exposed, the cell will cease to divide.

Snake's body, created as a clone of Big Boss, contained telomeres intentionally engineered to be short. The same was true for Liquid and Solidus.

And even though all three were the same age, Solidus had looked a decade older than Solid and Liquid—something that helped give him a presidential air suited to his office. It seemed he had been created with an even more fleeting life span than the other Snakes.

The Patriots' project, Les Enfants Terribles, sought to mass produce copies of history's greatest mercenary, Big Boss. The Snakes were warped, artificial creatures created for one purpose—war.

The clones were to designed to be saleable commodities, and in order to prevent misuse by clients or theft by enemies, their life spans were limited and a terminator gene inserted to prevent natural reproduction. None of the Snakes could ever father a child, and even if they survived their battle, they didn't have long for this world. It was a safety mechanism to prevent the sons of Big Boss from escaping the control of the Patriots. A cruel fate written into Snake's body.

Snake sat up on the CT scanner's bed.

"The truth, Naomi," he said. "How long is my body going to hold out?"

Naomi looked at the floor. "Your cells, blood, organs, nerves, skeletal system, muscle tissue—every part of your body is aging rapidly. If you were an ordinary man, by now? You wouldn't even be standing. The only thing keeping you together is your strength of will."

Snake was tired of roundabout answers. "How long do I have?"

"Half a year."

I gasped.

The doctor had said one full year, and now it was half?

She knew more about the Patriots, about Big Boss, and about Snake's body than anyone. My heart sank.

With the doctor's opinion, there had still been room for hope. Yes, we had to prepare for the worst, but he didn't really understand Snake's body. Snake was special. Not ordinary. The doctor's calculations—or his diagnosis—could have been wrong. To tell the truth, that's the hope I'd been clinging to, an excuse to turn a blind eye to my friend's fate.

Snake, on the other hand, took the news as coolly as ever. He took out a cigarette and searched for his lighter. I'd been ignoring his fate, sheltering myself from it, but Snake had accepted it. Of course, I couldn't claim to really know what was going on inside his head. It could have been Snake putting up another of his strong fronts, like with the injections.

Whether he truly was steadfast or was just shielding us from his inner turmoil, I didn't know. But wouldn't either option require the same strength and kindness of will?

Naomi looked away from the test results on her computer screen and back at Snake.

"Listen," she said. "There's something I have to tell you."

"Now what?"

"FOXDIE only kills its victims when the infected person's genetic code fully matches the genetic sequence programmed into the virus's receptors. In other words, it only attacks targets with specific genes."

We knew that already without her having to tell us again. That was what killed both the AT president and the original Liquid.

"Yeah," was Snake's empty response. He had found a light and raised the cigarette to his lips. Naomi snatched it out, and Snake dejectedly watched as she threw it into the trash bin.

"The receptors on the FOXDIE virus inside your body are breaking down. The rapid aging process is changing the environment within your body, and as a result, the virus is starting to mutate."

Two microscopic images appeared side-by-side on the display. In one, the object was smooth, but the subject of the other image was broken down. Mutated.

"This mutated version of FOXDIE could activate even if the infected person's genetic pattern doesn't perfectly match the receptors. Which means the virus will begin to indiscriminately kill the infected."

I was dumbfounded. Snake had unwittingly spread FOXDIE all over Shadow Moses, but the virus was programmed to kill only FOXHOUND and the AT president. By working alongside Snake, both Meryl and I had likely contracted the virus ourselves. The only reason we didn't suffer the apoptosis, the heart attack, and the death, was that we weren't its targets. FOXDIE (which was just a tiny little bit of protein, if you thought about it) was clever enough to discriminate between its intended victims and everyone else.

And it was losing that ability.

And it was happening right now. Inside Snake.

His body was an incubator for history's deadliest virus, one to which there were no antibodies and no cure.

"How long," Snake asked, "will it take for the receptors to wear down?"

I noticed the question wasn't *Will the virus go away after I die from old age?*

"Three months."

Snake gasped.

Naomi looked away with a pained expression. "Ironic, isn't it? You've spent your whole life saving the world from Metal Gear—from nuclear annihilation. And now you're becoming a doomsday device yourself. If it were up to me, you'd be quarantined already."

Snake said nothing at first. He looked out the window at the carpet of blue flowers. A vase of the roses sat on Naomi's desk.

"It's just like me," Snake said. "The botanists of old obsessed over creating a blue rose. But roses lacked the capability to produce the color blue. Thanks to advances in biotechnology, now there are fields of blue roses, created from the mixing of rose genes with those of other species of flowers."

Blue roses were impossible. So the existence of blue roses was proof of the impossible made possible.

"Unnatural flowers. Unnatural Snakes. We're all the same," he said to Naomi.

"It's not over yet," Snake said. Not to Naomi, but to himself.

She nodded. "I know. You still have a job to do."

We couldn't quit yet. Snake had to banish his sins. And the sins of his brother by blood, Liquid. And the sin of my participation in the creation of Metal Gear REX.

"I have three months," said Snake. "If I choose death first, will that stop FOXDIE from spreading?"

"If the host dies, the virus dies with it. You'll have time to think once this is all over."

There, waiting ahead of what I'd thought to be the worst possible fate, was an even worse one.

For the first time, Snake looked truly shaken. He retrieved another cigarette from his breast pocket, and as he held it, his fingers trembled. And not because of old age.

Because of fear.

But then he regained his calm. Who could consider ending his own life and not be terrified of it? Even beset by unnatural aging, Snake had never contemplated suicide. No matter what form it took, death would come by the hands of his genetic destiny.

And now that comfort, cold as it was, had been stolen from him.

By then, I was already in tears.

Why?

Why had he been burdened with such a cruel, terrible fate? He'd saved the world. Not just once, but many times over. He ushered the people of the world past the threat of nuclear war.

I was biting my lip so hard blood began to flow. But it was a necessary pain to keep my cry silent. Sunny was on the second floor and I didn't want her to hear. Not my crying, not my tiny, tiny scream.

As my tears fell, I bit my lip hard.

Snake lit his cigarette, and this time, Naomi didn't stop him. I just prayed the smoke would grant him some peace.

"Snake," Naomi said. "Tell me one more thing."

He simply looked at her.

"Have you been to a hospital lately? Been given an injection?"

"Why?"

"Take a look at this."

Naomi brought up another microscopic picture on her computer screen. The object looked like FOXDIE.

"Isn't that just FOXDIE again?" Snake asked.

"It's a new strain of FOXDIE—one I've never seen before. Someone must have put it in you recently. Do you have any idea who?"

*What, you don't like shots?*

Snake put his hand to his face and groaned.

"Drebin."

"The new FOXDIE strain is starting to multiply rapidly. I can't say what's in it for sure without further tests…"

Naomi walked to a medicine cabinet and withdrew a syringe like the one she'd injected herself with in the Middle East. She tossed it to Snake.

"Here, take this. It contains the same substance the soldiers' nanomachines secrete inside their bodies. It's a drug that inhibits the nanomachines' ability to regulate the senses."

"But I'm not linked to the SOP."

"Interference with the System can cause the older generation of nanomachines within your body to malfunction. That's what happened to you in the Middle East—the malfunction manifested itself as a seizure. Give yourself a shot whenever they get bad."

Snake stared at the autoinjector in his hand. The cylinder was divided into blocks, each a separate use.

"It's potent, so use it sparingly—unless you want to end up an invalid."

Now Naomi gazed out the window. "I've been a fool," she said. "I let myself drown in nanomachines, and now I'm trapped by them. I can't escape my fate."

Snake grabbed her firmly by the arm, as if to pull her free.

"Then I'll free us both. Where's Liquid?"

"He left last night. As for where to, I can't tell you yet. Not until you free me."

"Do you even know?"

Naomi brought her lips to Snake's ears and whispered, "Liquid has altered his plans." Snake frowned. The room was bugged. "Removing the System will only cause his army to collapse from within. So he's chosen to seize control instead. Liquid's objective is to hijack the SOP System. He'll use it to create the ultimate army of perfect soldiers and launch his insurrection against the Patriots."

She paused, then solemnly said, "He calls it 'Guns of the Patriots.'"

"Guns of the Patriots?"

Directly between them, something rolled to a stop on the floorboards.

A grenade!

"Naomi, run!"

He dove for her and pushed her aside. But before he could get away himself, the grenade went off. A flash of light. An earsplitting burst of sound. A flashbang grenade, like those favored by special ops forces on rescue and capture missions.

Snake knew he had roughly half a second to act. For the moment, he was blinded, but still conscious. He dropped to the floor and, bullets sailing overhead, rolled into the next room.

Over the ringing in his ears, Snake heard a voice say, "This place isn't safe. Come with us."

He poked his head up through an interior window but was forced back down by another wave of gunfire. The barrage threatened to tear through the wooden walls like paper, and Snake sought cover behind a metal desk.

In the brief moment he'd been at the window, he saw a Pieuvre Armement mercenary ushering Naomi out of the building.

Snake raised his M4 above his head and fired his own burst in the general direction of the window.

An eerie calm fell over the clinic. The PMC didn't fire back.

Were they gone? Snake gritted his teeth and stood up from the desk.

Nothing. He ran from the building and past the rose garden to see a steep slope leading down. The medical facility was atop a tall hill with a good vantage over the forest below, where a Pieuvre Armement APC roared down the winding path away from the building.

"This sector has been brought under the complete control of Pieuvre Armement. Pieuvre Armement, for all your future needs. Pieuvre Armement. Unfailing soldiers, unfailing strategy."

The infomercial voice echoed from the distance. Snake squinted at the retreating vehicle, sighed, and half ran, half slid down the nearly vertical slope.

## 5

SNAKE CAME OUT onto the road as another armored truck drove up, then skidded to a stop in front of him. The camouflage pattern on the side of the vehicle faded to reveal the words EYE HAVE YOU!

"Yo, Snake, need a lift?"

Drebin popped halfway from the top hatch, can of NARC soda

in hand. For some reason, the man looked goddamn merry. An honest-to-God jack-in-the-box.

Snake climbed atop the APC, pushed Drebin's head back into the vehicle, then lowered himself inside.

Drebin said, "It's gonna be a bumpy ride!" He slammed on the gas, and soon Snake was tossed about the cramped quarters, sandwiched among Drebin's wares and personal belongings. The gibbon, Little Gray—so named because the hairless monkey looked like a little gray alien—hung freely from a metal pipe that ran down the length of the vehicle.

"I'm following a Pieuvre Armement APC. It should still be up ahead on this road."

"I know that, Old Snake. Why do you think I came to pick your ass up?"

Crawling his way back to the front of the vehicle, Snake asked, "How did you know?"

"Your partner told me."

"Otacon?"

Just five minutes earlier, I'd asked Drebin to support Snake. In no time, we settled on fair terms—Drebin was eager to help.

Snake regarded the arms dealer. "You look like you're enjoying yourself."

"Aren't you?"

Drebin urged the APC faster, and Snake was tossed back to the rear of the vehicle like a load of laundry. Little Gray shrieked with glee.

Snake's codec chirped.

"Snake, can you hear me?"

"This is Jack, isn't it?"

"I am Raiden. Jack is no more."

The voice was emotionless. Snake slowly shook his head.

Something had come over Jack—was it the very same darkness that had once consumed Big Boss, Liquid...and even Solid Snake?

Snake asked, "Where have you been all this time? What have you been doing?"

"On a mission. Finding something. For someone."

That didn't help clear things up much.

"Finding what?"

"Something important. Something that holds the fate of the world."

A pause.

"Pandora's box, perhaps."

After Raiden saved Sunny from the Patriots, he'd simply said, "There's something I have to do," and vanished. Was this what he was talking about?

"What are you searching for?"

"The corpse of Big Boss."

For Snake, time froze.

The corpse contained the genetic code of the legendary soldier, the greatest warrior. At Shadow Moses, Liquid demanded it delivered to him. Even after his death, Big Boss continued to hold people under his spell.

Jack said, "I was asked to do this in exchange for Sunny's location. I was following the only lead I had to find her."

Liquid wanted Big Boss's corpse before... could he be the one who sent Raiden to find it? Snake feared it too, and asked Jack.

"Liquid?"

"No. The leader of a small resistance group. She can be trusted."

"Who is she?"

"Her followers call her Matka Pluku."

Snake recognized the words. They were Czech. When he was younger and a member of special ops, his training took place in the shadow of the end of the Cold War. Naturally, his studies included Slavic languages.

"Great Mother..."

"Big Mama," Jack corrected. "She seems to have some connection with the Patriots. She said she had plans for you."

Snake didn't know anyone called Big Mama, but it seemed like she knew him. It wouldn't be the first time he was contacted by a mysterious person.

"Snake!" Drebin yelled back. "I see it!"

Snake crawled up to the front cabin, somehow navigating the inside of the violently rocking car.

The other vehicle was still distant. A clearing far ahead had been converted into a makeshift heliport—probably Pieuvre Armement's doing. The PMC's armored truck was parked next to a transport helicopter, and armed personnel stood at the ready. Snake's quarry had already reached their destination.

Then Snake saw them. Standing at the open rear hatch of the large transport helicopter were Naomi and Vamp, that bloodsucker.

I yelled over the codec. "They're taking Naomi away!"

Drebin slammed on the gas, and the Stryker picked up speed— a feat only possible because the road had been freshly paved near the heliport. Even with the more level road, Drebin's speed was too great for the ride to be a smooth one, and Snake was again tossed into the back of the vehicle.

But as Snake tumbled, he grabbed onto Little Gray to keep himself from hitting the back of the APC. The gibbon, itself barely hanging on, let out a cry of anger in protest to the affront.

Snake flipped himself upright, hefted himself up through the top hatch, and found the rooftop gunner's seat.

He pulled out the DSR1 he'd purchased from Drebin and aimed down the sniper rifle's sight—right in the middle of Vamp's forehead. The road straightened, and the Stryker was pointed straight at the target. Maybe the shot would kill the wannabe immortal, or maybe it wouldn't, but there wasn't time to find a better option. All he could do was shoot.

Through the magnified rifle scope, Snake watched Vamp slump to the floor of the helicopter.

But he hadn't fired yet!

Snake lowered his gun and upped the magnification on the

Solid Eye. The PMC troops hadn't reacted to the sudden collapse of their comrade and likely commander. The rear hatch remained open as the helicopter slowly lifted off the ground.

"Drebin!" Snake shouted down through the open hatch. "Faster!"

Drebin raised his voice over the noise of the engine and the rattling APC.

"Hey man, I was just looking out for your senior citizen ass. Hang on tight, Old Snake!"

The g-force pressed Snake into the back of the gunner's seat as his body fought against the very last burst of acceleration the Stryker could muster. His dilapidated arms and back felt as if they were about to snap. The APC crested the last tiny slope before the helipad, and the tires left pavement, the Stryker practically diving into the compound.

"Naomi!" Snake yelled.

Then the world fell apart once more.

Just like in the Middle East, the world collapsed onto Snake, and everything descended into chaos. The PMC soldiers on the ground writhed in agony. Only those in the helicopter seemed unaffected, impassively ascending like angels abandoning mankind.

He still clutched the sides of the gunner's seat, but how long could he keep that up? He was going to fall, he knew it.

Snake looked up at Naomi, who stood still in the back of the helicopter. She pointed a finger at her neck. Even as Snake's consciousness began to crumble, he understood the signal. He took the autoinjector from his pouch, pressed it against his neck, and pushed the button.

Then everything came back.

The connections between the neurons in his mind reformed, bringing back meaning, state, existence. He could breathe again. The nausea faded.

"I'm going for it!" Drebin yelled, but Snake couldn't hear from where he sat. It didn't really matter—there was only one way to get the Stryker to the helicopter. The rear of the APC slid, and the tires left faint tire marks on the helipad as the car drifted to a stop directly beneath the helicopter.

Drebin shouted, "Eye have you!"

Snake called up to Naomi, and she leapt from the open hatch to the APC several yards below. The helicopter had been too high for her to jump to the ground, but the Stryker's height—and Snake's waiting arms—allowed for her safe landing. She made it inside the vehicle, and Snake followed.

"Now let's get the hell out of here!" Drebin's voice teemed with excitement.

This time, Snake grabbed onto the central bar to hold himself in place.

"It happened again," he said. "Like in the Middle East."

Naomi nodded. "Another of Liquid's tests. The emotional control isn't stable yet."

"What about Vamp?"

"He injected nanomachines to put himself to sleep and escape the effects."

Drebin cut in. "Look behind!"

Snake poked his head back out the top hatch.

When I saw them through the Solid Eye, I thought they were a pack of T-Rexes. When I designed the Metal Gear REX, I named the machine after the dinosaur, so I could understand the association, but still, I felt silly. I knew better—they were Gekko.

That said, the pack of IRVING chasing after the Stryker was straight out of *Jurassic Park*. I'd heard reports of the IRVING's effectiveness, but I didn't know their legs could propel them across the dirt that fast. They were like giant athletes.

Snake positioned himself at the mounted machine gun attached to the gunner's seat and fired at the Gekko. Although the mounted gun shot large caliber rounds, they didn't seem nearly enough to penetrate the thick armor plating of the IRVINGs' heads. Instead, Snake focused his aim on the exposed bits of sensory and nerve equipment at the top of their flat, tanklike heads, on the less heavily armored connections where their weapons were mounted, and on their fleshy, organic legs.

His strategy proved successful, and the Gekko tumbled one by one. But for each he felled, another sprang into its place.

"I can't believe the numbers of these guys," said Drebin, in awe. "This is way over the war price here."

The "war price" was a kind of market price that fluctuated according to the demand for PMCs and munitions industries as well as the demand for production, distribution, and energy. As fighting became increasingly intense and prolonged, the war price for those commodities went up. With the prices growing by leaps and bounds, investors had started to take notice.

Therefore, with the numbers of Gekko clearly disproportionate to the war prices for that region, Liquid's war must not have been motivated by profit.

Snake, who was becoming gradually overwhelmed by the swarm, called out to Drebin. The head of the pack edged closer and closer to the Stryker.

Now, some readers might be wondering where I was at that moment. I was in a helicopter.

When I saw Liquid launch his second test, I flew the combat helicopter out from *Nomad*'s cargo bay and monitored Snake's mission from there. Factoring in my helicopter's speed and Drebin's, I calculated the fastest possible interception vector.

"Head for the city!" I said to Snake.

Drebin spun the wheel and went off the side of the road and onto a side route leading toward a nearby town. One minute, houses began to dot the landscape, and the next, the Stryker was inside the city.

Still piloting my own helicopter—only possible thanks to a liberal usage of the autopilot functions—I sent a map of the city to Snake's Solid Eye and said, "I'm going to land just on the other side of the marketplace. Please, somehow, just make it there!"

Piloting his APC in a mad dash between buildings and pedestrians, Drebin drove with a skill inimitable by any ordinary man. Luckily, they'd entered the city through a less-populated area, but as they approached the market, crowds became thicker, and this feat became increasingly difficult. Even more unsettling than the Stryker's swerving maneuvers was how, as the situation became more and more dangerous, Drebin smiled all the bigger.

Naomi noticed it too and managed to whisper, "You…" but had no words to follow. What could she say?

"Whoa!" was all Drebin had to say, his grin nearly as wide as his face.

Drebin guided the APC around a corner in a sideways drift to see a flatbed truck blocking the street. He flicked the wheel, and the Stryker rolled on its side and bounced into an acrobatic flip over the flatbed.

I expect most everybody goes their whole life without seeing a giant hunk of steel the size of the Stryker roll through the air looking like a whale swimming in an aquarium. For all the trouble we caused the fair citizens of that city, at least we gave them a sight to remember.

Of course, we couldn't expect the tires to just land back on the ground, and they didn't. The Stryker landed on its side and slid down the stone pavement with a shower of sparks. Eventually, the friction of metal on stone slowed the vehicle to a stop.

Snake had reacted quickly and leapt from the roof of the APC before it left the ground. His knees and hips protested angrily, but that was better than being thrown from the Stryker. Soon after the vehicle came to a rest on its side, Drebin, Naomi, and Little Gray crawled out.

Naomi limped over to Snake. The cries of the Gekko—like those of pigs, or maybe crazed cows—rang through the skies. Then, moments later, a group of them appeared at the corner Drebin had turned in from. There, inside the city, it was easier to estimate their massive size—just compare one to a building. Three, maybe four stories. Just barely within the range a person could comprehend—probably a calculated decision to increase their effectiveness.

Drebin saw them. "Ah, shit."

The Gekko came at them. One giant step. Another.

Then they noticed a man standing in front of them.

Some bystander who took too long to run?

No, that wouldn't explain how still he was, or the complete lack of fear toward the creatures before him. He was so small in comparison to the giants that Snake's group hadn't realized he was there until now.

He wore a black trench coat, and a visor covered his face. But what got Snake's attention was the glowing blade he held in his right hand. Just like Frank's sword.

The visor slid up, and steam sprayed out the sides of his mask.

I'd seen those eyes before.

The man who killed Solidus.

"Raiden..." said Snake.

Raiden pointed his sword down the road as if to say, *Run!*

For a moment, Snake forgot to breathe.

I didn't know what had happened to Jack. Only that something happened. Something, some terrible thing had mercilessly torn at his youthful body. In a word, ruin. A dreadful air of desolation radiated from the top of his head to the tips of his toes.

I didn't know if Jack—or Raiden, as he had become—had moved beyond whatever events had changed him or if he was still in the middle of them.

Drebin's delighted cry, "He made it!" cut through the tension.

Snake looked at Naomi and asked, "Can you move?"

She took off her heels and said, "Yes. Let's go."

Snake and Naomi left the crash site, but Drebin and Little Gray climbed back into his toppled car. He threw his handkerchief in the air as if part of a magic trick, and the OctoCamo activated, the Stryker now a part of the road.

The arms dealer and the gibbon were safe inside, where the Gekko could no longer see them.

~~~

"Snake," I said, "I'm setting the chopper down at the market square. Hurry!"

Snake and Naomi burst into the market and its panicking crowds. I landed the helicopter in an open square in front of a church and kept the rotors turning.

Soon I sighted them amid the chaos. I waved them over. Knowing that the pack of Gekko would not have the courtesy to wait, I ran through the pre-takeoff procedures.

Naomi cut across the grass yard and made it to the helicopter. With her twisted ankle, she was having trouble climbing the waist-high step into the chopper. Snake was behind her, providing cover, and I couldn't leave my place at the controls.

"Sorry," I said, "I'm a little busy right now."

I disabled the Mk. II's stealth camouflage. Naomi noticed the little robot and used it as a stepping stool to successfully make it inside.

Snake scooped up the Mk. II and got in, and I lifted off. Naomi let off a pinched shriek at the sudden downforce.

I turned to make sure they were both all right. Snake was battling some severe fatigue, but otherwise he seemed mostly fine. Naomi had twisted her ankle when the Stryker rolled over, and I looked at it with concern.

That was when I noticed she had been staring at me.

Her gaze shot right through me, and I reflexively drew back. But she wasn't staring at me, not exactly. She was staring into my eyes.

I didn't have time to process it. I had to focus my attention on the instrument panel and what was outside the cockpit.

I still had a comrade to pick up.

"Where's Raiden?" I asked Snake.

He pointed at a street corner.

"Hang on to something!" I pulled the control stick and put the helicopter into a sharp turn. We could get to the point Snake indicated in mere moments. The problem was the pack of Gekko that surrounded Raiden. Thankfully, I didn't see any IRVING armed with anti-air guns, but attempting to pick Raiden up would bring the helicopter within range of the weapons they did have.

Even though the helicopter was built for combat, it wouldn't stand up to a barrage of Gekko fire without consequence.

All at once, four Gekko shot out probe arms and grappled Raiden's limbs. He looked like a medieval prisoner about to be quartered. But he held steadfast against their probes with an inhuman strength. Jack didn't look human.

So that was what was underneath his coat.

Ruin.

Now I apprehended the reason—or one of the reasons—that word had popped into my head when Snake and Raiden were reunited. He looked like Frank Jaeger. There were little differences in the details, sure, but I had no doubt: Raiden's body had been augmented by a high-tech exoskeleton.

I wonder what Naomi thought as she watched him fight.

Was she thinking about how this young man was burdened by the same fate that took her own brother away? Did she still think about it each day?

Naomi pointed at the pack of Gekko. "It's Vamp!"

A tall figure in a black coat slinked through the group of machines. He weaved around the Gekko and their extended probes with the grace of a ballet dancer.

Raiden stood with arms stretched straight out as if inviting crucifixion.

With a fierce stare, the nosferatu said, "Yet again, our paths cross."

Raiden clicked his tongue. I too owed Vamp my revenge, but the bloodsucker had made Raiden live with the guilt of failing to protect his charge. Raiden had been escorting my sister Emma to the computer room at the Big Shell when Vamp ambushed them. Raiden wasn't able to stop him from sticking a knife through her stomach.

Vamp threw off his coat. He was bare-chested, his very skin the embodiment of a soul born from a boundless cascade of evil begetting evil. A dead man. But my eyes could see that the man was very much alive, not sleeping under the dirt.

Powered armor—developed by the army—covered his legs. Vamp pulled a combat knife from its sheath at his crotch and thrust it into Raiden's chest.

"Raiden!" Snake shouted.

I brought the helicopter within sniping range—which, given the harsh vibrations inside the vehicle, had to be quite close. I knew it would risk taking gunfire from the Gekko, but I didn't see any other option.

Vamp made a show of pushing in the knife all the way to the handle.

Then he noticed the white blood seeping from the wound. He looked up and saw Raiden's twisted smile.

"You too," said the nosferatu. "Immortal?"

Vamp put his nose up to Raiden's face and took in his scent— or rather, noted its relative absence. Vamp seemed to be thinking, *This man is like me.*

"No," said Raiden. "I just don't fear death."

Vamp snorted. He yanked his knife out of Raiden's chest, then thrust it into the restrained man's stomach. As Raiden coughed up more white blood, Vamp retrieved his knife, turned to face Snake in the helicopter, and drew his tongue across the blade with a slow, sensual lick.

Snake leveled his DSR1 and fired at the probe arms holding Raiden down. At our distance, the probe arms seemed as thin as strings, but Snake—aged eyes or not—snapped them one by one.

With the last probe severed, Raiden drew his sword and kicked into the air. His blade flashed toward Vamp's face, but the immortal was inhumanly fast and blocked the strike with his knife.

But Raiden was already making his next move, kicking at Vamp's feet to trip the bloodsucker. Vamp dodged the attack with a graceful backflip, casting out a barrage of throwing knives to cover his retreat.

Raiden's sword danced in an attempt to deflect the knives, but several struck his shoulders and sides. Undeterred, he closed in on the backpedaling nosferatu. But Vamp suddenly moved forward, the maneuver so sudden it seemed to break the laws of physics. In an instant, he was right at Raiden's face.

Suddenly, Raiden found his foot pinned to the street. A knife penetrated through the top of his foot and into the ground. Vamp jumped over Raiden's head, flipped in the air, and landed behind him. The nosferatu wrapped one arm around Raiden's throat and thrust his knife into Raiden's back.

He pushed the blade deeper and breathed into Raiden's ear, his breath heavy with pleasure.

Raiden's eyes opened wide.

Then he took hold of his sword with both hands, gripped it tight, and shoved it through his own stomach.

*It's a shish kebab*, I thought. Naomi drew her hand to her mouth. A sensible reaction to the nonsensical sight before us. This wasn't a battle, not anymore. If I had to call it something, make it mutual destruction—the mutual destruction of two people no longer human but something beyond.

I don't think there are many who could face such a sight.

Snake hadn't the option—the surrounding swarm of Gekko required his full attention as he attempted to hold them back with sniper fire.

Vamp released a long sigh that hung in the air. He was in ecstasy.

"Yes...could you be the one to finally kill me?"

Raiden pulled his sword free and jumped onto Vamp's back. In a feat impossible for anyone lacking a powered exoskeleton, he sprung in two quick leaps from the ground to the top of a Gekko and from the Gekko to our helicopter.

Snake reached out the open cabin door and caught Raiden's arm. Artificial blood poured out of the man's wounds and rained white upon the South American city. Snake heaved him up and inside.

"You okay?" he asked.

"Fine," Raiden said, but his wounds were clearly severe.

"Hang in there!" said Naomi.

Raiden began to cough blood. Even though his blood was artificial, his pale face lost even more color and turned as white as fine china. He wasn't the same kind of immortal as Vamp.

Why wouldn't Vamp die? His body hadn't been replaced with synthetics as with Frank or Jack—Vamp's flesh remained that of a man. Tears welled up in my eyes as I faced the disappointment of being once again unable to avenge Emma.

"Vamp," I said. "He's got to be immortal."

Then Naomi, tending to Raiden's wounds, said softly, "No... he's not immortal at all. I'm the one who made his body that way."

"Huh?" I said.

She looked into Raiden's face. Maybe she was trying to see her brother in there somewhere.

"I'm responsible for Vamp," she said. "He's one of my sins."

I thought back to her syringe in the Middle East. Before she left it with Snake, she had injected herself with it.

Snake asked, "Does your body have the same nanomachines?"

She didn't answer except to say, "I brought a monster into this world...and myself too."

Raiden began to cough blood again. The spray of liquid, white as pure milk, splashed against the ceiling. The deck was a sea of it. This blood was white, and made of plastics, but to his organs, it was the same as the blood in my veins, or yours.

And if he lost too much, he would die.

Although artificial blood taxed the human heart tremendously compared to the natural kind, the amount of oxygen it carried was greater by magnitudes. Even after losing as much as he had, Raiden was probably still all right. But if we couldn't stop the flow, he would soon cross a line from which he would not return.

"Hold him down!" Naomi yelled.

I put the helicopter on autopilot and pressed my hands over his wounds. Immediately, the slippery white liquid engulfed my hands. This was Raiden's life. Life, created by man, different from the red blood inside us.

But looking at Snake and Raiden, I couldn't bring myself to celebrate the achievement. The only difference between the curses those two men bore was that Raiden was born normal. Snake came into the world a clone of Big Boss, already bound to the fate in his genes.

"He's losing too much blood," Naomi said. Her hands pressed against the white tide. Beads of nervous sweat formed on her forehead.

"Can you save him?" Snake asked.

"I don't know. He needs a blood transfusion. No—an infusion of artificial blood."

Raiden's coughing fit continued, and the blood kept on pooling under him. If he had still been a normal human, he'd have been dead by now.

Then Raiden squeezed the words out from his throat, "Snake... Europe."

His chin hadn't moved, and it took a moment for us to realize he had spoken. His mouth overflowed with his own blood, and the white liquid bubbled with each breath. I couldn't believe he had been able to speak at all.

"Go meet...Big Mama."

With that, Raiden slipped into unconsciousness.

All we could do in the helicopter was press against his wounds.

As we gritted against the realization of our helplessness, I sent the helicopter to El Dorado at full speed.

## ACT 3: THIRD SUN

LET ME TELL you a story about a flower.

The most beloved flower in America.

No one knows her real name. "The Boss" might be her most famous.

Back when the world was in flames, when Adolf Hitler led the Nazis against Britain and France as Japan bombed Hawaii half a world away, her talents blossomed.

Those who knew her well, and those who lavished her with honors, often gave her stars-of-Bethlehem as a token of their admiration. Flowers with pure white petals. Flowers with a meaning—virtuous.

Her talent was her ability to fight on someone else's behalf.

I don't know when people first started to call her The Boss. But from what I've gathered, in World War II, she created a new class of fighting unit—the special forces unit. Before The Boss, armies had long performed operations far behind the battlefront into enemy lines—cutting off supply routes, destroying weapon stockpiles, inciting resistance movements in enemy-held territories—but those kinds of covert actions hadn't been conceptualized as an organized function of the military.

That was The Boss's modest revolution in the history of war.

She was involved in the founding of many special forces units across the globe, from the British SAS—considered by some to be the world's best—to America's renowned Green Berets. The last would go beyond the scope of special forces as they had been known. She took a group of operators—nothing more than dogs of war—trained them in the art of espionage, and created a new class of agent.

Alongside Major Zero of the SAS, who sought the ideal next generation army, she put all of herself into the foundation of that unit—Force Operation X. Later, the unit became known as FOX, and its existence was revealed to US government leaders along with its new focus: to cultivate the world's number one agent—to create a young soldier inheriting the traits of the "Mother of the Special Forces."

The man chosen for this task was named Jack.

Whether that was his real name I can't say for sure, but The Boss and Major Zero called him Jack.

For more than a decade, The Boss and Jack had shared fates. They fought in many dangerous missions and witnessed many wrongs. Their experiences had undoubtedly shaken their faith in God and humanity more than once. Jack had already lost the ability to father a child. Before he met The Boss, back in the days when we were still ignorant of the effects of radiation, he was involved in America's hydrogen bomb tests. The cursed ash blanketed his body and denied him the chance to create a life for the next generation. Then, in the world's battlefields and in hells unknown to the public, he learned the fragility of the human conscience. He saw how war could twist a man.

But Jack never wavered. He absorbed all of The Boss's teachings and all of her knowledge. Maybe she had seen the latent ability within him. But he only survived that cruel training with his soul intact (I call it training, but most of it was on real battlefields in real wars) because of the example The Boss set for him—purity, righteousness, and a nobility that could stare into the abyss and feel no fear.

Her code name in battle: The Joy.

She gave herself to fight for others, to protect others. And in it she found her joy. Her soul stood pure white among the pools of blood, but in the end, she was buried among the graves of the nameless.

And Jack, her cherished apprentice, was the one who stole her life.

Upon Major Zero's orders, he undertook an official FOX operation called Virtuous Mission. Its goal was the rescue of a defecting Soviet scientist. But Jack failed after the sudden betrayal of one of the FOX specialists—The Boss herself. She revealed to Jack her defection to the Soviets and escaped with the researcher and a Soviet colonel.

Events turned even worse when a Davy Crockett nuke destroyed a research facility near the operation, and US-Soviet relations, already jeopardized by the Cuban Missile Crisis, were only moments away from disaster. Unless America could prove it wasn't behind the explosion, the two superpowers would soon enter a war capable of global destruction.

Then the president gave FOX one chance to clear their names of the failed mission—and of the defection of their founder.

To prove America's innocence, they were to assassinate The Boss.

Jack—under the code name Naked Snake—again infiltrated Soviet territory. The USSR's first secretary, Nikita Khrushchev, cooperated with the mission and provided FOX's communication system. With the aid of KGB comm satellites, Jack returned to the site of the failed mission to kill the woman who had been his life.

In a certain sense, to kill The Boss was to kill himself. The two had been inseperable. When the government ordered Jack to kill her by his own hand, they might as well have ordered him to cut a pound of flesh from his side and offer it on a platter.

And if you're wondering why Khrushchev and the KGB would want to help America, even covertly, it was due to a complex power struggle within the Soviet ranks.

Khrushchev had been building a relationship of trust with JFK, the previous American president. When the Cuban Missile Crisis brought the world to the brink of nuclear war, the two leaders came to a chilling realization—global destruction was at hand. Both sides had already amassed great numbers of nuclear weapons out of concern for their own safety.

More than just fine words, compromise and détente were a singular approach necessary to avoid the annihilation of the world. Their attainment would be difficult, but this wasn't a matter of idealism, rather of realism—and survival.

Yet in both America and Soviet Russia, many equated the concepts with weakness. Such people have existed in every age—vulgar voices shouting, *Strike them down before they come for us!*

This was a new era, however, one in which war between the two countries would imperil not only their own futures, but the future of the entire planet.

The man who engineered The Boss's defection, Colonel Yevgeny Borisovitch Volgin of the GRU, firmly fell into the war-mongering camp. A hawk, the colonel believed Khrushchev weak and that too much compromise with America meant danger.

Volgin wanted a way to deliver Soviet missiles across the divides of the Atlantic and Pacific oceans to American soil—one that didn't rely on giant missile silo complexes dug into the earth. He sought a mobile weapon that could be moved freely through Soviet territory, striking swiftly and decisively while hidden from enemy satellites. He found it in the Shagohod.

Volgin had now acquired the aid of both Dr. Sokolov, the developer of the Metal Gear's precursor, and The Joy, the legendary soldier known to the Soviets as Voyevoda (Warlord). In a remote fortress, he rushed completion of the Shagohod. But he did so without the funds of the Soviet army. Rather, Volgin paid for it with his own wealth.

Snake infiltrated the fortress to rescue Dr. Sokolov and terminate The Boss, but once there, he found himself in the middle of an unconventional battle for control over those finances. Volgin's funds had once belonged to his father. To state it more accurately, his father had stolen them. This reserve was known to few as the Philosophers' Legacy, an unimaginably large sum of money belonging to certain members of the global intelligence community.

Before the Great War, twelve of the most powerful figures in America, Russia, and China—collectively known as the Wisemen's Committee—founded an organization called the Philosophers. The men pooled their money together to fund the reconstruction efforts that would be needed after the inevitable outbreak of world war. The likely core of this effort was an underground mail network, known by its symbol of three postal horns, created to compete with the House of Habsburg's commissioned House of Thurn and Taxis, which itself served as the basis for modern-day postal service systems. Volgin's father was in charge of money laundering for the Philosophers, and upon his death, he left the means to access those funds to his son.

In short, Volgin drew the clandestine attention of many powerful players.

With the Philosophers' Legacy, he constructed a fortress in remote Groznyj Grad, where he stationed his own army and began development of the Shagohod. In a way, Groznyj Grad was its own empire located within Soviet borders, and Volgin was its ruler.

His actions weren't entirely unprecedented. A commander named Mikhail Tukhachevsky, who had pushed for the industrialization of the military and was instrumental in the development of several advanced ideas on military strategy, once raised his own army in Siberia. Stalin feared his growing power and had him executed. Back then, a surprising number of officers throughout Soviet Russia had their own private armies.

After Khrushchev's failed agricultural policies brought hardship to rural areas, the hawks ascended to prominence in the Soviet leadership. Meanwhile, Volgin scooped up farmers from troubled soil across the territory and brought them into his army—paid for by the Philosophers' Legacy.

EVA, the woman sent by Khrushchev to assist Naked Snake, had been tasked by an unknown entity to obtain the stolen fortune. And when Volgin captured Naked Snake, he subjected his prisoner to cruel torture and interrogation, certain the man had been sent by American strategists to reclaim the Legacy.

In the end, Naked Snake carried out his mission—the rescue and the assassination. He destroyed Shagohod and defeated Volgin. He killed The Boss.

By his own hand.

With hands The Boss herself had forged. With techniques she had taught him. With a soul she had imparted to him.

After the long and brutal battle, she collapsed into a bed of stars-of-Bethlehem beside a lake. And when Naked Snake fired the killing shot, something inside him died. And something else was born.

When EVA and Naked Snake parted, she told him about The Boss's final joy, her desolate desire—that if she had to die for her duty, let her life be ended by her beloved disciple.

Of course, that hadn't been The Boss's plan from the start. Her death had been part of a top secret op—so secret that even its instrumental player, Naked Snake, was unaware of it—to secure the Philosopher's Legacy.

When she captured Dr. Sokolov and defected in front of her own countryman, The Boss's deception of Volgin was absolute, and she cemented the ruse with the gift of two American-developed small-scale nuclear warheads. But when Volgin fired one upon Soviet soil, the scenario changed.

The Boss couldn't abandon her mission—and her cover as a defected agent—without leaving the Legacy in foreign hands. But in order for America to prove its innocence in the bombing, she had to be killed. And if America couldn't prove its innocence, the world would be consumed by a nuclear blaze.

Therefore, she could never be allowed to return home. Neither could she take her own life.

But even with all hopes dashed, The Boss never gave up. She accepted the responsibility that came with her gifts—to love someone, to fight for someone.

She loved the world, this world in which we live. This world in which a few billion small and foolish souls live in a mixture of misery and despair. Those were the makings of the world she held dear. She possessed too much love for too great a thing; but she was so great a woman, with strength enough to bear that burden to the end.

But nobody can carry the weight of the world by herself.

As the events played out, her last joy was a prospect so sorrowful it couldn't even be called a wish—for death to come by the hand of her own disciple.

And on the far-off Russian lakeside blanketed with stars-of-Bethlehem, Naked Snake made her wish come true.

Upon his return to America, he was summoned to the White House. There he met the praise of his assisting team—Major Zero, weapons and technology coordinator Mr. Sigint, and medical coordinator Para-Medic. President Johnson personally bestowed him with the title of Big Boss.

"You have surpassed The Boss," stated the president.

Naked Snake stared at him, as though thinking, *What the hell do you know about her?*

But he wasn't angry. He had nothing left in him to feel anger. He had killed his own mentor; she was killed by her own disciple. Sure, there was a difference between killing and being killed, but for two souls bound together so tightly as to be seamless, either was nothing more than suicide.

Naked Snake lost a part of himself, and in its place remained only a void.

The White House seemed distant, dreamlike. Snake regarded the substitute president as he would a wax figure. When Kennedy was assassinated by a former Marine in Dallas, this man was pulled up into the highest office in the United States like he'd won the lottery.

~~~

"The trick is to keep the lid on," said Naomi. She looked over Sunny's shoulder at the frying pan.

Sunny peered quizzically at the face of this woman who'd been suddenly added to the crew. A single rose in Naomi's hair exuded an air of artificial beauty. A single blue rose.

Naomi took a lid from the kitchen cabinet and placed it over the pan. The lid dampened the soft sizzle of the butter and oil.

"Now let it cook for one minute," she explained. "You like cooking, don't you? Good for you."

"Th-this? It's my Sunny-side-up fortune telling. When it t-turns out good, it means something g-good is going to happen."

I don't know what exactly Sunny divined from her eggs. She never told me.

Naomi leaned in. "So that's why you don't cook them over easy."

Sunny suddenly realized she hadn't set the timer. She quickly grabbed the kitchen timer, a yellow cartoon duck, and turned its dial. To Sunny, cooking eggs meant timing them. It's important to do things by the book—recipes exist to help make a delicious meal, after all—but when the guides become rules and rote, cooking loses all meaning.

"The secret to good cooking," Naomi said, "is to keep in mind who's going to eat it."

Sunny tried to say something in reply but couldn't find the words. Naomi looked around the room in search of a new topic.

On the wall was a framed photograph of a young woman with short-cropped silver hair and willful blue eyes that gazed at some distant point in the night sky.

"Is this your mother?" Naomi asked.

"Y-yes." Sunny stared down at the frying pan. Less because she was worried about the eggs than she was unable to meet the woman's eyes.

"She's really beautiful," Naomi said, meaning it. The woman in the picture was beautiful.

*This girl is like me*, Naomi probably thought. She knew of Sunny's loneliness. Both had lost their parents at a young age and were left alone out in the world. The child would likely never feel truly at home with her surrogate family aboard *Nomad*.

Naomi turned to face Sunny, put her hand to her own hair, and said, "May I?"

Without lifting her head, Sunny watched Naomi's hand as it took out the blue rose and placed it behind the girl's ear.

"See, Sunny? We girls have to look our best."

Sunny blushed. She'd never received a flower from anyone before. Nor had she been treated kindly by a woman.

"Her name," the girl said, "was Olga."

At first, Naomi didn't follow, and just said, "Hmm?"

"My mother."

"Oh...I see."

Naomi and Sunny were starting to get to know each other, even if by baby steps. In just a little more time, I imagined Naomi thinking, maybe the two of us could sit around a dinner table with Snake and Otacon, like a family.

But she knew that time was one thing that neither she nor Snake had.

*I won't be there. I won't make it to that table.*

Smoke came from the edge of the lid, and Sunny scrambled for the spatula.

We pulled together whatever equipment we could find on *Nomad* to provide Raiden some makeshift treatment, but it wasn't going to be nearly enough to keep him alive.

Not that any doctor would know what to do with him, caught somewhere between man and machine. Carrying him to a hospital would only serve to inconvenience their staff. So we sat among our dark moods in *Nomad*'s cargo bay, powerless to help as we watched Raiden slipping away.

Snake wasn't faring too well either.

He was reclined in a deck chair, holding an oxygen mask to his face like Michael Jackson, his aged body distressed by the thin air up in the mountains. The ability to rapidly adapt to changing environments belongs to the young, and personality isn't the only thing to become rigid with age.

Snake could probably have been on the oxygen treatment sooner, but until now, he'd endured to protect us from seeing him in his weakened condition. To break down his strong front, the climate and the battles in South America must have been incredibly severe.

Putting up that front was his way of showing us kindness. And that kindness had become more than I could bear as well.

Raiden moaned. Naomi and I ran over to the cot where his exoskeletal body rested.

"Raiden," I said, "are you all right?"

He still seemed unable to move his lips. Instead, a computerized voice spoke from his throat.

"Take me to Eastern Europe."

"What are you talking about?" Naomi asked.

Raiden, only barely conscious, turned his neck a fraction of an inch toward her and said, "There's equipment there that can heal me. Dr. Madnar. He saved my life."

What little strength he had was expended, and his head went limp on his pillow. Naomi leaned forward and reached out to caress Raiden's head, as if touching the memory of her brother.

I'd heard Dr. Madnar's name before. Not a single engineer involved with robotics didn't know about his career. Rumor was that he was working on underground cybernetic research.

"We're in luck, then," Naomi said. "We're going to Europe."

My eyebrows shot up.

"What do you mean," said Snake, his voice muffled by the oxygen mask, "by 'We're in luck'?"

Naomi stood up, ready to explain.

"Liquid is in Eastern Europe."

Snake and I looked at each other in surprise. This couldn't be a coincidence.

"And what's he doing there?" Snake asked.

Her next answer was an even bigger shock.

"He's after the corpse of Big Boss."

I practically shouted, "What?"

Nine years ago, when Liquid's group claimed Metal Gear REX and the stockpile of nuclear warheads, they demanded the legendary mercenary's remains. Their goal was to analyze his genes and find the cure for their genetic maladies.

The members of the rogue forces in the rebellion at Shadow Moses had already begun to express symptoms of their diseases. They—like the clone Liquid—had been genetically enhanced with Big Boss's soldier genes, which imparted to them increased efficiency in battle and situational awareness.

But now Liquid inhabited Ocelot's body. Only Liquid's transplanted arm still contained his original genes. In a certain way, he'd been freed from the curse of Big Boss's genes that had plagued the three brothers.

So why did he need Big Boss's corpse?

Naomi answered the question that was on our faces.

"It's the final key he needs to gain access to the SOP. The keys to the System are Big Boss's genetic code and biometric data. Without them, there's no way to gain access."

Then how had Liquid been hacking into the SOP?

In the research facility, Naomi said the chaos had not been a failure, but a success. With her help, he had taken temporary control of the SOP.

"What's Liquid been doing all this time?" I asked.

"In the first test, in the Middle East, he used the genetic code from his own DNA chip. In South America, he used the DNA code and biometric data extracted from Snake's blood."

That meant the results of tests she ran on Snake had been transmitted to Liquid. With a sidelong look, I studied her face for any traces of guilt or reticence.

It was Liquid's facility, so it would only be natural that he keep her equipment under surveillance.

But what if she had deliberately passed on Snake's medical data? Was she here as a part of Liquid's plan?

Snake lowered his oxygen mask and shambled toward us. On the way, he casually scooped up his pack of cigarettes from the desk. He lit one and drew the smoke slowly into the back of his lungs.

"What's the need for the original," he said, "if a substitute works just as well?"

"Neither your genetic pattern nor Liquid's is a hundred percent match for Big Boss's."

Snake coughed, choking on the smoke. "What do you mean we don't match?"

I rubbed his back until his coughing fit subsided, and Naomi continued her explanation.

"There's the markers implanted during the cloning process, the mixing of mitochondrial DNA within the egg cell, the deliberately altered terminator genes. Scientifically speaking, both you and Liquid are as similar to Big Boss as you could possibly be. But there are still differences."

Snake and Liquid had always been told they were Big Boss's clones, born as reproductions of the legendary mercenary. But while it was correct that they carried Big Boss's genes, those genes had undergone numerous alterations.

Liquid had shouted it in the Middle East—*We're not copies of our father after all!*

Snake asked, "So that's what Liquid was talking about?"

Naomi nodded. "Which is why they created Solidus."

President Johnson, before his death at the Big Shell decontamination facility, described Solidus as a well-balanced masterpiece—one neither Solid nor Liquid. From what Naomi was saying, Solidus was a higher-precision clone of Big Boss. He was far closer to being identical to his father than either Solid or Liquid—at least genetically speaking.

Solidus was born at the same time as his brothers, but he aged far more rapidly. Not necessarily because of the alterations to his genetic code.

There's something called clonal aging. The (supposedly) first cloned mammal, Dolly the sheep, was found to have shortened telomeres at her birth. Clones inherit their telomeres from the donor at the time the genetic sample was taken—they are born with cells that have already aged.

Solidus was born from the cells of a Big Boss already in his fifties. He wasn't programmed with a shortened life span like his brothers—he just aged faster than them. Not an engineered fate, this represented the natural (or at least, expected) fate of any clone.

"But Solidus is dead," Snake said.

"Listen carefully," Naomi said. "This is the most important part."

Naomi summoned a diagram on the monitor. The graphic was the outline of a computer network, which at a quick glance resembled the inside of a living organism. Functions of life might well have provided the basis of the security construct.

"The AI that controls the System employs a highly aggressive, advanced Intrusion Detection System, or IDS. By using a special code to inspect all data and commands circulating within the network, any data that fails to confirm is treated as a foreign object and expunged—like a virus killed by white blood cells."

Think of a network as the blood flowing through an organism's veins, with red and white blood cells and all the other essentials of life circulating within. The immune system watches for harmful bacteria and viruses hidden among the essentials and eliminates any material found swimming through the blood network without the proper codes.

The Patriots' System was modeled after the human immune system. Attacking foreign objects required a method of distinguishing them from itself. The System needed to contain a self-definition—a form of code that specifies what it is.

Naomi continued, "The authentication program this IDS uses is based on a genetic identification program—one I helped develop for FOXDIE. It's set up so that host commands only execute properly if the key matches perfectly."

Should an intruder gain access to the Patriots' network and inject rogue code, that code—without the proper genetic sequence— would be ignored by the System.

"However, if the IDS suspects an unauthorized user, the intruder's genetic code is registered on a blacklist. That code is then blocked and can never again be used to access the System. So, with our substitute codes, we've had to use a new genetic access code with each of our trials."

Snake exhaled smoke. "So when Liquid accessed the System in the Middle East and South America, those were only tests."

When Liquid used first his own code and then Snake's, the System initially accepted them as that of Big Boss. But upon detecting the slight variances within, it added them to the blacklist.

I took a long, deep breath to ease my nerves. "I can't believe this—that Snake and Big Boss don't have the same genetic code."

"Strictly speaking," Naomi said, "Snake and Liquid don't have the same genes either. Which is why FOXDIE only affected Liquid at Shadow Moses...and spared you, Snake."

That was a mystery that had puzzled Snake ever since the moment when FOXDIE froze Liquid's heart, and Snake watched his brother sink into the snow. He could still remember that moment as if it had just happened.

"Why did Liquid die," he'd wondered, "and not me? Weren't we the twin Snakes?"

Now he knew why.

Now Liquid had only one option left—Big Boss's true genetic code. Snake's and Liquid's codes were irrevocably on the IDS's blacklist.

"Let me put it this way," Naomi said. "If Liquid uses Big Boss's genetic code—the original—he'll have the System completely under his control."

"Hold on." Snake took the cigarette from his mouth. "I thought having his code wasn't enough. You need his biometric data at the same time, don't you?"

Big Boss was already dead.

Snake had killed him himself—in Zanzibar Land, the new country for mercenaries after the destruction of Outer Heaven.

Genetic code could likely be harvested from Big Boss's body, which had been cryogenically preserved by the Patriots. But no amount of effort could restore his breathing, his pulse, or the flow of blood to his eyes. Particularly not when the man had been dead for fifteen years.

But Naomi hadn't run out of revelations. Plainly, she stated, "No. He's alive."

What could we say to that?

Big Boss was alive. But Snake was supposed to have killed his father—no, his original—in Zanzibar Land.

The man—who Snake had just thought to be some war-crazed lunatic—told him he was his father.

Snake stood beside the fallen fighter and watched him die. In a certain way, he watched himself die.

"Big Boss is alive?" Snake said. "Ridiculous."

"His body is. Or rather...his cells. He's a brain-dead shell sustained in a lab."

I guess that could be called living.

I glanced at Raiden lying on the medical bed. Most of his body had been replaced with a strengthened exoskeleton. The blood that flowed through him wasn't red. But although he'd lost his body, he still had his mind. And if that could be called living, could I say that Big Boss, with his mind dead but his body alive, was really dead?

Perhaps that was nothing more than a problem of definition—a nebulous boundary between the phenomena of life and death. Whatever the case, if the System acknowledged the code, Big Boss was alive as far as Liquid was concerned.

The concept of life means different things to different people in different places.

"Liquid has already left for Europe in search of Big Boss's body. Even from the start, he never expected his experiment in South America to work. If he obtains the body, he'll be primed to make his final move."

If the Middle East and South America had been rehearsals, this would be opening night. Liquid would take command of the System and control each and every movement of the vast array of military forces around the globe. We had to stop him, no matter how.

Snake and I looked at each other. Snake's eyes held the same resolve as mine. The battle in Eastern Europe could be our last.

The trip to the other side of the world was a long one.

From America to the Middle East, from the Middle East to South America, and now to Eastern Europe, we went across the globe and back again, coming and going over the Atlantic Ocean. We—and Liquid in tandem—kept going halfway around the world and back.

The sound of wind rushing past machine. The sound of metal creaking under pressure. And lest I forget, the hum of the air conditioner. We were packed in between air and metal and machine.

Not that the trip was unpleasant. It wasn't. Rather, we were like children in the protective womb. Snake and Sunny were asleep, recharging for the next day.

I, on the other hand, had much work to do to prepare for the mission. I built a list of information I wanted Colonel Campbell to have for us by the time we were four hours from landing. I took data from current maps as well as satellite and aerial imagery and constructed a 3D view compatible with Snake's Solid Eye. Traffic reports, weather forecasts, language trends, network statuses, PMC reports—I needed to gather a great amount of information, and I fed it through an automated filtering system to extract the most useful data.

For my programs, sometimes I took snippets of useful open source code from the Internet, and other times, when I had to, I wrote them myself. Snake often joked about how he was blue collar and I was white collar. But white-collar work wasn't necessarily easy work.

The maintenance of the Mk. II was my job too. Sensors, wheels and leg joints, the autobalancer, and stealth camouflage—I had a checklist a mile long for that demanding, but cute, little guy.

"Who's this?"

Naomi's voice startled me. I turned to see her standing behind me, her finger pointed at a picture on my computer screen.

"Oh, her?" The sudden question caught me by surprise, and my heart was beating a little fast. "That's my sister."

I had Emma's picture on the edge of my terminal's desktop.

The sister I hadn't been able to save. The sister to whom I hadn't been able to give my love.

The sister I killed.

I kept her picture there so I'd never forget. No, that's not true. Of course I could never forget—but I wanted her image burned into my brain every single day.

Naomi knew none of this. Not about Emma. About my guilt.

"Really? I never knew you had a sister. For a moment I thought she might have been your girlfriend."

Terribly embarrassed, I deflected my attention to the Mk. II on the edge of my desk, which only served to make Naomi even more curious.

"Ah," I said. "I don't have a girlfriend."

I reached inside the Metal Gear's maintenance port and switched on the benchmark mode. The robot began its self-test sequence and started to bend and stretch.

"Emma was a brilliant programmer," I explained. "She wrote the worm that destroyed the Arsenal Gear AI."

"Where is she now?"

*Where is she?* I wondered. Wherever she was, our father was there, and even her mother too, acting like a typical mother. Somewhere, they sat as a family around the dinner table, and there I could call Emma by her name.

I hoped there was a place like that. I hoped she was there.

A place I hadn't been able to give her. A place where I hadn't destroyed everything important.

"She was murdered by Vamp," I said. That was the simple truth of it, and I couldn't find a better way to put it.

Naomi's expression darkened as she realized she shouldn't have asked. She turned away and said, "I'm so sorry."

"No, there's nothing for you to be sorry for." I looked at her. "I'm the same as you."

She looked back at me, ready to listen.

"I used to be an anime otaku," I explained. I wasn't being entirely honest—I still was one. But that was beside the point. "I was always fascinated by sci-fi anime. That's what got me into robotics."

Back then, I delighted in my work designing Metal Gear REX for AT Corp.

"But reality wasn't so simple," I said. "I never even imagined that my science—that my own research—could cause so much misery."

Naomi appeared perplexed. Perhaps because my story was similar to the same sense of guilt she carried. I wanted her to know that I was the same as her—that she wasn't the only one that felt a duty to atone for her wrongs.

"It's not like we scientists are Satanists or anything," I said. "But even when we have the best of intentions, we end up being used by others for evil."

Naomi just looked at me and let me talk. And I was able to meet her gaze because I knew we had the same guilt, and the same duty.

She drew her hand to the pendant around her neck and squeezed it tightly.

"Dr. Emmerich, I…"

As soon as she spoke, all my embarrassment flooded back. I sought refuge in the Mk. II, pretending to work on its preparations.

"You see this?" I said, changing the subject. "Sunny helped me build it."

"Really? Sunny helped you?"

As if she were my own child and I her proud parent, I boasted, "We built it using top-secret docs and patents dug up from intranets at a bunch of research labs. She wrote most of the controller source code. To tell you the truth, I think she's better at it than I am."

Naomi released her pendant. Maybe she had taken an interest in hearing me talk about Sunny. Although now that I took a closer look at it, the object at her neck wasn't a pendant like I'd thought—it was a memory stick. I chuckled to myself. If she was using computer memory as an accessory, she really was a geek.

"Sunny was taken in by the Patriots right after she was born. She never even met her parents. She's spent her entire childhood inside the Internet."

Naomi gave an understanding look and said, "That's why she has trouble speaking."

"Her home is the Internet. She can only look out from the inside. She's always in there, searching for herself. Searching for her family. She's trying to figure out who she is and where she's going."

Naomi quietly listened to me talk—perhaps she saw herself in Sunny just as she'd seen herself in me. (Although, Sunny wasn't old enough to be burdened by any sins save for the original one, so the connection was probably different than with me.)

"She believes she can find the answers inside a machine hooked up to the world. She spends every day inside the net, exploring. For Sunny, this is home."

"No," Naomi spoke. "It shouldn't be like that."

I was a little taken aback by her seriousness. "What?"

"It's time you let her go outside."

My heart seemed to cower within my chest. I hadn't expected to hear her say the same thing Snake kept telling me. She had cut straight to the core of the situation, but all I could do was pretend not to understand, and say, "What are you talking about?"

"She hasn't even been born yet. She's still in the womb. You need to give her a real life."

Her eyes were grave. I realized I wasn't going to be able to get away with playing dumb. I turned to face the cargo bay and spread my arms wide. "Sunny's never shown any interest in leaving *Nomad*."

It was the truth. Sure, I knew I was being overprotective. I'd admit it. But more than my denying it to her, Sunny refused to connect herself to the outside world. I didn't know if it was because of her time in captivity with the Patriots, or if it was because of Snake and me, or both.

"Frankly," I admitted, "I'm worried about letting her go out there."

I was the one who was scared. I couldn't help but worry about her being exposed to all the irrationalities of the world. I'd already lost my sister. I didn't want to lose anyone else.

But Naomi simply smiled at me, as if to say, *Sunny is stronger than you may think.* Then she said, "I have a feeling she'll do just fine."

"You really think she'll be okay out there?"

"That's not what I meant. I think she's got a good handle on her science."

And with that, I was thoroughly lost from the conversation. I'd thought we were talking about whether or not I could let Sunny outside, but she suddenly shifted to our earlier talk about the sins of our science. Had we been talking about different things all along? Had we just assumed we'd been holding a conversation, piling one misunderstanding upon another?

I took off my glasses and rubbed the bridge of my nose between my fingertips as I tried to think of what to say next.

"Sorry," is what I came up with. "Go on."

"Huh?"

I was lousy at changing the subject. Mentally kicking myself for my continued social ineptitude, I said, "You were about to say something earlier?"

Naomi nodded, but she fell silent. Perhaps she was nonplussed by the sudden shift in the conversation. That was probably why I could never get a woman.

Then she smiled and said, "Would you mind if I helped Sunny with her cooking?"

"Of course I wouldn't," I said, but judging from her earlier severe expression and the relative lightness of her question, I doubted that's what she'd originally intended to ask. (That said, improvement in Sunny's fried eggs would be a revolutionary bit of culinary news.)

I started to put my glasses back on, only to be stopped by Naomi's hand.

The sudden sensation of the coolness of her skin startled me.

I'd always heard that women get cold more easily than men...was this what that meant?

Her skin was cool and delicate.

I liked it.

"Leave them off," she said. "You're more handsome this way."

"You think so?"

Naomi's hand guided mine back to the desktop, where I set down my glasses.

She stared into my eyes, but unlike when we were talking about our sins, this time I found her gaze hard to meet. The look in her eyes held a different meaning now.

Had she kept staring much longer, I truly would have fainted. Mercifully, she looked away from me and over at the military helicopter stored in the bay. "Dr. Emmerich, is it okay if I sleep in there?"

"Oh. Um. Sure."

Her lips turned into the slightest smirk. "Sorry. I know it's selfish of me, but I'd like to be alone for a while."

"Right. I understand. I'll show you in."

I led Naomi past the sleeping Snake and Sunny and to the helicopter's side hatch.

*Nomad*'s cargo bay was incredibly large, but with the military helicopter stowed away, not much room was left on the sides. I slid open the hatch and moved aside just enough to let Naomi in. As she climbed up onto the waist-high floor, her chest brushed by me. There were only thin layers of clothing between us. An awkward moment.

She got inside the helicopter, thanked me, and said good night. The blockhead I was, instead of some normal reply, I simply said, "Yeah." I wanted to do better than that, but I couldn't think of the words. After a moment, I said, "If you get uncomfortable or anything, just let me know. I'll be out there working."

"Thank you."

Now both of us were thinking of what to say.

I spoke first, still unsure of where I was going with it. "And..."

"Yes?"

"Call me Hal. Good night."

Naomi closed the hatch. I sighed for what seemed like the umpteenth time that day.

The hatch suddenly slid back open. Naomi's hand reached out and grabbed me by the shoulder. She pulled me toward her, and our eyes were barely an inch apart.

She wrapped her arm around my neck. I climbed in and shut the hatch behind us.

2

SNAKE LOOKED OUT the window to get a view of the European countryside, but since this was the last train, Eastern Europe had already slid into the gloom of night, and all was darkness.

What he did see was a brightly lighted billboard alongside the rail line. The ad featured a raven with wings spread across a backdrop of advertising copy. Raven Sword. An American PMC. One of Liquid's, of course.

According to Campbell's report, the local government had declared a state of emergency in the historic capital. A curfew was in effect, and armed soldiers—provided by Raven Sword—patrolled the empty streets.

Their goal: to hunt resistance forces. The government was making a concerted effort to halt the constant rebel attacks against its capital.

Campbell found a list of groups naming the government as an enemy of peace. The list included organizations in support of the parliamentary opposition party and NPOs opposed to specific policies. The whole thing reeked of political reprisal.

One of the names on Campbell's list was the Paradise Lost Army.

But the odd thing about the group was that its political goals and strategies were completely unknown. Even the locals' knowledge, or lack of knowledge, of the organization was strange. If they were a terrorist organization with public attacks, some level of information would get out.

Big Mama—possibly the caretaker of Big Boss's corpse—was the leader of this mysterious resistance group.

On a mission. Finding something. For someone.

That was what Raiden had said in South America. Followed by three other words: *Pandora's box, perhaps.*

The train slowed and entered into a space under a giant roof.

The disembarking travelers were few, even considering the late hour. With the state of emergency, the number of visitors to the city had plummeted, including those from other European countries. And even though Snake came disguised with a trenchcoat and a leather travel bag, the local PMC had enough resources to run a careful check on all passenger IDs.

According to Drebin, Liquid's PMCs had been given a top-secret order to kill Solid Snake on sight. The local army and police forces wouldn't know about the order, but Snake knew he couldn't turn to them for aid.

But Campbell told us he had a way for Snake to get past the checkpoint.

Snake walked the lonely train platform to the door leading inside the station, where a group of PMC soldiers were checking IDs. They had a large white walk-through biometrics scanner with an AT logo on the side. The scanner read retinal patterns, fingerprints, and nanomachine identifiers.

What now?

Snake had no choice but to believe in Campbell. We hadn't prepared any dummy fingerprints or retinal spoofers, and there was nothing to be done about his nanomachines. Snake stuck a cigarette between his lips only to realize he'd forgotten to bring a lighter.

"Next," said a soldier standing in front of Snake.

Well this was about to get interesting.

Snake glanced at the biometric scanner, which was probably connected to some central server. Small lights blinked on and off, and it perched before the doorway like an eager executioner. If Snake walked through, a lot of trouble would follow.

All he could do was wait. Campbell had said it would be all right. But how long would the PMC let him stall?

"Hey, you, I said next!"

The soldiers raised their guns. Now there was nothing more

Snake could do. He just wished he had a damn light. At least then he could face the circle of rifle muzzles with a little calm and the pleasant puff of smoke.

"That's enough," said a soldier from one of the side doors. Her uniform didn't match the others—it was American. A familiar emblem was on her chest. "I'll take him from here."

One checkpoint guard confusedly said, "But…!"

Her reply was firm. "We've been looking for this man."

"Yes, ma'am."

The American waved Snake over. He walked around the scanner and through the side door.

Inside was the station lobby. At several coffee tables, a few scattered groups of soldiers and civilians chatted. The American withdrew a lighter and set it to Snake's cigarette.

"You're looking younger," Meryl said. "What's your secret?"

She was looking at Snake's face, circa nine years prior. His face before the wrinkles spread from his eyes and mouth to cover everything else.

"Face Camouflage. The same stuff as the OctoCamo, I was told."

Snake briefly switched off the face texture, and for a moment, the old, tired face she saw in the Middle East reappeared. A sadness appeared in her expression.

"The PMCs seem to know you well enough," he said.

"You may not believe it, but I'm in charge of overseeing all PMC activity here as well. Having connections can still open doors."

Snake exhaled smoke. "You alone?"

Meryl nodded in the direction of the back of the lobby, where the members of Rat Patrol 01—Ed, Jonathan, and the man with the poor intestinal fortitude, Akiba—all sat around one of the tables.

"Snake!" Akiba stood and waved at Snake. "Hey, Snake! Over here!"

Meryl and Snake sunk their heads in their hands. Ed swiftly

elbowed the kid to shut him up, but the PMC soldiers had already noticed the commotion.

With a look of disgust, Snake said, "Him again?"

"Him again."

From all around the room, eyes were upon them. Meryl led Snake to an adjacent lounge where no one was around. They sat at a table.

"Listen to me, Snake. After reporting what happened in the Middle East to my superiors, I wrote up a threat assessment. The president's finally realized the danger Liquid's rebellion poses. Now I've got more bodies than I know what to do with—a whole joint Army-Marines team. They're already on-site, mixed in with the US forces here."

She looked into Snake's eyes. "We're ready to capture Liquid at any time."

Snake let out a small sigh. This young soldier still didn't know there were things that strength of force could achieve, and there were things it couldn't.

"You're planning to take him by force? That's crazy. Look, things aren't that simple," he said.

"Listen, old man. I don't take orders from you, or from your Colonel Campbell."

Snake knew that would be her response before she said it. She was stubborn—like Campbell. Still, he had to warn her, even if it was futile. "It's gonna be the Middle East all over again."

Meryl shook her head. "No, it won't. If things get out of hand, we can put a total lock-down on the PMCs' weapons. They won't be able to fight back. Don't forget—we control the System."

First force and now the System. Snake knew all too well how fragile those could be. Often those who believe themselves masters of the system—capital S or no—end up finding out they were the ones being exploited by it. Meryl, Liquid—hell, even me—we were all nothing more than the context for the formation of the Patriots' System.

"I wouldn't rely too much on the System if I were you," Snake said.

"Even so, we've got them beat in sheer numbers."

"Meryl..."

Some things are too complex to be solved by force. But Snake knew it would be nearly impossible to convince her to back down.

Then she softened and spoke with a voice he hadn't heard for nine years. The voice of the Meryl he once knew.

"Snake, just leave this to me." She wasn't crying, but there were tears in her eyes. "Don't throw your life away."

She laid her hands over his. "What you're trying to do... it's not a mission."

"I know. It's not justice. It's a hired hit."

"But then," Snake wondered, "have I ever fought on behalf of justice?"

After Outer Heaven, Snake had distanced himself from the concept. Justice is never more than someone's idea of justice, and never in history had "justice" made the world into a better place.

Liquid and Snake were brought into the world by the Patriots—one controlled by their System. So while this operation might have been a personal killing, wasn't it also part of a global battle? Snake's birth had been too strange, and his life too extraordinary, to separate the personal from the global.

Meryl watched him smoke his cigarette. "Look," she said, "our ways of thinking might be different, but to me, you're still a legend... a hero. I know all about the things you did when you were young. It was what kept me going."

Then she added, "I can't bear to watch you die over something so pointless."

Snake chuckled. "Don't worry about me. Old soldiers never die."

Before Snake could say the rest—they just fade away—Meryl started to cry. He'd meant it as a joke, but now he could see there was nothing funny about it.

"I'm sorry," he said. "I'm no hero. Never was. I'm just an old killer hired to do some wet work."

Meryl wiped her eyes, and the resolve returned to her expression. Any trace of sadness or doubt was gone.

"Fine. Then we'll just have to catch him before you do." Meryl stood and turned her back to him. "I may have loved you once. But now you're just a obstinate old man."

She walked back to her squad, not once stopping to look back. "Wake up and face reality, Old Snake. And stay out of our way."

By the time Snake left the station, I had already made contact with Dr. Madnar. Naomi briefly explained Raiden's injuries, and the doctor said he thought he could help. I sent Naomi and Sunny with Raiden to his location—safely inside a noncombat zone—while I provided support to Snake.

Although we were using the face camo to project Snake's younger face, its primary function—just like the sneaking suit or Drebin's APC—was to scan its surroundings while mimicking the background.

A member of the Lost in Paradise Army arrived on a train a little over ten minutes after Snake's. The man had a criminal history, so with minimal effort, I hacked into the police database and retrieved his background and facial recognition data.

Snake wasn't wearing the Solid Eye—it wouldn't exactly help him stay low profile inside the station—and I couldn't send him the resistance fighter's picture. But I could access the face camo's live image data, providing a full 360 degree view of everything around Snake. I fed that stream through a facial recognition filter and watched for the match.

Just as Meryl was walking away from Snake, I saw him.

"Snake, he's leaving the station through the exit directly behind you."

Snake acknowledged, put out his cigarette, and stepped out into the foggy cobblestone street.

"He's walking away to your right. Don't let him see you."

"I'm used to sneaking right past someone's back, but it's been a while since I've had to tail anyone."

Now that he mentioned it, he'd never had to shadow anyone in any of our missions together.

The streetlights were lit, though only for the benefit of Raven Sword patrols. With the curfew, the streets were empty.

Even if Snake kept a good distance, all the resistance fighter had to do was turn and see him, and that would be it. Only someone incredibly careless would notice someone behind him, when no one was allowed on the streets, and think it a coincidence.

Supposedly, Snake had done tail work in Zanzibar Land, and I wouldn't be surprised if he had done it as a matter of routine for the CIA, with all the dirty work they forced on him as an undercover operative. He might have done something of that nature in the Outer Heaven op as well.

The streets were covered in fog. Snake switched off his face camo—no need for it now—and strapped the Solid Eye around his head, and its enhanced optics helped him see through the darkness and fog. Now he could stay farther back without losing the other man.

Snake steadied his breath, and as he had done in South America, he matched his body's rhythm with the baseline of his surroundings. The ambient urban noise faded, and his focus attuned with the city.

The man he followed, of course, also needed to avoid being spotted by the PMC. There wasn't much Snake could do to assist without giving away his own presence. The most he could do was hope the resistance fighter would navigate the streets wisely.

Meanwhile Snake had to hide from not only the man he followed, but also from any PMC patrols. It's hard for me to imagine how difficult it must have been.

Snake was reminded of *The Third Man*. All that was missing was the Ferris wheel and the underground tunnels.

At the edge of the mist, the resistance fighter's figure looked like a ghost. He was young. In his twenties. Without his youth, it would have been hard to throw himself into the rebellion against the System.

But me? Well, I am where I am, but back in my twenties all I cared about was anime and robotics and hacking—well, cracking. I never would have even thought about rebelling against the world. I never romanticized my cracking as an action against the system. In my work for the world's largest manufacturer in the military-industrial complex, I never questioned my masters.

I did it because it was fun. Because it gave me an escape. That was it.

I think the reason I joined the fight later in my adulthood was to compensate for how long I'd spent running away from my fate. It was the retribution for so many in my family, including my own my past self.

Snake spoke over the codec. "Otacon, he's going into a building."

The young fighter stood at the service entrance to an old monastery. A guard in the doorway was looking around to see if the man had been followed. The sentry didn't seem to have any special equipment. He checked the young man's dog tags and waved him in.

"Now!" I said, but Snake had already rushed from the shadows.

Snake was one with the city, and he closed much of the distance without the guard sensing him. As he ran, he tossed his trench coat to the ground. The guard turned, stepped inside, and started to close the door behind himself. Snake jabbed the toe of his boot inside the doorway, and when the sentry finally saw him, he was already inside.

Snake locked his arms around the man he'd followed and pressed a knife against his neck.

The sentry cried out, "Who?"

Inside the service entrance were three guards, including the one at the door. They quickly raised submachine guns and pointed them at Snake. But with their comrade a human shield, they dared not fire.

Snake put his back to the wall and started moving farther inside.

"I'm here to see Big Mama," he said.

"Is this the guy?" said one of the men.

The fear drained from the hostage's face. Then, calmly, he said, "I didn't hear him coming at all. He's gotta be the one."

But the other three weren't convinced. Yes, the man in front of them had followed one of their own, who wasn't without skill himself, and made it into their hideout undetected to hold a knife at their comrade's throat. But this intruder was coughing.

Even with his coughing fit, Snake kept his focus, of course, but his face was old. The guards pressed toward him.

Snake kicked out his prisoner's legs and shoved him at the nearest guard. The other two guards lifted their guns, but in those close quarters, the advantage was with the knife and CQC.

How quickly young people turn to guns for help. I was the one who hacked into the CIA and found the CQC manual developed by The Boss and Big Boss, then gave it to Snake.

My point being that until recently Snake had been one of those soldiers who relied on guns—he even said once that he "hated knives." Of course he'd been trained in basic close combat techniques, but he almost never used them. I think I can get away with revealing that much since, after I discovered the CQC techniques, Snake had used me as his training dummy. It was terrible.

Although he hadn't practiced CQC long, he was a warrior with Big Boss's genes, and in a flash he dropped the three guards as well as his captive.

Another soldier, who had heard the scuffle, appeared at a side doorway, his gun drawn. Suddenly, more men—and more guns—

appeared around him in numbers dwarfing his first welcoming party.

From behind the mob of armed young soldiers came a woman's voice.

"Very impressive CQC, Snake."

Like the Red Sea parting before Moses, the group of men moved aside. Through the opening, Snake could see into a sanctuary.

The woman was blonde, with a brown leather jacket and black leather boots. She knelt at the altar, her back to Snake.

"No doubt about it," she said. "He is the legendary soldier."

She rose and, under the watchful gaze of the angels and apostles painted on the ceiling, slowly turned to face Snake. As if by signal, the soldiers simultaneously lowered their weapons.

The woman was at least as old as Snake's body looked. But she stood with poise, and the straight line from her spine to her hips to her knees held no tremor. Her face held enough sparkle to make it easy to imagine the beauty it once held. The light in her eyes, if nothing else, couldn't have changed since her twenties.

"Call me Mama. Big Mama."

She walked toward Snake. He entered the sanctuary and approached her.

"I need to talk to you," he said. "Raiden sent me."

Big Mama surveyed him from head to toe. "My, how you've grown...David."

Snake froze. Not many knew his name. Just me, one small fraction of his many foster parents, and those with high enough security clearance in the US government. Snake lived his life as Snake.

"It was you," she said, "not I, who was created from the rib of man. But I gave you life."

She looked down at her stomach and softly patted it with a gloved hand. Then she looked up and fixed her eyes upon Snake. He could just barely see they were wet.

"I am your mother."

Snake was speechless. He tried to say something, but what? He'd hardly ever given thought to his mother. As far as he'd been concerned, Big Boss, his father, was the cause of his existence and his curse.

Somewhere out there was the woman who gave him birth—that was only natural.

"Les Enfants Terribles," Big Mama said. "You can't grow a human being in a test tube. Not even a clone. You need a woman's body to give it life."

"You mean, a surrogate mother?"

Her smile was mixed with irony, sadness, and self-scorn. "That's an awfully cold way to put it."

The angels on the ceiling watched them—the woman who lent her body to the insubordinate imitation of God's work, and her creation. On Shadow Moses, a native Alaskan American member of FOXHOUND on the verge of death said to Snake, "You are a Snake that was not created by nature."

"I gave birth to all of you," Big Mama said. "For the Patriots."

From her womb came Snake and Liquid and all of their tragedies. Perhaps Big Boss's corpse *was* a Pandora's box. But considering Big Mama was the beginning of everything, then she was one too. If so, then what happened to the hope that was left inside?

*Maybe she's the hope*, I thought.

"Follow me." Big Mama waved Snake to follow her into the next room. "I'll explain everything."

## 3

IN THE BEGINNING, there was Zero.

Big Mama started talking from there—with the man named Zero who was at the start of it all.

She had once been known as EVA.

It was only one of a number of aliases, but she spent most of her life under that one.

EVA was a spy with many names, raised in the ways of espionage by the Philosophers, the group of twelve powerful figures from America, China, and Russia, in one of their operative training schools.

She met Big Boss during Operation Snake Eater, as a Soviet agent sent by the KGB to assist him on his mission.

But that was only a cover—she was an operative of the Chinese faction of the Philosophers' post–World War II split. Her true goal: to acquire the microfilm, stolen by Volgin's father, containing the only means to access the Philosopher's Legacy.

But in the end, she failed her mission.

The Boss faked her defection to get close to Volgin, and put her life on the line for that tiny bit of plastic. She handed over the microfilm to Big Boss, and EVA stole it from him.

But the film was a forgery. Afraid of reprisals from the Chinese government, the triple agent fled to Hanoi at the height of the Vietnam War.

So who ended up with the Philosopher's Legacy?

The man who had founded and led the CIA's experimental special forces unit FOX—the man who was given charge of Operation Snake Eater.

He was a former member of the British SAS alongside The Boss. He was known as Zero. When he first met Big Boss, his rank was major. Like EVA, he had many names—among them Major Tom, David Oh—but most called him Zero.

∿

Then it was born.

With the enormous fortune of the Philosophers in hand, Zero brought into being a new organization to follow in the legacy of the legendary hero, The Boss. The other founding members were Mr. Sigint, Para-Medic, Big Boss—with Zero, the four core members of the FOX unit—and a young man who had infiltrated the GRU to get to Colonel Volgin and covertly help Zero. Ocelot.

They called themselves the Patriots.

EVA joined them when Ocelot helped her out of a dangerous situation in Hanoi. They revealed to her their purpose: to unite a world divided between East and West, Soviet and America, communism and capitalism. A unity of thought and awareness, so that all might share the same one view of the world.

The Patriots believed their vision to be the world The Boss had hoped for—a utopia where no soldier would be cast about by the changing times or have his life senselessly stolen. United, the Patriots shared in The Boss's dreams.

That had been the world she envisioned behind those sincere, yet sad eyes.

With The Boss's noble martyrdom, Zero felt a need for a new icon to propel the new organization.

He made Big Boss that icon. Zero gave rise to new legends, some wildly distorted and more fiction than reality, and added them to Big Boss's famed achievements. The great mercenary. The strongest warrior in the post-war world.

But Big Boss wasn't so callous a man that he'd accept those false honors without feeling he'd done The Boss wrong. It didn't take long for the tiny fissure between Big Boss and Zero to grow irrevocably icy and deep.

He left Zero when the man became consumed by a thirst for control. He didn't desire power or money themselves, but simply pursued his desire to join all the people of the world to one single dream—and he did so relentlessly and to grotesque ends, reaching extremes of paranoia with ideas of universal monitoring and control, and power through environmental simulations.

Big Boss couldn't watch Zero distort The Boss's ideals into a simple one-sided dogma.

When Zero noticed Big Boss growing ever more distant, he started a new project in secret. Dr. Clark, known at the time as Para-Medic, headed the efforts.

What Zero really wanted was another Big Boss, but the warrior had been exposed to radiation in his youth and could not father children. If Zero wanted another fighter with Big Boss's genetic traits, he needed to create one outside the normal methods of reproduction.

The project's name was Les Enfants Terribles, and its goal was to clone Big Boss, the ultimate soldier. After dozens of failures, they finally, miraculously, succeeded in producing a fertilized egg—an imitation life born from somatic cells. EVA volunteered to serve as the surrogate mother, to protect the egg inside her body until birth.

Her joy was to give birth to Big Boss.

But the project would split Zero and Big Boss once and for all. When Big Boss learned of the births of his two copies, Solid and Liquid, he left America and, after years of drifting, founded the private military company Outer Heaven in South Africa.

In this way, Big Boss declared war against Zero—and any who would twist The Boss's "joy" into an appalling dogma.

One wish, two interpretations.

Everything stemmed from that. One thought order and control were all, and he grew obsessed with exercising total control.

He amassed a fortune through countless wars. His words influenced decision-making all the way up to the Oval Office. He believed people's inner selves could be governed by an outer force—the System.

The other was angered by the obsession with limitless control, a vision far remote from what had once drawn them together. He launched a battle against the would-be global control.

At the end of the Cold War, this second cold war broke out.

None knew of its full scope, and none could possibly comprehend its real meaning. This world, so out of phase with our own, could only barely be perceived by slightly shifting the meaning to each war, conflict, and incident.

Big Boss's battle was put down by none other than his own son. After he was defeated by Solid Snake, a man with his own genes, Zero recovered his battered body. Big Boss had once been the icon of Zero's movement. He had once been Zero's friend. The fallen man represented everything Zero had once believed in, as well as the inevitability of betrayal.

Zero was no longer willing to place his organization in the hands of the next generation.

He built four AIs—GW, TJ, AL, and TR—to be the final centerpiece to fulfill his mad aspirations.

There was one more artificial intelligence, a core unit called John Doe, or JD, that regulated, monitored, and controlled the other four. Our efforts on the Big Shell resulted in the destruction of GW, but the remaining AIs continued to set forth the future envisioned by the Patriots.

EVA and Ocelot began working to free Big Boss from Zero's clutches. They enlisted Naomi Hunter, an authority in the field of nanomachine research, into their organization. They helped free Frank Jaeger, the test subject of exoskeletal research who lived a cruel existence, in hopes they could use him to kill Para-Medic, the head of the Patriots' cybernetic exoskeleton research. And EVA and Ocelot prevailed.

Ocelot infiltrated FOXHOUND, getting close to one of the Snakes, Liquid, and helped them on Shadow Moses. There, he killed Donald Anderson, the DARPA chief and the man at the core of the development of Metal Gear REX—also known as Mr. Sigint.

Liquid had raised his army in rebellion and demanded Big Boss's body in hopes that with it, he could do something about the genetic disease that afflicted his men, the Next-Generation Special Forces, who had been genetically enhanced with Big Boss's genes.

Of course, Ocelot had given Liquid the idea. Ocelot's sole purpose was to use the island's capture to kill Donald Anderson, and if he could get Big Boss's body at the same time, all the better.

But with that mission came the end of Ocelot and EVA's alliance.

Ocelot lost his right arm on Shadow Moses, and when he grafted Liquid's arm in its place, his body was taken over by Liquid. Now entirely alone, EVA had nearly lost all hope when Raiden came to her with GW's data and gave her a new path.

Among the data was the location of Big Boss's body.

Snake and Big Mama walked out the front of the monastery and into a courtyard.

The rain had stopped. The stones in the courtyard were still wet, sparkling in the moonlight, and smelled of the rain.

The fog had lifted and few clouds were in the sky.

Big Mama walked Snake to the back of a van. Two identical ones, droplets still clinging to their black paint, were parked on either side.

"They look like hearses," Snake said.

"This is his pyx," Big Mama said, "his Holy Ark."

Slowly, she opened the van's rear door.

Seeing the figure inside, what Snake felt wasn't anger, much less hate, but pity. He felt a sadness akin to despair toward the man, who even in his current state was considered alive.

Big Mama stepped back. "His body is alive, but his conscious-ness is locked away by nanomachines. So technically speaking, he's not really brain dead."

Snake had trouble appreciating the difference.

Covering the body was a translucent black sheet of sealed plastic that seemed to Snake like a body bag. The man inside was without limbs—a sadistic sculptor's idea of a bust.

Judging from the missing left eye, and the shape of his face, he had to be Big Boss.

The skin Snake had burned away in Zanzibar Land had been stitched together with skin grafts so completely that no seam showed. But his cheeks were deeply sunken, and his lips had lost their fat, taking the shape of the gums beneath. If someone were to slap a layer of skin over a bare skeleton, the result would likely look about the same.

Medical equipment installed inside the van kept those skin and bones in a state of life. The dutiful machines regulated the breaths of the man who would never be able to breathe on his own again.

Snake muttered, "Why did Zero keep him alive?"

Why had he gone to such great efforts to cling to this body, the body of the traitor, the enemy who had hindered his great aspira-tions and the man he had grown to hate?

With a sad smile, Big Mama said, "People need legends." She looked past Big Boss and into some distant place. "Zero wanted to create a messiah. A legend that would never die."

She closed the door, and Big Boss was again shut away inside with his ventilator.

As Snake followed her back to the church, he pondered his fate. Perhaps committing suicide would be a better end to his life than the eternal quasi-death Big Boss suffered.

Meanwhile, in *Nomad*, Naomi had disappeared.

4

STANDING BEFORE THE altar, Snake tried to absorb what he'd just learned.

A statue of Christ on the cross looked down upon Snake and Big Mama from its place above the altar. Blood flowed from where the crown of thorns cut into his forehead.

*I'm just like that statue.* Is that what Snake thought as he looked upon it? A powerful symbol for the apostles.

Needless to say, Snake wasn't Jesus Christ. He hadn't died for all the sins of mankind. Snake was just a living statue born from one man's obsession.

But Big Mama hadn't fought on behalf of that faith.

"You fought for Big Boss," Snake said. "But what about Ocelot? Why did he join with you? What did he fight for?"

"The same as me. Big Boss. He didn't fight for the Pentagon or the Russians. And certainly not for Zero. Ocelot was dedicated to Big Boss. He idolized him."

When I think about it, Ocelot had a terribly complex role on Shadow Moses. He participated in the rebellion with FOXHOUND and was a spy for the Patriots, but his real goal was to outmaneuver the Patriots, bury one of their founders, and retrieve Big Boss's body.

But now his body was controlled by Liquid.

Big Mama said, "We can't allow Liquid to inherit the same sins that corrupted Zero—manipulating people's minds for the sake of his own ego."

Just then, the sanctuary doors opened.

Snake and Big Mama reflexively spun to face the intruder, a lone man in a buttoned-up trench coat and a hat lowered over his eyes. He looked like he'd just walked in from a noir movie. The resistance fighters raised their guns, a hive of bees ready to strike.

But Snake felt something was wrong.

The coat fell to the floor and the silhouette of the man crumbled and split off.

The rebels yelled in surprise. I couldn't blame them. The supposed man was really three small surveillance robots standing on each other's shoulders, like three kids in a trench coat pretending to be a grown-up.

Each robot was a black orb the size of a bowling ball with three long, slender humanoid arms. They shed their disguise and scattered across the floor and up the walls.

Big Mama said, "Give," and took a gun from one of the young fighters. Immediately she shot one of the robots on the wall. Then she moved her gun in one smooth arc and fired shots at the other two. The robots skittered around the room with infuriating dexterity, but within seconds after the first had fallen, Big Mama's unerring aim finished them off.

The resistance fighters exchanged troubled looks, some biting their lips.

"Scarabs," one said, "Unmanned scouts."

Without emotion, Big Mama said, "They've found us. We're moving out."

Either this was a frequent occurrence or she was handling it gracefully so as not to rattle her men. Her reaction impressed Snake—now he knew why this woman who called herself his mother had so many followers.

From the satellite image feeds and the density of wireless transmissions, I could see the PMC were quickly converging on the monastery. I told Snake they would be on him in less than five minutes.

Big Mama headed outside to the vehicles. The resistance fighters were already preparing their escape. She walked up to the driver's side of one and asked the driver, "Are they ready?"

"As they can be."

Big Mama lowered her voice. "We'll send the real one through the canal route. Get it ready. Hurry!"

"Yes, ma'am."

The Gekko's cries rang through the air, and all eyes turned to the bright moonlit sky. The howls of man-made beasts filled the empty streets.

Snake knew the situation was about to get bad. There wasn't even time for a smoke.

Big Mama called him over to a row of motorcycles beside a garage. Some already had riders warming up their engines.

As she walked into the garage, she said, "We've got decoy vans set to draw some of our pursuers away."

At the rear of the space, a motorcycle slumbered beneath a tarp. EVA threw aside the cover. Dust flew off the plastic and danced across the beams of moonlight coming in through the windows.

"She's a Triumph," Big Mama announced.

The bike was a T120. Designed in 1959 and the first of the Bonneville models, it had retained a persistent popularity. Even in the twenty-first century, its parts were still sought for tuning. At one time, Auto Race riders, believing the Triumph engines would bring out the best of their racing abilities, competed over Triumph Engineering engines. A vintage bike suited Big Mama. Beauty and power combined.

She rolled the motorbike outside and indicated the resistance fighters' quiet, frenzied preparations with her eyes.

"They're all orphans," she said softly. "As children, they all worked in arms factories, and when they grow up, they want to join a PMC. They seek revenge on other companies—the PMCs that killed their parents. Their pay goes to support their younger siblings. There are countless child soldiers in the PMCs."

Much like Raiden.

What happened to Raiden as a child seemed to me the worst act one human could do to another, but that was only the very beginning. He was sent to America, where he joined the army. He was put in the Patriots' fake FOXHOUND unit and underwent endless VR training.

"Nowadays," Big Mama said, "anyone with access to the net can get combat training. The PMCs distribute popular FPS games for free. Of course it's all just virtual training. It's so easy for kids to get absorbed by these war games."

In order to recruit personnel, the PMCs had to lay the proper groundwork within the culture. They needed a culture that raised children who were ready to leap into war. By cultivating that culture, they could secure the manpower to carry the future of their industry.

"And before they know it, they're in the PMCs holding real guns. These kids end up fighting in proxy wars that have nothing to do with their own lives. They think it's cool to fight like this. They think that combat is life." She gave Snake a hard look. "They don't need a reason to fight. After all, for them, it's only a game."

"It's the war economy." Snake's face twisted with disgust. That's not to say that past wars weren't about making money. When kings and lords reached past their own borders, it was always about money. What Snake abhorred was the hiding of the seas of blood and the stench of rotting meat under a sterile cover. What they called an economy was really just war—same as always.

The children had been blinded to the nauseating realities of war. The image of the battlefield became sterilized. The groundwork was being laid for a world in which all people fought in proxy wars.

Big Mama spoke with a low, forceful voice. "Zero is the cause of all this. Defeating Liquid won't change things. Unless we stop the Patriots' System, the cycle will continue unbroken."

She stepped on the pedal, and the vintage bike roared to life, its engine humming and vibrating, a noise wholly unlike the creepy, unnatural roar of the Gekko. This was a real machine, rough-hewn and comforting. Big Mama beckoned Snake to sit behind her, and he did.

She took a moment, absorbed in the noise of the idling engine, then let out a sigh of ecstasy and said, "With so many wars being waged, oil and biofuel have become as precious as diamonds. It's been a while since I went out for a ride."

"You sure about this?"

She threw him an over-the-shoulder grin. "I only get off my bike when I fall in love...or fall dead."

Then Snake saw it in her eyes. *Saudade*—yearning for something that is lost. Perhaps she saw Big Boss's face in the man who was both her son and a clone.

"Call me EVA."

She signaled the departure, and her fighters raced out the open gate.

They split into three teams—one for each van.

Motorcycle squads ran alongside each vehicle. The one led by EVA was likely the real one, with Big Boss's body inside. If the enemies got their hands on it, everything would be over.

With the curfew in effect, the streets were empty save for PMC troops, and there was no reason for the Paradise Lost to watch their speed. But the European city, with its long history as a fortress town, was built with a complex network of twisting roads—much to the detriment of both past-day invading armies and the present-day commuters.

The city had been untouched by Allied tank battalions during World War II, even escaping Hitler's wrath. So the streets remained perfectly preserved in all their nuisances. The narrow, winding roads held back the speed of EVA and her men.

But the same was true for the PMC forces. And they probably didn't have motorcycles either. Hard to imagine them gaining much ground in their armored personnel carriers.

A sound cut through the air, and something flew by overhead.

"A Slider!" I yelled.

A birdlike unmanned combat aerial vehicle like the one we saw in the Middle East, gliding around with wings like a raven and coming at Snake head on.

"Snake!" EVA shouted. "Do something!"

He took out his submachine gun and fired on full auto. But head on, the Slider had a slim profile and was exceptionally hard to hit.

"Shit!" Snake said.

The Slider's mounted gun began to shoot. The weapon was located where the bird's head would be—unlike the wings, that part of the machine could remain steady during flight.

"Hang on!" EVA yelled. She deftly maneuvered the Triumph to the side in a movement so quick the bike didn't seem to turn at all. The drone's machine gun fire passed beside them. The rear van and bikes managed to evade the attack, but their riders hadn't managed to fire back like Snake.

"I'm turning!" EVA threw her kickstand into the ground and spun the bike around in a bowel-wrenching turn.

The rest of the squad managed to follow, but Snake felt sorry for anyone having to keep up.

They came onto a thoroughfare with PMC patrols stationed here and there alongside the road. Those quick enough to notice the resistance's motorcade fired whatever weapons they had, but the vehicles shot by too quickly. Nearly all of their shots missed their targets.

A high-pitched shriek made Snake turn to see a Slider fly out onto the road, right on their tail, firing indiscriminately after the resistance forces. Several PMC soldiers were struck down by the bullets. The Slider gave no regard to friend or foe.

"Snake," EVA said, "in front!"

Another Slider was rapidly approaching.

"What do we do?" Snake asked.

"Push through, what else? Just pray for luck!"

"What about that side road up ahead? Can you make the turn?"

"That goes backwards! It can't be more than a thirty degree angle!"

This was essentially a U-turn. Not even EVA, and that maneuver she pulled before, could make that turn at their speed—let alone the rest of their entourage. It was as EVA had said—all they could do was try to pass under the oncoming Slider.

Then an APC came out from the side road. Its loudspeaker cheerfully called out, "Snake! You need me?"

"Drebin!" What got Snake's attention even more than Drebin's sudden and surprising entrance was Little Gray, standing atop the APC, an RPG-7 in hand. The vehicle slowed to let EVA's motorcycle catch up.

"You think we can make a deal here, Old Snake?"

"Please!"

The APC pulled right up next to the Triumph, so close they were almost touching. Little Gray stretched out his long gibbon arm and handed Snake the rocket launcher.

EVA yelled, "Snake, it's coming!"

Snake stood on the back of the bike, lifted the RPG-7 to his shoulder and took aim at the Slider in front.

"I'm throwing this one in for free," said Drebin.

Snake glanced at the APC. Sitting in the gunner seat was Little Gray, another RPG-7 at his shoulder. He was aiming at the Slider in back.

"I'm not sure what's going on here," said EVA, laughing. "But you guys are really fucking weird."

Snake didn't have the time to laugh, but he was bemused by the idea of a monkey and a Snake fighting together.

"Fire!" Snake said.

The monkey and the Snake simultaneously fired.

Just as they had launched together, so did both rocket-propelled grenades find their targets. Before and behind the racing squad, orange flames burst into the night sky and cast their light upon the city.

"Well, Snake," Drebin said. "Gotta run!"

The APC turned down a side road and parted with the convoy. I wasn't sure if he activated the OctoCamo or not, but I lost sight of him within seconds.

"What an odd man," EVA said. "Who is he?"

"A gun launderer. For some reason, he seems to like me."

Another howl. This wasn't over yet.

Then came the hailstorm of grenades.

It was practically a carpet bombing. The two Sliders shot down by Snake and Little Gray had been nothing more than decoys. Amid the battle, a third Slider had stealthily flanked them.

The van rolled over from the force of the explosions. The vehicle came careening at EVA's bike, and just as it was about to flatten them, she yanked the handlebar to the side.

The Triumph tumbled sideways. Snake and EVA were flung off, smacking against the wall of a building partially destroyed by the bursting grenades. The van brushed past them and slammed into another house.

Snake had been battered against the stone wall, but most of the impact was absorbed by his sneaking suit. He stood, coughing violently, and looked at EVA. Under her leather jacket, she wore only thin clothing. Not enough to protect against that amount of force.

Her face was chillingly pale.

Beads of sweat ran from her hair and down her forehead. Her right hand reached across her stomach, clutching at her side, trying to hold her life inside while it slipped away. I couldn't see if it was a fragment of a grenade or a chip of pavement, but whatever the thing piercing inside her was, it looked fatal.

She gazed up at Snake, her eyes distant. "My children?"

He looked down the street. The motorcycle squad had been wiped out. One rider had a caved-in skull, another had bones protruding from all over his body, another was covered in shrapnel—their bodies still upon the drying pavement.

Snake walked over to where the van rested on its side. The rear door hung open, empty. EVA's hearse was a decoy. With a deeper appreciation for her strength, he walked to the driver's side door. He checked on the limp bodies of the driver and another youth in the passenger seat, but it was already too late.

Snake turned to EVA and shook his head.

"I'm so sorry," she said and closed her eyes.

He walked back over to her and said, "So it was a decoy. I'm impressed."

"Not just this van—all of them were decoys. The pyx is safely floating down the river."

"EVA, are you all right?"

He inspected her side. Her gloved hand was wet with her own blood. A bird cawed in the distance. Was it a sign of morning's approach—or was it Death's scout?

"Big Mama, can you stand?"

"Snake," she said, her voice fevered and weak. Her eyes were vacant, unfocused. "Is that you?"

What she saw in her half-conscious state wasn't the Snake in front of her, but another man who once had the same code name. A man who had once saved her when she was gravely injured in the forest in Soviet Russia—coincidentally, that wound too had been in her side.

"The man I once loved. The man whose eyes I knew were only for that strong, righteous, great woman, yet who still I couldn't stop myself from falling for.

"That's why I gave birth to them, to your children. To you. Something that not even the woman you loved could do. Yes, maybe I was jealous. What I felt toward her was beyond the concept of love versus hate.

"Maybe it was wrong of me, Snake. To bear your children. Snake…"

"EVA, I need you."

Then EVA came back to reality. She curled her lips, blood

trailing down from the corners, into an unnerving smile. "A mother's work is never done."

With one arm still to her side, she pushed herself up with the other. Drops of blood dripped from between her fingers.

Snake gave her his shoulder and asked, "What now?"

"Land and air routes are cut off, but a cruiser is waiting for us at a rendezvous point on the riverbank downstream."

"Good thinking."

As she leaned against him, he let her lead the way. But after a few steps, she stopped. She took a few moments to look at her overturned Triumph.

"I don't need to feel the wind anymore. I don't need to keep lying to myself." She pulled away from Snake's shoulder and walked by her own strength. "I only get off my bike when I fall in love—or..."

She walked to a manhole near the side of the road. She looked down at it, and Snake understood. Together they lifted the cover.

"The underground aqueduct leads to the river. There should be fewer of them down there."

They climbed down the ladder.


5


FOR THE MOMENT, they seemed safe.

Snake and EVA walked through the aqueduct toward the river. She was moving slowly, and Snake matched her speed. Snake, of course, remained on alert for any sign of danger, but I thought it the best chance we might have to talk.

Over the codec, I said to him, "Snake, I need to tell you something."

"What is it?"

"It's Naomi—she's gone. She's not in *Nomad* anymore."

Snake didn't say anything. I took the moment of silence to scold myself for my lapse in caution. I gritted my teeth.

Then he asked, "When did you notice?"

"Right after she and Sunny got back from Dr. Madnar's place."

"Why weren't you watching her?"

"I wasn't wearing my..."

The words caught in my throat. Naomi said I looked handsome without my glasses. She'd manipulated me. She used my feelings to trick me. I felt the anguish of it in every cell of my body.

"...my glasses."

"Naomi said it herself—the experiment can't succeed without her."

As soon as I saw she'd left, I had the same thought. As I felt the sting of her betrayal, my mind went straight to the absolute worst scenario. If I assumed she was that evil, then maybe my shame could be lessened if only by a little bit.

Even though I'd already mostly convinced myself that was the case, I asked, "You think she went back to Liquid?"

Snake didn't answer. He must have known I believed it myself. I felt awkward. After working together for a decade, we pretty much knew all there was to know about each other.

He changed the subject. "What about Raiden?"

"Good news on that front. We managed to get our hands on a dialysis machine and set up an ICU on *Nomad*. Sunny's keeping a constant watch on him and is handling the dialysis and the treatment of his wounds. But the dialysis is probably going to take forty-eight hours. Until then, Raiden can't move."

"Wait, Otacon."

Snake tensed. I switched over to the Solid Eye's live feed and saw light up ahead.

Snake readied his M4 and moved ahead of EVA and toward the exit. Outside, a boat was silhouetted by a flickering light in the distance. Was it the cruiser with Big Boss's ark?

Snake advanced.

A lone figure emerged from the ship, stepped down onto the walkway, and took something from his pocket. Snake watched down the sights of his M4. The figure flicked open a lighter, lit the object in his hand, and put it to his mouth.

A cigar.

"Liquid!" Snake said.

The man himself—Liquid Ocelot.

Snake moved out into the open where he could clearly see the boat. Not the cruiser Big Mama had mentioned, but rather a military patrol boat. On its deck the main cast had assembled—Liquid's armed private guard, along with Vamp and Naomi.

Just as we'd thought. My predicted worst possible scenario had been dead on, but I was wrong about one thing: my shame and guilt weren't lightened in the slightest.

Liquid triumphantly exhaled a mouthful of smoke and said, "Not bad."

With unsteady steps, EVA moved forward and grabbed Snake's shoulder. She knew Ocelot's face well. He was her comrade once. Together, they freed Big Boss from the Patriots and left Zero truly alone.

But his behavior, his mannerisms—those didn't belong to the man she once knew.

"Where's the pyx?" she asked.

Liquid replied without bothering to look at her. "That no longer matters."

With the last tattered bits of her strength, EVA yelled, "Where is it?"

On the ship's deck, Vamp had turned to face the flickering light across the water. That was when we realized what it was. Fire.

"EVA," Snake asked, "is that your boat?"

She removed her hand from his shoulder. Her legs lost the strength to carry her, and she slumped to the concrete. Keeping his M4 aimed at Liquid, Snake glanced down at EVA, now on her knees within a slowly spreading pool of blood, her face lit by the flickering light of the sinking cruiser's blaze.

Snake gritted his teeth. "Naomi…"

"She told me everything," Liquid said, his voice calm and composed, with no trace of the triumphant boasting he had displayed in the Middle East. "And now, thanks to her, I finally have him. The one I've sought for so long—Big Boss."

Snake moved his eyes to Naomi. She turned away out of guilt—whether actual or feigned, I couldn't tell.

"Put down the gun," Liquid said. "It's already too late. You almost did it."

Half a dozen of Liquid's elite guards in power-assist armor similar to Snake's sneaking suit appeared from below deck. Snake lowered his weapon.

Exuberance edged into Liquid's voice. "Looks like I win after all, brother." He let out a puff of smoke. "This brand was Father's favorite. What do you say? Care for one last smoke?"

"You think you're Big Boss now?"

Liquid blew smoke into Snake's face. Now he was just being childish. Snake coughed.

"Guilty as charged." He tossed the cigar to the ground. "But all that ends today."

As Liquid put out the cigar with his boot, Snake raised the M4 and aimed at him. But before he could squeeze the trigger, Liquid had stepped to the side. In one swift movement, he lunged forward and stole the gun out of Snake's hands.

He pulled out the M4's magazine and ejected the chambered shell. At the same time, Snake drew his Operator, but Liquid just snatched it away. In a flurry of elbows and knees, Snake was sent to the ground.

"Nice try, brother, but when it comes to CQC, I've got the upper hand."

The private guard stepped out of the boat and encircled EVA and the disarmed and powerless Snake.

Then Liquid pointed the Operator at its owner's face.

Snake looked his brother in the eyes.

*So this is it,* he must have thought. *It's been nine years since our hand-to-hand battle on Shadow Moses Island. And he's dogged me ever since. I shot down his HIND D, threw him from the top of Metal Gear REX, killed him with FOXDIE—but each time he found a way back to life and back in my face.*

*I don't think I'll be so lucky.*

But Liquid turned the Operator aside and threw it into the river.

*Why won't he kill me? Does he just want to prolong his enjoyment? Or is there some reason he needs me alive?*

Snake glared at Liquid. "Even if you do get ahold of the System, you'll only have one part of the Patriots' AI—the military part."

Liquid shrugged. "What of it, brother? It's only a matter of time before I'll have everything."

He lifted Snake by the shoulders and threw him against the wall of the aqueduct. With the wind knocked out of him, Snake slumped against the bricks and struggled to breathe. Liquid leaned his arm on the wall and put his face right in front of his brother's, so close they could smell each other's breath.

"Remember GW?" Liquid said. "The AI you think they lost? It's mine—a part of my army."

I yelled at my computer screen. "Impossible!" My sister's worm destroyed it. Emma gave her life for it.

"Your worm only managed to cut GW into little pieces. Tiny, functionless, disconnected fragments. Fragments we were able to reconstruct and stow away inside JD's network.

"Revolver Ocelot's body has served me well. He was, after all, one of the founding Patriots. It allowed me to pass every security barrier between me and GW. Now GW is like a ghost inside JD. They used to be separate entities, like brothers, but as bits and pieces of GW were added to its information network, JD could no longer recognize it as an external threat."

Liquid pulled Snake from the wall.

"Once I destroy JD with a nuclear strike, the Patriots' network will be mine. And then, I'll build my Haven, free from all forms of control. I'll cast aside my old identity and take my own name for the first time."

"You're planning to take the place of the Patriots?"

The punch landed hard in Snake's stomach. He spit out every last bit of air from his lungs like a boxer who had just taken his finishing blow.

But Liquid wasn't finished with him yet.

"Snake, we were created by the Patriots." He sent another punch to the same place. "We're not men. We're shadows in the shape of men."

Snake was utterly defenseless, with no strength left within him. Liquid pushed him back.

"We're freaks who never should have existed!"

This time the punch came straight at Snake's face.

"We're a system to stifle the prosperity of future generations."

Another punch. But this time, somehow, Snake was able to stop it, wrapping his hand around his brother's fist.

"The Patriots saw fit to create us, and in doing so became our only raison d'être."

Liquid drew back his other hand to strike.

"I won't fight my fate any longer."

Snake narrowly blocked the punch. Snake had each of his hands around Liquid's, and they stood posed like wrestlers testing each other's strength.

"I'll kill Zero and Big Boss and become a Patriot myself."

For a few tense moments, Liquid resisted Snake. Then suddenly he relaxed his arms and let Snake go. He turned his back to his brother and started walking to the patrol boat.

As he walked away, he said, "It all began with Zero and Big Boss. Our purpose in life is to fulfill our destinies. And once all is returned to nothing, the world can be reborn."

When he reached the side of his ship, he turned to face his brother. Snake, exhausted from the struggle, was helpless to do anything but stare into the eyes hidden behind Liquid's sunglasses.

"So long as we both live," Liquid said, "there is no future. If we're to pass the baton to the next generation, the only choice left to us is death."

Between the fatigue of old age, the loss of breath, and the damage inflicted by Liquid's beating, Snake was only half conscious, no longer able to tell which emotions showed in his brother's eyes.

Vamp said something to Liquid, who nodded. Snake and I both got the feeling that something big was about to happen.

The nosferatu made a signal, and the soldiers surrounding Snake quickly backed into the boat, their weapons still trained on the wheezing old man.

The ship began to distance itself from the concrete walkway, and Liquid hopped aboard. "The players have all assembled, Snake. The time has come for you to witness our moment of triumph!"

Snake could only watch as the boat withdrew to the river. Liquid stood on the deck, his arms crossed, the wind across the water blowing his—that is to say, Ocelot's—long gray hair.

Naomi stood beside him. Her eyes, brimming with sadness, settled on Snake.

Then a bright light flooded over everything.

Liquid's ship was in the dead center of the river when the beams of light hit it from all directions. American helicopters hovered in the night sky, their floodlights aimed at the patrol boat. In an instant, the pitch dark of the city transformed into the glare of a concert arena.

"Hold it right there, Liquid!"

Meryl's amplified voice, practically a howl, echoed off the bridges.

Her shout came from a line of five American patrol boats that blocked the width of the river as they sped toward Liquid. A similar force blocked the other side.

US forces poured across both shores of the river and the bridges to either side of Liquid's boat. In an instant, the bridges were covered with APCs, Jeeps, and Humvees with mounted heavy machine guns—so many that the combined weight of troops and equipment might send the beautiful stonework crumbling into the river.

"Drop your weapons and stand down. Now!"

The roar of whirring rotors multiplied. Liquid looked up to see a fleet of helicopters bearing down on him of such number he must have found it a bit ridiculous—and most of them had sharpshooters on deck. They were like a swarm of flies buzzing in circles around Liquid's ship.

Liquid was ecstatic—like a struggling artist finally thrust into the limelight.

His boat made a loop in the center of the river, while Meryl led her ship to the docks near Snake and EVA.

Snake put his arm around EVA's waist. He led her onto the Rat Patrol's ship and past Ed and Jonathan, who stood guard. As for Akiba, he was slumped at the edge of the deck, taken out of commission by seasickness.

"All of you," Meryl shouted, "drop your weapons and put your hands up!"

Snake kept on telling her to stop, to run, but his voice was drowned out by the cacophony of rotors and engines—or perhaps she did hear him but chose to ignore his pleas. She believed her show of force would meet with certain success.

She piloted the boat after Liquid, moving in for the arrest.

The horde of machines howled from the land and the sea and the air. To the pilots and snipers, Liquid, bathed in the searchlights, must have looked like a helpless man surrounded by a hundred wild beasts.

Liquid took a deep breath.

It was like the pensive moment when a musician pauses before his audience before launching into his most beloved song with no introduction.

He raised his right arm. His fingers formed an imaginary gun, as if he were a child playing pretend. He pointed its barrel at one of the helicopters.

"Bang."

What the hell was Liquid doing?

At first, nobody—not Meryl or any of the American soldiers—knew what the gray-haired old man was trying to accomplish with his childish display. He kept pointing his fingers at the helicopters. Bang, bang, bang.

The first to notice something amiss was the pilot of the first helicopter "shot down" by Liquid. All of the chopper's instruments simultaneously went black, and the navigation display in his head-set winked off. Within moments, he realized the control stick had ceased to have any effect.

One after another, the helicopters lost control and were thrown into erratic spirals. The falling vehicles made a sad, absurd dance.

The first scream came from that same pilot. "Metal Slave 01 has lost control! We're going to crash!"

The SOP's tactical link was flooded with a continuous noise of shrieks and cries, with new voices coming in waves, filling in for the ones that fell silent.

Liquid aimed at a soldier on the bridge.

"Bang."

His target groaned and collapsed to the ground. The Marines next to the fallen man didn't know what had happened.

Meryl yelled, "Fire!"

The US forces raised their weapons in unison and squeezed their triggers.

Click.

The metallic chorus rang through the night sky.

Scores of weapons were pointed at Liquid's boat, from small arms to light machine guns, to the Humvee-mounted large caliber guns. But none with a hammer willing to fulfill the needs of the inhabitant of the chamber.

Meryl went pale. "What?" She stared at the Desert Eagle in her hands. Reflexively, she checked its mechanical safety, even though she already knew it was off. It was.

Finally she realized what was happening.

Her patrol boat was slowing down, its engine no longer running.

In the distance an explosion violently blossomed. One of the helicopters had crashed.

"The System is mine!" Liquid boomed.

His personal guard opened fire from the deck. This time the attack was with real guns and real bullets. The other helicopters lost their battle against gravity, crashing into the buildings and streets. Amid the thunder of explosions, the helpless soldiers were cut down by an onslaught of lead.

The ones who reacted quickly enough to get behind cover experienced the world falling apart. Their suppressed and compressed residual emotions, suddenly given free rein, became a raging storm battering at their nervous systems.

Blood streamed from their ears as they vomited relentlessly into their masks. With hands to their heads, the soldiers screamed unintelligibly, their wailing every bit as loud as the gunfire. They convulsed like wind-up toys. Everything crumbled—consciousness, meaning, the world, the landscape, words—into grains of sand blowing in the wind.

Most of the fighters hadn't made it to cover behind their vehicles. They either collapsed on the spot into a twitching mass, threw themselves over the guard rail, or were shot in the back.

Liquid pointed four fingers straight out and mimicked a Gatling gun with each hand.

He started with the ships to his left and his right.

He aimed at them, *Bam-bam-bam-bam-bam.* His arms shook with mock recoil.

The ships' engines exploded.

The searchlights were destroyed by the blasts, but the flaming wreckage lit the river orange, painting a beautiful light on the canvas of the water's surface.

Next were the vehicles on the bridges and riverbanks.

Liquid swept his arms in a 180-degree arc, *Bam-bam-bam-bam-bam*, and the vehicles launched into a neat, orderly line of explosions. The grenades and ammunition of soldiers caught in the fire ignited, and the earth looked as if it had been napalm bombed.

The city burned.

Golden embers fell from the sky like snowflakes. Liquid raised his arms and bellowed in triumph. "Do you see this, Zero? We are victorious!"

This would only be the first of the flames. These deaths were only the beginning.

A bigger fire was coming, and it was coming soon.

"These are the Guns of the Patriots!"

Like the rest of the soldiers, Ed, Jonathan, and Meryl were fighting off the crushing weight of their emotions and the destruction of their nervous systems. They were helpless to fight back, and the two large men had taken bullets from Liquid's men and fell to the deck.

Meryl called their names. Ed and Jonathan couldn't do much but moan through the pain. At least that meant they were still alive. Amid the crumbling world, Meryl lifted herself up on one knee and managed to find her balance. She withdrew a combat knife from a sheath at her hip.

The knife didn't have any clever mechanisms. There weren't any ID tags, just a blade, a primitive instrument to cut and slice and take the lives of its victims. Simple and beautiful. True. Meryl held it at the ready and glared at Liquid's boat drawing ever closer.

But still, her mind hung by a thread.

The thread snapped.

Somebody shouted, "Meryl, get down!"

Somewhere in her hazy thoughts she might have wondered, *Was that Snake?* but she and everything and everyone she knew fell apart. In that state, she couldn't parse the command, let alone follow it. Her consciousness stretched infinitely thin, and waves of headache and nausea, like from an endless fever, pulsed through her body with every heartbeat and tore her down from within.

Then someone tackled her. Gunfire echoed in her ears. It took some time for her to realize the person covering her had been shot. His face looked remarkably like Johnny Akiba's.

"You're..." she whispered. "You're okay?"

"Yeah, I'm fine."

"Akiba? But why?"

Akiba sensed something and looked to the port side. Liquid's patrol boat was bearing down straight at the side of their ship. But Meryl's ship was dead in the water.

"Out of my way!" Ocelot yelled. The ship cannon spit fire.

Akiba grabbed Meryl and dove to the starboard side. In that instant, the port side of the boat was blown to pieces. The blast flung the two to the opposite side. Jonathan and Ed fell to the river where they floated. Akiba made a quick decision and dove into the water with Meryl in his arms.

Just before the explosion, Snake was about to use Naomi's autoinjector to alleviate the System's interference with his nanomachines. But when the shell tore a hole into the side of the ship, he was knocked back, and his only salvation slipped from his hand and onto the deck. EVA seemed to be holding on to a part of the deck, and she was still slumped over in the same spot. But now hardly any life remained in her eyes.

Liquid's ship slowly glided past theirs.

Liquid stood atop its cannon, his arms crossed. He cast them a glance and said, "Let them have it. We don't need it anymore."

Vamp picked up a large black bundle. Snake and EVA watched helplessly as he threw it into the starboard fire on the Rat Patrol boat.

EVA let out a tiny, pathetic scream.

Inside the bundle was Big Boss's body. Disconnected from

life support, it was likely no longer alive. The corpse rolled to a stop inside the blaze. Its skin began to wither and shrink in the flames.

Snake struggled to his feet and took unsteady steps toward the body. The deck was enveloped in smoke. Snake's lungs, already weakened by age and a lifelong cigarette addiction, had no way of coping with the particulate cloud. He coughed ever more violently and nearly blacked out.

"So long, Snake!"

Liquid drew his pistol and fired at Big Boss's body.

The deck was engulfed by another blast of flames. Fully half of the ship was now on fire, and Snake's OctoCamo turned orange to match the blaze. Snake raised his hands to protect his exposed face from the incredible heat.

Through the gaps between his fingers, he could see that Big Boss was already halfway gone.

I don't know where she found the strength, but EVA jumped into the fire to save the body of Big Boss. But it was hopeless. Snake reached into the flames and pulled her away.

For one brief moment, EVA and Liquid met each other's eyes. Then another explosion disintegrated the burning half of the ship.

The fireball licked across EVA and Snake. The flames burned through the back of EVA's leather jacket and charred her skin. Snake's left cheek burned off in an instant. Snake screamed in pain only to be choked by the stench of his own burning flesh.

Snake fell to the deck, defeated.

And then Snake realized that everyone there was his family. His mother, his father, and himself, their son—all reduced to ashes while only Liquid remained, the last of the Snakes, to throw the world into chaos.

That couldn't be allowed to happen. It wasn't over.

Snake shouted, "Otacon!"

I snapped to my senses and drew back from the horrors on the screen. I sent the Mk. II across the deck on full throttle and built as much momentum as I could. It rolled past Snake and EVA, aimed directly at the back of Liquid's boat, and jumped.

I engaged the stealth mode in midair, and when the tiny stow-away landed on Liquid's deck, no one noticed.

The city was filled with light.

Not daylight—helicopter crash sites blazed like bonfires. Columns of black smoke rose in the gaps between the roofs. The roar of noise—cries, curses, gunfire, and explosions—had fallen silent.

There were more men dead than alive. When the nanoma-chines threw their bodies and minds into disorder, they were rendered incapable of firing a single bullet in their defense. The soldiers faced down a whirlwind of automatic fire. If you could have looked down at the streets from up high that day, you would have seen their blood over everything.

But some yet lived. There were many only on the brink of death.

Johnny dragged Meryl's body to the shore. He checked her pulse. Nothing.

He lifted her chin and checked her airway. He removed his mask, pinched her nose shut, put his mouth over hers, and breathed air into her. Out of the corner of his eye, he could see her chest rise. The air was reaching her lungs. He breathed again. No response.

Her lips were cold. He nearly lost himself in fear.

"Meryl, don't give up on me!" he cried, partly in case she was still conscious somewhere inside—in case she would hear it and find her way back to the land of the living—but mostly just to pull himself back together.

Despite the pain of the many injuries he'd received protecting her, Johnny worked the entire upper half of his body, pushing re-peatedly into Meryl's chest.

"Don't die, Meryl!" he repeated again and again as he continued the chest compressions. There was no one else around who could help. Ed and Jonathan were nowhere in sight. On the bridge were only the dead and those who, like Meryl, were near death.

The only one who could possibly save her was him.

*Come back, come back.* Johnny's hands, one atop the other, pumped against her sternum.

*Come back, come back, come back, come back!*

But she didn't respond.

He stopped and returned to the artificial respiration, putting his mouth over hers.

Her eyes opened.

Their eyes met, not even inches apart. Johnny hurriedly removed his lips from hers, which had already started to regain their redness.

"I...I..." He tried to explain but stumbled on the words. His cheeks burned. What was Johnny embarrassed about anyway? He did what he had to do to save her life, that was all.

But he couldn't lie to himself. As much as he struggled internally, his reaction was plain enough to anyone watching. Very few could have seen him and not understood. *That's not all, is it?* he seemed to be thinking. *That isn't why I cried out to her to come back from the other side.*

"Thank you, Akiba."

She pulled him down and put her lips to his.

At the end of the kiss, he gently whispered, "If it's all right, call me Johnny."

Snake and EVA were on the opposite riverbank, not far from the smoldering husk of her cruiser.

Its nose had already begun to sink under the water's surface, and most of the fire had died out. The corpses of EVA's men had grown cold. Though their lives were lost, Snake wanted to do something to save their remains. But the swim to the shore had taken the last out of him. There was nothing more he could do.

Her men weren't the only bodies left to the river. The surface was littered with them. Some were thrown into the water by explosions on their ships, and some fell accidentally from the bridges, while others jumped of their own accord just to get away from the pain.

Scores of corpses floated downstream, but others, like those who had strapped heavy weapons to themselves or were weighed down by too much body armor, just sank to the bottom of the river.

And this was only one fraction of the field of the dead, with countless others on the roads and bridges.

Snake was sitting with his back against a guardrail post and EVA cradled in his lap. She opened her eyes, and in a voice so soft Snake had to lean forward to hear the words, she said, "You and your brother are together a monster—a shadow scorched into the world by a light shining upon a monster. Unless the light is put out, the shadow cannot be erased. As long as there is light, there will be shadow."

She looked at Snake with unfocused eyes. Her gaze kept drifting and returning, making her seem hollow.

"To return everything to normal...the light must be extinguished."

Her voice was barely a scratching in her throat. Snake put his ear as close to her pale lips as he could.

Her eyes closed, and a single tear ran down her cheek as if it were her own life leaving her.

"And when that happens, you...will be too."

And then she was gone.

Snake watched her face for a time—the face of the woman who loved Big Boss, who bore his children, and who rescued him.

"When I kill Liquid and end my own life, the last of EVA's

children will vanish from the face of the earth," Snake said, to himself more than to me. "That's our fate."

Snake heard the sound of a running engine up above. He looked up to see Drebin and Little Gray leaning over a guard railing at the side of the road, each with a can of NARC in hand.

"Hey, we pride ourselves on service. Let's get you to your friends."

## ACT 4: TWIN SUNS

LET ME TELL you a story about a Snake.

He was one of the twin Snakes, a fragment of the whole. Some called him a shadow.

Like his brother, he grew up knowing nothing of his birth parents. Like his brother, he had a name few were allowed to know. I don't know what people called him before he was given his code designation. Having never called his twin brother by his birth name, he might have died not even knowing his own.

So I can only call him by his code name:

Liquid Snake.

Liquid was raised in the UK to be Solid Snake's shadow. And like Snake, the young Liquid was not aware of, or allowed to learn of, the genetic fate he carried within his DNA. Like Snake, he went into the military at a young age. Then he joined the SIS, a British foreign intelligence service also known as MI6, where he proved as capable a spy as he was a soldier.

Back then, the price of oil was consistent and cheap, and the precious liquid was abundant all over the globe. But the market became flooded, and Iraq saw revenues from the sale of oil—the nation's only commodity—shrink, crippling their efforts to rebuild an economy ravaged by the Iran-Iraq War.

With Iraq and Kuwait's history of conflict over oil fields, tensions heightened between the two states. War was clearly only a matter of time, and the nations of the world sent their intelligence agencies into action.

The only country in the G7 with an existing intelligence network in the region was Great Britain, who had maintained theirs since the colonial period. Although America later came to see Iraq as an enemy—despite having supported Iraq in the Iran-Iraq war—the US government had not yet been able to create an effective network in the region.

Therefore, the SIS sent Liquid to infiltrate Baghdad, and there he remained as a sleeper agent. By nature of his birth in the Les Enfants Terribles project, Liquid was part Japanese and could pass as half Turkish and half Caucasian. More importantly, his language abilities were a match for his brother's, and he achieved a near-fluency in Arabic.

Liquid was gifted. Once inside Iraq, he quickly built connections with resistance fighters among the oppressed Kurds and Islamic fundamentalists repressed as part of Saddam's pan-Arabist agenda.

With the aid of his contacts, Liquid was able to remain inside Baghdad even after the beginning of the Gulf War, amid the heavy presence of Mukhabarat (the Iraqi Intelligence Service) agents and counterspies within the secret police forces known as the al-Amn al-'Amm.

Liquid was productive. He uncovered the locations of Scud missile mobile launching platforms, details of mustard gas production, and the movement of Republican Guard tanks. He sent reports to coalition forces, who used his information to plan a number of missions. For a short time during the war, both Snake and he were in Iraq and not far apart—one an American Green Beret, and the other a spy for the British SIS.

Liquid never understood how he, so adept an agent, got captured. Inside the van, headed for the secret police's headquarters, with a canvas sack over his head, he appraised his situation from every angle.

"Where?" he whispered to himself. "Where did I go wrong? Surely I haven't made a mistake. Did someone rat me out? Did they work backward from the list of bombed installations and find a common leak?"

What it just came down to was this: before the end of the Gulf War, Liquid's luck ran out.

Liquid was trained to resist interrogation. But reality wasn't as easy as training. The tortures of the al-Amn al-'Amm interrogation squads were beyond imagination.

There, Liquid learned how far humanity was capable of going.

A man could become boundlessly cruel. Even a revered figure, once named an enemy, would be seen as less than human. The soldiers who gleefully rubbed salt into Liquid's wounds were Muslims, but everything they did, they did for Saddam. There's not much difference between gods and men.

Given absolute freedom, humans will sink to any depth.

Liquid witnessed what pitiful creatures chains made of men. Prisoner camps were designed to brainwash captives into believing themselves powerless and insignificant. Liquid abhorred all that would constrain life to no purpose but to live.

After the war, he vanished. Not once did he make contact with London. Nor did SIS ever attempt to find him. Maybe the situation was just too uncomfortable for the agency—for you see, they had used him as bait, and allowed his capture in order to secure a new informant valuable to Britain. Liquid was, essentially, a human sacrifice to get intelligence from a man close to Saddam.

Four years later, Liquid was rescued by the US military. I don't know to where he drifted in the intervening years—from what I gather, he wandered the world, building his own international network. He never returned to Britain. Instead, he was scouted by the American forces and selected for the High-Tech Special Forces Unit FOXHOUND. By that time, Colonel Campbell had already left the unit, and when Liquid joined, he effectively became their new commander.

Under his new leadership, FOXHOUND—once a sizable, albeit hand-selected, group—was reformed as a selective ultra-elite force of a limited number of soldiers with superhuman abilities. Their ranks included Sniper Wolf, Psycho Mantis, and Decoy

Octopus—presumably he met them in those four years he spent building his global network.

I don't know if Liquid found Revolver Ocelot himself or if someone else introduced them. Either way, Ocelot was seen at Liquid's side from the very beginning. Whether Liquid went to Ocelot or Ocelot approached FOXHOUND, the result was the same.

Liquid learned of his own secret origin.

Why he had been born. That his father was the legendary mercenary. That the man known to all in the underworld, Solid Snake, was his brother.

When he learned these truths, Liquid again felt the enmity he'd discovered inside the Baghdad prison camp. Anger toward his creators blossomed into a fiery rage.

He revered no gods and no heroes, and had come to feel contempt toward those who did believe in something.

But now he came face-to-face with the knowledge that he had been born nothing more than a mere reproduction of the genetic code of a person he neither revered nor respected.

Suddenly he found himself a prisoner of a fate he'd never wished for.

Idols and gods might be forgotten, but his genes were inescapable. His mind, his personality, his intellect, and his skills were all nothing more than traits inherited from his father.

The prison camp was nothing compared to this realization:

*I'm imprisoned in my own body—and my genes make it a life sentence.*

Surely a certain element of jealousy was involved. He must have surely thought it idiotic that his identical brother, his figurative cellmate trapped with the same DNA, came to be known as the legendary hero and as the man who made the impossible possible.

The accolades bestowed upon his brother were absolute proof of his imprisonment.

Liquid started to fight against his fate—to find freedom from despair and to put his very life on the line; to shout at the world, "I am me! I am myself and no one else! I am here!"

And he would do it by fulfilling his father's dreams.

He saw it not as inheriting his father's fate.

He would do what his father couldn't. And what his brother couldn't.

If he were successful, he would find liberation from his curse.

That day, the earth was quiet.

A world once filled with the ceaseless gunfire of manufactured revolutions found a moment of peace. All across the surface of this big blue marble we call home, wars fell silent, as if mankind's wholesale butchery against his fellow man had been nothing more than some distant lie.

In Africa, in the Middle East, in Russia, and in Southeast Asia, soldiers all across the globe looked up to the skies.

*What happened?* they must have wondered. Their weapons, along with those of their compatriots and their enemies, suddenly locked and became inoperable. The bewildered combatants fiddled with their rifles before ultimately giving up and retiring from the front lines. A few with naked guns were still able to fight, but their opponents only folded and surrendered with their arms in the air.

In all the varied combat zones across the world, soldiers falling back to their bases looked up to the heavens. In some places, they looked up to the blue, cloudless sky, while in others they saw countless stars, but all were filled with the same feeling—even those of no faith.

Had God, or some godlike being, descended upon Earth?

Had we angered Him with our foolish ways?

Sure, even with their guns disabled, they could still have done battle with hatchets and bayonets, even knives, but to most of the soldiers killing another man at close range with their own hands was unimaginable. Even only a small fraction of front-line troops in World War II ever fired at the enemy.

Even when their own lives were in immediate danger, people

tended to avoid shooting one another. The Vietnam War saw the development of new training methods to condition soldiers to overcome the natural resistance to shooting, but many of them suffered for it after their return home. Psychological damage threw their lives into ruin.

That day, not one single fighting unit anywhere in the world attempted to fight by bludgeoning skulls or thrusting blades into hearts. All conflict had ceased.

I was in the cargo bay of *Nomad*, concerned about Snake's condition. He had already started to recover from the mission, but half of his face was badly burned, and his airway, ravaged by the smoke and the intense heat, sent out an endless torrent of coughs and phlegm.

A call came in on the monitor. I accepted the connection, and Colonel Campbell appeared on the display. A woman—off-screen, probably Rose—was just finishing straightening his tie. The conjugal display stirred up a flash of irritation in me. Sunny remained tirelessly at Raiden's side. His dialysis and treatment would still take a little while longer.

I asked the colonel, "How's the White House responding? And the public?"

"The president has yet to make an official announcement. But the media are starting to pick up on it."

Between coughs, Snake added derisively, "He probably thinks he can still keep information under control."

Despite his dilapidated state, Snake's mind was still sharp. And yet at times I couldn't bear to look at him anymore—to see my friend possessed of the will to fight, to see him even now attempting to fulfill his duties.

"No, not this time," Campbell said. "The war economy has ground to a complete halt. It's tough to downplay a crisis of these proportions. War economy-related stocks are already going into a free fall."

Snake laughed. To think that the extinction of war was a crisis.

He said, "They must be shitting themselves at the White House right now."

"In any case," said the colonel, "the people of the world had better sleep soundly while they still can. Liquid's insurrection is about to begin."

Indeed, Liquid's control over the System had created the calm that fell over the world. The PMCs weren't the only forces controlled by nanomachines and ID tags—the US Army, Navy, Air Force, and Marine Corps were also crippled. America's entire armed forces were at the mercy of the System.

Liquid would become known in the history books as the man who simultaneously brought peace to the world and unleashed global war upon it—although I guess that would depend on someone still being around to write history books.

Campbell continued, "The first thing he'll do is try to destroy the System the Patriots built to control the US."

I narrowed my eyes. What good would that do him? He'd already seized the System—that was essentially the same as destroying it.

When I said as much, Campbell explained, "Supreme authority still resides with JD, which the Patriots still command."

The three remaining AIs of the Patriots—TJ, AL, and TR—constantly gathered information from the global networks—taxes, family registers (births, deaths, marriages, and so on), medical data, economic indicators, biological data from nanomachines, and of course, the SOP. The computers collected exabytes of information each day and utilized them to create the proper context in the world and to construct the narrative for the human race—and by proper context, I mean the context the Patriots thought proper.

No single core was able to handle the massive amount of data alone. The workload had to be spread out in some way. But the Patriots didn't want to give the AIs a free hand. They created a central unifying core AI to make the adjustments necessary to prevent any discrepancies from arising between the three narrators.

Liquid had reconstructed GW, the AI we thought we'd destroyed years before. Even when disabled, it had maintained a hidden connection with JD.

To explain it in simpler terms, Liquid shrewdly disguised himself as GW to get into JD's family. Once he had been accepted, he showed them Big Boss's genetic information and declared himself the rightful heir.

All that was left was to kill the master of the house, JD, and then Liquid would take over. Once this was accepted by the rest of the family, no one could stop him.

So far, Liquid had only seized the SOP, which controlled the soldiers and their firearms. Without higher authority, he had no access to American nukes and ballistic missiles.

"Which is why," said Campbell, his face grave, "Liquid plans to launch a nuclear strike on JD. In orbit."

We had overheard that bit of information thanks to the stowaway Mk. II on Liquid's patrol boat.

Liquid had discovered JD's location.

Outer space.

The Patriots' core AI quietly floated through the cold void within a cloud of space junk, hidden among the countless fragments and metal husks of abandoned Cold War-era spy satellites.

I don't think I could think of a better refuge for the Patriots—after all, they were born out of the Cold War. Amid the drifting refuse of the past, the satellite looked down, godlike, upon the tiny wriggling humans below.

Liquid had announced his intention to use REX. They were going to take REX and use its nuclear missile launcher to destroy JD. With the destruction of the control AI, the master authority would transfer to the System, just like the order of succession in the event of a presidential assassination. The System itself was created upon the foundation of the S3 Program tested on Big Shell, which was controlled by none other than GW. If Liquid's attack were to succeed, GW's priority within the AIs would rise to one.

The only obstacle was the nuclear warhead needed for his plan.

Nuclear weapons weren't under control of the SOP—the Patriots hadn't allowed that—and remained fully within JD's grasp. It wouldn't matter if he had REX if he couldn't operate it.

That was when I remembered. "Oh," I said.

"What?" Snake asked.

"REX was scrapped before the Sons of the Patriots System was implemented."

"Of course. The railgun."

Metal Gear REX was outfitted with a shoulder-mounted railgun that could fire nuclear warheads undetectable by radar. When I headed up REX's construction, I had been led to believe the railgun was designed to intercept nukes, not deploy them.

"Indeed," said Campbell. "REX's railgun can launch a stealth nuclear warhead into space, unconstrained by the System. In short, it's the only device they have that is able to launch a nuke. Liquid's going to use it to kill JD and deliver the coup de grace to the Patriots' reign."

Nine years ago, I created the Metal Gear–class mobile nuclear launcher. Told by AT Corp that it was a defensive weapon, I leapt at the opportunity to create a two-legged robot like the ones I'd seen in anime. I never questioned my bosses.

On Shadow Moses, Liquid described it to Snake as "the demon weapon that will drag the world into the twenty-first century." But now the robot was about to change our twenty-first century into something entirely new.

I asked Campbell, "Where's REX now?"

He lifted his shoulders and looked at me as if it should be obvious. "I think you know. A long-forgotten base, in US territory, outside the Patriots' control. The place where Liquid made his debut. The place that serves as a monument to him. Off the Alaskan coast, in the Fox Archipelago."

Snake spoke first. "Shadow Moses Island."

Where Snake and Liquid's battle began. Their ground zero.

"If Liquid destroys JD," Campbell warned, "and his GW

assumes total control over the System, he'll have the world groveling at his feet. And no one will be able to stop him. Not even the Patriots."

I looked to Snake. His face, as I'd expected, showed no emotion. He already knew what he had to do.

I turned away. Hadn't he already done everything he could?

I hated myself for being unable to do anything more for my friend, this old man who would have to end his own life in three months.

Campbell said, "You're the only one who can save the world now. Snake, I'm counting on you."

I hated him for saying that.

The world? When had Snake ever asked to be responsible for the entire world? My friend—my best friend—would be dead soon enough. Couldn't you let him be?

Campbell cut the transmission.

Snake stood and tottered over to Raiden's medical station at the side of the cargo bay. The cyborg was covered with cables hooked to monitoring devices, and tubes filled with white liquid wove in and out of his body. Thanks to QR codes, Dr. Madnar had quickly been able to locate the access shunt to the bloodway that substituted for his arteries and veins.

A computer hooked up to a bar scanner could read the tags covering Raiden's exoskeleton and display any relevant information for each part—its capabilities, related components, the manufacturer, the production date, even URLs for online help pages. Just as nanomachines filled soldiers' bodies and constantly monitored data about their health, labels covered Raiden's artificial body and contained data about his manufacture.

Sunny was thankful for the tags. In fact, they might very well have saved Raiden's life. If she had needed to stop to look up each and every part, he might not have survived. Still, something about the shroud of wireless ID tags rubbed Snake the wrong way.

Sunny must have thought Snake had come to take Raiden,

because she turned to him and said, "N-no! Jack can't go. He's not ready yet."

Then Raiden spoke.

"Let me go, Sunny."

He slowly shifted his arm. The movement was sluggish; he clearly hadn't yet recovered. His voice wasn't even his own, but that of a speaking device in his throat.

"No!" Sunny said sternly. "Your dialysis isn't done yet."

"I'll be fine."

Raiden was strapped to the medical bed by several data cables. As much as he tried to move, the cords held him in place. The sight made me think of Gulliver captured by the Lilliputians. Except Raiden had been so weakened, I couldn't imagine he had the strength to snap free from his binds.

When told he wasn't ready yet, Raiden looked straight into my eyes. I shrank back, overpowered by the force of his gaze.

"From now on," Raiden said, "I'm living my life by my own will. Not a proxy life, as a slave to someone else's scenario."

Snake stared at Raiden, remembering what the young man had said in Manhattan—how Solidus killed his parents and turned him into a child soldier, and how he fled from that nightmare to America, where the Patriots, as part of the S3 Project, used him as a pawn and manipulated him into becoming another Snake.

None other than Solid Snake himself freed Raiden from that life.

Only after he met Snake did Raiden begin to walk his own path.

So Snake felt responsibility for meddling in another's life and skewing its direction. He let out a sigh, quiet, but heavy with his thoughts.

"I'm a shadow," he said. "One that no light will shine upon. As long as you follow me, you'll never see the light of day."

Perhaps Snake felt responsible for Meryl too. And I didn't want to think about it, but maybe he even did for me. Maybe my friend had always carried a sense of guilt: *These young people who look*

*up to me, can I even begin to tell myself that their lives are blessed for it?*
*If I'm the Legendary Hero, wouldn't the legend be of bringing nothing but*
*misfortune upon others?*

Those feelings were a part of why he now fought for an ending.

Raiden spoke more to himself than as a response to Snake's words. "You and I are both just pawns in this proxy war. But once this is over, we will have our freedom. I'll release you. It's the only way I'll ever be free."

"Raiden," Snake said firmly, "what I said five years ago…that's not what I meant."

"I've got nothing to lose."

I shook my head. He said he had nothing to lose, and yet he still clung to something—maybe to the fight itself. The sight was too painful to watch.

His near obsession must have tortured Snake, who leveled stern eyes at him and remonstrated, "Don't be an idiot. You know you've got someone to protect."

"Snake," he said, putting on a smile so awkward he looked like he was choking on it. "I'm the rain. The light of day holds nothing for me."

"You've got it all wrong," Snake said. He was still young; he should've still had the strength to bring light somewhere.

Snake put his hand on Raiden's shoulder. "You're the lightning. You can still shine through the darkness."

"The lightning…"

"Raiden, look at me."

Suddenly, Snake ripped the bandage from his left cheek and revealed the scorched skin beneath. "Do you see this? I have no future. In a few months, I'm going to be a weapon of mass destruction."

Raiden looked into the face of the ragged old soldier, skin battered and burned and peeling off. This close, his flesh gave off a distinct, unpleasant odor—the stench of old age, perhaps. Heavy, sagging eyelids crushed the spirit from eyes that had been so astute and fearless when they first met on the Big Shell.

This was the face of a man with no future, an old man held up solely by a longing for the closure only atonement could bring. Snake wasn't fighting for the future. He wasn't fighting to hold on to something. Snake fought for what he had already lost. This was the face of a man who had nothing left to lose.

But Raiden still had a woman who cared for him.

He had something to hold on to—a place to come home to.

"You have a family," Snake said.

Raiden's eyes flew open. "I have no family!"

With his outburst, the medical observation systems sounded a warning in unison.

Raiden's hardened exoskeletal body began to convulse. I dashed to his bedside, and Sunny wrapped her small arms around him, holding him down, while Snake shook his head with finality.

Again Raiden shouted, "I have no one!"

His wounds were already life-threatening—if it continued, Raiden's agitated state could prove fatal. Sunny worked the infusion pump to temporarily increase the flow of painkillers.

Then Raiden spoke. Not with the artificial sound from his throat, but from his own mouth, he said, "I have always been alone."

As his chin moved, the oxygen mask, only loosely held in place, slipped to the floor. Teardrops ran from his white eyes down his cheeks and onto the bed.

And then the drugs pulled his consciousness back into a opiate haze.

His unsteady breaths regained a steady rhythm, and his eyelids grew heavy and shrouded his eyes. I let out a relieved sigh, and my tensed back muscles returned to normal.

Softly, Snake spoke Raiden's name. The man whom Snake, albeit unintentionally, had torn from a better and rightful life to further his own cause.

Just as he fell into sleep, Raiden squeezed out the raspy words: "Don't leave me here alone."

Snake got on one knee, drew close to Raiden's ear, and gently whispered to the unconscious man, "This is my fight. My destiny."

Snake's words seemed as much directed at himself, reaffirming: This fight isn't Raiden's. It's not Meryl's. You don't have to get hurt.

Snake stood, removed the bandages covering his injured body, and retrieved his equipment and maintenance tools from the storage area at the rear of the bay. Just as I decided to help him, he began to cough violently. The noise was terrible and sickening, like the depths of his lungs were convulsing.

I ran over and went to pat his back, but he shook off my hand and put Naomi's autoinjector to his neck. Its contents had mostly calmed him down, but clearly the drug's effectiveness was diminishing.

I couldn't take it anymore. The emotions I'd suppressed through Campbell's call came out all at once.

"Snake, stop," I said. "You can't handle any more of this."

He put his hand to the wall and tried to steady his breathing. "I'm not dying right this moment."

"That's not what I mean. You can't beat Liquid. He's got the Patriots' own control system on his side. Not only are weapons useless, but the US military is in shambles. And even if it weren't, Liquid's has the men and machines to match it."

All else aside, our opponent controlled sixty percent of the global military might, but now any forces that would stand against him were frozen as if by magic. So why did this man alone have to fight?

"Things can't get any worse, Snake. Face it. We've lost," I said. "We never stood a chance."

I'd let my emotions vent, and Snake just looked at me. He never appreciated becoming the subject of concern. Although he might have jokingly complained at times, he always dealt with everything himself. Snake, of all people, knew he couldn't fight this by himself. At Shadow Moses and the Big Shell, he learned that there were situations in this world he couldn't make it through alone.

That was all the more reason for him to fear others getting hurt on his behalf. Even when the battles had been too much for him alone, as long as he could make any of the responsibility his own, Snake always carried the guilt.

Having seen the crossing of Snake and Raiden's lives, I don't think I ever found Snake's tragic sense of responsibility so painful as with Raiden, who had come to embrace battle.

Snake, eyes still at the wall, put his hand on my shoulder.

"It's not about winning or losing," he said. "I—no, we—started this. And it's our duty to finish it."

Then, having nothing left to say, he returned to his equipment check.

As I helped him prepare for combat, I quietly cried. I'd known that would be his response; I'd known I couldn't stop him no matter how hard I tried. I think Snake noticed I was crying, but he didn't speak. The two of us worked together in silence.

With the fate of the world and that of humanity at stake, I prayed for one single thing: for the noble soul of my friend, who continued to fight despite a body covered with injuries, to find peace.

## 2

THE PLACE WHERE our battle began.

A small lump of rock surrounded by the sea.

The Aleutian Islands stretched like a necklace across the Pacific from the chin of Alaska to Russia's Kamchatka Peninsula. The Aleutian low-pressure area drew in Arctic air and often left the chain of islands exposed to tremendous cold.

But despite being so close to the North Pole, the climate of the archipelago was milder than Siberia or Anchorage, partly due to volcanic activity along the Ring of Fire and the Aleutian Current flowing along its southern edge. The Arctic was generally warmer than the Antarctic also because the surface of the ocean has a tendency to retain heat. The temperature above frozen ground and thick layers of snow differed from that above water.

The Fox Archipelago sat on the Alaskan side of the Aleutians, and the island, birthed from the volcanic fires of Old Moses after World War II, lay close enough to the island group that a ship would need to take care when sailing between.

The Aleutian fishermen considered the area a place of great evil, and none came near. Even if they had, there were no natural harbors. Sheer cliff face surrounded the land on all sides.

The fishermen called the island the Shadow of Moses.

Snake rode the freight elevator from the cargo dock and arrived at the island's surface.

A blizzard awaited him. The fury of the Aleutian Low spread

across the sea. Because the weather made landing an aircraft too dangerous, Snake had approached the island first by submarine, then by a smaller submersible called an SDV, or Swimmer Delivery Vehicle. For the last stretch of the icy Bering Sea, he swam. An injection of peptides temporarily boosted Snake's blood glucose level and lowered his body's freezing point to below zero, preventing him from freezing in the Aleutian water and drowning at sea. The concept worked the same way as mankind did during the Ice Age—essentially cultivating diabetes.

Despite the severe weather, the island's occupiers seemed determined to fly a helicopter. Snake hid behind a stack of containers beside the elevator and watched incredulously as the helicopter's rotor spun up. The Soviet gunship had once been the terror of Afghani jihadist fighters.

"A Hind D..."

Shadow Moses was supposed to be an American base, yet here was this attack beast built by their former adversary.

"Colonel, what's a Russian gunship doing here?"

"I have no idea," the colonel said over the codec, "but it looks like our F-16s got their attention. Now's your best chance to slip in unnoticed—"

Another voice, sounding incredibly out of place, cut in.

"Wow!" she said. She sounded like a teenage girl. "He must be crazy to fly a Hind in this kind of weather."

"Who's that?" Snake asked.

"Oh," the colonel replied, "sorry, I haven't introduced you two yet. This is Mei Ling. She designed your Soliton radar system."

"Nice to meet you, Snake." Mei's voice possessed a childlike, innocent quality. "It's an honor to speak to a living legend like yourself."

That, of course, was nine years ago.

Snake's infiltration of the nuclear warhead storage facility captured by FOXHOUND began there. Mei Ling, who at that time had still been a young undergrad, now captained *Missouri*. Her transfer might have been a sinecure, but the position still enabled her to wield a significant portion of the military's resources. She had used the position of the Mk. II's last transmissions to predict the course of Liquid's ship.

Just as we'd thought, Liquid had come to Shadow Moses. Mei obtained photos of the island taken by a civilian—and free of SOP control—imagery satellite. A large, dark shape resembling Liquid's ship had hidden within the rocky shore.

The US government had sidelined Mei's and Meryl's careers out of a desire to leave Shadow Moses in the past, forgotten. All records of the incident had been falsified or erased with no trace left behind, as if nothing had ever happened. Metal Gear REX's broken husk remained there, abandoned, along with its stealth nukes and the stockpile of warheads left over from the Cold War.

Mei offered to give us support. The decommissioned USS *Missouri* survived less as an actual battleship than as a training vessel. There had been no need—or funds—to retrofit the ship to be compatible with the System, and now *Missouri* was the only craft in the fleet still able to move. Once, I jokingly told Mei it reminded me of the *Galactica*, but she never watched much TV and didn't get the reference.

Now Snake had returned to the same heliport where he'd been introduced to Mei over the codec. We never looked back fondly upon the many hardships that led up to this day, and yet Snake standing here, back at the same place, stirred up strong feelings of nostalgia. The facility looked mostly unchanged after all those years.

Alone in the helipad, Snake remained still.

"Snake," I said. "Are you all right?"

"I was just thinking how different this place looks during the day."

I had spent a long time on the island through REX's development and testing, and was familiar with the facility at any hour. But now that I thought about it, this was Snake's first time encountering the heliport in daylight; the infiltration op had taken place in the middle of the night.

The cargo dock he'd entered by had since been reclaimed by the ocean, a victim of global warming. The elevator was frozen over, no longer usable. But that wasn't an obstacle for us, because this time Snake didn't come by sea. I had rented a civilian helicopter and brought Snake, and the Metal Gear Mk. III, to the island.

FOXHOUND and the Next-Generation Special Forces Unit of Genome Soldiers were nowhere in sight. I think Snake was a little spooked by this empty, daylight version of the heliport.

If not to put him at ease, I gave Snake a word of advice.

"I don't see anybody around, but there are unmanned sentries patrolling the area. Be careful out there."

"Yeah."

His voice sounded more pained than ever.

In a few short days, he'd traveled the world from the Middle East to South America, to Eastern Europe, and now Alaska. Snake's body had aged too much to withstand the severe changes in temperature and air pressure. The cold air carried by the Aleutian Low sent the temperature to twenty below. The lungs of a seventy-year-old couldn't last long.

Snake crossed the heliport and stood before the facility's giant doors.

When he was last here, the front gate was shut down tight, and he had to find entry through an air duct. But now the doors had been left wide open, and Snake found himself feeling oddly crestfallen and unsatisfied.

And wasn't there a surveillance camera here?

Snake turned his eyes to the right of the door where a CCTV camera had once kept vigilant watch for intruders. Left exposed to the ocean wind and the cold, without anyone to maintain it, the camera had gradually rusted away, and fell to the ground where it now lay half buried beneath the snow.

Snake stepped into the building.

*This is so gothic horror*, I thought. Inside, the sound of snow striking the building became an eerie howl echoing inside the empty space of the former tank hangar.

This was our era's version of the old abandoned castles of Eastern Europe. The only way I'd have felt it more surely would be if Count Dracula himself showed up. Him or Frankenstein's monster.

The room had been part of the armory, where tanks stood in rows, with the infirmary and weapon storerooms below ground. Meryl and Snake first met within the building. She had been part of the training exercise and was locked in a cell by Liquid when she refused to cooperate in his uprising. Meryl escaped by tricking her guard.

"Keep moving, Snake," I said. "Head to the nuclear warhead storage building. There's not much time left."

"No, there isn't," Snake said, his voice heavy. Though I hadn't meant to, perhaps I had sent his thoughts to his own body.

The FOXDIE virus Snake unknowingly carried had left both Decoy Octopus, who had taken on the guise of DARPA chief Donald Anderson, and ArmsTech president Kenneth Baker dead beneath this building.

Now that same virus was undergoing a terrible transformation. Within his blood, the viral signatures that detected Baker and Decoy Octopus were eroding.

As Snake exited the hangar and began to cross the snowy canyon that led to the warhead storage building, a thought came to me. Viruses, like influenza or HIV, could experience sudden mutations to withstand antimicrobials and medicine. As far as modern medical science had come, the viral variations numbered in the billions and trillions—surely one would slip through the net and continue to evolve, and survive.

Every virus evolved. Why would anyone expect man-made nanomachines to behave any differently?

No matter how careful the creation, how strict the parameters—

only kill people with these specific genetic patterns, for example—once the virus was released into the wild, it would someday escape from the intentions of its makers. For viruses, that's simply the natural way.

The researchers should have seen this coming. Men weren't gods; we could never hope to control billions—no, trillions—of separate viruses. Taking the capability to suddenly mutate into account, the creation of nanomachine viruses was not a technique mankind was capable of mastering. An independent life-form, once beyond the expectations of its creators, could not be stopped.

The SOP could be said to be a virus with more hosts than any other. It couldn't be contracted through the air, but with this many carriers, the System could someday evolve far beyond the Patriots' imagination.

Snake walked across the field where he had first confronted the FOXHOUND member Vulcan Raven, a giant man with Inuit blood. The ground itself echoed with Raven's dying words:

*You are a Snake that was not created by nature.*

*In the natural world, there is no such thing as boundless slaughter. There is always an end to it. But you are different.*

*The path you walk has no end. Each step you take is paved with the corpses of your enemies...*

He might have been right. Just as the shaman predicted, Snake's battle had continued. Raven foresaw a new world created by a man-made snake. His memory followed Snake across the field and into the nuclear warhead storage facility.

I shuddered.

The hundreds of nukes kept here for disassembly remained in racks along the walls and stacks of boxes in the middle of the room, and not under a particularly close watch. Anyone who knew of this location could easily obtain the warheads.

But was that fear groundless? With the Patriots' control of information, almost no one knew of the facility. For military reasons, the island had never been marked on a map. Unmanned weapons, like Gekko and Scarabs, hired from a PMC would provide sufficient security. Beyond the storage room would be another snow field, where two twin transmission towers stood like miniatures of the former World Trade Center, and across that, the entrance to the deep underground service bay where Snake once destroyed REX.

I spurred Snake on. With the frost-covered rows of last-generation warheads left untouched within these ruins, the space seemed to me a catacomb stuffed with buried relics of the Cold War. Snake walked straight through the room to the security door on the other side.

The gate had frozen over, still locked. Snake asked me what he should do, but I was already thinking of an answer.

*Security is shut down altogether. He can't release the lock without activating it.*

*He'll have to go there.*

*There, he can log in to the security system.*

"I've got it, Snake. My old office is close by. If the power's on, you should be able to unlock the door from there. And if you check the facility records, we can find out REX's status and who's been in and out. You remember where it is?"

"I'm not senile yet," Snake snapped.

He knew I was making fun of his strong front. I laughed at the expected response and said, "Just to be safe, I'm marking it on your map, Old Snake."

∿

By the time the young man noticed something was wrong, he was already too late.

From the hallway outside the lab came otherworldly screams. The walls were soundproofed, and the doors, governed by the Personal Area Network, were bomb-proofed and made of thick metal. The screams must have been unimaginably loud to make it into the lab and the young man's ears.

And there was only one door from the lab to the hallway.

These days, scientists had to maintain the physical fitness and self-confidence of a lawyer or a pro athlete in order to keep their patrons. But this young man was an exception: lanky and without apparent regard for his health or allure. His hair was as frazzled as a bird's nest, and he hadn't bothered to shave.

He quickly scanned the room but saw no place to hide. Sparks flew from the door's security panel. The door opened in a cloud of smoke, and a lone figure stepped into the room.

The figure's silhouette was shockingly beautiful. But the young man couldn't tell if *body* was even the right word. Any way he looked at it, the intruder was no normal man.

"A powered exoskeleton?" the young man said. "Who are you?"

What at first had looked like muscle was an exoskeletal shell with complex detailing running in all directions. The intruder was a cyborg straight out of anime.

The cyborg spoke behind a mask. "Where is my friend?"

His voice, strange, and clearly modified by some machine, echoed eerily behind the full head mask devoid of all feature save for a single, glowing orange eye.

But none of that mattered. The young man's attention was focused on the long katana-like blade in the cyborg's right hand.

Was this the source of the guards' screams?

The young man stammered, "What…what are you talking about?"

The sword-wielding half man, half machine steadily advanced, backing the young man into the corner.

The young man was frozen, with nowhere left to run, when the cyborg suddenly stopped in place and slowly turned away. Another man, in a full bodysuit, stood in the middle of the room. His suit appeared to have some sort of body armor, but at least it wasn't a powered exoskeleton.

The cyborg ninja cried out, his voice trembling with joy. "Snake! I've been waiting for you!"

"Who are you?" the man in the bodysuit asked. The cyborg had called him Snake, but Snake didn't seem to recognize this twenty-first-century ninja.

"Neither enemy nor friend." The cyborg's voice possessed an unsettling tinge of intoxication. "I am back from a world where such words are meaningless. Now you and I will battle to the death."

"What do you want?"

"I've waited a long time for this day. Now I want to enjoy the moment."

The young man muttered nervously to himself, "What's with these guys? They're like something out of anime."

The two men standing before him, their attire, and the words they exchanged contained no trace of reality. Only the terror of that blade was real. Only the unadulterated feeling: *I don't want to die.*

"What is it?" the man called Snake asked. "Revenge?"

"No. Nothing so trivial. A fight to the death with you. Only then can my soul find peace. I will kill you, or you will kill me. It makes no difference."

The young man, hearing the ecstasy in the ninja's voice, ran. But his mind was so overcome with fear, he had only escaped straight into the open locker behind.

"Hah! Fine," the cyborg laughed with a glance at the witless hiding job. "He can watch from inside there."

"I need that man. Keep your hands off him."

Snake emanated defiance, and the ninja drew joy from it, coursing through his body.

"Now, make me feel it," the ninja said. "Make me feel alive again!"

Nine years had passed, but the lab hadn't changed a bit.

The room had been untouched by the wind and snow, and went unexposed to the sea air. Only a layer of dust had deposited itself in the solitude. The workspace remained in the same disheveled state from the battle between Snake and the cyborg ninja, who was later revealed to be Gray Fox.

For nine years the dust had settled—on top of the work desks, the supercomputer racks, and the locker where I had hid—and now the stirred-up particles sent Snake into a fit of coughing. When the violent coughing showed no sign of stopping, Snake pulled out Naomi's autoinjector and hurriedly pressed it against his neck. While he took a few moments to collect himself, I scouted the room with the Mk. III.

Much had happened here.

At a computer behind a glass partition, many times I had run calculations in order to strengthen REX and simulations for his walking algorithms. I built mathematical models and made modification after modification. I calculated and recalculated and recalculated again, until finally, one day, REX took its first step. I could never forget that day.

An incredible number of man-hours went into the formulae that maintained REX's balance in motion—how the robot's enormous parts should connect, how much pressure should be put where, how much strain the parts could withstand. A mind-boggling array of hundreds of interconnected operations comprised REX's ability to walk.

When Snake had recovered, I asked him to lift the Mk. III on top of the workspace. The terminal's input jack was still operational, and I jacked in the Metal Gear's manipulator arm.

I probed the electrical system. Most lines on the island were still active, and I wouldn't have too much trouble rerouting the necessary power. I started by restoring the lab's lifeblood.

One by one, the monitors came back to life. The climate control exhaled for the first time in nine years and sent dust dancing into the air.

"This version is totally obsolete," I said to myself. "This is going to take a little work…"

Using the password from when I hacked into the system to save Snake, I bypassed the security. As I worked, Snake sat on the edge of the desktop and glanced at the corner of the room with the locker, door still open.

Embarrassed, I said, "This room isn't conjuring up any unpleasant memories, is it?"

"No," Snake said, but I couldn't help but wonder if the carpet where I wet myself as I cowered in fear still carried the stain. How could I not think about it?

"You saved my life," I said.

Until this moment I hadn't realized that I'd spent all this time with Snake never having expressed my appreciation to him for rescuing me from Frank Jaeger. I was profoundly grateful to have finally said something, and to have come back to this place, remembering everything—including my life—Snake had given to me.

There were a mountain of things I needed to thank him for before he passed on, yet amid the day-to-day struggle, I'd forgotten them all.

Snake, as if I hadn't said anything, was absorbed in his own memories.

"Naomi hated them for what they did to Frank's body," he said, "but it was I who crippled him in the first place. She must have hated me too."

Deep regret overcame me. Some serious introspection seemed required into what exactly I had expected out of her. And yet the sin I carried was so similar to hers. Our own technological creations had twisted the world, and we shared a common guilt.

And so, carelessly, I trusted her.

I said to Snake, "But she was only using us to atone for her sins."

"So what?"

Snake's response left me confused. "You forgot already? She betrayed you! She stole your blood!"

He shook his head. "If that was all, she would have been done with us in South America. Why'd she join us afterward?"

"Well, I..."

I didn't know what to say. Snake's observation was dead-on. Naomi had seduced me. She used me. Blinded by shame and regret, I hadn't seen anything else.

"She has us come rescue her," Snake said, "and then she turns around and goes straight back to Liquid. Why would she do that?"

"I don't know," I replied. It didn't make any sense. If her goal had been to obtain Snake's blood for the SOP, she could have escaped South America with Vamp. And I had trouble believing she'd boarded *Nomad* to plant some transmitter or bug. She might have come to kidnap Sunny, but she hadn't done that either.

There were a great many things she could have done for Liquid's benefit, but didn't. So what was her aim?

Now it seemed she was back with Liquid.

I pulled the security access logs. The passageways had remained nearly empty over the nine years since we left the island. Now, just a few hours earlier, two others had come to the facility. I routed the security footage to the Mk. III's flip display and showed Snake the two visitors.

Naomi...and Vamp.

"The beauty and the beast," Snake said.

The hallway was dim, and the feed was low-res and filled with static, but the tall man in the long coat and the woman in the dress couldn't have been anyone else. They walked down the underground passage to REX's hangar. Into the Cold War gothic ruins entered the vampire and the beauty. I rubbed my eyelids, fighting back a wave of impatience at having been beaten to the facility.

We were late. Like always.

But this time, if we failed to catch up, there would be no future.

Not for us.

And not for the world.

~~~

Snake emerged through the unlocked security door of the warhead storeroom and onto another field of snow.

The raging wind sheared off the top of the snowpack and kicked up clouds of white. Visibility wasn't even ten feet. So as not to get lost, I guided Snake with the Mk. III.

We passed between the twin transmission towers and onto a comparatively flat plain. Then I realized where we were: where Snake had defeated Sniper Wolf.

"Wolf," I said to the computer screen.

The Mk. III's camera showed only the blowing white snow, but this was where the woman I once loved now rested.

When I was in FOXHOUND's captivity, she had looked after the island's resident wolf-dogs. She was different from the rest of her group—she was kind to the animals, and to me. Maybe you'll laugh, but that was enough to make me fall in love. At the time, Snake called it Stockholm Syndrome, the psychological tendency for kidnap victims to feel a sense of closeness or friendship toward their captors.

Whatever the case might have been, Wolf was the first woman I'd met in a long time whom I could approach without feeling scared.

Without evoking that despicable relationship with my stepmother that broke the bond between brother and sister.

For so very long, women scared me. Whenever one entered my life, my world came further unhinged.

But Wolf was different. She was born a Kurd—the name of her people came from the word for wolf—and to be born a Kurd was to live on a battlefield. She was raised fighting against Turkey and Iraq in the defense of her very existence.

Through the scope of her sniper rifle, she watched the battlefield, both a part of it yet at the same time distant. Perhaps I sympathized with her. Burdened with painful memories of my family, I too kept the world, and all its people, at a distance.

And here on this field I lost my first love in a long time.

There had been no avoiding the confrontation. Snake needed to defeat her, and Wolf needed to kill him. Neither had any cause to hesitate. I never even factored in.

If I mistrusted Naomi because she had reason to hate Snake, I guess I had reason to hate him too. He'd killed the woman I cared for. Of course, I've never even entertained the sentiment, but I'd bet there were more people who hated Snake for a similar reason than there were fingers on my hands.

Snake never wanted to fight, but he lived with the consequences of his battles. Those he killed might have had people who loved them. People left with enmity and the lingering pain of having lost someone dear. Their revilement, viscid and rotten, worked into his being and refused to let go.

Perhaps their concentrated emotions were the cause of Snake's age.

It wasn't Snake's fault. Snake had never asked for this.

No matter how many times I said it, I doubted the dead, joined with the gods and no longer with mortal reason, would ever understand.

Snake was a sacrificial lamb. He attracted the world's ire, but like the lamb up for offering, the responsibility wasn't his own.

Through the wind and the snow came sorrowful howls, as if the wolf-dogs were still in mourning after these nine years.

Did the dogs that gathered around her body that day still hate Snake?

I found that hard to believe. I hoped they didn't.

I prayed the wolf-dogs had forgiven him and come to understand as I did; there had been no other way.

3

HIGH ABOVE STEEL frames intertwined in intricate arches, recalling a great Buddhist temple.

*Or perhaps a cathedral for the Cold War*, I thought. Though REX itself might have been, as Liquid had said, the demon weapon that ushered in the twenty-first century, the ideas and thoughts that birthed it belonged decidedly to the previous era. A ghost of the Cold War, the architecture of REX's maintenance bay a testament to its nature.

Atop the platform as large as a sandlot baseball field, REX had once stood. When we were still working on the robot, catwalks extended from all sides of the sanctuary, surrounding it like a building under construction.

But now that space lay vacant, and the catwalks littered the floor where they had fallen nine years ago when Liquid raised the platform to take REX to the floor above.

The aboveground entrance room to the supply tunnel became the graveyard for my largest creation. To my astonishment, Snake had soundly destroyed that monster. Though he benefited from my advice and Frank Jaeger's self-sacrifice, the victory could still only have come at the hands of the legendary hero.

"Hop on, Snake," I said. "I'll send 'er up."

Snake lifted the Mk. III and set it on top of REX's platform. The Metal Gear's remains awaited at the lift's destination, the supply tunnel entrance. I opened the cover to the floor access panel and inserted the Mk. III's manipulator into the jack.

With a heavy shudder, the massive lift awoke from hibernation. Alarms reverberated through the chamber.

"If everything's been left the same," I said, "REX will be here."

Snake watched the upper floor draw closer.

The weapon Snake destroyed. The weapon that stole the life of his mentor and friend, Frank Jaeger. The weapon I created, and my sin.

After another large shudder, the alarms quieted.

We had arrived. The platform fit neatly into the floor.

"REX," I whispered.

The supply tunnel entrance was a dim space, roughly the size and shape of a gymnasium. REX's corpse leaned against a wall, unmoved since Snake had destroyed the machine. The robot's head was askew, like a confused puppy dog unsure of what just happened. Despite a massive frame, the Metal Gear looked small now.

As we got closer, I realized why REX seemed to have become so diminutive.

"Look," I said. "The railgun's been removed!"

I clicked my tongue. Had Liquid already left with the railgun? He didn't need the whole REX to launch his nuke, only the naked cannon, free of the System's control.

"Damn," Snake said. "Have they already taken off with it?"

I said, "I'll check," and sent the Mk. III around the back of REX's giant legs, to the maintenance port that would provide access to REX's work logs.

Perhaps the railgun had been taken much earlier. The Patriots could have recovered it after the incident. But given the abandoned state of the rest of the facility, I didn't have high hopes.

The voice came from above.

"I'm afraid so."

Snake looked up to the second floor walkway to see Vamp standing there.

"Unfortunately for you," Vamp said, "the railgun is no longer here."

In defiance of the cold, the nosferatu discarded his jacket, exposing his bare chest. But more shocking was the hollowness in Naomi's eyes. She stood behind him, wearing a dark brown coat.

Then I noticed something about her mouth—and his—that gave me chills. Both were missing something in the below-freezing air: the white clouds of exhaled breath.

At the sight of her, Snake just said, "Naomi…"

I know this might sound fanciful, but after seeing Vamp killed so many times and yet remaining alive, the bloodsucker's lack of white breath seemed only natural. Snake and I had come to expect his body to operate in ways beyond all reason.

But Naomi, there at his side like a vampire bride, deeply unsettled us. She and Vamp didn't seem much different at all.

"This place will be your grave," Vamp said, adding, "as Naomi wishes."

The confidence in his smile was unnerving. If Vamp and Naomi had already sent out the railgun, why were they still here?

I routed queries to the security system via REX's access port and found readings of a large number of entities headed toward the supply tunnel entrance at a great speed.

I warned Snake, and Vamp flashed us a satisfied grin.

"The Suicide Gekko are on their way," he said. "We've rigged their heads with explosives. Soon, there'll be nothing left of this place."

"We've been had," Snake said. "Otacon!"

Snake needed help. I initiated a scan of REX's drive system. I ran the self-diagnostics and got back a full report of damage to each of the robot's components. I didn't have time to look at every detail, but drawing on old sense-memories of testing the Metal Gear, I managed a rough diagnosis of REX's state.

"Snake," I said, "I think I might be able to get it working!"

I disconnected the Mk. III's manipulator, switched its wheels to magnetic mode, and climbed REX's leg. If I could get into the cockpit on the front of the Metal Gear's nose, I could put the robot's knee-fired antitank missiles to use.

"Now," Vamp said, "amuse me until they arrive."

He leapt down from the second floor and stuck a four-point

landing. He held in a crouch and stared at Snake, licking his lips. Snake cursed, raised his M4, and began to fire.

Vamp evaded the gunfire with astonishing agility.

Some of the nosferatu's speed might have been from the US Army power-assist armor he wore over his legs. But the movements of his back and legs easily surpassed mortal limits, mechanical aid or not.

Snake needed to get close. He and I had come up with a plan on *Nomad* to handle the deathless man. If my conjecture were correct, Vamp's immortality could be stripped away.

Snake could only succeed if Vamp remained unaware. My idea wasn't a sure thing—far from it—but Snake understood that the fight's outcome hinged upon a single moment. He fired the M4, shrewdly orchestrating the opening we needed.

The next crucial step came: Vamp wielded a knife.

The bloodsucker sent out a volley of throwing daggers. Snake twisted to the side, evading them by inches, save for the one aimed at his head, which grazed the burn wound on his face. The shallow cut into Snake's scarred skin let out a trickle of blood. Seeing the line of red across Snake's cheek, Vamp licked his lips—perhaps anticipating the taste.

Vamp pressed in on Snake. Our plan required luring the immortal in, yet the closer he got to Snake, the greater the danger.

Our sole chance of defeating the nosferatu would come at the moment of greatest risk. When the M4's magazine ran out of bullets, Snake didn't reload. Instead, he dropped the rifle to rest on its sling, brought out his knife, and took the CQC stance. Vamp accepted the invitation and closed the distance. The moment we'd been waiting for had finally arrived.

Snake's knife was only a front.

Hidden in his other hand, the autoinjector was Snake's holy sword and holy water—perhaps even the stake to drive into the vampire's heart. Snake stuck the needle into Vamp's exposed neck. Compressed air pushed the piston down, and the swarm of nanomachine inhibitors rushed into Vamp's bloodstream.

Taken by surprise, the bloodsucker leapt back. He put his hand to his neck and, with agony in his expression, dropped to one knee and said, "What have you done?"

"There," Snake said. "Now you're a dead man too."

He displayed the autoinjector to Vamp before putting it back in his pouch. Vamp didn't seem to yet know what was about to occur within him—only that something was changing inside his body; something long asleep was awakening.

Could this be…life?

As the frozen life began to stir, Vamp looked afraid.

I took Vamp's moment of confusion to slip the Mk. III inside REX's cockpit, where I connected the robot's manipulator arm to a data port on the side of the control stick. This could work.

The moment I initiated REX's boot-up, the south wall crumbled like cardboard, and a Gekko lumbered like an elephant into view. The machine had crashed through the composite partitioning wall.

"Snake," I said. "Look out! They're rigged to self-destruct."

Snake looked from the Gekko back to Vamp. Though Vamp had been momentarily discomposed when the nanomachines thawed his frozen life, now he slowly arose, ready to fight. He put his hands behind his back, then, after only an instant, they reappeared wielding knives.

Not even Snake could hope to stand against both Vamp and the Gekko. He was trapped. The muscles of his half-burned face tensed. The Gekko lifted one sausagelike bird leg and stepped over the rubble and into the room.

Then the robot's head and legs split apart.

The cut was that of a master swordsman slashing through a bundle of straw. The Gekko's head, packed with explosives, slid lopsided down its back. The robot, its sensors disconnected, inoperative, could no longer determine when it should explode.

A figure alighted on REX's back. His right hand grasped the sword that had split the Gekko in two.

Raiden.

"Snake," he said. "Sorry to have kept you waiting."

Raiden flourished his large sword as if it were a baton, then slid the blade into its sheath. No trace of confusion remained in Vamp's expression—only rapture: *If it isn't the man I've been waiting for...*

"You ready for this?" Snake asked with worry in his voice.

"Yeah," Raiden said. "Sunny gave me the go-ahead."

With a freakish cry, Vamp jumped to REX's knee, then he was atop the steel giant with Raiden. He presented Raiden a heartfelt grin and said, "How about it, undying man? You want to die too?"

"Sorry," Raiden said, his eyes locked on the vampire's, "but I can't die just yet."

"Then... kill me!"

Vamp drew throwing knives from their holders at his forearm and thigh and displayed them, fanned out between his fingers like a magician's deck of cards. Raiden grasped his sword sheath.

"Wait," the nosferatu said. "They say you consider yourself some Native American scout. Knives, then? Let us duel with knives."

Raiden released the hilt of his sword and, keeping his eyes on Vamp, withdrew his *yoroi-doshi*, a thick, straight-edged dagger. He held the weapon in a reverse grip and pointed the blade's tip at Vamp.

"Snake," he said, "this one is mine. You keep those Gekko at bay."

From behind the Gekko destroyed by Raiden came reinforcements. Snake readied the sniper rifle he'd purchased from Drebin in South America, pulling back the bolt and sending the first round into the breech. If he could hit the Gekko in their comparatively weak armored heads and sensory equipment, he might be able to stop them.

"Otacon," Snake said, "we're gonna buy you some time."

I went back to work. I needed to get REX's systems back online to stop the oncoming Gekko.

"Kill me," Vamp said. "Kill me!"

With a scream, Vamp unleashed a volley of knives from both hands. Raiden, unable to dodge or deflect, took the weapons into his body, the knives sinking into his sides, his shoulders, and his arms.

Raiden used his free hand to swiftly pluck out the daggers, returning them at Vamp with machine-gun speed. The bloodsucker dodged them with his characteristic ballet grace and unsheathed his finest and largest knife from its sheath on his thigh. He smoothly transitioned forward, and Raiden, reading the nosferatu's movements, rushed in to meet him.

Their blades crossed. The sharp clang of metal on metal resounded through the space, their music reaching even Snake's ears below.

Suddenly, the concert cut silent. Raiden and Vamp separated and stared each other down, ready to make their next clash the decisive one.

*Now.*

The two flung themselves forward as if propelled by magnetic force. Directly between them, their swords flashed one final time, and in each man's chest, a blade sank deep into flesh. White blood dripped from Raiden's wound, dark red from Vamp.

For a few seconds, neither moved.

Vamp's lips formed a taut grin, no longer the hopeless smile of an immortal that might suggest, *Not even this will kill me.* No, Vamp felt pain now. He felt life pouring out of him.

This smile was from surprise, and from happiness.

The two men separated, and Vamp breathlessly pulled the yoroi-doshi out of his chest.

"This thing spouting from my chest—this, this is my life."

As Vamp fell from REX and down to the floor, his thoughts ran to the life force flowing from his wound. *Where have you been hiding? If you've been there all along, why have you denied me death and decay? Don't you know how much suffering you've inflicted upon me?*

I shouted, "Snake, get down!"

Snake dove away from the partitioning wall the Gekko continued to smash through. The next instant, missiles I fired from REX slammed into the top of the wall.

The concussive blast and debris rushed past Snake. He lifted his head to see the destruction, the mountain of rubble blocking any surviving Gekko from getting inside the supply tunnel entrance.

Surprised myself, I said, "This thing might come in handy after all."

Snake had thought REX utterly destroyed, and sure enough, the radar dome and cockpit interior had been largely done in. But when the Mk. III ran a system check, I found the joints and support systems at nearly full strength. Even the cockpit's manual controls appeared to be operable, provided I could reassign the control systems among any remaining functional input devices.

To give Snake room to fit inside the cockpit, I steered the Mk. III back down to the floor and found Naomi standing there, solemnly looking down on Vamp as he contorted in pain. Snake put away the sniper rifle and went to her side.

Through the Mk. III's camera, I stared into the face of the monster who took my sister's life. But the face was no longer that of a monster but of a human, fragile. No longer a nosferatu, no longer a monster, now a man once more. A mere man, as he had been born.

I had reviled him as a monster, but this ordinary man left me bewildered.

"Vamp was never immortal," Naomi said. "His natural healing abilities were enhanced by the nanomachines inside his body. But after so many battles, he's finally reached his limit."

She didn't have to tell us. We had already realized this when, inside the helicopter escaping from South America, she confessed her sins, saying, *I'm responsible for Vamp.*

That was when Snake and I knew. Vamp's immortality was not

innate but rather granted by Naomi's nanomachines. If we could only inhibit them, we could restore the inevitability of death.

Raiden descended from REX and joined Naomi, looking at the man he defeated. After Snake had made Vamp human again, he was vulnerable to Raiden. Returned to his natural flesh and blood, Vamp would die now.

In turn, Raiden's victory evidenced that he was no longer human. Perhaps Vamp had been transformed into a monster by technology. But Raiden was the same. Raiden was now a monster—as was Snake.

But, as with Vamp, Raiden had been the baby of a man and woman like any other. And Vamp, at the end, had been able to regain his humanity.

*It shouldn't be too late for Raiden*, I thought. *It mustn't be.*

Because Snake, born as a monster, wouldn't be granted the same good fortune.

Raiden said to Naomi, "Sunny asked me to tell you something." White blood still flowed from where Vamp's knives had cut him.

"What?" Naomi asked.

" 'I cooked them right.' That was it."

"I see."

Naomi closed her eyes. Tears silently streamed down her cheeks as she seemed to reach an understanding. Whatever was going through her mind, I sensed there was more going on than satisfaction at teaching Sunny how to make fried eggs correctly. I could sense her emotions of fulfillment and relief, and they unsettled me.

"Good for you, Sunny," she said. "You finally did it."

At her feet, Vamp let out a painful moan. Naomi went to her knees and stroked his forehead with the scarred-over bullet wound.

"Doctor," he said, afraid, "ease my pain."

Faced at last by the real death he had so desired, Vamp now battled a terror that was hard to contain.

A pitiable sight; all too natural a response for any man.

I had been possessed by the notion that by defeating this monster, by killing this inhuman thing, I would be freed from my hate. But the figure on the ground before me was just a man, tragic in his normality, now nothing more than an inhabitant of a body on its way to death.

I wanted to scream. *Why? Why do you have to be like that now? Why do you have to be human again? I reviled you as a monster, and I wanted to kill you as a monster. Why is your face so human with fear?*

Naomi took out an autoinjector and said to Vamp, "You must have been so lonely."

Vamp reached for the syringe, his hand trembling, pleading for the promised land sealed within the cylinder. But Naomi's hand also trembled.

"I can't," she said. "I haven't earned the right to save you."

His eyes yearned for help, but Naomi felt too much guilt to provide it. *I stole his life,* she thought. *I robbed him of death. I destroyed within him the peace which no living being should be denied.*

*Can I grant him salvation?*

*Who do I think I am? That's supposed to absolve me of my sins?*

Naomi would not allow her hands to provide his mercy. Instead, she came to the Mk. III and said, "You have to trust me, Dr. Emmerich."

She put the autoinjector up to the robot's camera. I didn't know how to react.

"Give this to him," Naomi said. "Not for revenge, but to put an end to his suffering."

For a time, I stared at the syringe, unable to move. This man killed Emma. This monster took her from me. Now, I doubted anything could rescue Vamp from his anguish. All that remained was a lonely sinner burning in the blazing flames that lay in the space between life and death.

Still in a daze, I operated the Mk. III's controls. The next thing I knew, the robot held the autoinjector within its manipulator arm. The misery that had been propelling me was gone now; without it,

I no longer knew what to do, bereft of my anger, of malice and the desire for vengeance.

Where had they gone—the anger and the hate? While I struggled with my confusion, Vamp snatched the autoinjector from the Mk. III and jabbed it into the side of his neck.

Vamp began to writhe in agony. The life—and death—long sealed away now raged within his body. He was at the opening of a new life. And with life came the possibility of death.

"Now you can return to your true self," Naomi said. "You can be at peace."

"I can...die?"

Though his body contorted with pain, Vamp exhaled in relief.

"Forgive me," Naomi said.

The nanomachines washed through him and restored old wounds to their rightful places.

*Here*, he seemed to think. *Here is the place I've longed for. Dark and painful, and warm.*

Vamp's breath became visible in the cold, his life force taking root in soil long left fallow.

Pain filled his existence—the sweet, precious pain of being alive.

*I don't have to be anymore. I don't have to suffer in the gap between life and death, refused from either.*

In his last moments, his muscles seized tight, and his back arched.

Then, Vamp found what he had been seeking.

Gently, Naomi closed his eyelids, covering the eyes that no longer held fear or joy. For a time, I gazed at the Mk. III's monitor feed, unable to find the words I should say. I remained empty, a discarded shell.

Vamp was dead. And nothing had changed.

"Why?" I whispered.

But I didn't have to ask. Everything was clear now. This wouldn't bring Emma back. This wouldn't redress all the things I should have done for Emma but wasn't able to do. Vamp's death didn't mean anything. The revelation left me astonished—I should have realized this from the beginning, so why had I never been able to accept it?

Emma couldn't forgive anyone, not anymore.

Vengeance. I had been looking outside myself, while my true enemy had always been within.

"We can't erase the past," Naomi said. "Nor can we forgive it. And so…the only thing we can do is end it."

I don't know if she spoke to me or to herself. Either was the same. If only I had understood sooner.

*Emma, I'm sorry. Why am I always so foolish?*

Retrieving the autoinjector that had delivered Vamp's death, Naomi stood and faced Snake. Just as I could never receive Emma's forgiveness, no matter what I had done or might do, neither would Naomi ever find atonement. But she still carried unresolved sins, and her journey was not yet at an end.

"Snake," she said, "Liquid's down below us. He's stolen the Patriots' System, slipped out of their grasp, and taken their ark."

"Their ark?" Snake asked.

"A warship unfettered by land, law, country, or computer network. The only place where they are truly released from the shackles of the Patriots. The place where they can be free. *Outer Haven*. From where Liquid plans to launch the nuke."

Haven. Drebin had mentioned the word back in South America. Tax havens, data havens—places outside the System, safe from supervision and control.

"Snake," she said solemnly, "your life has been prolonged so that you may fulfill your purpose."

Was his accelerated aging a brief stay granted to him to complete his mission? Without it, would he already be dead—perhaps nine years earlier, on this island, stricken down by FOXDIE?

Naomi continued, "When all of this is over, you'll have no choice but to accept death. We are given life only so that we can atone for our sins. Your life was created for that very purpose."

Gently, she touched her hand to Snake's burned cheek and said, "We ourselves must atone for our sins. We must not pass them on to the next generation. We must not leave them for the future."

Tears falling from her eyes, Naomi looked like Mary Magdalene at Golgotha, witnessing the agony of the man crucified for all the sins of the world.

"That is your true fate," she said. "One that cannot be defied."

She put the autoinjector to her neck. With her thumb, she pressed the button, sending nanomachine inhibitors into her blood just as they had been sent into Vamp's.

"Naomi?" I said.

I sensed something was wrong. From her peculiar calmness when she reported Sunny's words to her handling of Vamp's passing, Naomi seemed to be settling her unfinished business one piece at a time. I turned the Mk. III's camera to her and caught a fleeting, contrite smile.

"Snake," she said, "Vamp and I are the same... living corpses, bodies kept barely alive by nanomachines."

"Then you..."

"Cancer. I shouldn't even be alive right now."

"What?" I yelled. I remembered shivering at the touch of her lips inside the helicopter, wondering, *Why is she so cold? Why is her skin so lacking in warmth?*

But when I had joined my body with hers, I fled into the reassurance of feeling loved by someone, and I pushed any such doubts aside.

"The nanomachines kept my cancer from progressing," she explained. "But there's nothing more they can do. With the nanomachines gone, my time will unfreeze and begin to flow again."

Her breath had become visible in the frigid air.

Just like Vamp. Life blighted her body. The nanomachines that had once sealed away the realities of life and turned aside death's gaze were now swiftly stripped from her lungs, her organs, and her arms and legs.

"Goodbye, Hal," Naomi said, hugging herself as the frozen air of Shadow Moses robbed what little warmth remained from a body that should already be dead. She held herself as if cherishing the cold.

She smiled at the Mk. III and said, "Give my best to Sunny."

Far removed from Shadow Moses, I was helpless. I couldn't hold her steady, and I couldn't put my arms around her. "Naomi," I yelled at the computer screen, "don't do it!"

I cried and I screamed, unreservedly; it was all I could do. Racked by feelings of powerlessness, I could only observe through the Mk. III's video feed.

*Why? Why did you betray us, to die so selfishly?*

Ignoring my tearful cries, Naomi gave herself another nanomachine injection. She slumped to the floor like a marionette whose strings had been cut. At last, her body had regained its natural state: inflicted by a cancer, spread from lungs to liver to lymph nodes to everywhere else—a cancer that should have long since killed its host.

I brought the Mk. III to Naomi's side. With effort, she lifted her head and touched a finger to the robot's flip-out screen, tracing my face on the mini LCD.

"You have such beautiful eyes," she breathed.

I choked up. Through the Mk. III's cameras, our eyes met.

"Forgive me," she said. "And forget me."

Deep down, I refused to accept it.

*I can't.* It had been the same with Emma, and with Wolf. Not once had I been able to save anyone I loved. Not when Snake and Wolf battled on that snow field, not when Emma was stabbed on the Big Shell.

What was I fighting for when I couldn't protect a single person important to me?

Then, as if in disregard for my despair, a wall I thought I'd blocked off with REX's missiles burst open. Raiden turned to see a leg protruding lazily from the rubble, large and still like an elephant's. A Gekko had self-destructed to reopen an entrance.

"Now go!" Naomi said, pushing away the Mk. III with the last of her strength. For a moment, I thought the robot might tip over, but somehow I maintained balance. I tried to send it dashing back to Naomi, but Raiden had seized the tiny machine. I moved the MK. III wildly, but its legs only flailed at the air.

Keeping his gaze on the advancing Gekko squad, Raiden warned, "Snake, we need to hurry."

The leg of the exploded Gekko was tossed into the air like a chicken bone—one of its comrades had kicked its remains aside to clear a path into the space.

*Why does it always end this way?*

I stared at Naomi's motionless body, frozen by feelings of powerlessness.

Just when I thought I was ready to fall in love.

Just when I thought I could protect her.

"They're coming!" Raiden shouted.

Snake took the Mk. III from him and sprinted toward REX. I could only watch Naomi pass into the distance.

The three of us reached the Metal Gear and clambered into the cockpit. I helped Snake start up REX, while sadness, and the magnitude of all I had lost, crushed down on me, relentlessly.

I understood that the instant I allowed my concentration to falter, I would break down into despair.

Certainly I knew what I had to do. I had already lost two people close to me—if I hadn't grown accustomed to loss, I at least had learned how to endure.

I could calm my emotions—to a certain extent, at least—simply by closing my eyes and steadying my breath. Emotions follow the flesh. The minds and bodies of man possessed an inherent, and perhaps cruel, insensitivity. I felt a fleeting yet fierce contempt for myself for not being any different.

"I understand," I said. "I haven't lost everything yet."

From REX's cockpit, I connected to the facility's network and sent the command to open the supply tunnel door. I remembered something else I learned through all my losses.

Those women were real. They were a part of this world. Emma, Wolf, and Naomi. Everything I gained through them—the sadness, the joy, the hate—proved that they had indeed lived, and now they continued to exist in a different form inside me.

Regret didn't have to mean being imprisoned and paralyzed by loss. By holding onto these thoughts—of what I hadn't been able to do for Wolf, what I hadn't been able to provide Emma—I could keep the women alive inside myself.

And as I did, my duty of regret had another purpose: to ensure I wouldn't repeat the past.

"Snake," I said, "I've still got a job to do."

Naomi still existed within me. Her life might have been gone, but my love for her remained.

For now, that was enough. Later, there would be time to spare for tears. I've had nine years of many battles to learn how to stave them off a little bit longer.

Snake nodded at the Mk. III. "That's right. We need you."

"I'm done crying. My tears have dried up."

Then Naomi's body disappeared within the stampede of Gekko.

I had to move forward. There was no stopping here.

I went back to my efforts to bring REX back to life.

To keep giving meaning to everyone I'd lost.

To preserve the meaning of their existences.

## 4

I OPENED THE Mk. III's storage port and withdrew a modified video game controller. I had already revised REX's control programs, discarding any functions not immediately required, and mapped the rest to the controller's limited inputs.

"Let's go," I told Snake.

Gekko swarmed below, their heads packed with high explosives. We didn't have time for a leisurely explanation of the controls.

"I'll fill you in as we go," I said, and Snake faithfully took the controller in his hands.

At the push of a button, REX sprang to life, bypassing any typical warm-up maneuvers, and the sudden acceleration slammed Snake's back against the pilot's seat. Considering its massive size, the Metal Gear moved with incredible speed. REX, the slain dragon now ridden by the hero who had vanquished it, steadily ascended the slope of the supply tunnel.

REX continued to gain speed, trailed by the pack of Gekko, with one particularly impetuous machine leading the rest of the herd. Raiden leapt from the Metal Gear's back, and his sword flashed in midair.

The leading Gekko's head slid to the ground and exploded amid the trailing swarm. The robot's legs, seemingly unaware they had lost their head, continued to run for a few seconds, then faltered, and finally went limp and fell.

With a laugh, Snake said, "Not exactly an intelligent bunch."

From the other end of the tunnel more Gekko appeared in small groups. I fired missile salvos from the Metal Gear's knees while Snake used the twin XGAU-8R rotary cannons to dispatch the distant foes. I wished I could do more, but I had my hands full keeping the wrecked robot together. To keep REX operational, I had to coax cooperation out of components that either kept breaking down or would cease to function altogether.

As REX rushed onward, Raiden and his sword managed to stave off the Gekko behind us. He leapt from one charging machine's back to another like a ninja, sinking his blade into sensors and core systems.

"Otacon," Snake shouted, "help!"

I looked at the monitor to see that one Gekko had slipped past Snake and Raiden's defenses and was nearly upon us.

The machine was so close it had evaded the field of fire of the twin cannons. REX had a single weapon suited for close-range combat, and I had chosen it: the free-electron laser, which had caused Snake considerable grief nine years ago.

The self-diagnosis program reported that the weapon, my version of a lightsaber, was still operational. Whether I believed that to be the case or not, I didn't have any other options.

I fired the laser.

The beam of amplified energy pierced through the head of the suicidal Gekko, and REX stomped on the robot to finish it off.

Each of us faced a challenge. Snake urged the faltering Metal Gear forward at full speed, while simultaneously operating the twin cannons to deal with the Gekko ahead. Behind us, Raiden leapt from back to back amid the stampede, dispatching one machine after another.

And while I wasn't there with them, I was glued to my monitor, struggling not to get washed away by the waterfall of data streaming from REX.

We were like pieces of an airplane split apart midair yet still somehow managing to fly. As the self-diagnosis program squawked at me every few seconds, I sorted through the torrent of damage reports, closing off circuits and rerouting systems to mitigate the damage.

I wouldn't be able to keep up like this. Bookkeeping can only do so much.

About to exhaust the very limits of my ability to sustain concentration on the data and to keep my fingers flying across my keyboard, I heard Snake shout, "The surface!"

At the top of the ramp, I saw sky and the gray clouds of the Aleutian Low.

Snake squeezed even more speed out of REX, sending the Gekko scattering. Two clawlike appendages at the base of each foot dug into the metal floor, providing the Metal Gear's giant-sized legs purchase on the incline. Leaving a trail of pockmarks in the supply tunnel ramp, REX scrambled out into the open.

We barely had time to notice that the blizzard had ended before the impact struck us. A shock wave slammed into REX's back and sent the massive machine lurching forward. The blast rocked Snake and the Mk. III, and for a second, I thought we'd be flung from the cockpit.

The throng of Gekko packed in the tunnel exploded in a chain reaction with ferocious energy. Sensing their attack, Raiden had separated himself from the leader of the pack as best he could before their self-destruction, but the brunt of the pressure wave pounded against his back.

Bathed in countless bits of shrapnel and the plasma from high-temperature gasses, Raiden was sent flying and landed just inside the tunnel entrance. I dug REX's talons into the earth to keep the Metal Gear from tipping over.

But Raiden's body, without REX's weight or thick armor, had no way to evade or withstand the violent cascade of energy. He could only take it, and was sent rolling to the floor like a knocked-over bowling pin.

The simultaneous explosions produced the force equal to several cluster bombs. Each Gekko had been equipped with several explosives, and for the first second or two of the chain reaction the air inside the tunnel compressed. Then the squeezed-in energy pushed back, expanding rapidly, and burst the composite walls of the facility like a balloon.

Pillars of flame shot from the ceiling, and the supply tunnel collapsed. Broken beams and concrete crashed down on Raiden in a colossal mass. In an instant, he was gone, swallowed up by dust and debris.

"Raiden!" Snake yelled, but no reply came from the swelling cloud.

The passage had been completely buried by the rubble of the destroyed facility. Even if any Gekko remained active below, I didn't think it could make it to the surface. We wouldn't have to worry about any more self-destructing Gekko, but we had no way of knowing Raiden's fate.

Snake called out to Raiden again.

Slowly the haze thinned. Raiden's body stuck out from the rubble. His lower body and right arm were completely buried. Only his left arm was free, but his sword had tumbled just out of reach and wouldn't be of any use.

Just as Snake moved his hand to release his seatbelt and go help his friend, he heard a noise. I heard it too and turned the Mk. III to face the sea. We were in a cargo port, with generators, a waterworks, and several smaller structures including a few warehouses and observation towers. Concrete piers provided space for large-scale cargo vessels to dock. The wide roadway linking the facility with the harbor doubled as a landing strip.

Trepidation coloring my voice, I asked, "What is that sound?"

The ground rumbled, carrying vibrations from the water. Something was coming—something gigantic, and approaching fast.

The ocean swelled, and a massive, streamlined form resembling a killer whale sliced through the water's surface and leapt into the sky. And then it kept on going, until it was over the land and coming straight at REX.

This was no whale.

It possessed long, massive fins—more like arms, really—enough to make those of any killer whale seem miniscule. Besides, whales didn't have legs and weren't so ridiculously large as to be on par with REX.

RAY.

Metal Gear RAY had been designed by the US Marine Corps as a counter against Metal Gear derivatives built by the other nuclear powers of the world. RAY landed and braked by digging talons into the ground, breaking pieces of the runway as if the asphalt were a bar of chocolate. The Metal Gear was massive, yet graceful, and when it slid to a stop, tilting forward, the robot's head opened to reveal Liquid Ocelot inside the cockpit.

"Brother! It's not over. Not yet."

Snake yelled back, "Liquid!"

RAY raised a piercing howl into the Aleutian sky—not an animal's howl, of course, but a thunderous noise of metal parts clashing and scraping.

"Moses," Liquid boomed, "where our fates were born. And where yours ends, Snake!"

I looked back at the rubble. Raiden still lived, but his right arm was pinned under the debris.

We'd have to rely on REX.

We faced an anti-Metal Gear Metal Gear. In a way, RAY had been built to destroy REX. Liquid's machine was an apex predator.

Snake looked into the Mk. III's camera and nodded. I faced the camera in my monitor and returned the gesture. With a glance at Liquid, Snake charged at RAY.

I noted that Liquid rode in a new model RAY. Unlike the clunky, tanklike REX, RAY looked alive, with a sleek appearance and components that glided with precision. This manned version of RAY had a long tail, much longer than the one on the AI-piloted version we previously encountered in the waters of the Big Shell. REX, in comparison, had no tail, and held a deep squatting posture to retain balance.

The unmanned RAYs were originally designed to protect the Arsenal Gear, a giant submersible missile carrier with access to the communications networks of all five branches of the US military. A commander on board could issue orders to all US armed forces across the globe. Despite the ship's importance as a functional center of government, radar and threat-detection systems were absent, presumably left to accompanying Aegis cruisers and the air force's AWACS sentry craft.

The Arsenal was equipped with few means of self-defense. Without its escort, the vessel was nothing more than a giant floating coffin packed with fireworks. The short-tailed RAY-class Metal Gears were built to protect the vulnerable Arsenal.

The RAY piloted by Liquid had been modified to be manually piloted, but its basis was the unmanned model. The machine would have a fairly short operational range. Was the big one nearby, underwater?

*Bang!* went the staccato noise, like a starting gun, and a cluster of smoke trails rose up from RAY's back.

"Missiles," I shouted. "Snake, dodge them!"

But Snake kept advancing into the missiles' paths. Then, at the last instant, he slid REX to one side in a maneuver so quick, had I been inside the cockpit myself, I might have gotten sick. Keeping REX pointed at Liquid, Snake moved sideways, using a water tower as cover. A missile struck the tower, destroying it and sending the tank's contents pouring down on Snake.

*We have a chance.*

RAY had been designed to be unmanned, with the robot's peak performance delivered through the orders of the Arsenal's AI. Whatever the effects retrofitting the machine for human control might have been, the results couldn't have been beneficial.

I designed REX knowing a human would operate it with human judgment. Perhaps such complex and unconventional machines were better off in the hands of an AI. That was why, for the Arsenal project, the navy moved away from the manned designs created for the Marines to autonomous robots, like the Gekko, guided by combat AIs.

But as far as I was concerned, for giant mechs, nothing could replace a human.

Again Snake charged ahead. RAY was clearly shaken. Occupied with trying to keep REX from falling apart with each step, I couldn't offer any help with attacks or defense, but Snake skillfully piloted the robot and closed in on Liquid.

They were too close now for Liquid to fire a missile without risking damage to himself.

One reason I had designed REX to be manually operated was due to my inability to find a suitable AI among the currently developed autonomous weapons systems. But there was another reason: I loved Japanese anime, and with REX the realization of that passion, I couldn't bear to see a giant mecha without a human operator.

The original RAYs might have been anti-Metal Gear weapons, but when the designers chose to go the unmanned route, that decision would have necessitated a great number of alterations from the manned design. Even if Liquid's machine appeared similar to the other RAYs, the robot's insides would have to be vastly different. AI command enabled an array of controls far more vast than a puny human brain could handle.

To put it another way, the unmanned RAYs could never truly be retrofitted for a human pilot. This RAY was being forced at great lengths to bend itself to Liquid's commands. If REX had any chance against the superior machine, this would be the reason. REX had been designed from the ground up to be piloted by a human being.

I shouted, "Grapple him!" but Snake already knew what to do. REX crashed into RAY, the two colossal bodies colliding beside the water's edge like giant monsters in a Japanese kaiju film.

With the two cockpits close together, the two men came face-to-face. Astonishment registered in Liquid's eyes as he took in Snake's confident grin. Liquid's human command was REX's curse. Snake fired the free-electron laser mounted beneath his robot's chin, and the amplified energy pierced the surface of RAY's armor. The light reflected off RAY's specialized coating and left traces of an iridescent glow.

Liquid raised a war cry and fired a laserlike beam from RAY's head.

"Otacon," Snake said. "He's using a water cutter!"

"Don't worry, REX is a tank. Don't lump it in with some puny whale-looking thing."

Powerful enough to cut through metal, the pressurized water cutter was RAY's primary close-combat weapon. The jet could easily cut through walls and would split a man cleanly in two.

But however strong the water pressure, no water cutter would so easily pierce the armor of the nuclear-armed bipedal tank. Before RAY's jet could break through REX's armor, REX's laser fried RAY's insides. The supposed Metal Gear killer, bested by its own prey, howled a death cry.

At the same time, REX had been pushed past its limits. The mighty dragon, engine shrieking, finally succumbed to the wounds Snake had inflicted nine years before. With the last of the robot's power, Snake withdrew from Liquid. With a few dozen meters between them, REX fell silent.

Snake let out a moan. For the first time since the clash, I looked at Snake and lost all words. Blood flowed steadily from his mouth and his forehead. He breathed heavily, painfully, the frozen Alaskan air piercing his aged lungs like shards of glass.

"Liquid," Snake panted. "Is he..."

Snake would be helpless were Liquid to attack. When RAY and REX collided, Snake had taken a terrible blow to the chest. The two giant metal masses had crashed into each other at tremendous speed. Had it been a traffic accident, I wouldn't have expected any survivors. Snake tried to move his body and screamed in pain, his left shoulder dislocated.

RAY had collapsed, and from its cockpit Liquid's arm reached out. He grasped at the machine's surface to pull himself free.

Slowly, he crawled out of the Metal Gear. Like Snake, Liquid had been severely injured by the crash, but he had a gun grasped firmly in his hand, and he staggered toward REX's wreckage.

This was bad. Somehow, I managed to free Snake from his seatbelt, but his wounds and fatigue left him in a stupor. Liquid was in a similar state, except he could walk while Snake wasn't going anywhere.

Liquid, in Ocelot's body. And Snake. The two old, worn-down, and wounded men confronted each other, each resolute in a shared goal: to put an end to their entwined fates. But one had taken his body to its limit and could no longer move.

Suddenly, Liquid grasped at his chest as if trying to gouge out his heart.

Snake had seen this before.

Nine years ago, when Snake escaped in a Jeep from the underground base and was trapped under that Jeep, unable to move, the original Liquid stood before him with eyes wide.

Snake's own eyes said, *I know this. I've lived this.*

As if it were a magic curse, Snake apprehensively uttered the syllable, "FOX—"

Then Liquid, delivering his own coup de grâce, finished, "—DIE!"

His knees hit the ground, followed by the rest of him. His hand clutched at his heart in agony, nails digging into skin.

Was it over? Could their lengthy battle have ended so abruptly?

Snake gaped at Liquid, forgetting his own pain for a moment. His foe lay alone before him. Once known as Ocelot, the man had taken Liquid's name and regarded himself as Solid Snake's shadow and the son of Big Boss.

"Think again!"

Liquid sprang up, and his face radiated delight, even more so than on that night in Eastern Europe when he had cut down the surrounding US forces.

Had his injuries just been an act?

"What?" Snake said.

"Sorry, but that won't work this time. Behold!"

Liquid pointed to the sea from which he and RAY had emerged. A rumble filled the port, beyond comparison with the sound RAY had made. Snake and I watched in astonishment as the gunmetal sea rose up, erupting into pillars of spray as if in celebration.

What I saw next made me doubt my own sanity.

A giant mass split the ocean, seawater cascading off the front in waterfalls. The mist cleared to reveal the four granite presidential heads of Mount Rushmore rising from the frozen Alaskan sea, faces unperturbed. Snake and I were caught dumbstruck by the sight, absurd, utterly ridiculous, and oddly magnificent.

Moved by the brazen irrationality and sheer shamelessness of the display, I worried that the Naval Hymn might start playing in my head. Snake recovered his sanity ahead of me and began to struggle free from the cockpit.

Not only did his body not work as he expected it to, but age and injury strove to crush his consciousness. Biting down a cry of pain, Snake crawled from the pilot's seat of the fallen REX.

Seeing Snake on the ground, Liquid did a childish caper back to the water's edge. He walked jauntily, pointing at us, every bit a picked-on little boy who'd just gotten back at his bully. I guess it could have been worse; at least he wasn't jeering at us. Still, his gleeful immaturity disgusted me.

Perhaps incited to action by the juvenile teasing, Snake willed his pain away, raised his M4, and got to his feet.

Even so, the dislocated joint of his left shoulder wouldn't cooperate. Snake could handle the pain, but he couldn't get his body—not just his shoulder, but all of it—to move.

"Liquid . . ." he said, trying to lift the seven- or eight-pound rifle in one arm to get a bead on Liquid, but his biceps and shoulder muscles refused. Snake no longer had the strength to shoot anything higher than the ground fifteen feet ahead.

His bronchial tubes and diaphragm had grown too weak to

deliver oxygen into his lungs. He was on the verge of asphyxiation. His breath came out in wheezes and gasps. In the cold, his metabolism struggled to convert his stored-up energy into heat.

Snake's stamina had been depleted. As for the Mk. III, the robot was wedged in the back of the cockpit, the tiny legs flailing pitifully in the air.

At last, the structure beneath the Mount Rushmore heads appeared from the water.

It was a giant submarine at least two thousand feet long. The shape of the vessel, like a whale born the wrong size, marked it a relative of the Arsenal Gear.

Between the Arsenal-class submarine and the wreckages of RAY and REX, I felt I was in a land of giants. Snake and Liquid looked terribly small surrounded by the towering machines.

With a better look, the effigies on this Mount Rushmore weren't the fathers of our country, Washington, Lincoln, or otherwise. The four faces resembled each other so closely at first I thought they were all copies. Which was only natural, for these were the likenesses of the family of Snakes, including Solid Snake himself. With him were Liquid, Solidus, and the man at the beginning of it all—Big Boss. When I really studied the sculpture, I realized that Big Boss's face occupied Washington's place among the four.

I found Liquid's delusions of grandeur appalling. Was he suggesting the Snakes decided history—that only the line of Snakes would free the world from Zero's obsessions of monitoring and control?

Then the Mount Rushmore began to fade. This was something I had been too stunned to realize sooner, but now seemed obvious—the image was only an OctoCamo texture projection.

At the edge of the harbor, Liquid stopped and turned to face us. He spread his arms wide, just as he had done after his victory in the Middle East, and proudly proclaimed, "This is the liberty we've won for ourselves: *Outer Haven!*"

Revealed beneath the OctoCamo Mount Rushmore was a gentle slope rising from the deck—the ship's bridge had been unified into the hull for improved stealth capabilities. That said, *Haven* was so ridiculously gargantuan its bridge alone was easily three times the size of a typical nuclear submarine.

That huge bridge began to slide open as though the vessel were removing a hat. Inside the exposed interior of the ship stood a city-like cluster of rectangular structures, between which thrust a cannon familiar to me. The barrel angled upward, glaring at the sky.

The weapon was REX's railgun—a nuclear launcher outside the Patriots' governance.

"Behold," Liquid shouted. "With this weapon, I will destroy JD. Then...everything ends, and everything begins!"

A cargo crane extended from the open bridge. Wheezing from his constricted windpipe, Snake struggled to catch up with Liquid.

"Not again," Snake muttered. "I've done nothing but fail to stop Liquid. In the Middle East. And in Eastern Europe.

"But I don't have any more time. No longer can I afford to let Liquid get away. If this keeps up, my old and dilapidated body will stop moving before I can put myself to rest."

His lips moved in a silent prayer. *God, the will of the universe, fate, whoever is out there. Please let me complete my last mission. Let me, and then I'll give you my soul, my life, or whatever it is you want.*

But Liquid stepped onto the lowered hook and parted from the quay. Like an ascending angel he gazed down at Snake, then, with a triumphant pointing of a finger, he said, "But as for you, brother...You'll stay here to mark this island's watery grave."

Snake gritted his teeth and forced strength into his wavering legs to somehow raise the M4 and stop Liquid. He wrung out the last of his stamina and planted his feet.

Suddenly, his windpipe went into a violent fit.

He coughed with no sign of stopping, as if to expel every last gasp of air from his lungs. Every muscle in his upper body, from his back to his chest to his sides, already ached from all the coughing induced by the harshly cold air since he'd set foot on the island. Now it felt like his muscles were tearing themselves off his bones. As Snake began to black out from the convulsions in his chest, Liquid slipped into the ship.

Snake slumped forward, clutching at his chest, helpless, while Liquid's voice boomed, announcing the death sentence: "I'll crush you with *Haven!*"

Just then, a deep explosion like that of a launching firework went off in the distance, followed by the high-pitched sound of an object cutting through air.

A white pillar of water burst into the sky just off *Haven*'s starboard.

The spray fell in a downpour, drenching Snake. Cannon fire. Coughing, Snake lifted his head and looked to the horizon line, where the cloudy Aleutian sky met the Pacific. He could see the outline of a single ship. Judging from the size and distance, the vessel had to be quite large. Two more shots landed right next to *Haven*.

The projectiles belonged to the three-gun, sixteen-inch, fifty-caliber cannons mounted on Mei Ling's *Missouri*. The battleship lacked digital navigation and relied on last-century analog fire control computers to direct the main battery.

I wondered if Liquid realized the unfavorable situation he was now in. Not even *Haven*'s double-layered submarine hull could take a sixteen-inch shell unscathed. And *Missouri*'s initial attack hadn't even been intended to hit target, but were test rounds fired to determine distance, air pressure, and wind speed. If *Haven* remained still, the next volley might well hit.

*Haven*'s canopy hurriedly began to close. If a shell through the hull would be bad, a direct hit on the exposed interior would be disastrous. Then there was the all-important railgun. The Arsenal's bridge closed, and the vessel pulled away from the dock at full speed.

Snake, still coughing, raised his M4 and aimed at the quickly receding *Outer Haven*. Blood flowed from a cut on his forehead and stained his face red. He used one hand to wipe the blood from his eyes, but his vision remained blurry, and he couldn't tell what he was looking at.

Then something deep within him snapped.

Something that had been barely holding together his overburdened body.

In a terrible spasmodic fit, Snake dropped the rifle. Unable even to fall over, he stood there in a daze, watching the indistinct outline of *Outer Haven* turn back toward him. He realized the shape was growing larger. The ship had returned to smash through the harbor—and Snake with it.

*Missouri* opened fire, but *Haven* moved too quickly. The giant steel whale charged between columns of spray. I didn't think the impact with the harbor would put a scratch on *Haven*'s hull.

The harbor would be crushed—and the frail human body standing upon it.

I urged Snake to run, but he appeared not to hear anything. He stood frozen, like a scarecrow, with no prayer of moving, fettered by fatigue, injury, and age.

The rumble filled my ears. Snake closed his eyes and awaited the final moment.

"I'm a loser. I'm no one's hero. I'm defeated."

He accepted his humiliations.

"Liquid was right nine years ago. I can't protect anyone. Not even myself."

Then came the scream. Surprised the voice wasn't his own, Snake slowly opened his eyes.

Even after all the incredible events he'd witnessed over the years, Snake still couldn't believe his eyes. Standing between *Haven*'s bow and the crumbling quay was Raiden, feet planted wide, his back holding the ship at bay. He only had one arm, having severed the other to free himself from the rubble.

"Raiden," Snake said.

The sight was incredible. Who could have believed that—even with the powered exoskeleton manifesting strength beyond compare with a normal human—a lone man could halt a vessel two thousand feet long? And yet Snake had seen something similar before. He knew this. He'd been saved like this before.

Shadow Moses, nine years ago. *When Liquid went to crush me with REX's foot, Frank saved me like this. My comrade in arms, code name Fox. Naomi's brother.*

Resisting the vast mass of *Haven*, Raiden said in a guttural voice, "S-Snake, hurry."

"He's right," Snake said. "I can't die yet. I can't give up here. I can't concede to humiliation or defeat. At least not yet," he said to me over our link.

"I have been granted an extended life so that I can atone for my sins. That's what Naomi said to me. Maybe she was right. Maybe I continue to live so that I may fulfill my fate. But don't I carry an even more serious debt—an incontrovertible duty I had to see through more than any abstract concept such as fate or sin?"

Then, Snake spoke to himself, or to someone long dead. "Frank, I wasn't able to protect your sister. I couldn't free her from the bindings of her fate. The one thing I cannot do is betray her wishes. You saved my life; to betray you further would be unforgivable."

As *Haven*'s prow drove into the crumbling concrete, what propelled Snake to escape didn't come from some reserve stamina or mental fortitude, but rather pure duty. Snake's body moved out of an unfulfilled responsibility to the man who'd saved his life, Frank Jaeger.

Raiden's cybernetic frame shot out sparks like it had gone haywire. His powered exoskeleton had twisted in places and been crushed in others. Sent down pathways with no destination left to receive the energy, volatile electricity arced across the outside of his body. His back and his left arm, bearing the full force of *Haven*, strained to withstand it. If he kept holding back the ship much longer, his body would be crushed along with the quay.

Liquid's mocking voice came from a loudspeaker on the side of the ship. "Give me a good show at the end, like Frank did."

Snake's blood boiled with rage. But as he called out to his friend, Raiden's powered exoskeleton finally exhausted the last of its strength. Raiden collapsed, electricity discharging in a violent cascade of sparks. His arm fell slack, outstretched, wedged between *Haven*'s hull and the crumbling pier.

Snake shouted, but his voice disappeared within the rumble and the screams. Raiden's fingers snapped, his hand squashed, his wrist crushed, then his elbow, then his entire arm. This pain wasn't anything like the brief instant of fire when he cut his own right arm off. This pain, the meat grinder slowly working its way up from his fingertips, exceeded anything he'd ever experienced.

Not even Vamp skewering him like a shish kebab compared.

Flesh fused with bone, and his shoulder was pulverized beyond recognition. Bathed in white blood, Jack screamed a name.

The place he belonged. The woman he belonged with.

Jack called out the name that hadn't passed his lips in years and fell into darkness.

## ACT 5: OLD SUN

SO FAR I'VE told you stories about many people.

The two Snakes who changed the world; the young man who became caught up in their struggle and was nearly turned into a Snake himself; and the woman who gave birth to those Snakes—and thereby to our world.

My last story belongs to another woman, the woman who ended that world.

Just as everything began with a woman, so too did it end with one.

~~~

As with the first woman, I don't know the real name of the one who brought about the end. I don't think she ever learned what name her parents had lovingly called her. Perhaps she herself died not knowing.

But her name wasn't her only mystery. She had been orphaned by the time of her first memories. Her smooth, burnished brown skin suggested from where she may have come, but provided no real answers. From her sharp, chiseled nose, she was likely of Indian rather than African descent.

Lending further credence to that conjecture was the history of the nation from which she had been adopted—Rhodesia.

Rhodesia never received formal international recognition as a state, not from the time the nation existed as a colony of the British Empire until its rebirth as Zimbabwe.

After World War II, independence movements grew in colonial territories such as India. The British Empire decided holding on to those lands would be too dangerous and chose to give up control over the Dominions of the Commonwealth, recognizing the peoples' right to self-rule.

Rhodesia, however, met this policy with a public outcry. That is to say: the *whites* of Rhodesia were the ones doing the outcrying. The ruling class, of European descent, comprised not even one tenth of the colony's population. To that elite group, a free republic was beyond consideration. Such independence would signify the total destruction of their way of life, built upon oppression of the locals.

In an ironic turn of events, the ruling class decided to sign a unilateral declaration of independence from Britain to prevent the crown from creating a republic by decree.

As a former colony of the British Empire, Rhodesia saw significant immigration from another former colony, India. Perhaps the nameless woman carried the blood of these people, possibly mixed with Anglo blood. Regardless of her own provenance, she was born amongst the many races of a colonial populace. Soon, she was orphaned.

A mercenary hired to fight in the civil war took the child in. Indigenous peoples rose up against the white government in the hope of creating an African state, of Africans and for Africans; a nation whose people could live with dignity, and not under the false republic of Rhodesia or the apartheid state of neighboring South Africa. For the name of their land the African nationalists suggested Zimbabwe, after a kingdom that once ruled the region.

To oppose the nationalist factions—such as the Zimbabwe African National Union and the Zimbabwe African People's Union—the white government strengthened its army through the employment of great numbers of mercenaries. At the same time, some among the wealthy class fled from Rhodesia with their assets and used their fortunes to hire soldiers as private bodyguards.

The teenage soldier who found the girl on the Zambezi River was one of these dogs of war.

She was born in a country that officially didn't exist. She had no name and no parents. On the banks of the Zambezi the helpless girl hungered and thirsted until the hired gun took her to his home in America. He provided her with documentation, education, a living, and a life. Everything she had lost in Rhodesia, he gave to her freely.

With her new life came a name: Naomi Hunter.

She began a new life in an unknown land. She was neither white nor black, nor part of America's rapidly growing Hispanic population, nor was she Chinese or Korean. Not even sure of her Indian descent, she kept her distance from that community as well.

In the great melting pot, people of all races came together, yet each lived with the help of their own racial peers. Not belonging to any race, or even knowing who she was, Naomi faced many difficulties in her new life. A multiethnic society did not mean a person could live without ethnicity or religious belief, but rather the opposite—society demanded of its participants a clear and constant expression of their blood and their God.

Despite her hardships, Naomi adored the soldier who had taken her in. He loved her as a younger sister, and she respected him as an older brother. The two shared nothing in common, yet they supported each other. They were a community of two. In this lonesome world, this one man accepted who she was, and for that she loved him deeply.

He never spoke much of his past, but even the young Naomi could easily sense that he too carried loneliness inside, and she knew intuitively that, like her, he was a war orphan. She understood him.

Naomi felt thankful to her brother and thought of him as an inseparable part of herself. He was her purpose for living, and for him she would have done anything. She never pried into his past and never asked why he had taken her in.

I think this was a form of self-deception.

Naomi was acutely aware that only tragedy would come the moment she asked *Why me?* Whenever she laughed with him, or shared her troubles, or cried with him, she sensed her brother's heart was somewhere else, almost as if he were saying that here was not where he belonged.

Naomi felt deep shame that she couldn't provide a place for her brother. She realized that no matter how completely she loved him, she couldn't become his strength. She saw the way he never looked her in the eye, and as they played their contrived roles as brother and sister she gradually realized the answer to her question, *Why did he take me in?* With confirmation would come true understanding, but so might come the destruction of their family.

Naomi ran from the truth. She refused to ask. If there was any chance the question could hurt her brother, she'd swallow the words and hold them deep inside.

Perhaps she was scared by the slightest possibility that he didn't really love her—or even worse: that upon learning the answer she would lose her own love for him.

Naomi didn't want to lose either his love for her or her own love for him. She ran from the answer until one day, her brother suddenly disappeared.

He had returned to the battlefield. Rather than playing at being a family, he chose life under fire, praying amid the gunpowder smoke to see the next day.

Because of her brother, she had been able to survive. Because of her brother, she had found a life in America. In a world so malicious her very existence seemed threatened, her only comfort was the brother who loved and protected her—Frank Jaegar.

Until then Frank had provided her a foundation, a guarantee of her identity. No matter what else, at least *he* knew who she was. But now, having lost her brother, she needed a new basis for her identity. To seek it, she started down a new path—the study of genetic engineering.

Maybe she believed that by studying her own genetic makeup, she would come to understand who she was. Within the fragmented genetic codes awaited knowledge of her father and mother.

Naomi made many revolutionary discoveries in her field, but each was nothing more than an accidental by-product of her personal journey. And the deeper she searched, the more unclear and elusive her answer became. Science was often like that—the pursuit of a clear, distinct, and unchanging truth brought only a vast ambiguity neither black nor white.

Yet Naomi persisted, resolute on finding her true self from within her genes. Her ever-growing list of contributions to the science of genetic engineering—and its offshoot, nanomachine technology—brought her no closer to discovering a new foundation for her self-identity and instead amounted to nothing more than tiny, incidental wounds acquired amid the struggle to find herself.

Naomi found not the answer she sought, but rather an array of professional accomplishments she neither desired nor found fulfilling.

Then she reunited with her brother.

He was barely alive.

When secession movements erupted in the Soviet republics of Central Asia, one territory remained crucial to the motherland as a religious cushion between the neighboring Muslim states, and the reformed Russian government wasn't about to let it go. As the Soviet military had invaded Afghanistan, the Russian armed forces were detached to the territory of Tselinoyarsk.

Yet the child state, certainly no major military power, somehow prevailed in the conflict. According to rumor, one man had organized a mercenary army, supplied a torrent of arms, and provided training on the ground. The newly independent people named their country Zanzibar Land.

And Naomi's brother came back from that failed nation nearly a dead man.

As much as she loved him, faced with his tragic transformation, she couldn't make herself feel glad that he had survived. Not only had Frank Jaeger been at the brink of death, his heart had stopped several times.

He had become the test subject for a powered exoskeleton prototype.

Fighting off terrible pain with a cocktail of drugs and nanomachines, he existed in a state that couldn't be called life.

The man who had done this to her brother was an American operative sent into Zanzibar Land. Naomi never uncovered the agent's real name from deep beneath the veil of classified information. But after single-handedly toppling the fledgling nation, his reputation as a "legendary hero" spread quickly through the underworld.

His code name was Solid Snake.

And he was the man who had destroyed the one she loved and the foundation of her being.

~~~

In *Missouri*'s briefing room, Mei Ling gestured at the slides with a pointer.

"*Haven* is headed southward through the Pacific at a speed of thirty-three knots. We're falling behind at a rate of about two nautical miles every hour."

Displayed on the projection screen was an aerial view composited from several dozen images. Far ahead of *Missouri* and its trailing hyphen of white wake, a faint whalelike shadow could be seen beneath the ocean's surface. But the shape, at more than two times *Missouri*'s size, couldn't have belonged to any whale—not even one from a Japanese monster movie.

I asked Mei Ling, "Can't this thing go any faster?"

She smiled tightly, the expression part umbrage at my lack of respect toward her relic of a ship and part apology.

The situation wasn't without irony. The US Navy's Arsenal Ship Program had aimed to create a battleship for the twenty-first century. Now the last of the old battleships pursued its modern counterpart like a father chasing after his runaway child.

"I'm afraid not," Mei Ling said. "This is as fast as she'll go."

In other words, we would never be able to catch up with Liquid and blast him out of the water. But all was not hopeless. We didn't have to overtake him on the way.

"Liquid's target is JD, a US military satellite disguised as orbital debris. *Haven* will have to surface in order to use its railgun."

As she gave her briefing, Mei Ling regarded the room. Seated among the gathered soldiers were members of the Rat Patrol—but only Meryl and Johnny. Ed and Jonathan hadn't recovered from the events in Eastern Europe and remained shoreside.

In a chair beside Meryl, Johnny began typing on his wrist computer and said, "If we have JD's orbit, we can predict where *Haven*'s going to surface."

Mei Ling nodded and advanced the slide. On the screen, the earth was enveloped within a particulate haze—every satellite, whether military, weather, communications, or any other kind, under NORAD's watch. Gradually, the dots and orbits winked out until only one remained.

JD.

Adding the locations of *Missouri* and *Haven* to the simulated globe, Mei Ling said, "JD is in a synchronous elliptical orbit. So its next perigee should be in..."

"Got it!" Johnny read the results from his wearable computer. "Fifteen hours, six minutes, and twelve seconds."

At that time, the satellite would be closest to sea level.

"Right," Mei Ling said. "In fifteen hours, JD is going to be over the Bering Sea, 494 nautical miles from the Bering Strait. *Haven* will be in holding position in that area."

Meryl asked, "Do they really have to get that close to launch?"

REX's railgun could launch a nuclear warhead to any location on Earth. So why did Liquid need to wait for the satellite's perigee? I stood and approached the screen to explain not just to Meryl but to the rest of the team.

"REX may be armed with nuclear ordnance, but JD floats in

an orbit high enough to be called outer space. Why is this important? Because up there, there's virtually no air, and without air, there's no stuff to envelop the fission event, absorb the massive output of energy, and turn into plasma.

"In terrestrial nuclear explosions, whether fissile or fusional, a certain amount of the destructive power comes from forces external to the initial blast, including shock waves, fragmentation, and thermal waves. Even assuming that all of the energy will radiate, between the distance of the satellite's orbit and the yield of REX's nukes, the effective damage radius won't be much larger than a thousand feet, or approximately three hundred meters.

"Some of you may be thinking that a two-thousand-foot blast radius sounds impressive. But your typical satellite is always moving forward, so as not to be pulled down by Earth's gravity, and maintains an orbit traveling at a relative velocity that can exceed ten kilometers per second.

"Down on Earth, in the presence of air resistance, producing such a ludicrous speed is impossible. An object moving that fast wouldn't even be captured by a twenty-four frame-per-second movie camera, passing by entirely in that instant between frames. To put it another way, without sufficient acceleration, the satellite would be pulled down by gravity and crash.

"Say REX's nuke manages to explode precisely on JD's orbital path. The satellite, moving at ten kilometers per second, will pass through the six-hundred-meter blast diameter within six hundredths of a second. That's barely the blink of an eye. Even with the Arsenal-class targeting computer, the only chance of shooting down such a high-speed object is to reduce the range as much as possible. Though the elliptical orbit means that JD will be at peak velocity at its perigee, the possibility of a close or direct hit is maximized at relatively short range.

"So even when Liquid reaches the firing location, he'll have to wait to launch his nuke until he has the highest probability of success, when JD is at its perigee. Time enough for *Missouri* to catch up."

Mei Ling made sure everyone understood my explanation before moving on to our battle plan.

"*Haven* will need to open the outer cover to launch the nuke via the railgun. That's our one and only chance to board."

The next slide was a photograph of *Missouri* firing upon *Haven*'s exposed bridge back on Shadow Moses. The two electromagnetic rails of REX's stolen weapon looked like a pair of chopsticks.

"To board?" Meryl asked. "Why can't we attack it from the outside?"

*Missouri* didn't have digital guidance systems, but the ship did have large caliber cannons. She was a relic from the last century, but new or old was inconsequential: a giant mass of metal and explosives would punch a hole in even the newest of vessels.

Meryl's question was reasonable, but the problem rested in the source of Liquid's power.

"It wouldn't do any good," I said, then stood and again made my way to the front of the room. "As long as Liquid has control of the System, physically destroying GW would still leave supreme authority over SOP in his hands. We can't simply blow *Haven* apart when she surfaces."

Mei Ling nodded. "Yes. Dr. Emmerich is right. That's why we need to destroy GW from the inside before attacking *Haven* itself."

Snake, who was leaning against the wall at the back of the room, removed the oxygen mask from his mouth to joke, "Liquid's very own Death Star."

In the nine years I'd known Snake, this was the first time I'd heard him reference *Star Wars*. If he had been hoping for a reaction from the room he was disappointed, for as soon as he had made the remark, he began to cough painfully and reaffixed the mask.

When his coughing quieted, Mei Ling continued. "We know *Haven* will have to surface in order to fire the railgun. When it does, we'll know, and *Missouri* will make a quick approach and deliver our strike team. Our goal is twofold: prevent that nuke from launching and wipe out GW's programming. The enemy relies entirely on electronic means of threat detection, so they won't be able to see the *Missouri* until they surface."

Mei Ling gazed across the dark room at the faces illuminated by the projector's light. All thought this talk preposterous at least to some degree. Liquid's elite guard of *Haven* troopers were a death trap in waiting. This wasn't a plan but a suicide mission—that much was as clear as day.

But they all knew there was no other way.

Mei Ling explained the plan. "We'll launch the strike team from catapults at the exact moment *Haven*'s armored cover opens. They'll then penetrate GW's physical server room and infect it with Dr. Emmerich's worm cluster."

Johnny, watching a simulation on the display of his wrist computer, asked, "But what if Liquid turns off GW before we get in there?"

Even if the team made it inside the server room, the computer terminal needed to be powered on and functioning in order to receive the virus. Of course, Mei Ling and I had already thought of all the potential problems and contingencies, so she was ready with an answer.

"Liquid is already entrenched within the Patriots' network. He needs to maintain his link with the SOP, or destroying JD won't serve any purpose. They can't afford to shut GW down."

Meryl, sharing Johnny's concerns, bleakly said, "Liquid will throw everything he's got at stopping the strike team."

She was right, of course. It was easy for us to propose the infiltration, but the strike team—Meryl, Snake, and Akiba—would be the ones facing the gunfire. Mei Ling and I hadn't been able to think of anything we could do to help them once the mission began.

Now Mei Ling broached the biggest danger facing Meryl's team. "Exactly," she said. "The corridor leading to GW is defended by directed-energy weapons that emit a type of microwaves."

Johnny leaned forward. "Did you say microwaves?"

Mei Ling's report seemed to have unsettled the other soldiers in the room too, including Snake, who lowered his oxygen mask and sent his eyes to me.

Disregarding her audience's unease, Mei Ling calmly continued. "The waves will immediately begin to vaporize any living person within range."

Snake started to say something but coughed instead, and kept on coughing until he finally regained himself.

"A giant microwave oven," he said. "You'd have to have a death wish to go in there." His lips twitched into a ghastly smile. "Sounds like the perfect job for me."

"Snake," Meryl scolded, her voice tinged with sadness, "this isn't time for your stupid jokes."

Within three months, this man whom she had loved would have to end his own life, perhaps with a gun to his head, or with a can of gasoline and a match.

The grim reality was that some situations required the risk of life and limb for any chance of making it through.

Only natural for the task to go to the one man who had already accepted death.

But Snake's resolve came not from some passive acquiescence to circumstance but rather an outraged rejection of forcing someone younger—Johnny or Meryl—to take on his ills and die for it.

"If somebody has to die today," he said, "it has to be me. No one else." Everything about this briefing grated on him. "Why bother with all this when I should be going in alone?"

Meryl and I could read his emotions all too well. I was pained to see him like this, intent on finishing everything unaided. I wondered if Mei Ling felt intimidated by his heroic determination. Not knowing how to respond, she proceeded with her briefing.

"Outside the corridor, Liquid's soldiers will be out in full force. Inside, unmanned weapons will wait."

A new slide revealed a detailed schematic of *Haven*. Under the Patriots' control, the Arsenal-class ship was supposed to be a highly guarded state secret. Few even knew of their existence, yet this was an incredibly detailed report.

Snake's eyes tightened. "Where are you getting this information? You really think there's a way to destroy GW?"

Mei Ling tossed me a glance. I had shared with her all the intel so she could develop a battle plan. She knew the identity of the source, but her eyes told me Snake needed to hear the name from me.

I took a moment, then said, "Naomi had been making preparations."

Naomi's original reason for boarding *Nomad* had been none other than me. She needed someone to whom she could entrust her plans, who had the ability to fulfill her hopes.

But in the end, that person wasn't me.

Naomi chose a little girl, not yet ten years old.

Naomi had nearly completed the program to destroy GW. But she knew that she couldn't grant herself enough time to finish—that her life, extended artificially by nanomachines, would soon end; that death would shatter time's icy prison, and she had to accept it; that she might pass from this world without seeing the worm cluster finished.

And she had chosen Sunny as the one who could realize her wishes. The child's message, delivered by Raiden at Shadow Moses: *I cooked them right*, her words a message to Naomi. Sunny had finished the worm.

Naomi left us more than source code. She had provided accurate and precise internal data on *Haven*, upon which we based our plan of attack.

Snake asked, "Whose side was she on, anyway?"

He stared me straight in the eyes. Maybe he thought I would know the answer because I'd had feelings for her. I might have found the inquiry offensive coming from anyone but Snake.

Our friendship had long since crossed any such barriers, and I would have happily told him—had I known the answer myself.

But sadly, despite what I felt for Naomi, I hadn't the slight-est idea. If she wanted to defeat Liquid's plans—by giving us the unfinished code to a program that could electronically destroy GW—then her actions in Eastern Europe were inexplicable.

"I don't know," I said, "what her true intentions were. But..."

If Naomi had wanted to stop Liquid, she wouldn't have needed to escape *Nomad* and help him take over the SOP. In doing so, she gave him control over the world's armies—a terrible power—and then told us to stop him. Neither Snake nor I had a cohesive expla-nation to resolve the clear contradiction in her behavior.

And now, neither of us could know what Naomi had truly wanted.

I made myself recall her fleeting expression of relief when she heard Sunny's message. *I cooked them right.* I tried to feel what Naomi must have felt.

What purpose for living had she found after learning of her cancer, as the fear of death threatened to break her each night? What had she needed to accomplish before passing on? What would be her penitence? Her sins—among them Vamp, Snake, and Liquid—had brought irrevocable change to the world.

Naomi knew her borrowed time would be far too short to settle her debts. And so she imposed on herself the artificial life she had given to Vamp, and she made contact with me and Snake—and Sunny.

As she died, Naomi said to Snake, *Your life has been prolonged so that you may fulfill your purpose.* She had been tied to the same fate. Snake wanted to know whose side she was on, yet I sensed that she had long since passed any notion of allegiances.

"But," I continued, "one thing's for sure: she was determined to stop Liquid."

Snake's gaze seemed to soften, if by only a bit. I don't know if he believed me, or if he had simply decided to take the gamble. Naomi was gone from this world; whether he believed in her or in Sunny and me, who had taken up her cause, the result would be the same.

In that manner, Naomi wasn't unique. Wolf and Emma, and all of the dead—for that matter, the living too—existed in a way, nestled inside other people. I was Wolf, I was Emma, I was Naomi, and I was Snake. I was, in part, all of those gathered at the briefing.

"There's a saying in China," Mei Ling said. "When a bird is upon death, its cry is heartbreaking. When a man is upon death, his words are right."

Even Mei Ling's formidable command of quotations had misfired here. If sorrow could be found in a bird's death cry, a person's dying words were worthy of attention. Perhaps Mei Ling was suggesting we should trust Naomi. But none in the room provided any reaction, not even Meryl or Johnny.

But her words did make me think.

People never truly ceased to be. Like a river flowing through those who speak for us, human existence endured within both the physical body as well as stories passed down. As long as somebody continued to tell our stories, none of us—not Snake, not Meryl, nor any of the soldiers here with us—none would truly go.

*His words are right.* What was spoken on the verge of death were not mere words but a facet of our lives, a seedling to sprout branches into the future.

Mei Ling asked if anyone had any other questions, but a dark mood had fallen over the room. No questions were necessary. Snake had said this mission was for a suicide squad, and he was right: some might die. Then, breaking the heavy, seemingly eternal silence, Snake casually raised his hand.

"Anybody got a smoke?"

2

AS WE ALWAYS did before a job, Snake and I walked together.

Where we went was never important, whether a park or the streets near a hideout. Before engaging in a dangerous mission, as part of our anti-Metal Gear or anti-Patriots activities, the two of us went on a walk. As long as the sky was above our heads, we didn't care where.

This time, we strolled *Missouri*'s deck. I was never a believer in the so-called "good old days," but the wooden deck was top class and top quality, well polished and pristine. A museum ship in Hawaii until recently, the vessel had been carefully preserved. In terms of pure aesthetics, the meticulously polished deck was in a class apart from the modern metal numbers, slathered with a mixture of shoddy-looking blue paint and coarse sand for better traction.

Snake asked me, "How is Raiden?"

Raiden had severed his right arm to escape the rubble, and the Arsenal had crushed his left. Obviously he wasn't all right.

"He'll live," I said, "but he's in no shape to fight. Best to let him rest."

Raiden likely owed his life to his body's cybernetic tissue closing capability. Losing an entire arm, let alone two, was a potentially fatal wound. But when the flow of blood and energy can be disengaged from the limbs, preventing any further losses, such injuries became vastly preferable to what Vamp had done to him in South America. With multiple stab wounds over his entire torso, closing down those tissues would have rendered Raiden immobile.

Snake seemed relieved to hear that Raiden wouldn't be joining the fight.

"The only people I have left to rely on," Snake said, "are Meryl and..."

He looked across the deck's expanse to the port side of the ship, where Akiba was walking, hunched over and unsteady. Perpetually at the mercy of his bowels, Johnny was a young man in great difficulty.

I shrugged and said, "Kind of an unknown quantity, isn't he?"

Akiba felt restless because of his ever-worsening stomach, but the other soldiers were similarly ill at ease, nervously fidgeting and glancing in all directions. Without the SOP's control, they were no longer able to hold back their fear of and excitement for battle.

"Everybody's losing their nerve," I said, "without the System to protect them. I hear that a lot of soldiers are deserting because the SOP's aftereffects are so bad."

Then I heard a familiar voice. "I hooked Akiba up with a naked M82."

I turned to see Drebin, sitting above us, atop the massive barrel of a sixteen-inch gun turret, his pinstripe suit appearing entirely out of place.

Drebin raised a can of NARC soda in greeting and said, "Fancy meetin' you here."

"What are you doing here?" Snake asked.

"I laundered these guys' IDs, then issued 'em new, naked guns. Including that catapult you're gonna be riding."

Drebin gestured with the can toward a row of what at first glance looked like antiaircraft guns affixed to the wooden deck— the human catapults that would launch the strike team onto *Haven*.

"Business has been slow," Drebin said, "ever since Liquid got his hands on GW. His extra orders stopped coming in. Now that all the weapons all over the world are locked, the only ones still looking to fight would be you and yours. Apparently everyone else thinks it's not economical to replace all their useless equipment with my stuff." He shrugged. "So I made an extra special trip out here, just for you."

*This guy must have some taste for danger*, I thought.

"Drebin," Snake said, "do you have even the slightest idea what's going on here?"

"Of course I do." Behind the sunglasses, Drebin's eyes narrowed in delight. He held out the aluminum can. "See, when it comes down to it, the world's like this soda here. Once the fizz is gone, I ain't got no use for it. It's got no worth."

He paused to let his message sink in. "I'm on the side of whoever needs me the most. You dig?"

Then Drebin made his trademark gesture, pointing first at his eyes, then at Snake.

Unable to decide what, if anything, he had up his sleeve, Snake and I left the peculiar man and resumed our walk across the *Missouri*'s deck.

To Snake, I remarked *sotto voce*, "He can't be here just for business. I shudder to think someone would be here for the fun of it."

Snake shook his head and said, "I strongly suspect this is more than a hobby for him."

Why was Drebin following us everywhere we went?

The man certainly seemed to be enjoying himself. But I'd have had to be crazy to think he'd gone across the world and back with us just for fun.

The horizon where Liquid would soon surface was quiet and still, without any large waves, perhaps in awareness of the gravity of the coming battle. As we cut through the peaceful waters, I turned my gaze back to the majesty of the aged battleship.

Maybe she hadn't half the Arsenal's stupefying size, but *Missouri*'s superstructure, with a unified bridge, smoke stacks, and rear rangefinder, stood stern and imposing, like a medieval castle. She was the epitome of a battleship, with a fatherly ruggedness—not at all similar to the Arsenal-class *Haven*'s rounded, stealth-oriented design. As befitting a sea vessel, *Missouri* would always be referred to as "she," but have no doubts: *Missouri* was a man, and a resolute father at that.

The ship carried scars from her many battles. Walking from aft to fore along the starboard side, Snake noticed part of the hull was significantly bent.

Snake patted his pockets for a cigarette. "That's a fairly large dent."

I nodded. "A Zero put that there. A kamikaze in the Pacific War."

"A Zero, huh?"

"This ship has many stories. She's been around longer than either of us. The Japanese foreign minister signed the Instrument of Surrender on this deck, you know."

"Where?"

Snake looked across the deck. Several of the ship's crew were working, busily preparing for the fight to come.

"I think there's a plaque somewhere," I said. "Mei Ling would know."

"A hull bent by a Zero, and a plate to show where Japan signed surrender—marks of the history she's witnessed..."

"Right," I said. "Everything has a tale—not just people, but ships, buildings, even simple objects. All of us."

"And you've taken on Naomi's story. You finished her worm cluster."

"Actually, Sunny's the one who finished it. Although she was only one of three to write the code."

Snake managed to find a cigarette and put it to his mouth. His lips tightened, his skeptical expression asking, *Sunny, Naomi, and who else?*

Snake was right to be curious. He knew I hadn't contributed any of the programming. I took out a lighter and, covering the flame with one hand to protect it from the sea breeze, lit Snake's smoke.

Then I said, "Sunny went fishing through the Gaudi's libraries to see if there was any source code she could use to complete the program. What she found was Emma's worm cluster."

Snake didn't say anything but just looked into my face. My sister, a specialist in high-volume data analysis, had written the program to destroy GW. And she knew well how to destroy the AI, having designed it herself.

"Sunny took my sister's code and worked it into Naomi's program. I didn't have time to look over every single line, but what I did see reminded me of Emma—like she had left traces of herself in the way she coded."

Even programming code could hold a story. Programs were more than numbers and instructions, but records of another world. The cluster was part of Emma's story—proof that Emma Emmerich Danziger had once lived, and she had told many stories.

Snake, engrossed in my talk, had forgotten to breathe, and began coughing on his own cigarette smoke.

I made a wry smile, patted his back, and said, "But this worm cluster that Sunny created... it's even better than Emma's. Sunny's worm destroys the AI's intellect by triggering apoptosis. Once uploaded into GW, it should do some real damage."

I continued to comfort Snake and was again struck by how terribly weak he had become. Touching my hand to his back, I could feel that the strength that had once roused the legendary man no longer remained in this aged body.

"You're dead set on going to *Haven* yourself?" I asked, but I knew there was no point in asking. When I tried to tell him to give up before we went to Shadow Moses, he wouldn't listen. *We started this*, he'd said, before descending to the island and the bitter cold his old body couldn't withstand.

"I still have things left to do besides smoke."

Snake moved as if to toss his cigarette into the ocean. He returned my disapproving look with a grin and took out his portable ashtray and used it. I hadn't made a face at his littering, but rather at why this man had to shoulder the sins of mankind, and at why he would be leaving us.

He was the same with Frank. Snake hadn't wanted things to end that way. Irrational fate brought the two men together, and in the end, compelled them to fight. Snake wasn't to blame for defeating Frank Jaeger, and Snake wasn't the one who made Frank the experimental subject for the powered exoskeleton project.

But Snake attracted tragedy. He stewarded the sins of others. At Shadow Moses, he drew Naomi's hate. And now he was ready to put a conclusion to it all before embracing his death.

Another coughing fit overcame Snake, and when it passed, he remained bent over, hands on his knees. He looked up at me and said, "What about you, Otacon? Have you thought about just leaving the ship?"

Snake had always brushed aside any concern offered him. Even in his current shape, he stubbornly pressed ahead to fulfill his duty. But now with Snake worrying about me, I found myself answering as he would. We were two pigheaded men.

"Stop it," I said. "I've still got things to do myself. And I don't even smoke."

"Snake," Campbell said, "can you hear me?"

On my notebook's screen the colonel's face appeared stiff. I had called Snake and Meryl back to the vacant briefing room to hear Campbell's report. Meryl didn't like having to meet with the man, even across the computer screen, but Snake asked her, and she couldn't refuse him.

"Liquid's warship, *Outer Haven*," Campbell said, "is a modified version of an Arsenal Gear model stolen from the Patriots."

The first Arsenal-class ship had been secretly constructed in New York Bay. Solidus's terrorist plot, intended to locate information on the Patriots hidden within GW, resulted in the ship grounding on the island of Manhattan, destroying several buildings.

The true story was hidden from the public, and the shocking event went down as the largest naval accident in history, attributed as a software error in the Arsenal's navigation systems—something akin to the divide-by-zero glitch that left a cruiser running Windows NT dead in the water off the coast of Virginia.

"After the Manhattan 'accident,'" Campbell explained, "public criticism of the military swelled, and between oversight committees and a spate of new laws monitoring safety and operations, the US Armed Forces were paralyzed. PMCs gained prominence, and the war economy pervaded the global marketplace. Looking back on the events, I wouldn't be surprised if Liquid—or the Patriots—had planned it all."

According to Campbell's information, the Patriots had built several more Arsenal-class ships—even after the original had been so publicly exposed. When Liquid took over Ocelot's body, he might have gained knowledge of the ships dwelling beneath the seas.

The colonel continued, "Liquid has the warship crawling with IRVINGs and other unmanned weapons. According to Naomi's data, *Haven* is crewed by a battalion of enhanced soldiers, each culled from the best each PMC has to offer, from Praying Mantis to Raven Sword."

Through the monitor, Campbell looked at Meryl. She stood some distance behind us, toward the back of the room, yet she became flustered under the gaze of her father and looked away.

His daughter, his own flesh and blood, was about to embark on a desperate mission, to infiltrate the ship where Liquid's PMC awaited. Campbell kept his composure as best he could, but I knew gut-wrenching emotion consumed him as he watched his daughter.

"Please bring her with you to the briefing," Campbell had asked me.

Lacking confidence that I could convince her, I ended up leaving it to Snake.

The colonel had much to say to her—to his unknowing daughter, to whom he had never permitted himself to confess his illegitimate fatherhood.

But now, as every man and woman aboard the battleship stood

ready before the fateful moment, this father and daughter had not been afforded the time to say what they needed to say. With or without the time, the two preserved a measured distance, unable to make themselves tell the tales they needed to tell.

"If Liquid succeeds in destroying JD," Campbell said, "and gains control of the Patriots' System, he'll make *Haven* his flagship, and his PMCs will spread like wildfire across the globe."

Still, Liquid's plan to destroy JD was undoubtedly a considerable gamble. The more I thought about it, shooting a railgun nuke at a satellite traveling ten kilometers per second bordered on the outrageous.

Missile-based antisatellite weapons were developed by both America and the USSR during the Cold War. The early twenty-first century saw China successfully test an antisatellite weapon system, and in 2008, the US Navy shot down a malfunctioning spy satellite with a missile launched from an Aegis cruiser. That satellite was traveling at a little under eight kilometers per second; the missile flew at it head-on at a speed between three and four kilometers per second, making their relative velocity somewhere around eleven kilometers per second.

But missiles could be controlled after launch. A railgun, however, was essentially a cannon. Once its warhead was fired, the trajectory was largely fixed. With terrestrial targets, stabilizing fins could provide a form of last-moment guidance, but at JD's orbit, the atmosphere was sparse, and fins meant little.

Moreover, this cannon floated on the ocean. No matter how large the ship, no matter what kinds of stabilizers were on-board, maintaining perfectly stationary firing conditions would be nigh impossible.

Liquid had everything riding on one moment. Just as we had everything riding on this one battle.

"This is our last chance," Campbell said, "to stop Liquid from global domination."

I knew that. Snake and Meryl knew that.

I couldn't bear to see Campbell making the same mistake I had made.

*Don't you have anything more important to say right now?*

In those last moments, I hadn't been able to call Emma by her name. I hadn't been able to tell Wolf how I felt. I hadn't understood Naomi's dying wish.

Not like this, Colonel. Time is something people never have. If you two keep up this measured distance, neither of you will ever tell each other anything. Yet still we languish and delay.

Then, as if in disregard for my exasperation, an alarm rang through the ship, and a voice came over the ship's speakers.

"A large object is rapidly surfacing. We can't verify the object, but measurements are in line with an Arsenal-class vessel. Proceed for visual confirmation."

Even behind the closed door to the briefing room, we could hear the footsteps of crew running down passageways to the deck. Amid the suddenly hectic mood, I sighed and shook my head, and looked to Meryl. As the alarm continued its grating clamor, Snake held his eyes on Campbell in silent criticism of his old friend's cowardice.

Meryl simply kept staring at the floor, with no indication she would return Campbell's gaze.

*You have to say something. Now is the time.*

I glared at the father on the other side of the computer screen, trying to spur him to action with my eyes. But Campbell's mouth was held half open, mute and frozen in search of words.

Snake jerked his head to beckon me. Liquid's ship was surfacing, and we had to get moving. Giving up on Campbell, we reluctantly turned our backs to the monitor.

As Snake and I left the room, we could hear Campbell softly begin to speak.

"Meryl," he said, "can you hear me?"

His was the voice of a father.

A father taking the first steps toward responsibility to his daughter.

## 3

THE MOUNT RUSHMORE had emerged from the ocean surface. Depicted by *Haven*'s OctoCamo in the presidential positions, the family of Snakes stared down *Missouri* head-on.

Clutching my notebook computer at my chest, I dashed up the ladderways, eventually parting with Snake and Meryl, who headed for the deck, and continuing up toward the bridge.

I flew into the bridge to hear Mei Ling shouting orders like thunder.

"Maintain full speed! Prepare for ship-to-ship combat!"

A young assistant officer echoed her commands. Mei Ling's voice had already gained the gravitas of a commander. People, when placed in a role, would fill it, whether they wanted to be in the position or not. The circumstances made the person, for better or for worse. The Patriots had used that truth on the Big Shell to put Raiden into Snake's role.

I started to say, "The Arsenal's armament is—"

Mei Ling, her stare fixed upon the distant *Haven*, cut in, "—eight hundred VLS missile cells on the upper structure, and countless MLRS batteries. It's practically a missile field."

"And we only have naval guns?"

"We have four CIWS guns. If one of *Haven*'s missiles gets too close, the Phalanx system will shoot it down."

I opened my notebook and connected to the Mk. III. Snake hugged the diminutive Metal Gear to his chest and sprinted with Meryl toward the catapults. I had given the robot two new upgrades: an antimicrowave coating on the outside, and Sunny's worm cluster in its internal storage. Now Snake had to bring the machine into *Haven*'s server room.

The catapults stood on the wooden deck, thrusting into the

sky like the swords of giants. The machines had been invented to rapidly deploy firefighters and antiterrorist squads to the rooftops of burning or captured buildings.

The compressed-air firing mechanisms would launch the unlucky guinea pig-cum-human cannonballs five stories into the sky—a prime example of a deranged engineering boondoggle unleashed by DARPA on behalf of the American taxpayers.

Snake, Meryl, and Johnny climbed into the seats of their catapults, facing the launch rails as if sitting on carousel horses. Once the air pressure was released, the seats would lift up and fling the strike team onto *Haven*'s inner deck. Back in the briefing, Snake hadn't seemed happy envisioning how ridiculous they would look midair—with arms and legs awkwardly bent like frogs in mid-hop.

With the strike team seated and defenseless, soldiers gathered around them to protect from possible sniper fire. The giant hulk of the *Haven* approached. Readying himself for the moment of the launch, Snake stiffened his aged muscles.

"Prepare to fire the main battery!" Mei Ling ordered.

Using a rangefinder and gyrocompass that were practically ancient relics, the gun operators began computing the necessary data to fire. Turrets swiveled to point at *Haven*'s frame.

We might have been beaten in terms of firepower, but the Arsenal was not agile, and the boat was both immense and close by. I couldn't believe our cannons would miss that kind of target. That was our solitary hope, at least.

When *Haven* surfaced fully, the bridge began to slide open.

The sight was of a titan rending open its stomach to reveal its guts to the daylight. Behind *Haven*, slashes of sunlight cut through the cloudy steel-blue sky, and as the colossal structure opened, the scene felt almost mythical.

Inside, the railgun's tip slowly rose, revealing itself from within the city of boxy structures.

Mei Ling stared through her binoculars, transfixed by Liquid's last gamble. "There it is," she whispered, "the naked nuke."

"Captain," said the young assistant officer, his voice trembling, "tiny hatches are opening all across *Haven*'s deck. They could be exposing VLS launchers. There's too many to count!"

Mei Ling needed to remain composed. She gathered herself, then steadily, decisively ordered the advance. "Maintain full speed. The CIWS will take care of the hostile missiles."

The officer shouted, "The enemy missiles are launching!"

Threads of smoke rose from *Haven*. The smoke climbed straight up, U-turned back down until just kissing the water's surface, then cut straight for *Missouri*.

"Fire!" Mei Ling roared, and the three-gun turrets spit fire. The crew members on deck had covered their ears, so no eardrums were broken, but the severity of the blast and intensity of the powder smoke left more than a few coughing—Snake included.

The fifty-caliber shells flew through the cloud of oncoming missiles straight for *Haven*. A few connected with missiles, exploding the warheads instantly and catching several more in a chain reaction.

The shells struck *Haven*'s bridge. But the gently sloping exterior masterfully repelled the projectiles. The barrage left visible but minor dents; nothing that could really be called damage. While in motion, the Arsenal-class vessel looked like a gently rolling hill gliding atop the waves. No matter which angle *Missouri*'s guns fired from, the projectiles would hit at a shallow angle.

Mei Ling clicked her tongue.

The bridge crew were on hand to provide rapid-fire reports on the battle.

"Even when we hit the target," said one of the young men, "there's only light damage."

Another added, "Missiles incoming!"

One missile that had survived the chain explosions grazed *Missouri*'s starboard hull, right where the kamikaze Zero had struck, and exploded at the water's surface. The rest either blew up near the battleship or were destroyed by the CIWS.

The sea burst and poured over the wooden decks, but *Missouri* didn't slow, her prow barreling straight toward *Haven*.

Mei Ling switched her microphone to broadcast through the entire ship and said, "All hands, prepare for impact. Brace yourselves."

I managed to wrap my arm around a handrail just as *Missouri*'s nose collided with *Haven*'s belly. The bridge shook like a drying machine, and even Mei Ling was knocked off her feet. My arm felt like it was being pulled from its socket, and I gritted my teeth in pain.

The two ships had met at a slight angle. *Missouri* cut toward the starboard side, and the two ships scraped past each other with the dreadful, deafening screech of metal on metal.

Even sent to the floor, Mei Ling held on to her microphone. She had something to do before climbing back to her feet. If she missed her timing, everything would be over.

"Now!"

The tightly compressed gas was let free, and the piston lifted Snake's seat. Fierce g-forces assaulted him, threatening to shatter his hip bone into pieces. The old man bore not only his own weight, but that of the Mk. III, and as the chair heaved him skyward, the muscles and trace amounts of fat in his backside felt like they would crush his pelvis.

But the sensation was brief. The next thing Snake knew, his body was tracing a parabola, and he could see the decks of *Haven* and *Missouri* below. Meryl launched next and seemed to be chasing his posterior through the air. Snake's hunch had been right—they *did* look ridiculous.

Just then, *Haven* rocked to the side and slammed into *Missouri*. The larger ship's mass bore down on *Missouri* and jarred the old battleship.

Unfortunately, Akiba's catapult launched at that moment.

His trajectory sent askew, Akiba flew in a direction far from Snake and Meryl. He didn't have much time to lament the turn of events beyond his control—by the time he knew what had happened, Solid Snake's titanic countenance occupied his field of view.

Johnny Akiba's screams silenced when he struck Mount Snakemore.

Meryl called out to him and looked over her shoulder to see Johnny, unlucky as ever, kiss Snake's lower lip, then tumble down *Haven*'s hull and into the sea.

Meanwhile, the real Snake had crossed into *Haven*'s exposed inner bow. In the moments before he struck the deck, he attempted to maneuver into a landing stance. Snake possessed some experience—when he had infiltrated the tanker where Metal Gear RAY was held, he'd bungee-jumped to the ship from the George Washington Bridge.

Snake thought he had the landing down, but his aged body wasn't able to keep up. He attempted a three-point landing with both knees and his right arm, but he couldn't absorb the inertia of his fall and tumbled to the ground, rolling a few yards down the deck.

Snake had done his best to roll out of the landing, but his body smashed against the inside of his sneaking suit. Of course, he didn't have time to lay on the ground. He put his hand on the deck to push himself to his feet, and the muscles in his shoulder and arm cried out in pain. Beneath the OctoCamo and power assist systems, his skin was battered and bloodied.

Gritting through the pain, Snake searched for a place to hide. He had to retreat before Liquid's soldiers came running. Snake swiftly took notice of his surroundings. Within *Haven*'s hull, the ship's bow was as it had appeared from afar: a labyrinthine city of rectangular, windowless structures some three or four stories high.

Snake saw no signs of Meryl or Johnny amid the sprawling blocks—but since his visibility was limited by the irregular and perplexing layout of the deck, the two might yet be close. Just as Snake began to worry about Meryl, the ring of an incoming call over the codec vibrated the bones of his inner ear.

"Snake," Meryl whispered. From the sound of her voice, she too was fighting pain. "I hurt my right ankle."

"Can you walk?" Snake asked.

Meryl tried to stand, but her sprained ankle buckled under the weight.

When Snake asked if she was all right, she laughed drily and said, "Hurts a hell of a lot more without SOP."

Before, the SOP would have quickly detected any injuries she sustained that were severe enough to impede combat performance and subdue the pain through sensory deprivation or increased endorphin output. Under the System, she had still felt pain, but only as a virtual sensation—a phantom pain in place of the real one, just strong enough to provide awareness of the injury without dulling her reflexes.

Now, for the first time in a long time, Meryl experienced the real thing.

Snake said, "Makes you feel alive, doesn't it?"

Long-forgotten sensations disoriented soldiers freed from the SOP's control.

Sensations imposed by flesh and brain were often unpleasant. Over their long evolutionary history, vertebrates acquired the ability to feel as a fundamental function for survival. Of course, such perceptions, however unpleasant, were a part of keeping alive, and since nobody could find someone else to experience the sensations for them, most people were content to take the bad with the good.

Snake asked, "What about Johnny?"

"He fell into the ocean."

Akiba was out of the mission before it even started. The guy was proving more hopeless than ever. And he had fallen between *Haven* and *Missouri*—that he had done so without injury was unlikely. Both Snake and Meryl worried for him, but they could do nothing now but hope.

Gunfire reported over the codec and the shots echoed through the ship's interior. Meryl was under fire, near enough for the battle to be heard.

"Snake," she said, "I'll catch up soon. You go ahead."

"Meryl!" Snake shouted, but she cut the connection.

Blocking out his pain, Snake ran in the direction of the gunfire.

"Otacon, can you trace her transmission?"

I compared Naomi's coordinates with *Haven*'s schematics. She was toward the ship's stern, near the server room.

Snake asked, "How long until JD reaches its perigee?"

"Fourteen minutes, twenty seconds. The worm takes two minutes to upload. You haven't much time."

Snake enabled his suit's OctoCamo and entered the maze of the ship's bow. He breathed quickly, and his body was tense.

The *Haven* troopers, on the other hand, were connected through the SOP and worked in coordination as they tightened their noose. The US military had been denied the SOP, but Liquid's forces had unrestricted use.

If Snake were found, he wouldn't have a chance. Even the legendary hero couldn't allow himself to be drawn into close combat—to be surrounded by the troopers' overwhelming force was to be caught inside a beehive.

In the end, he needed to rely on his stealth, advancing slow and steady like a tortoise to catch his enemies off-guard, to carefully search out an opening in their dragnet.

Only Snake didn't have time for a cautious approach.

I connected my notebook computer to Gaudi, pulled open a mathematical model I'd previously prepared, and began inputting any data I could predict. The ship's bridge still quaked from the collision with *Haven*, and a couple times my hands nearly slipped off my keyboard. But in about fifteen seconds, I'd entered the last of the numbers and launched the simulation.

The computer program was one of the many inside resources obtained through Naomi.

The code was a top-secret resource belonging to AT Security, and the leaked information could, in the wrong hands, be fatal to the US Armed Forces. The software analyzed information from the SOP and assessed the current battle situation to provide better command over the soldiers. The program suite could propose the most appropriate tactical actions to commanders on every level of the military, from lieutenants on the front lines to VIPs in Pentagon war rooms. The battlefield prediction software had been created under a 2008 DARPA initiative called Project Green Ball and was eventually merged into the SOP, enabling the System to perform even more precise battlefield management.

Of course, since each tactical pattern was mathematically generated on the fly, a perfect prediction remained impossible—unless you knew the equations.

The *Haven* troopers, under SOP control, would be efficiently hunting for Snake and Naomi following the oracles passed down by the System. But the pursuit of efficiency and the elimination of wasteful effort could also lead to predictability.

Gaudi's CPUs crunched through the numbers and, within thirty seconds of my command, reported its calculations.

"Snake," I said, "I've run a simulation of the enemy's movement patterns. I'll send their projected routes to your Solid Eye. Please don't get caught."

Snake dropped his stealth.

He stood from his prone position and began a mad dash, putting complete faith in my calculations. He slipped through the pathways, narrowly avoiding any contact with his pursuers. Time limit aside, something akin to pride swelled within me at Snake's trust. I was at the right hand of the legendary man. I was the partner of the man who made the impossible possible. Snake ran for his very life. One encounter with the enemy, and he would be killed in an instant—yet he left his fate in the hands of the simulation I created.

Snake reached the ship's aft without ever meeting the enemy.

He latched on to the bulkhead hatch and spun the wheel as quickly as he could. The effort strained his aged, weakened muscles and joints. But with the encroaching threat of enemy patrols, he couldn't afford a moment's rest.

"Snake," I shouted, "get inside!"

A *Haven* trooper unit came upon the open space at the ship's aft. Snake gripped the handle, gritting his teeth so hard one of his molars chipped. Just as the soldiers aimed their guns at his back, Snake unlocked the door, spit out the tooth fragment, and slipped inside with the Mk. III.

Snake closed the door and locked it. Outside, the *Haven* troopers unleashed a tremendous burst of gunfire—they were children throwing a tantrum. But the small arms fire had no hope of penetrating the thick metal of the watertight door. With the sound of denting metal echoing through the chamber, Snake leaned his back against the hatch and caught his breath, untouched by a single round.

"Snake, are you all right?" I asked.

I knew he wasn't. His telomeres had worn down and his cells approached their last divisions, and while his internal organs were still all there, they barely functioned. His lungs, half-incapacitated by pulmonary fibrosis, had grown too stiff to absorb enough oxygen. Snake slid to the floor, his back propped against the hatch, and he gazed vacantly at the ceiling; his empty eyes bespoke fading blood oxygen and consciousness.

The walls of his heart had swollen and lost elasticity and could no longer keep a steady pulse. His arteries and heart valves had hardened and were clogged with plaque. His organs and nervous system had been denatured by amyloid deposits. His heart was on the verge of bursting.

The entirety of Snake's old age screamed out to him, *This is it. This is the end of your fight.*

Between gasps, Snake's voice creaked out, "Otacon, I'm going to finish this."

But he wasn't saying it to me. Under his breath he was cursing his decrepit body to cooperate. *Move, you old bag of bones. Just ten more minutes. Just a little longer. Keep it together just that long and I can end everything. But not yet. I can't yield to pain and age until I've finished.*

"This will be our last battle," Snake said.

"Yeah," I said, not turning my eyes away from the image of the debilitated Snake on my screen, "it will…"

Seeing him like this pained me. I couldn't bear to watch my friend, the man who showed me a new way of living, spur his body from the verge of death and onto further suffering, in the name of completing his duty.

How many times had I swallowed back the words? *Enough. Who cares about the world anymore, if your spirit can find peace? This isn't Snake's fault. These sins aren't his to have to take, not a single one of them.*

I knew such thoughts were only falsehoods. These past nine years, nothing repulsed Snake and me more than the thought of pretending to be bystanders and watch as the world rotted. I wouldn't just stand on the sidelines anymore. That was what I told Snake at Shadow Moses; to betray those words now would go against all our time together.

"If we're responsible for Liquid's sins," I said, "then the onus is ours to bear."

Snake withdrew Naomi's autoinjector from a tactical pouch and pressed it to his neck. Compressed air delivered the liquid to his bloodstream, and his breathing steadied if only by a bit. He had used the syringe many times now, and the nanomachines were losing effectiveness. Snake's body was degenerating faster than Naomi's suppressors could work.

Snake stood and took unsteady steps down the ladderway to the lower decks, his hand finding the wall to support his tottering body.

〜

The entrance to the hallway leading to the server room was located in *Haven*'s CIC.

But this was nothing like any command center Snake had ever seen. He cautiously stepped into the room, M4 at the ready, shocked to find the space so wildly unreal. The initials CIC conjured an image of a stifling room stuffed with monitors and computers and a transparent plotting board standing in the center.

But this was like a stadium.

Each side of the octagonal, domed space descended down platformed levels to the central floor. Giant consoles, arrayed in tiers around the entire room, would have provided space for incredible numbers of operators to perform their duties. Floating above the eight-sided central space was our little rock, peaceful for the first time in a long while—a giant hologram of Earth.

The expanse of the room was ridiculous. Snake allowed his contempt to register on his face. The space felt less a command center than a stock exchange trading floor, or a conference hall at an international convention center. With some disgust, Snake stepped under the giant canopy.

In truth, the room wasn't for commanding *Haven*'s battles.

It was for commanding the world; the embodiment of so-called "super crunching," the distillation and homogenization of our surroundings into massive statistical datasets; the courtroom for our new gods to judge a reality extracted from exabytes of data. The space had been designed to compile data coming in from networks across the globe, and with that data chart the course of events, reshaping them into the narrative desired by the Patriots.

"Snake," I said, "be careful. I doubt this place is empty."

The walkway Snake had taken into the room cut through the tiers like the entrance to the seating in a stadium or a theater. Sighting down his M4 for threats along the side platforms and ceiling, Snake moved with silent steps.

Then, as he swung his rifle to the center of the hall, he saw her lying there.

Meryl.

Snake recoiled back to hide himself from possible threat. He cursed under his breath and used the Solid Eye's zoom lens to observe Meryl, curled at the base of the virtual globe. Her wrists and ankles were bound in cable ties, and she lay helpless on the ground.

"Damn. Snake," I shouted, "it's a trap!"

I was sure he already knew. This was a situation he'd encountered before. Nine years ago, on Shadow Moses, Meryl had taken point, when Wolf shot her legs to hold her in place, turning the woman into bait to lure Snake out.

Snake, who had managed to duck behind cover, couldn't do anything. Meryl was on her back, bleeding out, but Snake knew that the instant he poked his head out to help, the world's greatest sniper would send a bullet to open a hole in him.

That was how snipers worked. They hunted their enemies through their rifle scopes, out of range of regular soldiers. Regular infantry often killed in self-defense, but snipers shot only to kill.

Snake felt the same helplessness again.

You never can protect anyone. Frank's scream as Liquid crushed him with the REX echoed through Snake's mind. Emma, Naomi, all the people wrapped up in the Snakes' fates whom I couldn't protect.

"Is this the only way into the server room?" Snake asked impatiently, pulling up the ship's schematic on his Solid Eye.

I nodded. "Yeah. You have to get through the blast-proof door in the CIC. They know it's our only way in."

"The perfect place to leave their bait. The troopers must be waiting to see which entrance I come through."

"Should I send in a decoy?"

"The Mk. III is needed to upload the worm to GW. If I die, we haven't necessarily failed. But one hole in the robot's little body, and we're finished."

Meryl didn't appear to be in much pain. But once our unseen ambushers knew Snake had arrived, they wouldn't necessarily kill her in one shot. They'd riddle her with bullets, just as Wolf had done to draw Snake out.

This wasn't the time to be overcome by helplessness. Snake had to move. But Snake couldn't think of what to do, and in the meantime, anxiety sent adrenaline into his bloodstream, taxing his already overburdened heart.

Just then, a figure appeared in the opposite hallway, sprinting into the room.

"Meryl!" he shouted.

That fool. Snake clicked his tongue and ran forward.

It was Johnny. I don't know how he crawled out of the ocean, but here he was, dripping wet. He must have nearly drowned and been forced to ditch his weapon in the water, for he was completely unarmed, with only the bulletproof vest left to protect him.

Johnny's legs were much quicker than Snake's, whose hardened and attenuated tendons only permitted limited movement. By the time Snake took his first step, Johnny was already out of the entryway, beneath the dome, and in the snipers' field of view.

Snake shouted, "Johnny!"

Johnny dove to cover Meryl. In a flash, the space around his head was filled with a crimson mist.

To Snake, who was already struggling with the feeling of being powerless, the sight was like salt rubbed into the wound. The injuries spanning Snake's body and the pain of his heart seemed only illusory in comparison.

Seeing the young man collapse before him, Snake was torn by waves of self-loathing. But the instincts that made him the legendary man drove his body to action. In an instant, he deduced the bullet's trajectory and pinpointed the shooter's perch. He wrenched his upper body to face the direction and squeezed the trigger on his M4.

The shot pierced through the bridge of the sniper's nose

and passed out the back of his head, where the helmet remained intact, inside of which mixed brain and bone fragments like scrambled eggs.

Of course, more than this man alone awaited Snake. *Haven* troopers appeared from behind consoles and unleashed a volley of bullets. Snake, ducking behind the platform beneath the hologram, cut through Meryl's bonds with his stun knife, and the two dragged an immobile Johnny to the blast-proof door leading to the server room.

Meryl quickly inspected Johnny's injury. He had not been hit in the head, but rather in his shoulder. The bullet had passed straight through, though the wound was serious. Meryl withdrew a medical kit from a tactical pouch and stopped the bleeding.

The blast door was at the very back of the CIC, sheltered from the troopers' line of fire. But enemy reinforcements continued to pour into the room. If they pushed in with their numbers, Snake and Meryl wouldn't be able to hold them back.

Meryl drew her Desert Eagle, checked the chamber, and said, "Go on without me. This time, I'll protect you."

"Meryl…"

"Go. Destroy GW while there's still time. While I'm still alive."
*While I'm still alive.*

At those words, Snake realized his arrogance. He couldn't leave the sins of the Snakes to the world where Meryl, and everyone else, would live. He himself would take on the task and set things right. So he had rigidly believed.

But this young woman was fighting for her future—fighting to retake the future Snake and I had stolen from her. Not that I ever thought she blamed us. Meryl came to this battle believing it was her fight.

A world where we can live. A world where family and friends support each other, bear children, and pass down our stories through the generations.

Snake and I had been conceited to think the struggle to reclaim that world was ours alone. We had continued to fight out of a sense of responsibility. But while Snake fought for the past, Meryl risked her life for the future.

How much more value was within the setting up of guideposts to an uncertain future, over making up for transgressions already committed? This much was simple: pushing a heavy rock up a hill was harder than rolling it down. Snake realized, in the depth of his being, that this soldier at his side faced a battle far more difficult than his own.

And so he must complete his duty.

"Snake," Meryl said, "the corridor ahead is drenched in microwaves."

Snake nodded. The microwaves would wash over him from all directions and excite the molecules of water in his body. His skin, his muscles, his heart—every part of his body containing any water—would cook.

This was the end for them. Meryl held up her left arm. Snake wrapped his arm inside hers—a gesture between soldiers, and between friends.

"We'll meet again on the other side," Meryl said.

And Snake disappeared behind the hatch.

Meryl leveled her Desert Eagle at the *Haven* troopers and began to fire. Deep in her chest, she held on to what Campbell had told her after we left them in *Missouri*'s briefing room.

*As long as you have life, you must finish your duty.*

Not exactly a father's words to his daughter. Maybe more a commanding officer to his soldier. But Campbell had spent the majority of his life as a soldier, and those were the only words he could find. Believing them the only way to convey his true feelings, he shared them with his daughter.

*No matter what happens, I'll be with you till the very end.*

As he spoke, Meryl finally understood. With little time remaining before the battle, recognizing her as an able soldier was the only way he had of expressing his fondness for her.

*You are my pride and joy.*

Those were his last words.

She had to be worthy of his pride. She had to be the soldier Campbell believed her to be.

Under the overwhelming firepower of the *Haven* troopers, Campbell's words gave Meryl support, and she held steadfast, protecting the doorway to the server room. The woman there was no longer the little girl with a crush on the legendary man.

She was a soldier.

With eyes full of resolve, she gazed toward a future that needed her protection. She was strong, and she was a beautiful warrior. A true *sakimori.*


## 4


WHILE SNAKE RUSHED into the hallway leading to the server room, giants overran *Missouri*'s deck.

With *Missouri* clinging to her hull, *Haven* couldn't launch her VLS missiles. At this close range, any launched warheads might strike either ship. Even those that connected with *Missouri* could send debris flying to tear through *Haven*'s armor. Careless destruction of the battleship could send both vessels into the sea.

*Haven,* denied use of the tremendous firepower of the VLS and MLRS weapons, changed tactics, opting instead to tear *Missouri* apart. And *Haven* had a great number of machines on board that could do just that.

*Haven*'s guards, the unmanned RAYs, cut through water, shot into the sky, and landed on the old battleship's deck, their claws gouging into the wood. Again the ship rocked, and several of the deck crew were thrown into the sea. Some of the bridge staff hit their heads, suffering concussions, and lost consciousness.

"Dr. Emmerich," Mei Ling said, "it's too dangerous for you on the bridge. Get below deck."

She stared unflinchingly at the looming, ominous face of an unmanned RAY on the other side of the bridge window.

"But—"

"This is a military vessel, and I'm the captain. This is a military operation, and I have command. That was an order. Follow it."

I did. Notebook in hand, I fled down the rumbling ladderway. She was right, anyway; in those conditions, I wouldn't have been able to support Snake or to upload the worm. I worried for Mei Ling, but such attention would only get in her way. Besides, she was the captain, and this was her ship.

One RAY stood in front of a three-gun turret, which Mei Ling ordered to open zero-degree fire. The shell obliterated the robot's torso and split the RAY's body in two.

I wondered if I didn't need to worry about our younger comrades after all. Mei Ling was a real captain.

Of course, that didn't mean I felt Snake and I could abandon our reparations. As long as we could ease the battles of those who faced the future, even if only by a little, we had to. And since we had sown the seeds of conflict, the duty was ours all the more.

I descended from the bridge and ran back to the briefing room.

"Snake, what's your situation?"

Snake was surrounded.

I flipped open my notebook computer to see gun barrel after gun barrel after gun barrel.

While I moved down from the bridge, the Mk. III had been on autopilot, following directly behind Snake. The image on my screen was a direct feed from the robot's camera. A chill ran down my spine. At the inner entrance to the microwave corridor, Snake was in a hopeless situation.

The gray door isolated the server cluster from static electricity and even electromagnetic pulses. Thick sandwiched sheets of tungsten, gold, and ceramics stood like a monolith before Snake, who helplessly struggled against his own body. His legs had buckled under repeated spasms, and Naomi's nanomachine injection had lost any effect.

Gasping for air, Snake had just made it to the doorway when the *Haven* troopers rushed out of their hiding places. The armed soldiers, about ten or so in number, crowded the confined space and moved to surround the old man, who had dropped to hands and knees. Like a ghastly lynch mob, the soldiers closed in.

"Come on," I shouted, "get up. On your feet, Snake!"

He tried to stand, but the strength had left his legs. He slumped back against the doorway and slid down to the floor.

*If I don't do something, he's done for.* I steadied my resolve. I didn't think the Mk. III could win against the mob, but the little robot might be able to buy some time. I routed full power to the Mk. III's wheels and balancers, and sent the Metal Gear charging at the line of troops.

"Wait," Snake said, and a flash of light flicked above the soldiers' heads.

Like a ball of lightning, the thing spun through the air, emitting fierce electricity, and planted itself between Snake and the soldiers. It was a man. From head to toe, bolts of electricity emanated from him. He stopped the soldiers in their tracks with a murderous glare.

"Raiden," Snake said.

"I am the lightning...the rain transformed."

Raiden's muscles tensed, and an arc of lightning flew from his body. He was the god of thunder reborn. In his mouth, he held a sword by the blade.

After the events on Shadow Moses, he was left without arms. His tissues and circulation system remained closed at his shoulders, from which draped a long black leather coat. He had reached the depths of *Haven* in his condition. He held the long katana blade wedged between his lips as if to keep balance, and the sight reminded me of a balancing toy. To make it this far, he could scarcely be human.

"Snake," Raiden said, "leave this to me. I'll go to the server room."

The look in his eyes caused me to shudder—and probably Snake too. They glistened with a tinge of madness. *Here I fight, and here I die. My life is but for this moment.*

But Raiden's conviction was nothing more than an idea he'd quickly grasped to protect his own breaking heart. Snake understood this.

His voice raspy but firm, Snake said, "The corridor's awash in microwaves. It should just be me."

Jack's world of fighting as a child soldier, then as a member of FOXHOUND, was gone. Even Colonel, in command of the Big Shell operation, had only been a simulation, projected by the Patriots through nanomachines into Raiden's mind. The FOXHOUND unit he believed he'd recently joined was nonexistent, having disbanded after the incident on Shadow Moses. Then, when the new life carried in Rose's body met a sorrowful end, Raiden needed to find some purpose to hang on to, to preserve what he was.

"My body is a machine. I can—"

Raiden's burden was too heavy to bear. His despair dwarfed anything Snake or I could imagine; his loneliness, a thousand blades piercing his body. But to bury his despair and loneliness, he clung to his yearning like a feral beast. Someday, he would forget he was ever human.

Snake raised his voice, hoping to bring this young warrior, who Snake himself might have cursed to this condition, back to humanity—back to a life with Rose.

"Your body may be a machine...but your heart is human. You've got a life to go back to."

"She means nothing to me now."

"Raiden, look me in the eye."

Snake knew words wouldn't be enough. He found the strength to stand and presented to Raiden the battered countenance of an old soldier. Raiden's eyes, wild with obsession, perceived the magnitude of Snake's burdens and shrank back.

"You still have your youth," Snake said. "Don't waste it. You can start over. You're not saddled with your troubles—you're only clinging to them. You think destiny and fate to be burdens, but no shadow falls over your future."

Even now, despite being surrounded by enemies—no, *because* of it—Snake tried to sever the illusory bonds that tightly bound Raiden. This too was a duty Snake felt compelled to fulfill.

"From here on," Snake said, "this is my fight. I . . . *we* tore the world apart. We made your life a living hell. It's my duty to put an end to all of this."

Perhaps in this moment Raiden began to understand why Snake continued to fight, even in his current state. Perhaps Raiden finally comprehended the true meaning of Snake's words, in that early morning on Manhattan Island:

"Maybe you were only forced to play the role of Raiden in the Patriots' script, but everything you felt and everything you thought is yours."

After five years, Raiden—Jack—had taken in the deeper meaning of those words.

He had been fighting to free Snake. That was the reason, he told himself, that he had been born. That was the only way he could find meaning in a life once spent as a child soldier, and once spent as an imitation Snake.

But by doing so he only bound Snake.

Raiden realized that his intent to save the legendary man who had once rescued him, only added to the tired old man's burdens. What Snake wanted was for people like Jack to be free from Snake himself—to be relieved of the weight of Snake's memes, to have their own lives back.

"I'll release you," Raiden had once told Snake.

And the only way he could achieve that was to see Snake off to battle.

"All right," Raiden said. "I'll make sure they don't get through."

Raiden, possessing a newfound resolve, pushed back the surrounding *Haven* troopers with a razor-sharp stare. The intimidated soldiers edged away, their fanlike formation expanding as much as the confines would permit. I connected the Mk. III's manipulator to the identification reader next to the door, and with Naomi's passcode opened the way.

"Hold on until we insert the virus," I said. "You got me?"

Jack radiated lightning. If he couldn't hold the troopers back, we'd have no chance. As Snake staggered through the doorway, Jack spoke softly, his stare holding the enemy forces at bay.

"Snake," he said. "Thank you."

For a moment, Snake stood still. But he didn't say anything. He had no time to weigh whether his curse had truly been lifted from his junior. Yet hope remained.

*More is yet to come. A long struggle may yet await. But this young man has been given plenty of time . . . unlike me.*

Snake could only have faith in that hope, as slim as it might have been. He stumbled ahead. Raiden faced the *Haven* troopers' guns, and Snake went off into the corridor of death, and the solid, heavy door slid down between their backs, as if cutting the cursed thread that bound them.

∿

The moment he stepped into the hexagonal corridor, Snake was engulfed in microwaves.

Lethal electromagnetic waves emanated from all six faces of the hallway, their wavelength penetrating bone tissue and cell membrane and assaulting the water within every one of the sixty trillion cells within Snake's body.

Before the mission, I had applied a thick coating of aluminum dust to Snake's sneaking suit. The process was our best and only option against the microwaves. As in the door of a microwave oven, a metal plate—even if only a mesh—absorbed most of the energy.

I chose aluminum for the metal's nonmagnetic properties, since metal that reacted to magnets heated rapidly when exposed to microwaves. Aluminum has been used for shielding in microwave ovens because, besides absorbing microwaves, the metal was low cost and wouldn't radiate heat from dielectric loss.

Of course, I would have wanted to cover Snake's entire body with a metal shield and provide complete protection from the fatal radiation. But had I done so, he wouldn't have had the mobility to infiltrate the ship's interior, let alone the server room.

I could do nothing for the gaps and joints of Snake's suit. The suit was a complex assemblage of musclelike fibers, and the edges between them—the parts that moved—couldn't be coated. And even if I had been able to, the aluminum dust only absorbed a small amount of the radiation. The shielding on a microwave oven was maybe half a millimeter thick, but the coating's protection would not even be one one-hundredth of that.

A few steps in and the pain overwhelmed Snake and brought him to the ground.

I cried out to Snake.

His OctoCamo had gone haywire and turned the same red color as the burning floor. The sneaking suit began to change from its typical grayish blue to a deep crimson. The muscular design of the suit made Snake look like his skin had been stripped away to reveal the blood-red muscles beneath.

Snake couldn't even cough anymore.

He couldn't breathe. In his lungs and his heart, and every other organ in his body, Snake's blood heated, quickly approaching the limits a warm-blooded animal could bear. Broken blood vessels hemorrhaged within the confines of the suit, and the blood, unusually thick, painted dark red stains on Snake's skin.

Snake was boiling alive.

"Stand," I yelled. "Snake, stand up!" I knew he wouldn't be able to. But having the water in his body boil within him would not be a peaceful death. Through the intense heat, Snake extended his right arm.

He crawled. Excruciatingly slow, as if drowning in the inferno, he advanced, one arm at a time.

I thought I saw smoke rise from the joints in Snake's suit, then his left upper arm exploded.

Snake screamed a bone-chilling scream like none I'd ever heard. Reflexively, I closed my eyes. Somewhere, the heat had localized, and the vaporized water expanded until it had no place left to go, then blew through muscle and skin. I couldn't believe what I was seeing; a human body exploding bit by bit.

I fought down waves of nausea.

On Snake's arm, his muscles were exposed, and several tendons, detached from bone, dangled like crimson ribbons from which steam continued to waft. Again Snake fell to the floor, devoid of enough strength even to writhe in pain.

"Snake...please, don't give up on me."

I wanted to look away. How could I face such a sight?

My friend, who I had stood with through nine years of battles, was being cooked, broken, and mutilated. A mere three seconds of watching the dreadful scene was enough to drive me mad. So just for one second, I closed my eyes, selfishly hiding from the sight of the legendary man, pushed beyond his limits in the fight to fulfill his duty.

But Snake's moan required better of me.

More than an utterance of pain, it was a song, refusing defeat, rising above the hurt, continuing ahead. I couldn't close my eyes to his cry. He was trying to press on. To turn my eyes away from him now would be unforgivable.

"Otacon," Snake said, his creaky voice escaping from a burning throat. "Are you...there?"

Softly, I said, "Yeah, I'm here."

On the verge of weeping, I forced my voice to steady. "I'm with you, Snake. Now and always."

"Why...did you...decide...to fight...alongside me?"

I found it odd that Snake would ask such a question amid pain that would make remaining conscious a struggle. For a moment I was stunned, but I realized I needed to answer quickly and set my brain to work.

Snake needed my voice now. To retain his senses while his body was destroyed, he needed something to hang on to.

"I'm waiting for an answer."

I thought that might not be enough to jar his memory. I believed my answer honest, although in truth, this was only one of my reasons for sticking with Snake.

As I'd expected, Snake seemed not to understand. "An... answer?"

"On Shadow Moses, after we laid Sniper Wolf to rest, and you started off to destroy REX, I asked you, 'What was she fighting for? What are you fighting for?'"

The Kurdish wolf had fallen in the sniper battle on the snowy field. Standing beside her, the falling snow quickly engulfing her body, I asked those questions to Snake's back. Never before had I witnessed two people fight to the death.

Why do people have to fight each other?

I had lost the woman I cared for, and as I cried, I couldn't hold back that simple and childish, yet fundamental, question.

"And then, you looked over your shoulder at me and said, 'If we make it through this, I'll tell you.' But we escaped Shadow Moses alive, Snake, and you never gave me the answer. I've stayed with you to hear the answer you held back."

"Back then...I...I lived only for myself...because I didn't want to die...My survival...instinct...gave me reason to live."

"That's the same for everybody." That was likely true for everyone on that island—including Wolf, Psycho Mantis, Vulcan Raven, and Liquid.

*I live; I don't want to die yet.*

To feel that sense of being alive, we had thrown ourselves into battlegrounds to be close to death. After the end of the Cold War, Liquid feared that kind of world would be lost. He led the rebellion at Shadow Moses in order to build a world by warriors and for warriors.

"You're not the only one," I said.

"I only felt truly alive...when I was staring death in the face."

"And after we left that island?"

"I wanted to enjoy life...I really thought so."

"The nine years with me, have they been fun?" Snake kept crawling, as flesh burned and fluids boiled.

"It's like what Frank said...when he died...We're not tools of the government...or anyone else...Fighting was the only thing he was good at...but at least he always fought for what he believed in."

"I've heard you say something like that yourself, Snake."

"Thanks to you...I've remained...true to those words... through every battle...Thanks to you...I've seen...my battles through...to the end...I'm content with that."

After he finished speaking, it took me a moment to notice. Snake had reached the end of the seemingly endless corridor.

Steam and smoke rising from his body, Snake crawled out from the heat-ray hell.

~~~

The power-assist layer on the sneaking suit had frayed all over, exposing the inner material, the cloth stained red where Snake's skin had burst.

I attached the Mk. III's manipulator arm to the door's security panel and opened the way ahead. Finally free from the microwave hell, Snake attempted to stand, raising up to one knee, only to collapse immediately under his body's own weight. He fell forward into the server room.

Down on the floor, Snake vomited violently. He tried to inject Naomi's nanomachines, but his arm couldn't complete the motion.

I used the manipulator to press the autoinjector against his neck—just as I had tried to do on Shadow Moses, to deliver an end to the dying Vamp. Filled with those memories, I turned the Metal Gear's camera to look around the server room.

"This is GW," I said.

The room was a graveyard.

Tens, even hundreds, of black, burnished tombstones stood waist high in rows within a long, rectangular space the size of a football field. I felt like we had emerged into the Underworld. After further inspection, I realized that each tombstone was a server—although none shared any characteristics with my mental image of the servers I've used. None had even a single running indicator light.

With the quiet, orderly rows of ebony slabs, the room seemed less a server room than a cemetery, where the dead slept never to awake until their resurrection at the Last Judgment.

Before each tombstone, a cluster of pure white flowers waved, blown about by a breeze with no origin. They were holograms, stars-of-Bethlehem like those planted in the potter's field where The Boss and Big Boss's graves stood.

In a pained, raspy voice, Snake said, "Otacon...can you do it?"

The nanomachines had helped, but not much.

"Leave it to me," I said and piloted the Mk. III to one of the tombstones. I lifted up the cover to a maintenance panel in the floor and inserted the robot's manipulator into the access port.

Hurriedly, I searched for the best location to upload the worm.

GW comprised an unimaginably large system. Everything rested on my ability to find the right place to insert the first line of code. For that, I had less than a minute to search through the galaxy of information contained within GW's exabyte of data. At once, I launched several crawler agents—my scouts—and handled the stream of reports as they came in.

If I transmitted the worm into the wrong place, days—or even weeks—might pass before GW's ability to define and comprehend data would be completely destroyed. No matter how powerful Sunny's finished version of the cluster might have been, if the worm took too much time to overwhelm the AI, we would lose.

Less than two minutes remained before Liquid would reestablish connection with JD and fire the railgun nuke. After that, Emma, Sunny, and Naomi's stories would become meaningless.

Snake lifted his rifle and roared in pain.

He had sensed something. Even this near death, his senses hadn't dulled.

"Snake, what's wrong?"

Beyond the tip of Snake's gun barrel, which he had somehow managed to raise, rolled a single black bowling ball.

The object glided toward Snake to be joined by others like it, rolling out from behind the gravestones. The black swarm came at Snake and the Mk. III, carpeting the ground, and extended humanlike arms.

Scarabs—the small, unmanned scouts that had attacked Big Mama's base in Eastern Europe.

The carpet rose up, leaping at Snake, who remained on his back.

Snake squeezed the trigger, and the M4 kicked in his arms. His body, scorched, bled, and ravaged, no longer had the strength to handle an assault rifle. But Snake endeavored to protect the Mk. III from the Scarabs. Rubbery, jet-black arms grasped Snake, and in an instant, the bowling balls were all over him.

Somehow, Snake pulled his knife and stabbed at a Scarab at his side. The robot's red sensor eye flickered out, its arms slackened, and it fell to the floor. The rest of the swarm, in unison, shot out electricity, the sparks stabbing into Snake's body.

The machines attacked without mercy, striking at pieces of muscle and bone exposed by the microwave blowouts. I thought back to when Ocelot had interrogated him on Shadow Moses. Back then, Snake possessed the youth to withstand the pain, but now, his body cooked by microwaves, he struggled to remain conscious through these lethal shocks.

But if he fell, the Mk. III would be next.

"Otacon!"

As Snake released a deathlike cry
Sunny, Emma, and Naomi's self-replicating story
eroded through GW's core agent cluster.

In front of Meryl and Johnny, at the door in the CIC, the *Haven* troopers froze.

So did the soldiers bearing down on the armless Raiden at the entrance to the microwave corridor.

Throngs of Gekko filled *Missouri*'s deck.

Giant RAYs stomped through the wooden deck to split the battleship in two.

In an instant, the machines shut down.

"We did it!"

I read from my notebook's display to confirm we had taken over GW. The self-replicating worm cluster had practically exploded through the system. The program overwhelmed the core high-speed information-processing sectors and deleted nearly all the program units.

The Scarabs fell from Snake's body as if molting from his skin. The tiny robots had gone completely immobile and began to roll with *Haven*'s gentle sway atop the ocean.

"Wait a minute," I said.

I looked at my screen. Something wasn't right. I had set up a window to display the progress of the worm cluster's spread through a mapped rendering of GW's architecture. But the worm pushed farther than I'd anticipated. The program forced through every boundary and spread, like an insolent army, to every corner of the map, replicating with abandon.

"Is it removing the other clones?" I wondered, then rejected the hypothesis.

The worm's territory extended beyond GW's network. Not content with consuming GW in its entirety, the cluster reached its tentacles out toward the other AIs.

*It can't be...* Naomi.

I couldn't believe what I was seeing. As the worm expanded its influence, the display map of GW's network zoomed out. A planet retreated into a solar system, then a galaxy, and onto a nebula.

The worm was expanding into the entire universe of the Patriots' information network.

Noticing my unease, Snake asked, "Otacon, what is it?"

"JD is being erased."

"What?"

Already the worm cluster had nearly complete dominion over JD. The self-replicating tempest overloaded JD's central processor cores, destroying them. The AI's highest processing core, in effect the Patriots themselves, failed. The worm legion engulfed the immense neural network.

Then the worms, content at having entirely supplanted JD, solemnly engaged in their planned self-destruction.

It had happened so quickly.

Screams and whispers, innermost feelings, lies and confessions.

Every human story spoken or written, flowing through the networks of the world.

Every business transaction, real or virtual. Whether over the phone or by email, someone had declared love; someone had demanded a breakup.

Devouring every scrap of day-to-day information, the Patriots' prediction and control reconstructed the universe into a jail where everything was predetermined, woven by the biggest and most complex narrative in human history.

A book titled *Reality. A 1:1 Map.*

A single large tale written by coldhearted, arrogant, and lonesome gods in the belief that restricting the human narrative was the only path to preventing the extinction of the human race.

Effortlessly brought to failure, then destruction, by the stories of only three people.

This day, before my eyes, a universe perished.

The warm pulse of network traffic cooled in an instant, falling into eternal silence.

I felt like I had witnessed the last moment of time, the heat death of the universe.

*Snake, Hal. It's you, isn't it? I hope you're listening.*

Naomi's face appeared on every wall of the server graveyard.

I sank to my knees in astonishment. Naomi smiled at me.

She had smiled when she heard Sunny made the eggs well, and she had smiled many times when we talked together.

But I'd never seen her smile like this.

Of course, she wasn't actually looking at me now; this was a prerecorded message.

～ᗝ～

*The virus you uploaded used GW as a conduit to annihilate the entire*
*AI network—all four AIs along with JD, the core that tied them all together.*
*I've set this video to play once they're all gone.*

*Sons of the Patriots was only the beginning.*

*The Patriots were planning to use nanomachines to implement the*
*System to control the entire population.*

*I had an obligation to stop it.*

*With a little help from Sunny.*

*She believed her talents could help you all put GW to rest.*

*She created an anti-AI FOXDIE.*

*The virus's name is FOXALIVE.*

*It's the conceptual opposite of the nanomachines I created all those*
*years ago.*

*We wished to free the captured foxes . . . to let them run free in*
*the wild.*

～ᗝ～

Her expression showed no trace of darkness—no sense of tragedy, or the pain she must have felt. Her smile was that of one friend
talking with another. Her smile was that of someone nestling close
to the one she loved. Her smile held no cynicism and was so typical
as to become beautiful.

Naomi had reached the horizon of that smile.

Believing that the dead couldn't forgive, I had strived to live
a life without regret. Misdeeds, once committed, couldn't be un-
done, and so the only avenue was recompense. I thought the same
applied to Snake and Naomi.

But Naomi had come much, much farther than us. She had

arrived at the final destination for souls; a place accessible only after one's time on Earth had been spent.

And we saw it.

We saw the smile of a woman who had stepped into the world beyond atonement.

*By the time you hear this, I'm afraid I'll be gone.*

*This is a strange feeling. To be alive, recording a message for after I'm dead.*

*Hal...If you're listening...*

"I'm listening," I said. I'd never felt anything so nice as to hear her call me Hal.

*I'm sorry I deceived you.*

*It hurt me more than anything else, lying to you like that. I wanted to apologize to you before I died...but not even that was allowed me.*

*And yet, in the end, I finally can feel the joy of living.*

*Thank you, Hal.*

I realized that now, with everything over, I didn't need to hold back my tears.

Her choice couldn't have been a happy one. Afflicted by illness, she used the time she had left to make amends for her sins. Few would find joy in thusly spending their last days.

Yet her eyes were at peace.

*Snake...hear me.*

Still on the ground, Snake lifted his head.

*Our country is an innocent child once more.*

*A new dawn is rising. Now she can build a new destiny for herself.*

*Snake...the time has come.*

*You've earned your rest.*

Snake had mangled Frank and watched the man be killed. He had stolen Naomi's brother away from her, and I know he carried it with him. I know this from his doubts, during our briefing, when he asked if she was on our side. During the Shadow Moses Incident, Snake said to her, *Naomi, I don't blame you for wanting me dead.* He carried her hatred on his back.

But Naomi had forgiven him, after the incident nine years ago.

And now she had finally been able to tell him. She didn't hate anyone anymore—but to fulfill her duty, she couldn't let Snake know.

After she died, Snake thought he would never earn her forgiveness.

And now, to suddenly be granted that which he thought was lost, Snake felt bewildered. The legendary warrior was not used to such kindness—strange, since he had so much kindness within himself.

Her speech at its end, Naomi's gaze turned off-screen, to somewhere in the distance—as if she could see her next destination. Her eyes held no fear. Or maybe they did, only for an overpowering hope to scatter such shadows and lead her ever forward.

She looked not just to the past, but also to the future.

*The rose petal is about to fall.*

In the end, everyone went to the same place.

"Soon, I'll be there," Snake said. The man-made rose and the snake born not from nature. Our stories were near their end.

Another violent spasm racked Snake's body. He hardly had the strength left to even cough. His chest convulsed and his muscles clenched, and Snake curled into the fetal position.

"I've set things right. Now let me go."

And Snake slipped from consciousness.

5

HELICOPTER BLADES BEAT against the sky, and their sound slapped his eardrums.

The ocean's scent.

Snake tried to lift his eyelids, but they were as stiff as fired clay. Finally, he managed to force his eyes open—only to see Liquid Ocelot, arms folded, standing atop *Haven*'s bridge, gazing down at the calm, tranquil sea.

There were no sounds of battle; no gunfire, no shouts. Only Mei Ling's booming voice echoed from *Missouri*'s loudspeakers, announcing the battle's end and attempting to stop any remaining small pockets of hostilities. "Stop this pointless fight," she declared. "This is no war."

The low pressure front had been swept away, and the sunlight shone on the top of the bridge. The flat oval roof was covered in plates of stealth material and a layer of OctoCamo, and several transmission antennae stood like columns.

His long, black leather coat fluttering in the wind, Liquid kept his eyes on the ocean as he said, "Rise and shine, Snake."

Snake lifted his chin from the cold floor and moved his body slightly. He was still in pain, of course, but not more than he could handle.

"Look," Liquid said. "The war is over."

Snake got to his knees, and then to his feet. Surprised that he had been able to do so, Snake stood on the roof of the bridge and saw the battered *Missouri* along with several smaller craft, moving here and there to mop up after the finished fight. A US military helicopter flew overhead.

"Why?" Snake asked.

Liquid didn't act confused or angry about the defeat of his

plans. If anything, he seemed relaxed. He just stood there, gazing at the tranquil sea, and Snake couldn't explain why.

"If you had wanted to stop us," Snake said, "you should have been able to."

Any way I looked at it, a server room guarded merely by a swarm of Scarabs didn't make sense. I supposed a gunfight among the rows of the AI's exposed hardware would have been unworkable. But Liquid knew that the server room was his opponent's final target. Surely he could have prepared a more suitable line of defense.

Liquid shrugged. "Stopped you? Why would I want to do that? This is just as I'd hoped things would end."

Snake didn't understand. If Liquid was attempting to bluff at this point, he'd be a real fool.

"Our father, Big Boss," Liquid said, "sought to free himself from the Patriots' chokehold. His dream was to create an army of free citizens, one that answered to no government: Outer Heaven. But he failed...because of you."

During the two world wars of the last century, the Philosophers gained influence as an international group of people who traversed the halls of power. After World War II, the Philosophers disbanded, and the secret fortune behind the organization ended up in the hands of a former SAS major known as Zero.

Zero formed his own organization, the Patriots, whose members utilized the vast wealth of the Philosophers' Legacy to bring one woman's vision to the world. But what they brought about was a spiritual prison where supreme authority was maintained by means of prediction and control.

In the nineties, Big Boss sought freedom from that prison. Nine years ago, on Shadow Moses, Liquid sought freedom from biological destiny—genes. And five years ago, in Manhattan, Liquid and Solid's brother Solidus sought freedom from the Patriots' information control—memes.

All of this, until this moment, was nothing more than a process of trial and error resulting in *Haven*.

Everything until now had been a fight for freedom; resistance against any power attempting to restrict and belittle the human spirit within a confined narrative.

"Now we are free," Liquid said, "from the Sons of the Patriots, the ultimate form of external control imposed on the Patriots' soldiers. Free from FOXDIE. Free from the System. Free from ID control. Our minds free from their prisons."

Suddenly, Liquid thrust a finger at his cursed brother. Snake knew immediately what the action meant.

A part of Snake was not yet free, and a part of Liquid was yet imprisoned: the other's very existence. The bloodline of Snakes remained upon the earth.

"This is it, brother," Liquid said. "Our final moment. The battle has ended, but we are not yet free. The war is over, but we still have a score to settle."

Liquid discarded his coat. Caught in the breeze, it fluttered away. Liquid's bare upper body, now revealed, remained surprisingly muscular for the man's seventy-some years. Layers of exposed tendons were visible where Frank had severed his right arm. But the tissues weren't red and pulsing with life. They were synthetic, part of an augmented artificial limb, built from the same cybernetic technology as Frank's and Raiden's exoskeletal bodies.

At the end of the artificial arm, Liquid's hand balled into a fist. Liquid brought the fist to his chest and took a fighting stance.

I wondered what had happened to Liquid Snake's right arm, the arm that had taken over Ocelot's consciousness.

Snake raised his fists as best he could given his burns and injuries, and the two men measured their distance.

"Show me what you've got, Snake!"

Snake obeyed and charged at Liquid full speed. Liquid, stunned at the sudden, wild attack, took the tackle in the chest, and said, "Not bad!"

Snake, at his opponent's chest, jerked his head up, catching Liquid at the bottom of his chin, then followed up with a shoulder to the ribcage. Liquid had been overtaken at the very start, but he managed to shake Snake off and jab an elbow into his brother's back.

The impact penetrated through to lungs and gut and knocked the air out of Snake. For a brief moment, his guard slackened. Liquid seized the opportunity and delivered a knee strike. Snake recoiled in pain. His head cocked back, and in that instant, Liquid's artificial elbow connected with his burned left cheek and sent him reeling.

Pressing the attack, Liquid launched into a roundhouse kick, but before the centripetal force could accelerate the tip of his foot into the tender muscles of Snake's side, Snake jumped back.

The other time was in a place like this. Snake closed distance and struck at Liquid with everything he had. Chest, stomach, back, face. His elbows and forearms sunk into every bit of flesh they could find.

Nine years ago, Snake and Liquid's final battle on Moses Island, a masterful display of hand-to-hand combat, had been atop a similar giant platform. Back then, the REX's back had been the arena, and now it was on the back of a whale, but both times the two had stood on colossal weapons armed with the latest technology and punched at each other with their primitive fists.

No, it wasn't just that time. There was also that fistfight with Cyborg Ninja in the Moses facility. And the first time he exchanged blows with Frank, in the Zanzibar Land minefield. Just like then, this contest brimmed with a peculiar vigor—the sportlike purity of two men striking at each other, without malice or murderous intent, to prove each other's being.

As they pummeled each other, and as they wrecked each other's faces, Snake—and this may sound strange—began to *forgive* Liquid. Each strike was a display of his forgiveness.

Snake neared the place Naomi had already reached.

To find complete forgiveness and acceptance.

With his half-ruined arms, Snake reached out to that land.

Then came the final punch. Snake's fist brushed past Liquid's. Almost simultaneously, each man's cheek was smashed by the other's clenched hand.

Neither brother could move. Almost as if they were checking each other's temperature, each man's fist remained embedded in the cheek it had struck. After an endless moment, one figure fell slowly backward.

One man stood, and one man dropped. Fate had reached its end.

Here, at the last, no clear difference was to be found between victory and defeat.

"This is only the beginning, Snake."

Liquid lay on *Haven*'s bridge, his face to the sky. His body pulverized by Snake, Liquid's voice was feeble, and Snake strained his old, worn-out ears to listen.

"America will descend into chaos. It'll be the Wild West all over again. No law, no order. Fire will spread across the world."

What Snake had destroyed was not only a prison, but the chains that tethered the beasts called humans. The Patriots had attempted to restrict and control the world. They had guided and used the people, so each was compelled to action under the pretense of free will.

Yet in a certain way, the Patriot AIs were only possible as a projection of ourselves. The AIs, as the ultimate storytellers depicting the world around us, were our very own norms, customs, and lives.

People, as a group, followed customs without thought. That was the true stratgey of the Patriots.

"Through battle the people will know the fullness of life. At last, our father's will, Outer Heaven, is complete."

Liquid beamed proudly. The new era, the world Big Boss had sought, was to be created by his sons, Liquid and Solid, the two Snakes.

Big Boss reviled no place more than he did heaven. Absolute peace and total happiness only came about by the theft of thought, action, and responsibility. He deeply felt it his duty to break the reign of heaven, the world of Major Zero and the Patriots—that grotesque heaven he himself had helped create.

Big Boss fought against the system of control he had unknowingly helped build. He had taken responsibility for what he had begun. Unwittingly, Snake had repeated his father's battles.

Liquid whispered, "Somewhere out there, I know he's laughing."

His eyes were distant, perhaps not seeing Snake any longer. He stared blankly at the sky, as if searching for JD, still up there, in the coldness of space, having lost its heartbeat of information.

"We are beasts created by man," he said. "Unless the light is extinguished, the shadows will remain. As long as there is light, erasing shadows is futile."

Something was odd about Liquid—at least as far as anything could be considered odd about a man who had hijacked someone else's body. He now gave the peculiar impression that he wasn't being himself—like an actor losing his grasp on his role.

"I am Liquid's doppelgänger. And you are Big Boss's," Liquid said, then thrust his trembling hands toward Snake. "You're your father's son. You're...pretty good."

A small sound left his throat, and his arms fell to the floor.

Snake knelt beside Liquid and put his fingers to the man's neck. He could feel the body losing warmth, and the carotid artery delivered no blood from Liquid's heart to his brain.

Snake lifted his hand and touched Liquid's cheek. He closed his brother's open eyes.

*You don't need to see anymore. No more binds, no more fate.*

This was Snake's final parting from his cursed brother.

Sunny's program destroyed JD's brain but left the brain stem intact. She had analyzed Naomi's black box and separated the Patriot control system from the vital lifelines of society. Water,

air, electricity, food, medicine, communication, transportation—
Sunny cut off the Patriots' control while preserving modern
civilization.

Maybe it was her way of avenging her mother, Olga. Or maybe
she wanted to shape the future into her own ideal image.

Or maybe it was just one big defragmentation.

The Patriots' reign had crumbled away. That which we thought
to be control, and a prison, was destroyed. But that was a large part
of our world. With such a considerable loss, nothing would ever
be the same.

Some was destroyed, and some remained. Ironically, we en-
sured the survival of civilization's oldest cultivation since the times
of Genesis: war. I can only pray that the world you make will be
better than the one we fought.

What did we lose? What did we save?

To tell the truth, even as I compile the telling of these events, I
still don't know. I suppose those questions come at the end of any
battle.

In any time, in any war. In all the past, and all the future.

## EPILOGUE: NAKED SIN

HAVEN.

The sea breeze came in from the ocean at the end of the runway. By straining to listen, I might have faintly heard the waves. Seagulls flew overhead, perhaps thinking something was on the island.

This was a haven. Businesses buried their roots here to escape national taxes and located their servers here to ensure the physical safety of data they didn't want in their own countries. This was a tiny island, a nation only in name. The tropical isle, home to a scant few thousand residents, had been recognized as an independent state by the global community of nations who sought an air pocket outside the complex array of their interconnected interests.

The sun's gaze was strong here, but not uncomfortably hot with the unobstructed breeze blowing across the tarmac. The country provided little reason to visit, and the runway usually remained unused.

The airport itself was wholly adequate, paid for by taxes of corporations that had rushed to the island for its low tax rates and lax information laws. The locals seemed to be living comfortably. Where our society squeezed too hard, the benefits trickled down to this haven.

In the shadow of *Nomad*, prominently parked on the runway, we awaited the bride, who was changing into her dress inside the heavy transport plane. The scene was surreal.

Our intimate wedding party hadn't come all the way to this tropical island because the bride had wanted some flashy wedding. The ceremony was held here so that Snake and I might attend. Even though the Patriots had perished, the lengthy rap sheet they had framed us with lived on.

Yet the bride wouldn't hold the ceremony without us. Snake

and I declined, many times, but she insisted on having us two fugitives present, always saying (with such obstinacy as to make her father proud), "I can't imagine the wedding without you two there."

One month had passed. As for how much—and how little—the world has changed since those events, you probably have a better sense than I. As a wanted man, I flew around the world, apart from it. The outcome of our battle was only truly found amid the laughter, the tears, and the lives of the common man.

So, how about it? How much did the world change?

Or has it hardly changed at all?

The next time we meet, I hope you'll tell me.

Sunny told me what happened later. At a full-length mirror set up in the cargo bay, Mei Ling and Sunny adjusted Meryl's wedding dress. Her body was built to handle the terrific recoil of her Desert Eagle, with wide, firm shoulders and a well-muscled back. But replace Meryl's uniform with a dress, and her firm, utilitarian body flourished. Her well-honed figure was fundamentally beautiful.

"You look amazing," Mei Ling admired in wonder, her eyes tearing.

Campbell stood behind his daughter, cane in hand, watching over her as she prepared to embark upon her new life.

After Meryl returned from our battle alive, the colonel continued to avoid any opportunity to talk with her. Tortured by doubt—*Can I say to her face what I was able to over remote video? Would she even listen to what I have to say?*—Campbell remained unable to speak out to his daughter on her wedding day.

Perhaps acutely sensing the colonel's timidity, Meryl faced his reflection in the mirror. She took a step forward, her face devoid of expression. Intimidated, Campbell reflexively lowered his head.

There was something in his face. *I can't look away, not now.* Somehow Campbell found the courage to look at her face, ready to accept whatever she had to say and whatever words she would use to rebuke him.

What he got was a gun barrel pointed at his head.

Mei Ling and Sunny gasped. The Desert Eagle's frame formed a straight line that pointed directly at his temple. Campbell's eyes widened in astonishment, but after a moment, he closed them and waited for the muzzle to erupt.

"Colonel," Meryl said. "You're going to walk me down the aisle."

With the faint sound of metal rubbing past metal, the magazine released and dropped into Meryl's open hand. Campbell's eyes fell to the container. Not a single shell was inside. She slid open the action and displayed the weapon's empty chamber.

Then she took Campbell's hand in hers and gently deposited the Desert Eagle there.

"You're not angry anymore?" the colonel asked. The gun felt heavy. The pistol had a recoil strong enough to break the wrists of an average woman. Thick metal provided a frame and chamber suitable for powerful cartridge rounds. When considered in the context of modern close combat situations, the firearm produced excessive force and was too hard to wield. The Desert Eagle could only be called an unnecessary weapon.

To continue her soldier's life, Meryl had to carry such a thing. This was the weight she had borne until this moment.

"Oh, I'm still mad," she said. "But now...you've got a chance to win me over."

Campbell looked up from the pistol and returned his gaze to Meryl. Yes, there was still hope. As long as he could make that first step to change something. And this was his first tiny step—toward a new goal, and a new life. It was never too late for a new beginning.

"You're right. We have plenty of time now."

Campbell tucked the gun away at the small of his back, took Meryl's hand, and walked with her down *Nomad*'s cargo ramp and onto the tarmac. A wide red carpet led from the plane's hatch all the way to Johnny Akiba, waiting in a white suit, flowers in hand.

Johnny first met her nine years ago on Shadow Moses. Yet I doubt she even remembered. As a member of the Next-Generation Special Forces participating in Liquid's action, Johnny had been assigned guard duty on Meryl's holding cell.

The soldiers of the Next-Generation Special Forces had been brainwashed by FOXHOUND psychic Psycho Mantis. Because their participation in the Shadow Moses takeover had been unwilling, the Genome Soldiers were never officially prosecuted, but all either faced discharge or transfer to inconsequential duties. Johnny drifted from one armed force to the next, including a Russian mercenary group, until finally landing with the Army CID's PMC investigation unit, where he was reunited with the detestable gorilla of a woman who had once knocked him out and stripped him of his uniform.

Of course, she wasn't really a gorilla, and the moment he saw her again, he realized his feelings for her. But, hating needles, he ducked out of the mandatory nanomachine injections. Without the SOP, he could never keep in sync with the team. With Meryl only ever angry at him, Johnny remained unable to reveal his feelings.

If only he'd had the SOP, he could have controlled his weak bowels, and he wouldn't have been the target of laughter and disgust whenever he rushed to the toilet. His alienation from his squad had been a direct result of his refusal of the System.

But ultimately, his exclusion from the SOP saved his comrades—including Meryl—in the Middle East and Eastern Europe. Only Johnny kept his head through the chaos of the Guns of the Patriots tests.

During the fight on *Outer Haven*, Johnny was finally able to confess his love. After Snake disappeared behind the portal, Johnny woke up and helped Meryl defend against the *Haven* troopers. There, she realized that this man—who had already once rescued her in Eastern Europe and, only moments before, flung himself over her, snipers be damned—could be someone she could spend the rest of her life with.

Trailing the bride and her father, Sunny and Mei Ling descended from *Nomad*. Jonathan, Ed, and I stood on each side of the aisle and greeted Meryl with applause. Some distance away, on the side of the runway, a young boy watched, having been drawn in by curiosity. He must have been coming or going from the ocean and carried a fishing rod and a basket.

I noticed bells ringing. *Was there a church on this island?* But then I realized that the peals were growing louder. Ed and Jonathan also heard the sound and were looking around.

"The bells are getting louder," Johnny said. Then he saw something and surprise entered his voice. "It's coming closer!"

We turned to face the oncoming sound, and above the tarmac, the shimmering heat waves seemed to bend. Then, as if teleporting in, an armored vehicle appeared, first spreading from a single floating point, then quickly revealed in entirety as its OctoCamo deactivated.

The bell rings came from speakers on the outside of the Stryker APC. Having dropped its camouflage skin, the vehicle barreled straight toward *Nomad*. Just as the wedding party began to step back in alarm, the Stryker's mighty bulk turned into a drift and slid to a stop beside the red carpet.

I caught sight of the words EYE HAVE YOU! stenciled on the vehicle's side. The hatch opened, and Drebin appeared.

"Just in time," he said.

The green of the APC's armor was a little out of place amid the celebration. Though astonished by his showy entrance, I frowned, thinking, *Couldn't you have done something about that car?*

Drebin pulled a handkerchief from his jacket pocket and said, "And I brought gifts."

He waved the cloth, and the Stryker's green became the pure white of a UN vehicle—a wedding-themed OctoCamo pattern. Even Drebin's slogan changed to read DREBINS—WE HAVE YOURS. He touched the vehicle's rear hatch and looked over his shoulder at us with a smile.

Flower petals burst out from the open hatch.

"Incredible," Mei Ling admired.

They were white roses. Fans inside the APC sent white petals rising through the tropical sky.

Flowers blanketed everything around us—the runway, even *Nomad*; their pure white standing out all the more where they settled on the red carpet aisle.

"A shower of flowers, compliments of DREBINS. And—"

Drebin caught a single fluttering petal and closed his hand around it. He opened his fist again to reveal a dove, which took to the air.

"—a little something extra from me."

Then, Drebin's words a signal, in an instant the fluttering petals all became doves. The flock flew together, through the blue island sky, toward some distant place.

As the white birds danced past her, Meryl looked around for Snake. She wanted him to witness this moment over anyone else, but among the faces there, his wasn't to be found—even though she had the ceremony held in this Pacific haven, where no nation's laws would reach, so that Snake and I could be present.

Amid the applause, a trace of unease tinged Meryl's expression, and Mei Ling, the sole other woman here, was the only guest to notice. Mei Ling moved close to my ear and whispered for no one else to hear.

"Where's Snake?"

I faked a wry smile. I couldn't tell anyone he was still fighting a battle. This time, his opponent was himself, and this battle was far more difficult, tragic, and lonesome than any that we'd made it through in the past.

Now, Snake was about to face his last battle alone.

And so, just as Naomi had done, I lied—to keep secret Snake's battle; to let Snake slip off alone. This was our toughest choice, but we both understood it was for the best.

"Who knows?" I said. "That guy always keeps you waiting."

I didn't think for one second that Mei Ling believed a lie like that. I did my best, but I'm not an actor by anyone's standard. I made an attempt at a grin, but I couldn't help my lips from going taut. Only Campbell saw my oddly rigid smile and knew what meaning it held.

Campbell gave his unspoken words to the doves to carry with them to the heavens.

*Thank you.*

~~~

He spent the entire day in bed, gazing at the light that came through the blinds. The only time he ever left was when he needed to use the bathroom.

He was told he would be leaving the hospital soon, but he didn't know where he should go. Much might have changed in the world. A great many things out there might carry an entirely different significance, or may even have been rebuilt anew. But as far as he could figure, nowhere in that new world would there be a place for him. He spent the days lying in bed, unfeeling, taking a detached notice of Maryland's soft sunshine.

If only tomorrow would never come.

That might sound like a trite expression, but to him the dilemma was grave. How damnable the existence of time. Things came, then adroitly slipped past you, darting off to some distant place behind. With consciousness came the imposed nature of time.

To him, each day in this hospital was like a battle. A fight of not fighting. A fight of not doing. A fight of not feeling; of not thinking.

Troubled that tomorrow might be the day he could no longer keep up that battle, he slept on the bed, surrounded by the medical machines.

That was why, when the nurse came in and said he had a visitor, the man didn't do anything in response. When someone came, all he did was reaffirm his conviction that ultimately there was no place for him. Of course, even when the two passing through the door were Rose and a young boy he'd never met before, his reaction remained exactly the same.

Holding a white bouquet of her namesake, Rose approached Jack's bed. The boy hid warily in Rose's shadow. Jack rolled onto his side, putting his back toward her, returning to the Bethesda sunshine.

Rose smiled sadly and spoke awkwardly to his back.

"Jack, how are you feeling?"

Jack voiced a noncommittal sound. He didn't have anything more to say. When Rose asked if she could sit, he didn't respond at all. Without change, without a place, just the flow of time to let pass by.

Rose sat in a folding chair a couple of feet away from the bed and placed the flowers on the side table.

Standing behind her, the boy peeked his head out to stare at Jack. Sensing this, Jack glanced over his shoulder, only to meet Rose's eyes. He immediately regretted his curiosity.

"What do you want?" he said. "Come to laugh at me?"

Hearing the self-torture in his words and tone, Rose decided this was no time to worry about the distance between them. She stood from the chair, pulled the child over, and sat on the edge of Jack's bed. Jack tried to move away, but the wall on the other side of the bed provided no room to escape any farther.

"Jack," Rose said. "Look at the boy."

"Campbell's kid?"

Jack wanted desperately to run from the pain. There was the life that was supposed to have been his future, the life that was to lead him into a new world; the life that had not been granted birth.

Being stared at by the possibilities he had been unable to attain, Jack saw the depth of his despair as low as he thought it could ever be. This was the very bottom. This was when you were at the bottom and someone said *dig*.

Then, as Jack decided he might as well fall as far as he could and embarked on his way down to a new stratum of despair, Rose's words held him back.

"No...he's yours."

In that moment, when time stopped, the soft hum of the medical equipment felt harsh and grating. Time had simply streamed past. The void had been something only to pass through. But now all was still; time had been frozen by one sentence.

Frightened and confused, Jack said, "I don't have any kids."

Rose touched her hand to Jack's shoulder. The arms she'd heard he lost had been replaced with new ones without that purely functional aesthetic of the exposed combat exoskeleton. They were more like typical artificial limbs, coated with material that looked almost like real skin.

"He's your son," Rose said.

"You said you had a miscarriage..."

〜〜

Her display of kindness left Jack feeling exasperated—to be honest, he tried to feel that way.

But somewhere, some deep part of his heart beat faintly with the desire to believe that she was telling the truth. Jack despised the baseless optimism that even now reached out to that vague hope.

"The miscarriage was a lie. I had a healthy baby boy."

Rose lifted her hand from his shoulder, returned to the folding chair, and sat down. What her fingertips had felt might have only been a reproduction of human warmth, but Rose felt happy regardless to have touched Jack's body again. She didn't care if the flesh was only a replica as long as its heat came from the man she loved.

"Mr. Campbell pretended to be my husband to protect me—and our son—until you'd completed your mission...to shield us from Patriot eyes."

"What?"

Jack turned to look at her. Maybe her hope—*please believe me*—

was starting to get through. He still wasn't ready to accept the sudden revelation as the truth, but at least he had stopped being so intent on rejecting her.

"He didn't even tell Meryl. He sacrificed everything—even his family—to protect us. I'm sorry, Jack. I wanted to tell you."

Jack sat up. The bedsheets slipped down and left his chest bare. A faint groove along his shoulder indicated the edge between body and artificial limb. The boy ducked back behind Rose at the sight of him, but the child's eyes held on him, transfixed with curiosity.

"John... aren't you going to say hello to your father?"

Rose motioned the child forward. When John didn't make an attempt to move, Jack tentatively extended his arm out to the child.

"My son... little John."

With artificial fingers, he reached out toward the boy's face. His new limbs had been made to be as realistic as possible, but the minute differences couldn't be ignored. He was real life's version of the uncanny valley. Something was off about the texture of Jack's skin; a hint of ceramics, the sense of rubber. Almost human, but falling just short and thus inspiring revulsion.

John backed away from Jack's approaching hand.

"Scared of me, huh?" Jack said.

For a while, Jack hadn't been human. To protect Snake; to die for Snake—with that drive all he had left to cling to, the beast known as Raiden was born.

He didn't yet know if he could go back to being human again. And as long as he still remained in the realm of the beast, of course a child would be frightened.

Raiden studied his artificial body and said, "I don't blame you. It's okay."

"Nuh-uh," John said, the abrupt change of heart startling Rose and Jack. "I'm not scared."

The boy approached the bed, reached his hand behind his back, and pulled out a toy sword. He pressed a switch on the hilt, and the toy produced the familiar hum of a sci-fi laser sword.

John spread his stance, struck a heroic pose, and said, "I think you're cool—kinda like a comic book superhero."

Jack laughed. How long had it been since he had laughed like that, heartily, and without a hint of sarcasm? For a time, he had forgotten how good it felt to laugh.

To forget was to become the beast.

John was grinning back at him.

Jack looked at the boy longingly. Would he accept a hug?

The question wasn't one for the child—whether Jack could put his arms around his son rested entirely upon himself. Could he be a father? Could he take the boy into his life? Jack asked himself if he was up to the task.

Then Jack pulled his son in close, resting the child's head against his chest. This was his new life; one with responsibility, and with hope. In his arms he held his future, and he was ready for it, body and soul.

Suddenly, John began to cry—not afraid, but recognizing as much as a child could Jack's internal conflict, and his decision. He understood completely that this man was now his father and had chosen to take on a father's responsibility.

"Rose," Jack said. "I'm done running."

Jack became overwhelmed by how precious the child in his arms was to him. Emotions long suppressed now came to the surface. A tear ran down his cheek and landed on John's crew-cut silver hair. Seeing Jack crying, Rose too was brought to tears.

Rose leaned over their child to hug Jack and said, "And I'm not afraid anymore."

For John, this was the moment he finally found the father he'd been waiting for. Not every man could become a father. A man didn't become a father when the woman he loved began to carry his child inside her. Nor did a man become a father when the child was born. That moment only came when he accepted his child and decided, unconditionally, that they would share their lives together.

In a mirror in the corner of the room, Jack caught the reflection of their embrace. He chuckled and said, "We're like Beauty and the Beast."

Rose lifted her head and looked into his eyes.

"No," she said. "You're no beast. You're my husband...and his father."

Part of me thinks that in this moment, Rose truly became John's mother. She stopped fearing this man, the father of her child. She accepted him the way he was. As Jack began to acknowledge his role in their family, she too started down a new path.

How many detours had she taken before reaching this point? Much she had given up, and much she had lost.

Jack had come dangerously close to stripping all meaning from her sacrifices. He had selfishly rejected life and basked in the comfort of nihilism and despair.

"I won't lose my way again. I don't have time to waste in searching for myself.

· "I have too much to do now, as a father.

"And only by remaining true to my family can I repay the freedom Emma and Naomi gave me."


2


THE LONE MAN was placing a bouquet beside a gravestone.

The words inscribed upon the stone read: IN MEMORY OF A PATRIOT WHO SAVED THE WORLD. No dates of birth or death were to be found on the stone slab, nor any name.

This was, after all, a cemetery for the unknown. For unknown soldiers buried in solitude. For those whose identities were not permitted to be recorded. Carpeting the cemetery grounds were white flowers, called stars-of-Bethlehem, a name that evoked the light of heaven.

But the graves here belonged to those cast out from the world.

This was a potter's field, so named after the field of a potter that Judas purchased with his blood money and turned into a cemetery.

A graveyard for the outcasts, for the exiled, and for the abandoned.

The True Patriot, exiled, her name stolen, her remains lost, left nothing behind but her gravestone. Only the blanketing stars-of-Bethlehem, white and virtuous, reflected any memory of the grave's owner.

The Joy. That was her name.

She loved her country more than anyone, and her country was always in her thoughts. And yet this proud, beautiful woman was exiled, buried here, and stripped of her name. By all rights, The Joy's remains should have been properly laid to rest at Arlington, not abandoned in distant Russia.

At the site of that same grave, fifty years earlier, Big Boss's battle had begun.

Big Boss—who always hated that code name given to him by the president—had also come to the cemetery. Back then, the stars-of-Bethlehem had yet to bloom. Big Boss stood at her grave, his head tilted back to keep his tears from spilling. With that sorrow, that lonesome tableau, numerous battles were to begin. And fifty years later, those flowers he laid to rest there had spread to carpet the graveyard grounds.

And now, Big Boss slept beside her.

Snake stood before his grave. In southern Africa and Central Asia, Snake had fought this legendary mercenary and won. How had Big Boss felt, seeing his own copy turn against him? Could he have kept his head in battle, when the face of the man trying to kill him had once been his own?

But Snake and Liquid's fight had been similar. Aside from a

genetic marker, the two clones shared the same genes. In the end, perhaps Snake had only traced Big Boss's life. As Big Boss killed The Boss, Snake killed his father in Zanzibar Land. As Big Boss faced his clone in battle, Snake had fought Liquid. And the fulfilment of Big Boss's desires to free the world from the confines of prediction and control came by the hands of none other than Snake himself.

Snake offered a bouquet to Big Boss's gravestone.

To the fight he'd passed down to his sons.

*You are to infiltrate the enemy fortress Outer Heaven, then destroy their final weapon Metal Gear.* That mission, given to him upon joining FOXHOUND, must have come from the Patriots—no, from the machinations of Zero. Zero sent Big Boss's own clones against him. The spite beneath this act was now as clear as day.

This was the form taken by Zero's deep, seething hatred toward the comrade who had betrayed him; a twisted declaration of victory: *If I want to, I can create you.*

But in the end, all three Snakes created by the Patriots turned against their creators.

Snake had to wonder: if he remained, would history repeat itself again?

But that wouldn't happen. Snake had come here to end his life.

Snake lifted the hem of his suit jacket and withdrew the pistol from his waistband. He pulled open the action and confirmed the round in the chamber. Then, as if in prayer, he kneeled before Big Boss's gravestone and thrust the barrel into his open mouth.

The gun was terribly heavy. His hand trembled for more reasons than fear alone, as keeping an object that heavy in his mouth was a grueling task.

Snake may have spent more of his life holding a gun than not. In not one day since he first killed another man in the Iraq War had a gun ever felt light in his hands. Not the difference in heaviness noted from one specific firearm to the next, but the *weight* brought on by the gravity of the weapon's nature as an implement for killing and for war.

Perhaps the soldiers under the SOP hadn't felt that weight; the System had whisked it all away. But the Patriots' destruction signaled the end of the era of war without pain.

Each time had its own wars. War has changed. Our time has ended. Our war was over. But Snake still had one more thing he must do; one last punishment he must endure: to erase his genes, to wipe that meme from the face of the earth.

This was Snake's final mission.

Before he pulled the trigger, Snake spoke.

"At least I wasn't alone."

Nothing awaited him now. Snake feared going to a place of nothingness.

He remembered the faces of those who had fought at his side.

Emma, Mei Ling, Naomi, Meryl, Sunny, Campbell, Raiden, and Otacon.

"I can't allow myself to harm their world. If my death will prevent that, so be it."

His trigger finger tightened with conviction.

And finally Snake could pull the trigger.

I thought I heard a gunshot, and my muscles instantly tensed—though I knew the sound was only the cork popping out of a bottle of champagne. I became painfully aware that after my many years with Snake, the battlefield had worked its way into my very marrow—even if I had never been in combat myself. I sighed. I didn't want to admit it, but I was a green-collar worker through and through.

A short distance from where the rest of the wedding guests

drank champagne and celebrated Meryl's day, I stood leaning against the white APC and drank my own glass. Sunny had taken the Mk. III's remote controls and was playing with the robot, sending it scurrying around the runway—though she wasn't watching the robot with the same amusement a typical child might. Her interest was in things like the Mk. III's steadiness on one wheel—to discern the original coder's methods from the workings of the auto-balancing algorithm—and the coordination between spatial recognition and evasion systems when presented with an obstacle.

A bottle of champagne in hand, Drebin walked up to me and said, "Nothing beats a stiff drink, huh?"

"I didn't know you drank."

"It's not that I don't like the stuff," he said, the alcohol slightly edging into his speech. "Soda just agrees with the nanos better. The nanomachines break down alcohol before it has a chance to get you drunk."

That meant that Drebin was drunk because the nanomachines' control had disappeared, and the alcohol had been left unfettered to exercise its chemical effects. The time under the SOP must have been tough on the brewers and distillers of the world, their products having been stripped of their effects.

"So that explains it. No need for the nanomachines anymore."

Drebin swished back another mouthful of champagne. "Yeah, well, it ain't all sunshine and rainbows. Lotta folks lost their entire sense of being the moment SOP went offline."

Drebin was right. The effects weren't just limited to the US Armed Forces and the PMCs. In militaries of every country introduced to the battlefield control system, vast numbers of soldiers suffered from physical and mental breakdowns. The phenomenon, known as SOP Syndrome, or SOPS, was not, strictly speaking, caused by the SOP itself, but rather its absence—the outcry of a heart left bare against the onslaught of war memories.

More than one in ten soldiers worldwide were affected by SOPS, making it the most widespread disease in recorded history. We had eradicated the Patriots' control, but our actions had been drastic, with far-reaching consequences for human civilization. Getting rid of the Patriots wouldn't solve all our problems overnight.

"To be honest with you," Drebin said, "I'm not actually an employee of AT Security."

"Huh?" I said.

Drebin glanced at me out of the corner of his eye. He spoke matter-of-factly, a common technique for those making a guilty and serious confession.

"The Patriots raised me to be a gun launderer."

"The Patriots?"

"My earliest memories are of the Lord's Resistance Army. You know, the LRA? A bunch of wanton murderers and rapists in the Ugandan Civil War. They kidnapped me, indoctrinated me... forced me to fight. You're staring at a former child soldier. My parents, brothers, and sisters were all killed in the war. I was a war orphan."

He traced his finger down the scar on the side of his head. The long, straight slash was likely a knife wound. Like Naomi and Jack, Drebin had survived the chaos in Africa.

"After that, the Patriots picked me up and brought me into the family business. I was Drebin number 893. There's a whole lotta pawns like me all over the world. How do you suppose I laundered guns like I did? 'Cause they let me."

Drebin snorted with self-derision. "In fact, I was under strict orders to back you guys from the start."

"You what?"

I couldn't believe how careless I had been. He had gone one-and-a-half times across the world, from the Middle East to South America, from South America to Eastern Europe, and finally to the Pacific Ocean. Snake and I had never bothered to question why this man had followed us over such a distance. We had just filed him away as eccentric. I scowled, less angry at his lie than my foolishness.

"Hey man," Drebin said, "don't take it personally. I wasn't the only one under their orders."

Drebin glanced at me, then to the newlyweds opening another bottle of champagne on the runway.

"Meryl's unit?"

"They probably never realized it themselves, but..."

Drebin produced a piece of chalk from his cargo pocket and wrote on the tarmac: RAT PT 01. Then, a quick wave of his hand-kerchief over the writing, and the next moment, the letters had changed places.

PATR10T. This was a joke, but not the funny kind.

Apologetically, Drebin said, "You got played like a violin."

"But...why?"

If we were fighting the System, why had the Patriots lent support to pests like us?

"Obviously," Drebin said, "Liquid's plot was a threat to the Patriots. So they planned to have you guys take care of it."

Drebin spoke like he hadn't had anything to do with it. I guess to him, he really hadn't. He was green collar, enjoying the profits of war without ever participating in combat operations. He had watched our battle as a pawn of the Patriots, receiving orders that came down from a vague and nebulous above; a simple courier, a delivery man assigned to the principal players who would deter-mine the world's course.

"Only I guess it didn't quite turn out how they planned, with you crashing their System and wiping them out and all."

"Does that mean you're out of a job?" I asked.

"Are you kiddin'?" Drebin faced me, arms open wide, legs entirely unsteady now, and touched his champagne hand to the stencil on the Stryker's side. "I got the Drebins. All of the Drebins in the world are in on it. From now on, we're in business for our-selves. We are pawns no more."

I suggested he might want to take it easy on the champagne, but he ignored me and launched into a speech.

"The White House might've lost its taste for unilateralism and started to rebuild. But there's a lot of failed states out there that went bankrupt from their PMC habits, and they owe a shitload of money. Now the only question is, who's going to pick up the tab? I'm sure these new governments will try to keep it under control with PMC corporate reform laws, but it ain't gonna be good enough. They're all sunk up to their eyeballs in the war economy. It might not be a New World Order, but the old order under the war economy's gone for good."

Drebin was always a talker, but the alcohol sent him to a whole new level. For a moment, I considered that the nanomachines' control hadn't been entirely bad.

Drebin, who seemed to have forgotten I was even there, continued his monologue.

"I'm guessin' the UN is gonna be more important than ever, what with multilateralism and all. Then again, the UN itself's just an old twentieth-century relic. And if you think about it, it ain't that different from the Philosophers who went on to become the Patriots.

"A new war. New chaos.

"Then at the end, a new order. Whether it's the UN, or some new power altogether, I don't know. But it won't be anything more than a new context for the world in place of the Patriots. Crush, mix, burn, repeat."

I looked away from Drebin, who continued to expound to his own satisfaction, and turned my head in Sunny's direction. She had handed the Mk. III's controls to the island boy who had been watching the ceremony.

Yes, that was when you met Sunny. I can remember it now.

You were chasing around the Metal Gear, pulling Sunny after you by the hand. Nowadays, you take Sunny's lead, but back then, you were the one who stood in front of her and ushered her into the outside world, even if at the time you didn't know it.

I wonder what happened to the Mk. III after Sunny gave it

to you. I don't know if you can imagine my surprise when Sunny asked if she could give the Metal Gear to you, as new friends who couldn't even understand each other's language.

All right, I was a little—to be honest, a lot—taken aback, in part because the Mk. III was, despite being handmade, an assemblage of costly and detailed machinery built at considerable expense. But that was only one small part of my surprise. And if you want to know why, Sunny said it best when she told me, "I made a new friend."

She smiled, truly happy, and said that you were getting along. Struck by the radiance of her smile, I didn't notice at first that her stutter was gone completely.

You were Sunny's first brush with the outside world. You opened the door to a world that could be both overwhelming and weary, sometimes cruel and lonesome, but real, and where we would have to build our happiness.

And now, I'm surprised by how right she was about you. You have a power—the wonderful ability to gently lead others to greater things and greater understanding.

A power entirely unlike that of the Patriots, who used the human subconscious to bring about the reality they sought. You hold your fellow man in respect and possess the sense to awaken people, with a slight and gentle touch, to their inner strength and beauty.

"I like it outside," Sunny said.

That was the moment Sunny first started living her own life—a life where she stood on her own feet, saw with her own eyes, and from out of the vast sea of information called reality, picked out only that which she truly needed.

So when Sunny asked me when Snake was coming back, I felt a little relieved. I had known I would have to face that question from her, but now she didn't need Snake or me any longer.

Inside myself, I told Snake, who I thought was likely to be in the potter's field at that time, *Snake, at least Sunny will be fine now.* He had always been telling me I needed to let her go into the outside world, so I figured I probably wasn't the only one who worried about her.

"Snake is sick," I said. "So he went on a trip to get better."

I didn't tell her he was on a trip to kill himself. And not because I was worried the truth would hurt her. I didn't want to bring her tears, but I did want her to understand what Snake's choice signified, and how dreadful the terror was that he faced at that very moment.

For that, she'd need to grow up just a little more. She needed a deeper understanding of what it meant for a person to die, and how much value life held. Without that, I didn't think she could truly comprehend the battle Snake faced.

Sunny looked into my eyes and asked, "We're not going with him?"

I shook my head. "No. We'd...just get in the way."

"I wonder if I'll ever see him again."

She seemed to have some understanding.

I turned my gaze to the ocean, far away at the end of the runway. Beyond the edges of the airport, grasses swayed in the gentle ocean breeze, their leaves making noise as they brushed together. A single white rose swayed in Sunny's hair.

"Snake had a hard life," I said. "He needs some time to rest."

Though I wrote above that I wanted Sunny to understand, and not to cry, I have to admit that tears filled my eyes.

*I can't. I can't let Sunny see me cry.*

Acting like nothing was wrong, I turned my back to Sunny. But Sunny's sharp eyes didn't miss the trembling of my shoulders as I held back the sobbing.

"Are you crying, Uncle Hal?"

Somehow, I managed, "No," but in my emotional state, the answer came out curt. I smoothed it over by turning back to her and forcing a smile, adding, "I'm not crying."

Sunny pushed her index finger against the bridge of her nose. For a moment, I didn't know what she meant, but soon I realized my glasses had slid down out of place. I'd brushed them aside when I went to wipe my tears.

Sunny giggled.

Now she was the one comforting me. Perhaps she understood Snake's absence even more deeply than I. Perhaps she held back her tears to keep from making me feel sad. The possibility was considerable. After all, she had a far stronger and more caring and tender heart than I.

Of course, I don't need to tell you that.

You chose Sunny, and Sunny chose you.

## DEBRIEFING: NAKED SON

INSIDE THE CHAMBER, the metal pin struck the primer at the base of the cartridge.

The primer burst and ignited the powder charge, triggering an explosion inside the metal cylinder.

The explosive energy filled the cartridge and pressed against the rear of the bullet.

The projectile struck by the pin gained spin from the barrel's rifling, and therefore aerodynamic stability, and flew straight toward the muzzle.

The pistol, having fulfilled its purpose, slipped from Snake's hand and fell to the earth. The bullet, not hitting anything, not smashing anything, disappeared into the graveyard sky. Snake slumped forward onto his hands, feeble wheezes escaping from his worn-out body.

He couldn't do it. When the gun fired, it had been outside his mouth, the muzzle flash barely singing his cheek.

"Shit. How many times am I going to have to do this before I can finally die? How much practice does it take for a man to off himself?"

Exposed to this much fear, even old, dry, leathery skin formed beads of sweat. Cold sweat formed on his forehead and ran down in icy trails.

"Can I die?"

Snake never thought he would ask the same question that had plagued Vamp, even if the meaning behind it was different.

Snake was ashamed at the part of himself that felt relief now that the fear had lifted.

"What did I come here for today? If I can't pull the trigger now, when will I? If I put it off until tomorrow, then the next day, and the next, then one moment, my procrastination will bring me across the threshold, and my body will strew the deadly virus. The unpreventable, untreatable, heart-stopping virus. I suppose I'd be dead by then, but it would be a selfish death too late for the rest of the world.

"Life's more than just a game of win or lose, didn't you say, Otacon? Now I understand. Trying to compare yourself with someone else, competing for a victory like squawking myna birds is foolish. But in your inner struggle, victory and defeat do exist.

"And right now, I'm losing. I'm yielding to the terror that comes flooding from within.

"I don't believe in God, Otacon, so you're the only one to whom I can pray. Give me strength to do this now. Give me the resolve to protect the paths you and Sunny will take through life, and the world Meryl and the rest will build."

Battling the relentless, overpowering fear that beset his determination, Snake reached for the dropped pistol, when he sensed someone standing behind him and lifted his head.

"That's right," the man said. "Good. No need for you to go just yet."

For a second Snake thought he was seeing himself. The man's face was identical to his own aged countenance.

*I know this man.*

*Ever since I was sent into Outer Heaven as a rookie in FOXHOUND nearly twenty years ago, my brothers and I fought within his gravitational field. Running from the fate left to them by his genes, Liquid and Solidus had been reduced to live grotesque existences.*

"It's been a long time...Snake," the old soldier said.

But he was missing his iconic eye patch. He had lost his right eye during a mission in Soviet territory, yet here that eye was, right in place, and staring Snake down. His arms and legs and right ear, which had been lost in his battle to the death with Snake in Outer Heaven, were all firmly attached. I saw it all through the Solid Eye's feed later, as though it weren't a vision or a delusion, but a simple reality. And it was.

Maybe this man wasn't Big Boss but another clone hitherto kept secret—and who had been sent to kill Snake. But the Patriots had been wiped from the global information networks—what point would there be for the assassin to come out now?

Big Boss wore the long coat of the FOXHOUND unit he'd once commanded. The stars-of-Bethlehem parting at his feet like the Red Sea before Moses, he approached Snake with slow, deliberate steps. From neither his eye that shouldn't exist nor his shoulders that should have lost their arms could any malice be sensed.

But Snake saw the outlandish gun dangling from Big Boss's right hand. The man hadn't raised the weapon at Snake, but Snake sprang to his feet and reflexively aimed his pistol at Big Boss—the same pistol he had meant to use on himself only minutes before.

Big Boss, seemingly unconcerned with the muzzle pointed in his direction, drew in on Snake without faltering. He took one step, then another. Snake replaced his weapon's magazine. Then, just inside CQC distance, Big Boss stopped.

Snake's reason told him that Big Boss's eyes held no sign of violent intent. Even his unconventional weapon remained down at his side and pointing at the ground, utterly unthreatening.

Yet Snake was unable to lower his gun.

No matter what story Big Boss's lack of apparent aggression told, a former foe approaching, weapon in hand, posed threat enough. Odd for a man who had just been agonizing over his inability to die to find himself pointing a gun at his enemy. But such were the instincts of a man who had lived his life as a warrior and now approached his death as warrior.

Then Big Boss's gun fell to the sea of flowers.

Unable to comprehend Big Boss's intentions, Snake was confused. But before he had time to ask himself why Big Boss had dropped his weapon, the man who had created CQC alongside

The Boss had his hands around Snake's pistol. Taken by surprise, Snake attempted to counter the maneuver, but Big Boss pulled Snake's arm, drawing him close.

Big Boss hugged Snake tight, his strength far greater than Snake's despite their bodies being genetically identical, save for the telomeres and marker genes.

"Let it go, my son," Big Boss said. "I'm not here to fight."

Snake was dumbfounded. First the man showed up armed before the son who had supposedly killed him, and next he discarded his weapon and gave him a fatherly embrace. Still not understanding what Big Boss was after, Snake tried to resist, but Big Boss's arms were like metal hoops around a barrel and permitted no escape.

"Or should I call you brother."

"What?"

"It's over," Big Boss said softly. "Time for you to put aside the gun and live."

With that, Snake too let go of his gun. Now that both were unarmed, Snake finally accepted he had no reason to resist.

Big Boss hadn't come to fight. He hadn't come here to kill Snake.

Though the world had changed greatly with the destruction of the Patriots, Snake hadn't been able to escape the sins of the past. He pointed my gun at his former enemy, even though the causes that forced us into opposition were in that past.

As if sensing Snake's feelings, Big Boss patted Snake on the back, as if to say, *It's over. This was all the fault of us old fools anyway.*

"The old leaders have all passed away," Big Boss said. "Their era of folly is over."

Big Boss released Snake and looked at a gravestone that stood behind his brother—Big Boss's gravestone. The grave that should have held his bones.

"I'm the only one left," he said, "and soon...I'll be gone too."

His consciousness imprisoned by the Patriots, Big Boss's brain-dead body was supposed to have been incinerated by Liquid in Eastern Europe. We had secretly transported the charred corpse to America and buried it next to The Boss's resting place. With Mei Ling, Meryl, and Campbell's help, we had no trouble hiding his body among the coffins of the other victims and flew it from airport to airport beyond the reach of customs.

But this meant that those cinders hadn't really been Big Boss.

"How can you still be alive?" Snake asked.

"That body Liquid burned on the Volta wasn't mine."

The body was that of a clone—Solidus.

Solidus had been created as the perfect clone of Big Boss. Unlike Solid and Liquid, who had been given various customizations, he was created to be exactly the same as Big Boss. Zero and the proxy AIs that rewrote the world for him were convinced that Solidus's remains were those of Big Boss.

As for Big Boss, JD had implanted him with nanomachines and kept him in a state of eternal sleep. He was completely sealed away in both body and mind. Until the System was destroyed, he had been unable to wake. Ocelot and EVA wanted two things: to bring Big Boss back to life, and to end the Patriots.

EVA stole Big Boss's body from the Patriots and reconstructed it by replacing the missing parts from Liquid, who had died at Shadow Moses, and Solidus. With the limbs and organs essentially sharing the identical genetic code, the transplants weren't rejected by the immune response, as if they were happily returning to their former body.

But though Big Boss had been physically restored, his consciousness remained locked away. Then Ocelot, EVA, and Naomi put into motion a grand and complex scheme to free the world—and Big Boss—from their prisons.

First, Ocelot set about ceasing to be Ocelot.

His was a grotesque and woeful decision.

In order to revive Big Boss, Ocelot chose to sacrifice himself; to stop being Revolver Ocelot and become Liquid Snake. This was his ingenious ploy to deceive the System and hide his activities from the AIs.

Ocelot used nanomachines and psychotherapy to gradually transplant Liquid's personality onto his own. Each day, he became less and less sure of who he was. Eventually, he lost himself. One might say that his fate was akin to death. With a smile on his face, he destroyed himself for Big Boss's sake, believing, *If giving up my insignificant personality will obliterate Zero's repulsive world, the world I helped bring about, I will do so happily.*

Into Ocelot's vacant mind a fiction was planted. You are Liquid Snake, a clone born from Big Boss's genes.

The psychodesigners overwrote Ocelot's being with their version of Liquid Snake, created from a wide collection of bits and fragments; Gulf War reports on his interrogation by the AMN in Baghdad, the psychological test results from when he joined FOXHOUND, surveillance footage stolen from the Patriots, and, more than anything else, Ocelot's personal impressions of Liquid from their time together in FOXHOUND.

From the Patriots, EVA had stolen the technique, a prototype of the system to control human will that was later completed in Manhattan under the S3 Project; the protocol Jack—as Raiden—had been the prototype of, using environment and role to alter the personality of a specific person. Through that ghastly technique, Ocelot became Liquid's doppelgänger.

He became the son of that great warrior.

He had been born an ocelot but was now—even if only in fiction—a snake.

That might have been what he had always desired—to be the son of the warrior whom he respected more than anyone else.

~~~

As Big Boss told Ocelot's tale, something about him seemed lonely.

The two men were united by the depth of their losses; they were comrades in arms. They had helped give form to Zero's twisted delusions and paranoid worldview, and they would gladly pay whatever price to undo their misdeed. And Big Boss and Ocelot paid dearly.

Now Big Boss reached the source of his sins.

"It all started with him...Zero."

Snake looked in the direction of Big Boss's gaze. A small distance from the rows of gravestones, an old man was sitting in a wheelchair. The stars-of-Bethlehem danced in the breeze like snowflakes, and beyond them he looked sad and lonesome; desolate.

As Snake followed Big Boss to the man in the wheelchair, all he sensed was emptiness. The old man's face was covered with so many liver spots as to have been painted with them, and his wrinkles were ragged and deep enough to be called trenches. Whatever his face had been was buried far beneath. What remained of his eyes were hidden beneath encroaching eyelids; he couldn't see anything now. An oxygen mask strapped to his face forced air into his body.

Snake felt deep sadness upon seeing that a human being could age that much. Nothing was more precious than life, but nothing was more ugly than living too long.

Big Boss gently rested his hand on the man's shoulder. The old man's profile had long since ceased to resemble anything human. I doubt he wanted this for himself, to live this long. Zero wasn't the type to cling to life. But he had felt too much responsibility, and its flip side, suspicion, to die at peace.

Unable to trust the future to later generations, Zero was a lonesome man who carried everything by himself. Unable to believe in anyone else, he built a world of complete control, and to maintain that world, he kept living. Such was the only choice left to this visionary. His fate now, as a wrinkled ball of flesh taking feeble breaths from the oxygen tank on his wheelchair, was torture, cruel and meaningless.

Big Boss tenderly looked into the face of the man who had once been his commander and said, "Zero grew old, and by the end, his Patriots were being run by a network without shape or form."

"What do you mean without shape or form?" Snake asked.

"The proxies were only one small part of the vast cycle that Zero created. The corporations, for-profits, and research institutions that comprise the military-industrial complex were part of it too. They operated on budgets automatically allotted to them by the proxies—accounts maintained by the Patriots. The network covered everything from weapons R&D and investment to production and marketing. It encompassed the people, the companies—even the laws that protect them. Politics and economics became nothing more than iterations of the same oppressively uniform system. I don't think anyone realized that it was all a setup—a mere set of norms. The Patriots were those norms—a neural network reduced to its simplest form."

The Patriots had no room for reform or individual will. A type of cold universality formed the arteries of the Patriots' information bloodstream; a pattern from the flow of information brought visible by the political and economic networks that had gained complexity through advances in transportation, distribution, and communication. On the outside, the pattern seemed too complex to predict, but in reality its behavior was deterministic and followed a simple equation.

But a new pattern emerged. The stream of information suddenly diverged and took an entirely new course. The Patriots' network was to undergo a radical change; to go from their quiet existence to that of a primitive life-form, endlessly dividing and combining, and reproducing and propagating without limit.

A life brought on by Zero's delusions of a unified state.

A life called war.

The Patriots, now driven by Zero's obsession to unify the human consciousness, were quickly overcome by the new meme of the war economy. With the help of several catalysts—including the political cause of creating a cleaner, safer battlefield, and the move toward military privatization to reduce administrative costs—the war economy spread worldwide.

By then, the System was no longer being steered by Zero's will—or anyone else's.

Theirs was a world without ideologies, principles, or ideals—or even the loyalty The Boss had so treasured—and decided by the movement of intangible capital. The norms, intended by Zero to be only proxies, began to reproduce and take on a life of their own—the life of the war economy.

SOP, Gekko, ID guns, and more—these technologies appeared on the surface to have been developed by separate companies. But all had been directed into the world by the Patriots AIs, diverting funds from the Philosophers' Legacy to research groups and the equity investors backing them.

"But," Big Boss said, "with the American system in a state of collapse, the Patriots' society has reverted to a blank slate."

Big Boss gazed across the cemetery. The unvisited burial ground was the husk of the old, fallen world. Those interred within were soldiers who died in the old wars. Some had fought as agents of the Patriots, and some had fought against them.

"This man was the source of everything," Big Boss said.

He removed his hand from Zero's shoulder and stared at the man who had been the center of it all. He was the center of the world, yet possessed no recorded citizenship. To hide from assassinations and terrorist plots, he had thoroughly erased all traces of himself.

Thanks to Ocelot, EVA, and Naomi's plans, the moment we uploaded the worm cluster to *Haven*'s servers, and GW manifested physically in the Patriots' network, JD revealed Zero's location, which was information only the head AI knew. Ocelot, EVA, and Naomi had given their lives for that moment—to guide Snake and his team along the proper path.

One will. One thought.

Zero had tried to rewrite the world to bring all its peoples to his vision.

"And he doesn't even realize it. He's completely unaware of the fact that he led the world to the brink of ruin. He's practically dead."

Of course, the writer couldn't appear in his own story.

The world Zero wrote had no place for him. His was the loneliness of a writer; the loneliness of the creator of stories. That very loneliness transformed the world—his creation—to a desolate, sad backdrop.

And so the old man stopped writing the story himself. Zero built an automated system to produce the narrative he desired. Such was his only option; he had grown weary of aging and of storytelling. *I speak, therefore the world is.* If he stopped narrating, all his efforts spent toward the unified world would go up in smoke.

As Snake listened to Big Boss talk, he began to feel deep pity for the tiny figure sunk into the wheelchair. Zero could not write an ending to his narrative.

*Enough! Stop this here*, he cried out, but the machine he'd created paid no heed. Granted new, independent life through the war economy, the storyteller had begun telling its own tale now. Zero found himself on the receiving end of the story, blasting at him, drowning out all other noise.

"Now that I'm actually face-to-face with him again," Big Boss said, "the hatred is gone. All I feel is a deep sense of longing... and pity."

Before Snake was a lone man beaten by his own creation. Even the mighty Patriots began with a single man. One desire, one dream, grew huge and bloated, absorbing technology, manipulating the economy, until, before he could realize it, his creation had become a beast.

He made the System, but in the end he became just another of its victims. Big Boss gazed at him with eyes filled with tenderness and lacking any shadows of enmity or ire.

"Did Zero really hate me? Or...did he fear me? It's too late to ask him now."

Para-Medic, Sigint, EVA, and Ocelot, the original members of the Patriots, had all passed on. Only Zero, the man who started it all, remained.

Everything had its beginning. But the world didn't begin with "one," but long before, in chaos. From zero. The moment zero became one was the moment the world sprang to life. One became two, two became ten, and ten became one hundred.

Taking it all back to one would solve nothing. As long as Zero remained, one would eventually grow to one hundred again.

"Our goal was to erase Zero."

Big Boss closed his eyes and patted Zero's head as a nurturing father would his son. Occasionally, the wheelchair's life-support and nursing care systems made a sound as the suction-assisted equipment retrieved Zero's waste. His cranium had contracted, and his skin had wrinkled; his face resembled that of a newborn.

Big Boss crouched in front of Zero. Staring closely into that face, he softly spoke.

"We have our sins."

By we, he didn't mean Snake. Without realizing it, he had grouped himself with Zero, his former commander, comrade-in-arms, and the mortal enemy who had imprisoned him—and the world.

"And for that reason, I'm taking it upon myself to send Zero back to nothing."

Big Boss reached behind the wheelchair and switched off the life-support system. The old man's eyelids faintly trembled. Big

Boss stood, turned his back on his slowly dying friend, and started to walk back toward The Boss's grave.

A steady electronic tone could faintly be heard—the life support's warning alarm, turned down to its lowest volume, was Zero's loudest death cry.

What had ended? An old man, long past seeing, hearing, and possibly thinking, had been freed from a pointless existence. Snake couldn't understand how that signified an ending to anything. Hadn't this old man already been destroyed by his own creation?

By the time he realized it, everything important had ended.

Snake said to Big Boss's back, "You going back to zero as well?"

Big Boss froze in place, then looked over his shoulder at Snake and said, "You erased me two times before. Today will mark the third. The FOXDIE Zero planted in you has already begun eating away at my body."

It couldn't—

Then in an instant, Snake put the pieces together.

The FOXDIE colony Naomi found swimming in Snake's blood in South America had contained two variant strains. One was what remained of the FOXDIE virus he had been injected with on Shadow Moses. Its genetic pattern to distinguish the virus's targets had eroded and threatened to spread death indiscriminately to the people of the world. The other was a new, unknown FOXDIE that had been recently injected into Snake by somebody—possibly Drebin.

*I've been used again*, Snake realized. The orders he had been given at Shadow Moses—to eliminate the terrorists and intercept the nuclear weapon—were only a lie to deliver the virus into the captured facility.

"Truth is," Big Boss said, "the FOXDIE in you killed EVA and Ocelot. Naomi told me everything."

At the end, Big Boss's voice cracked and grew weak and hoarse. Just as Snake noticed something was wrong, Big Boss fell to his knees amid the sea of white flowers and clutched at his chest with his right hand.

Snake ran to him and asked, "What's wrong?"

Big Boss's face had turned pale, his aura of vigor vanished like an illusion. Sweat beaded on his forehead. Big Boss gritted his teeth through the pain in his chest.

Snake knew what was happening.

This man had been his commander and his sworn enemy. He was Snake's original, his father and brother. And now he was dying before Snake's eyes.

"They did it again. They used you to kill me. The Patriots... no, their proxies. To bury us, they did it again. In the end, they're a program, only capable of repeating the same pattern over and over again."

Through the pain, Big Boss forced out a wry laugh. Snake had kneeled beside him, and he put his hand on his son's shoulder and summoned the strength to stand again.

"Do me a favor, will you? Take me over to her. To The Boss."

Snake was nonplussed, unable to deal with the indescribable emotion that welled up within him, as the man he'd only known as an enemy asked for his aid. For a moment he remained unable to move, peering into Big Boss's eyes.

Yes, he was Snake's enemy, but he was also Snake's father.

Snake didn't know his father. He had been raised by many guardians, but none he ever considered his real parents. He was never abused or treated dispassionately. Rather, his surrogate parents had handled him with the utmost care. The young child was astutely aware that all of the love, and all of the severity, that as his parents they afforded him, was entirely calculated.

Now that I consider it, his upbringing followed the Patriots' playbook completely, just as Raiden had experienced. Through a manufactured narrative and environment, Snake had been put into the role of the child.

Big Boss, who had gone off the Patriots' script, appeared before

Snake as an enemy—a wall to be overcome, a constant presence binding him. Who could fill that role but a father? And wouldn't a father have the responsibility to fill it? Unknowingly, Snake and Big Boss had begun building their relationship as father and son.

Snake helped Big Boss walk across the carpet of stars-of-Bethlehem. Feeling the weight of his father's body on his shoulder, Snake laughed at the strangeness of their situation—a father and son bound as enemies. Snake had grown up only being given the fictional affection arranged for him by the Patriots, yet this was the man he faced as an adversary, as the sole person allowed to be the target of his hostility.

"There's one more thing Naomi wanted me to tell you," Big Boss said, his voice faint from pain. "About the old FOXDIE in your body...the one that mutated. The new FOXDIE inside you, that killed EVA and Ocelot, continues to multiply. At the same time it is preventing the old mutated FOXDIE from reproducing. The new FOXDIE is uprooting the old. Naomi confirmed it in her follow-up. The mutants are receding. Before long, they'll be gone entirely."

For a moment, Snake froze in place, astonished. Only minutes ago, he had been trying to end his own life, believing that he would otherwise become history's most terrible bioweapon and spread death across the earth.

"Does that mean," Snake asked, "the mutant strain won't cause an epidemic?"

"The mutant strain will only live as long as you do. But even then, the process will just repeat itself. One day, the new FOXDIE will start to mutate and become a new threat. That is... if you manage to live that long."

Suddenly the strength left Big Boss's legs. His sudden weight caught Snake by surprise, who let go. Big Boss fell to his hands and knees and let out a feeble groan. His right hand clawed at his chest as if to scrape out his heart.

The virus had recognized Big Boss and went to work on the

cells that kept his heart going. *Apoptosis.* The swarm of molecular machines went from cell to cell, spreading their falsehoods: *It's time for you to die now. Your work is over.*

Feeling as if he were watching his own death, Snake said, "Am I going to die?"

*This is my future.* Snake projected himself onto his original. Before his eyes, a man with his body and his face was dying. Snake felt as if he were having a near-death experience. Many who had been to death's door reported the sensation of floating above themselves, watching their body die.

This man was Snake's original, and a large and inescapable part of his life.

This man's death was Snake's death.

Possibly sensing Snake's fear, Big Boss lifted his head and said, "Everyone dies. You can't stop it. You can't run away from it. This is your notice."

Big Boss seemed to be telling him, *That's right, this is your death, whether it will come like this or not. There's nothing bad about seeing someone die who looks like you.*

To attend the death of a loved one is to have a practice run at your own. Mental images avoided through normal life are shown to you inescapably. And you're left to face the question:

How will you use the life you have left?

As if to drive home to Snake the significance of his own death, Big Boss put it in words.

"Don't waste the time you have left fighting."

Having somehow fought back the pain, Big Boss again borrowed Snake's shoulder and began to walk. He felt heavier now, weaker than before.

"I've never thought of you as a son."

Snake grinned, obviously thinking, *Yeah, and I've never thought of you as a father.* Until a short while ago, Snake had only regarded the man as the original source of his genes and as a longtime foe.

"But I've always respected you as a soldier...and as a man. If you'd been in my place back then, maybe you wouldn't have made the same mistakes I did."

And Big Boss accepted Snake—as the man who had surpassed him. As the man whom he, along with The Boss and Zero, had created, and who had overturned the world he had wrongly brought about. Though he might never have considered Snake his son, he respected Snake as a person. What could that be if not a father's praise for his son?

The man who had set everything right—all his sins, all his unfinished duties—was a man of his own blood.

"On the day I killed The Boss with my own hands, my own life ended."

Walking ever more slowly, the two men at last reached The Boss's grave. Big Boss removed himself from Snake's shoulder and slumped weakly to his knees. The words on the tombstone, IN MEMORY OF A PATRIOT WHO SAVED THE WORLD, struck deep into his regret.

"Boss... you were right," Big Boss said, as if at confession, then spread out his elbows and gave a military salute. "It's not about changing the world. It's about doing our best to leave the world the way it is. It's about respecting the will of others... and believing in your own. Isn't that what you fought for?"

Big Boss's heart was filled with regret, yet to have reached this place filled him with the greatest joy. This was the joy The Boss had understood; this was the joy she believed valuable enough to give her life for. Big Boss had taken a long road to get here, but finally, in the cemetery where he faced the end of his own life, he had been able to see.

"At last," he said, "I understand the meaning behind what you did. At last, I understand the truth behind your courage."

Using the last of his strength, Big Boss rose to his feet, still in salute—his proof to her that he understood. She had been a true patriot. She loved her country, but was never driven by present national interests. She had been intent on protecting her own identity, such as it was, and never looked down upon other countries or their peoples.

She loved not only the country of her birth, but the world as a whole.

That was something that Zero—and the Patriots—had never been able to accomplish. They were unable to believe in the wills of others, or themselves, and their fear manifested in the memes that expanded relentlessly, and in the narrative that used, exploited, and controlled.

But that had all ended. The country she wanted, the world she envisioned, could now be built by the next generation, and the last one wouldn't be around to see it. The past might yet repeat itself. Chains might again be discovered to deny love and forgiveness.

But hope always remained. Sometimes where you least expected it.

"It's almost time for me to go," he said.

Big Boss lowered his salute and faced the warrior and last remaining Snake. For Big Boss, Snake had been that hope. Many times he had confronted Snake as an adversary, thinking him an agent of the Patriots. But in the end, Snake had freed the world from Zero's curse. And not just Snake, but Liquid and Solidus; hadn't each fought the Patriots in their quests for their own freedom?

Their wills had not perished. Their stories had not disappeared. Hadn't the seeds of father and brothers taken root in Solid Snake? Hadn't they ultimately achieved the freedom they staked their lives to grasp?

The only task that remained was for Big Boss to fade away.

A task only he could do.

"With me, the last ember of this fruitless war dies out. And at last those old evils will be gone. Once the source of evil returns to zero, a new one—a new future—will be born."

Big Boss held out his hand, the gesture a farewell, an expression of gratitude, a declaration of peace to end a prolonged battle, and an order from a commanding officer.

"That new world is yours to live in. Not as a snake, but as a man."

Snake recalled the day he first met this man. It was the initiation ceremony to FOXHOUND. As the unit's commander, Big Boss walked down the line of new recruits and shook each soldier's hand. *The battle you face*, he had said, *is a war unlike any before. None will tell of your successes, or failures, or even deaths.*

*But know this. Whatever your battles, whether ordered by me or by country, each of you have been chosen. You who stand here today know no life but combat. In a way, you should be pitied. But these battles are not to be given to just anyone. You are not tools of the government or anyone. You fight for yourselves and to protect the things you hold dear.*

*Always fight by your own will.*

*Protect what you can't bear to lose.*

*No one else can fight that battle for you.*

Frank's last message to Snake, pinned beneath REX's foot, had been Big Boss's words at the start of it all. Snake smiled scornfully at himself for not having made the connection sooner.

Snake hadn't shaken Big Boss's hand since that ceremony, and as he did so now, he felt a sense of completion. In the future, an unknown world awaited.

Suddenly, Big Boss collapsed. Snake, responding quickly, caught him mid-fall. For a brief moment, their faces brushed against one another. Big Boss's cheek was terribly cold, and Snake reflexively recoiled. He had felt the life draining from Big Boss's body.

The pain seemed to worsen with each new breath.

But he still had more to say. From the pit of his stomach, Big Boss struggled to squeeze out his voice. He couldn't allow himself to die without saying it.

"Know this...Zero and I, Liquid and Solidus, we all fought a long, bloody war to be free. We fought to free ourselves from the limitations of nations, systems, norms, and ages. But no matter how hard we tried, the only liberty we found was on the inside...

trapped within those limits. The Boss and I may have chosen different paths, but in the end, we were both trapped inside the same cage. But you...you have been given freedom. Freedom to be outside."

Big Boss gasped painfully for air. Snake gently lowered him to the ground. Snake gently put his hand on Big Boss's side and guided the dying man's back to lean against The Boss's gravestone.

"You are nobody's tool now," Big Boss said. "No one's toy. You are no longer a prisoner of fate. You are no longer a seed of war."

Big Boss fondly recalled the anger he'd felt, rising up from the pit of his stomach, when he learned that the Snakes had been born. He had reviled his children. He hated the clones born in defiance of his will and without his permission. That they were raised and used as agents of the Patriots to defile The Boss's will made the hate only stronger.

But how about it? In the end, wasn't it those clones who lifted the curse Big Boss placed upon himself? He owed this man much. If his death would repay any of those debts, then he would gladly go.

"It's time for you to see the outside world with your own eyes. Your body...your soul...are your own. Forget about us. Live...for yourself. You need not be bound to me any longer, David."

Big Boss's words seemed an apology. *I'm sorry it took me so long. I'm sorry I shackled you so long. Yet few are able to live their own lives. Especially as the Patriots had people of the whole world within their grasp. Your future—that's your real life. Though it may be short, you get to live, and I envy you.*

"And find a new lease on life."

Big Boss pulled a cigar from his pocket. His trembling hand delivered the tobacco to his lips, then found his lighter, only to fall slack on the way back up. He was slipping into unconsciousness. His deep, ragged breaths from when he leaned on Snake's shoulder had become faint, and the slight rising and falling of chest and stomach could only be seen if searched for.

The cigar dropped from his mouth. His eyelids dropped, and he prepared himself to accept that which would soon come.

"Boss," he said, "you only need one snake. No...you don't need any snakes."

A transparent tear formed at the corner of one closed eyelid, followed his cheek down, and fell to the white stars-of-Bethlehem. Snake retrieved the cigar, returned it to Big Boss's lips, and lit it with the lighter. He caught a bit of the trailing smoke and coughed. Big Boss lifted his eyelids a tiny fraction and watched Snake softly cough.

Snake was his son, his brother, a soldier under his command, and an enemy.

To him, Snake's presence was complex and multifaceted. But now the many sides of Snake converged into one. Whatever anyone thought, wasn't that enough? Whether to dream of having a child. Whether to have another in the world who could take over his will. We are such stuff as dreams are made on, someone once said.

This dream, this hope, did not belong to the Patriots, and it did not belong to The Boss. This was his own. As was the coming death.

"This is good," he said. "Isn't it?"

The cigar fell.

As Big Boss's last breaths faded, Snake remained at his side.

Snake watched the white petals dance through the air. *They're like stars*, he thought. The Boss had been to space. How much like this view was what she saw beyond the earth?

~~

When Sunny asked me to write you my story—to write about the feelings that came to me then, the despair I felt, and the hope—I hesitated a little.

I remembered everything, but I feared I couldn't do a good

job telling such a sweeping tale woven by so many people. I never was much at talking. Even when Sunny introduced me to you, I was at a loss.

*But, Uncle Hal,* Sunny kept after me. *Tell Snake's story. Tell your story. I want the person I chose to spend my life with to know everything about me. I want him to know how amazing were the people who raised me.*

*You're my hero, Uncle Hal,* she said. She pushed me. I remembered how Snake's face got when someone called him the legendary hero. Of course, I wasn't a hero either—just a man who happened to be at that place at that time.

Snake always joked, *You're white collar, I'm blue collar.* As if spilling from a world put together so that everything was fate, a series of tiny coincidences brought me to Snake, and I followed him in his battles.

From here on you'll be sharing your life with Sunny. As you depart on your new adventure, I offer you not words of congratulations, but only this book. I can't be at your wedding, but if Sunny delivers this book into your hands, I think that will be enough for me. I've stuffed my thoughts into the lines within. I may have put in too much; if it's a little overwhelming, I hope you'll endure it.

Snake is gone now. Meryl and Johnny are off somewhere, fighting some fight just as The Boss had done—to protect what needs protecting. You know that war hasn't shown any signs of disappearing from the earth, but even now, I still do what little I can to limit it. While you're getting married, I'll likely be trying to put out the embers of some conflict.

I have new friends and plenty of little Metal Gears to be my assistants. But Snake isn't with me. The legendary warrior, the man who made the impossible possible, Solid Snake, is no longer part of this world. I won't tell you in this book how long he lived after Big Boss set off on his voyage from that cemetery, or what kind of life he had. All I'll say is that his last days were peaceful. He

passed gently, simply falling asleep with a smile on his face. When
I thought back to the days and nights he'd spent in constant battle,
I found great solace in this.

Snake affected the lives of many. Some, like Jack, misunder-
stood and strayed from their paths, but in the end, Jack too settled
into where he belonged. Any who witnessed the way Snake lived
his life could awaken their inner strengths. He had that effect on
Meryl, and even Colonel Campbell.

And ultimately even his father, Big Boss, was touched by Snake
and found the forgiveness and peace he had for so long sought.

I already told you that you have a power, antithetical to that
of the Patriots, to draw out the courage and the kindness within
others. Perhaps what the Patriots did was more simply exercising
control. But I bet you never even knew of their existence. The
Patriots were incredibly careful never to let the people they controlled realize under whose thumb they lived. Like how a busy
restaurant can provide chopsticks that are subtly more rigid, making the customers imperceptibly more uncomfortable and reducing
the number of people who linger over their meals and thereby
increase turnover. What the Patriots did was only an extension of
such contrivances. You could say they performed maintenance on
our environment.

The SOP was part of that. Militaries and PMCs actively sought
out the SOP because the System was useful. Though PMCs under
governmental contract were obligated to join the SOP, independent PMCs were not pushed into the System, but rather embraced
it to improve their war performance and protect their corporate
reputations. Once the SOP had become universal, those who
sensed something off about the System and refused to take part
in it would have no place to go—just as Johnny hadn't been able to
admit he wasn't in the SOP.

The Patriots used this to repress the populace; to control the
wild pack of animals from being let loose, to be able to act as they
pleased. Such was the System built from a fierce distrust of the

fellow man. The System wasn't a discrete existence to be found in any set of locations—the System hid in the relationships and connections between people. That's how that even after the death of Zero the System lingered, still able to keep the world under its control.

But Snake was different. He was not a system but one man, and by setting an example he changed many people. Including myself. I tried to express that through this book. *Just live. Live with sincerity, respect toward others, and belief in yourself.*

Actions speak. That was precisely the kind of man Snake was. He stoically fulfilled his duty and brought change to the world.

I'm not going to tell you to live like Snake. That would be the Patriots' way. Like how Jack had once been snared. But what I did tell you, through this book, was how Snake lived, how that affected others, and how the world turned out as a result. More than anything else, I tried to describe what his actions showed Sunny. I did what I could to express Snake's thoughts and the feelings of the people around him.

I want you to know why, even today, so many people are fighting for the world you live in.

At the end, Snake thanked me, but I was the thankful one. I know my decision to follow Solid Snake was the right one. If I had never met Snake, I might still be merrily developing weapons, my eyes and ears closed from the rest of the world.

True, I suffered great loss after I met Snake—Wolf, Emma, Naomi. With their deaths I became trapped in despair so deep I thought I couldn't go on living. As I wrote this book, nothing was harder than returning to those memories.

Still, I'm glad I met Snake. Through the days of our fight together, he taught me what it meant to be alive. And I learned that as you live, you etch your life inside other people.

People live to be remembered by others, no matter in what form. People die. But death is not defeat. For Snake and me, this is only the beginning. Even should our names become lost, the significance of our deeds will live on, passed like echoes from one person to the next.

That's why I don't want to forget a thing; not the happy recollections and not the painful memories.

Sometimes I think about how I wish I'd introduced you to Snake. You're a lot like him. Through your strength, your strictness, and your kindness, you have the talent to be a positive influence on others.

Perhaps Snake was a blue flower, a man-made beast.

And even though he couldn't leave a child, the testament to his life remains within many people. Jack, Meryl, Johnny, Mei Ling, and Sunny. Even this book I give to you is a testament to the man called Solid Snake.

After Big Boss died, Sunny and I went with Snake on his trip around the world—a world now free of the Patriots. To tell future generations of what Snake saw, we were witnesses attending to his last days. We followed him everywhere, no matter how exasperated his expression became.

Snake told me then, "I'm gonna be dead soon. You don't have to come."

But I insisted, saying, "You wouldn't let me suffer Sunny's eggs alone, would you?"

I wonder if Sunny's eggs have gotten any better since she met you. The last time I had them, they were...okay. In them I could taste part of Naomi's story, passed on to Sunny.

I wonder if you have to eat those eggs every day.

If they taste good now, not like the ones when she was eight, it's because Naomi helped her. Naomi was only with us on *Nomad*

for a fleeting moment, but a glimpse of her skill was passed on to Sunny.

Even atop the dining table, someone's story lives on.
This world is an aggregate of such modest stories.

## AFTERWORD

A NOVELIZATION. A book taking a story written as a movie, anime, or other media and changing it to prose.

"Will you do the novelization for *Metal Gear Solid 4?*"

To be entrusted with the novelization of such a monumental work was too great an honor for a novice with only one novel to his name. A newcomer might quietly undertake the job, receive the script, and dispassionately adapt it into a novel. A basic, sincere approach within the novice's abilities.

But I had reasons that made such an approach out of the question.

I had been a fan of the *Metal Gear* series' creator, Hideo Kojima, for twenty years.

Because I was a fan, I didn't want to treat this like a typical novelization. I didn't want to present a fleeting memory to be read and then discarded; I wanted to offer something that would remain forever on the bookshelves of whoever picked it up. I wanted a novel worthy of being read more than once. As Hideo Kojima's stories held a special place for me in my youth, I hope that this ending to the *Metal Gear* series will be special for you. That's what made this novelization what it is.

Perhaps I should have written shorter sentences. Perhaps I should have cut everything but the dialogue as much as I could. Perhaps I should have shortened the paragraphs and made it easier to read. As a reader, I've been under the care of novelizations like that. A rumination of the experience of the "real thing." Since this book tells the story of the game as it was, perhaps I didn't need to produce detailed descriptions.

But as long as the name *Metal Gear* was attached, I decided I wouldn't let this be something merely peripheral.

Yet I didn't at all want to make the novel special to myself by using the worldview and characters to assert myself through the narrative. How furious would I have been as a fan if some inexperienced nobody came in and asserted himself through the narrative and presented an original story with the same world and the same characters? Were it a famous, accomplished author, I might forgive, but someone new to the field like me couldn't do that, nor did I want to or feel the need to. It's easy to assert your ego through an "original" story. But I knew that the possibility of the novel lay in a place outside the story.

It was the choice to make Otacon the narrator.

How would the story be told? I know that a novel's essence resides in that *how*. Moses parted the Red Sea, and Jesus turned water into wine. The soldier put his life on the line for the princess, and the little boy left on a journey. *Once upon a time...* In the past, stories didn't belong to novelists, but to someone, somewhere. The passing down of another person's deeds. From the likes of minstrels, tellers of lore, and the faithful apostles came many styles of storytelling to pass on the tales to the future world.

The method of the telling has as much meaning and importance as the story itself. Though *The Lord of the Rings* films are loyal to Tolkien's creation, Peter Jackson's presentations of the stories make the films distinctly his own. One might say that Peter Jackson told his own story through the way he told *The Lord of the Rings*.

I thought the same might be possible with a novelization. Moreover, I thought that was the only possible avenue through which to make my novelization personal. I could faithfully tell the story Hideo Kojima painstakingly built without losing its emotional impact. A careful and thorough consideration of that method resulted in this novel. This is a book that stands complete on its own and can be read even by those who aren't familiar with the *Metal Gear* series, and yet contains new discoveries for those who have already reached the end of the *Metal Gear* tale.

My long deliberation on the nature of novelizations produced a story informed by the meaning of telling the *Metal Gear* story—a story about stories, a story about what the *Metal Gear* saga is, what it symbolizes about the structure of the world we live in, and even an evaluation of *Metal Gear*.

Nothing would make me happier than if you took from this novel the meaning of passing down another person's story. I hope this story will enrich your bookshelf and become a fond memory.

—*Project Itoh*
*June 2008*

## ON PROJECT ITOH

*Compiled from an interview with Hideo Kojima*
*February 12, 2010*

MARCH 1998. I remember first meeting Itoh-san during the Spring '98 Tokyo Game Show. I was in the exhibitor's booth for *Metal Gear Solid*, to be released that September, when a young man called my name. I turned to see who it was and saw his face streaming with tears. Here, amid the clamor and festivities of the Game Show, one young man was crying. Later, he would become the novelist Project Itoh.

At the booth, we showed a trailer of in-game footage I'd compiled and edited. The preview had brought Itoh-san to tears, and now he talked to me earnestly. Before that moment, I'd never met a fan who so loved *Metal Gear Solid*, and I remember being moved. From then on, Itoh-san sent me fan letters and even *Metal Gear doujinshi*—fanzines—created by him and his friends. I eventually heard he had a website, and I would take a look at it from time to time.

Still, my relationship with Itoh-san remained nothing more than that of a game creator and a passionate fan. This may sound cold to some readers, but I don't ever think of fostering one-on-one connections with my fans. And I feel this way even today—I'm just on the delivery end and mustn't directly exchange with the consumers. The messages and presents and web comments are the most crucial nourishment for my work, and of course I'm grateful for them each and every day. But I feel the only way I can properly respond to them is through my creations, my games. So I never did anything to encourage Itoh-san. For a time, our relationship wasn't mutual, it was one-way.

Change came to our relationship in September 2001, right before 9/11.

I heard from members of the Konami team that Itoh-san had been hospitalized, possibly with cancer. *I want to do something for him*, I thought, then when I thought of him on his sickbed, I wondered, *But what can I do for him?* The answer I came up with was, of course, a game. We had met because of my game, *Metal Gear Solid*. That provided the only answer. I recorded cut scenes from the still-in-progress *Metal Gear Solid 2* onto a MiniDV cassette and took it to his hospital room. He put on a composed front, but it couldn't mask his dark expression. An uncertain future left him depressed. It wasn't much, but from his bedside, I showed him the ending scene of the Tanker segment.

Normally, we can't show people outside the company even a portion of a work-in-progress. But it was all I could do for him, so I let him see it.

"I won't die until you finish the game." That was what Itoh-san said, to my relief, when the clip ended.

In November 2001, we managed to release *Metal Gear Solid 2: Sons of Liberty* as planned. I invited Itoh-san to the press conference, and he attended the reception. He had been through a serious operation, and I was pained to watch him walking with a cane, but I was glad to see him. He kept his promise. When I look back at it now, I think that was the moment he went in my mind from being a fan to a friend.

*Metal Gear Solid 2* was greatly anticipated, but the initial response to its release was sharply divided. The game has since gained a reputation, but at the time, I would become depressed when I saw what people wrote in comments and reviews—about the new character, Raiden; that the message at the end was too strong; and that the story was too abstruse for a gamer audience. Itoh-san was the first to understand me. On his personal website, he wrote an article saying, "I'm the only one happy with this kind of game!" Someone understood the riddles and messages I put into my games. I felt that simple fact saved me.

I think that was when Itoh-san had an awakening and set forth on the author's path. One time, Itoh-san asked me to look at a manga written by him and drawn by his friend. I was happy at the chance to read it, but to be blunt, his work didn't really do anything for me. True, he had abundant knowledge and an uncanny power of understanding. He was able to grasp points in my games that most of my fans missed. One of my works before *Metal Gear Solid, Policenauts*, featured as part of its theme the notion that a space colony would have to become a highly medicalized society, but very few understood its inevitability. But Itoh-san got it, along with the reveal in *Metal Gear Solid* that Liquid's group sought Big Boss's corpse, and the twist in *Metal Gear Solid 2* when Snake's NPO becomes designated a terrorist organization. He delighted in them, saying, "*This* is science fiction!" But I had doubts about his creative potential, as opposed to his discernment as a gamer.

Then he began to change. It started with the quality of his writings on his blog, followed by his online movie reviews. I can't quite find the right words to explain it, but I was seeing something like a new perspective within his writing. Looking back at it, I think the change came soon before he started writing *Genocidal Organ*. I can't give a solid explanation, but perhaps the experience of a severe illness awakened the author within him. I imagine as he lived with death by his side, his perceptions underwent a major shift.

When I read *Genocidal Organ*, I was shocked. It was something only Itoh-san could have written; delicate, yet dreadful, and even endearing. Project Itoh the writer was born. Apparently, in a later interview, Itoh-san said that the short story serving as the basis for *Genocidal Organ* had been fan fiction of my early game *Snatcher*. But in the novel I saw reflections of the *Metal Gear Solid* series. And so I didn't hesitate to approach him for the novelization of *Metal Gear Solid 4*.

We made the first plans for the novelization in January 2008. When Itoh-san entered the meeting room cane in hand, he emanated an author's aura. Gone was the fragility of the young man crying at the Tokyo Game Show booth just ten years prior. He had the dignified countenance of an author. I think this was the first time Itoh-san and I exchanged words as two creators.

Before we knew it, the plans had been made. I wanted the novel to be based on *Metal Gear Solid 4*, but also, so that those who hadn't played the rest of the series could understand, to include characters, history, and settings from the *Metal Gear* saga. I wanted it to be written and composed so that it would be accessible to younger readers, and I wanted the novel to express the themes of MGS4. He took our unreasonable list of demands and checked them off one by one. He came up with the ideas of making Otacon the narrator and omitting the Beauty and the Beast Unit, boss characters crucial to the themes and game design of MGS4, to instead let series regulars embody the themes. In almost no time at all, the basic concepts of the novel had been set.

Then, with tremendous enthusiasm, he went to work.

The first draft soon arrived, and it surpassed my expectations. There was even a feeling, I have to say a nice feeling, of entrusting my own creation to a third party. Of course he recreated the themes I'd put into the game, the emotions of my characters, and the turns of the story, but vividly present in Itoh-san's prose were different aspects of the story I'd never realized were there, and motifs hidden within the setting. There's a phrase, "reading between the lines." Itoh-san gathered meaning and details and feelings between the *letters* of the game script. This wasn't merely a carbon copy of the game in novel form.

After the game and the novel were released, I settled on the plot for my next project. After *Metal Gear Solid 2*, whenever I finished creating a game, I always first looked to see if it made Itoh-san happy. And not just then, but during production I would wonder, *Will he take to this story, to this setting, to these characters?* I had it in my head that my next game would be set in Costa Rica in 1974. On the timeline it would come after *Metal Gear Solid 3*. It takes place during the Cold War, when an unknown military group engages in secret operations within the peaceful, defenseless Central American nation. Naked Snake's *Militaires Sans Frontieres* are brought in to stop them. The game is *Metal Gear Solid: Peace Walker*.

I wanted to ask Itoh-san to collect my new story with *Metal Gear Solid 3* into a single novel. My next chance to talk with him came unexpectedly.

February 2009. In the hospital, Itoh-san's condition was not good. So far he had won every battle in the long fight with his illness, but I was told that this time he might not make it. I dropped everything and rushed to see him. Itoh-san was in bed, and I talked about what movies I'd seen and what books I'd read recently, but his expression was blank, and he wasn't able to say much in return. I thought, *I want him to get his spark back. I don't want him to give up living.* So I started to tell him about *Peace Walker.* I told him about Costa Rica and the theme of nuclear deterrence, about the secret struggle between intelligence agencies in the Cold War, about the AI weapon straight out of 70s' sci-fi, about Snake and the other characters, and as I talked he regained more and more of his smile. And then, just like before, he told me, "I won't give up until you're done."

At that point I hadn't publicly announced a single aspect of my plans for the game. Itoh-san was the first person outside the company to hear any details, just as it had been with *Metal Gear Solid 2*. The only real difference between the events of 2001 and 2009 was that this time, Itoh-san couldn't keep his promise.

There is a scene in this novel in which Naomi teaches the struggling Sunny the trick to making fried eggs. That scene, of course, is also in the game, but as Itoh-san writes it, even that moment is a story handed to Sunny by Naomi. Even in the morning's fried eggs a story dwells—a story not expressed in my game. I believe this novel is Project Itoh's *Metal Gear Solid.*

*Would this game make Itoh-san happy?* That standard is part of what the story of Project Itoh means to me. Therefore, Project Itoh already dwells inside my game. Itoh-san took this game, retold it, and handed me back his own *Metal Gear Solid*. Like a double helix. Such a wonderful game of catch.

Because of the existence of a man called Itoh-san, I've experienced a happiness difficult for a creator to obtain.

Project Itoh-san, thank you.

**Keikaku (Project) Itoh** was born in Tokyo in 1974. He graduated from Musashino Art University. In 2007, he debuted with *Gyakusatsu Kikan (Genocidal Organ)* and took first prize in the Best SF of 2007 in *SF Magazine*. His novel *Harmony* won both the Seiun and Japan SF awards, and its English-language edition won the Philip K. Dick Award Special Citation. He is also the author of *Metal Gear Solid: Guns of the Patriots*, a Japanese-language novel based on the popular video game series. All three of his novels are available in English from Haikasoru. After a long battle with cancer, Itoh passed away in March 2009.

# HAIKASORU

## THE FUTURE IS JAPANESE

### THE FUTURE IS JAPANESE BY HAIKASORU

A web browser that threatens to conquer the world. The longest, loneliest railroad on Earth. A North Korean nuke hitting Tokyo, a hollow asteroid full of automated rice paddies, and a specialist in breaking up "virtual" marriages. And yes, giant robots. These thirteen stories from and about the Land of the Rising Sun run the gamut from fantasy to cyberpunk, and will leave you knowing that the future is Japanese! With new stories by Bruce Sterling, Catherynne M. Valente, Hideyuki Kikuchi, Project Itoh, and many others.

### GENOCIDAL ORGAN BY PROJECT ITOH

The war on terror exploded, literally, the day Sarajevo was destroyed by a homemade nuclear device. The leading democracies transformed into total surveillance states, and the developing world has drowned under a wave of genocides. The mysterious American John Paul seems to be behind the collapse of the world system, and it's up to intelligence agent Clavis Shepherd to track John Paul across the wreckage of civilizations and to find the true heart of darkness—a genocidal organ.

### BELKA, WHY DON'T YOU BARK? BY HIDEO FURUKAWA

When Japanese troops retreat from the Aleutian island of Kiska in 1943, they leave behind four military dogs. One of them dies in isolation, and the others are taken under the protection of US troops. Meanwhile, in the USSR, a KGB military dog handler kidnaps the daughter of a Japanese yakuza. Named after the Russian astronaut dog Strelka, the girl develops the psychic ability to communicate with canines. A multigenerational epic as seen through the eyes of man's best friend, the dogs who are used as mere tools for the benefit of humankind gradually discover their true selves and learn something about their so-called "masters."

### ALSO BY PROJECT ITOH

#### HARMONY

In the future, Utopia has finally been achieved thanks to medical nanotechnology and a powerful ethic of social welfare and mutual consideration. This perfect world isn't that perfect though, and three young girls stand up to totalitarian kindness and super-medicine by attempting suicide via starvation. It doesn't work, but one of the girls—Tuan Kirie—grows up to be a member of the World Health Organization. As a crisis threatens the harmony of the new world, Tuan rediscovers another member of her suicide pact, and together they must help save the planet…from itself. Winner of the Japan SF and Seiun Awards, and the Special Citation for the Philip K. Dick Award.